The Dead Loop

The Dead Loop

Jason Tipple

ISBN-9781718196056

Dedicated to 'The Liquidators'

Those brave souls who put their lives on the line to clear up
the Chernobyl nuclear disaster.

Contents

Prologue

'Death aims only once, but never misses.' – Edward Counsel.

There was a time when I believed that those philosophical words were true. Not anymore though, because now I know differently...

Death is one of life's certainties – an inevitable absolution that we all have to accept. It is the instant when life is extinguished and your own personal spark fades away forever. Dying is your last experience and a final door closing on life's journey of existence. It's also supposed to be a permanent affair – and for you at least it will be. But dying isn't the end for me. It's just another opportunity to experience death again, but in a different way.

I've lost count of the number of times I have died and how often my body and spirit have surrendered to the darkness. Counting them seemed important at first and naturally it terrified me every time my life ended, but dying is part of my daily routine now. It seems as familiar to me as brushing my teeth or putting on a pair of shoes. Sometimes I even find myself smirking at the irony of death's apparent inability to finish me off.

My death feels insignificant now, just as my past has become irrelevant. Somewhere along the line dying became my way of life and living became meaningless. So I've stopped looking beyond today or thinking about the future, and I spend the moments wondering where my next death will come from. I'm trapped in an endless tiresome cycle where every time I die I seem to lose a little bit more of who I am.

I'm not some immortal being, it's just that life and death are the same to me – there is no distinction between them anymore. But this isn't the afterlife or some kind of reincarnation – it's something that I call the 'dead loop'.

So it seems that Edward Counsel was wrong, death doesn't only aim once and never miss, because I die every single day. The famous Roman philosopher Seneca put things better when he said: *'It is uncertain where death may await thee, therefore expect it everywhere.'* When you die as often as I do, those words seem to make a lot of sense and offer me a kind of ironic comfort.

I will always remember my first death clearly. It was some time ago in the Ukraine and long before I knew of Seneca's words, so back then – I never expected it.

PART 1

THE DEAD LOOP

1
The Fall of Pripyat

I can see the ominous bulk of the Sarcophagus in the distance, recognising it from books and the internet. Entombed forever inside its metal and concrete walls lay the shattered remains of the Chernobyl nuclear power station. The ruined plant will remain here forever as an iconic symbol of poison and death; a remnant from the 1980s.

The Chernobyl disaster is the worst nuclear accident in man's history and a permanent stain on the rich tapestry and fabric of the twentieth century. The highly radioactive reactor core lays silent and buried by the boron, sand and lead that was dropped by helicopters to quench the fire. This whole place is eerie and fascinating, but it's strangely calm and serene too.

It's intimidating to think that the danger now lurking here is completely invisible to my senses and only a Geiger counter would show me how close I am to being exposed to the silent threat that's all around me. But the worst radiation is contained within the fuel cells that were destroyed by the explosion and buried deep inside the Sarcophagus.

Books will tell you that the risk out here is at least tolerable now. Still it would be wise not to linger too long within the exclusion zone around the plant, lovingly known as the 'Zone of Alienation'. The perimeter and shape of the zone changes dramatically based on the levels of radiation that are continually monitored and recorded, it is no longer a simple 30km circle around the disaster site and you still need special permission to enter it.

All around me are the abandoned and decaying buildings of the lifeless Ukrainian city of Pripyat, scattered like the discarded toys of a playful child. The apartment blocks are generously separated, making the city feel spacious and open. But these buildings have been empty for a long time and are just another grim reminder of the desolation that radioactive contamination has left behind.

On the orders of the City Council 50,000 people were evacuated from this once thriving city in April 1986. As the scale of the Chernobyl nuclear disaster continued to escalate, authorities had no choice but to order an evacuation whilst deceiving the world that everything was okay. The residents were told that it was just for a few days, so most of them left everything behind – apartments full of their belongings, furniture, clothes, photographs and even their pets. But those people never returned.

But the city wasn't empty for long because the residents were promptly replaced by the 'Liquidators', the poor brave souls shipped in to try and clean this mess up. There were thousands of them, including power plant staff, fire-fighters, the Kiev Civil Defence, the military, construction workers, miners and helicopter pilots. Radiation almost certainly affected the thousands who served here demolishing villages, removing contaminated soil and metal and building the Sarcophagus. They all received a medal – the only one ever given out for participation in a nuclear clean up. But the Liquidators are long gone now, replaced by scientists and those who study the after effects of the disaster or monitor radiation levels.

Thorny vegetation and weeds all grow quite happily here though despite the radiation. Even the trees seem to be green and thriving. It's almost as if man has been banished for the damage he has caused to this place while other life was encouraged to stay. Mother Nature is slowly reclaiming the city as her roots and the weather gradually chip away at the concrete of a dead civilisation. I wonder how long it will be before Pripyat is swallowed up by trees and undergrowth like some ancient temple in a South American jungle.

I carefully pick my way through the shattered city streets, stepping over the weeds that grow through cracks in the concrete pavements. Walking makes me think about the people that once lived here. Mothers taking their children to school or the park, Fathers on their way to work at the Power Station, swimmers on their way to the Olympic pool to exercise or go diving from the boards. I feel like a ghost walking in their shadows, an intruder in the graveyard of their home. That's all Pripyat is now really – it's just a graveyard that no one visits.

As I approach the power plant I realise why people have never returned to reclaim this desolate and contaminated expanse of Eastern Europe. The enormous bulk of the Sarcophagus and the ventilation stack of the power station are a stark reminder of how close the city is to the disaster site. There is a huge abandoned crane here and piles of unused construction materials littering the vast industrial area. As I glance back towards the city it occurs to me how irresponsible the delay in ordering the evacuation was, how crucial and precious those extra days or hours could have been to the evacuees.

This place has always fascinated me, right back to 1986 when I had to wind up the windows of my first car as news came over the radio of the contamination cloud spreading over Europe. But why am I here in the Ukraine, is it just to see Pripyat and Ground Zero?

Upon reaching ground zero I stare in awe at the enormous Sarcophagus, drawn to its raw archaeological grandeur. A building uniquely designed and constructed for the sole purpose of protecting everything that was outside it. It is surely the largest and deadliest Pandora's Box in the world.

I know that the radiation is worse here because of my proximity to the reactor site but somehow the Sarcophagus is a reassuring symbol. Despite its age and hasty construction it is here to serve for as long as it remains intact, and to keep everything here safe from its deadly contents.

'Who the hell are you?' The blunt but muffled voice startles me, and I turn around to face a man wearing protective blue overalls. He has a surgical face mask covering his nose and mouth which explains his muffled voice. His pristine appearance makes him look oddly out of place here. The man pulls his mask down away from his mouth and repeats his question a little more politely. An impression of the mask remains on his cheeks above his rapidly greying beard. His frown is intense and his body language hints that he has authority.

'I'm Ewan,' I tell him.

He appears relieved that I speak English and relaxes his face noticeably. 'I'm Greg,' he replies. 'Are you with a team here?'

His question registers in my mind but I can't immediately find an answer. Who am I here with?

'Where's the rest of your group?' he asks, stroking his beard thoughtfully. 'I wasn't expecting anyone else here this week.'

'My group?' I respond doubtfully, 'I'm not sure where they are. But what about your team?'

Greg loosens the straps of the face mask hanging around his neck. 'Oh they're around the "Sarc" somewhere,' he says, gesturing with his hands. 'We're just taking readings for the research centre. There's only three of us today.'

For the first time I notice his clipboard and Geiger counter which only highlight the absence of any equipment of my own.

'The rest of our gear is back in the truck,' he says, 'where's your stuff?'

It's like he has somehow read my thoughts, but I can't seem to remember exactly what I'm doing here or even how I got here. I avert my eyes from him for a moment and turn to stare back at the crumbling ruins of Pripyat, hoping for answers but not finding any. When I look back at him I suddenly shiver at how cold it seems to be.

My cardigan is thin, inadequate and grey, not my colour at all but I can't even remember putting it on.

'No,' I murmur quietly, 'I'm not part of a team, it's just me.'

It's the best answer I can offer as Greg scratches his beard thoughtfully as if it's a habit.

'Just you?' he asks. 'So you're not part of a science or research team? I didn't think you looked like you work here.'

'Oh, I'm just looking around,' I explain.

Greg frowns and looks at me a little suspiciously. 'Well you know the zone is restricted right?' he asks while pointing to an ID card clipped near his chest. 'Tourists aren't allowed to be wandering around here.'

I shrug my shoulders dismissively at his statement and images of Pripyat suddenly flow through my mind. Somehow I know this place. Maybe it's only from pictures on the internet but I can visualise the city, the Sarcophagus and the abandoned villages clearly in my mind. He can't tell me that I shouldn't be here.

'I'm not a tourist Greg,' I protest.

He breathes a little sigh of impatience. 'Well how did you get here? How did you get through the checkpoints?'

But I'm through with trying to find answers to his questions.

'Do you know where the Ferris wheel is?' I ask.

But before he can reply, we are interrupted by a crackling voice from the radio hanging at his belt. Greg removes the radio and responds in what sounds like Russian, although the exchange is brief and I don't understand a word of it.

'Look mate, I have to join my team,' Greg says, 'you should get out of the zone. You can be arrested for sightseeing here if the Ukrainians catch you. Not to mention that it's dangerous without a Geiger counter, which you obviously don't have.'

But I have no intention of leaving, I want to see the Ferris wheel and the rusted remains of the dodgem cars that I know are close by it. Other than the Sarcophagus, those are the most iconic images I can remember about this place.

'Thanks, but I'm going to find the Ferris wheel,' I inform him.

Greg shakes his head in obvious annoyance. 'Look, we'll be pulling out for the day soon, I suggest you leave too. If you want a lift out of the zone, we are leaving in about an hour. We can squeeze you in and give you a lift.'

With that, he turns away and strides off briskly towards the Sarcophagus, cursing into his radio in Russian. After watching him leave I turn my back on the hulking Sarcophagus and start walking back towards the city.

Silence is the master of Pripyat, a deathly and lonely quiet. I've never experienced such a silent place in all my life. It seems to be devoid of any animal life, but I know they are out there somewhere; animals do thrive here in the zone now that man has gone.

The sun shines high in a cloudless sky, but it seems to offer very little warmth and my hands feel cold. I rub them together for a moment before continuing my search. The Ferris wheel proves quite easy to find. Like everything here the fairground is a strangely beautiful scene despite the weeds, the cracked concrete and the oppressing emptiness of neglect.

The Ferris wheel stands there like a painting, almost motionless except for a gentle sway of the rusty yellow gondolas in the breeze. It's the first time that I've seen it in the flesh and I wish it would turn, for music to play and the sounds of laughing children to be heard. But there is only silence here now. The wheel died a long time ago, taking the music, fun and laughter with it.

I close my eyes and imagine the wheel turning again and its twenty yellow gondolas rotating around the wheel. But hearing no response, I open my eyes and stare at it, trying to mentally force life back into its rusty frame but still it doesn't turn. The whole city has had the life sucked out of it but perhaps the dodgems can be resurrected instead.

The roof of the dodgem enclosure is a rusty, bare frame like the rib cage of some long extinct dinosaur. Patchy grass and thick clumps of stringy weeds grow underneath it. The dodgem cars themselves are surrounded by a dirty carpet of fallen leaves and spongy green moss and there are even a couple of young trees growing through the tarmac surface.

I carefully climb over the rusty metal fence to take a closer look at the cars, most of which lay on their sides like broken tanks on a funfair battlefield. The rubber rings around the front of the cars make them appear as if they're smiling despite their abandonment. The half a dozen cars are all yellow and look strikingly bright against the dullness of the concrete and weeds. The nearest one is missing its steering wheel, with just a rusty stump of metal where it used to be. I slide my hand along the car's body, feeling its cold, cracked surface and wonder how contaminated with radiation the metal is. Another car still has its steering wheel, but no seat and although the wheel still turns it offers only a mournful and reluctant grinding sound of defeat when I turn it. But then I notice her, a tiny figure lying behind the car.

She is long dead, her face blackened by dirt and exposure to the elements. One of her arms is all black and bent oddly. She seems so vulnerable, abandoned and alone here in the zone of alienation. Her dirty hair is thick, brown and curly, just like my late mother's, but with flecks of what looks like ash in it. I don't know why I pick her up but I feel an urge to rescue her from this place and to protect her. The little doll is broken and lifeless, with no clothing apart from a tattered pair of pink shorts. She doesn't belong here and I can't help but wonder who might have left her behind. Which little girl accidentally dropped her favourite doll as she was dragged away crying in the haste of evacuation? I picture her reaching out for her precious doll with a desperate outstretched arm, only to be dragged hastily away by her mother. But at least now the doll is safe now, with me.

As I gently cradle the lifeless doll in my arms and wipe her grubby face with my handkerchief, I suddenly notice movement out the corner of my eye. It was just a momentary flash, high up in the nearest apartment block – but something definitely moved up there. Maybe it was someone else like me exploring the ruins – or perhaps another scientist. It couldn't be one of Greg's team because he said they were all by the reactor, but I'm sure that someone moved past one of the upstairs windows.

There's no one else in Pripyat except for those studying radiation levels and the long term impact of the disaster. Are they gathering data so that they might be better prepared for next time? Thinking about a next time is a frightening thought while standing amongst the ruins of Pripyat. Have they learnt enough here to make sure that many more dolls won't be abandoned in future?

The dodgems begin to glide past me like they are sliding down a hill, but I realise they aren't moving at all– it's me that's moving over the soft mossy ground. I'm instinctively walking towards the apartment block to investigate the flash of movement while carefully cradling the little doll in my arms.

There is more of the familiar thick green moss on the concrete pavement and straggly weeds poke their way through thin cracks in the path. Most of the windows in the downstairs apartments are either open or broken and it looks dark inside the rooms. One of the windows even has a tree branch growing through it from inside the building.

The rotting double doors to the tower-block are barely clinging on and look ready to fall off. I push open one side and it groans inwards with a mournful sound of protest from irradiated rusty hinges. The sound seems out of place and disturbingly loud as it echoes across the silent city like it's trying to escape this place. There's no doubt in my mind that I have to go inside, no hesitation at all. That unexplained movement has given me a sudden purpose here other than sightseeing and converting images in my mind into real experiences. It's a moment of clarity that replaces my jumbled and ambiguous thoughts.

The lobby of the apartment block is dark, uninviting and the floor is covered with a fine layer of grey powdery dust. Paint peels from decaying walls and the floorboards are broken. I can smell the dry musty odour of mould and decay as I move further inside. There is graffiti scrawled on the walls of the stairways but even the writing is dull and faded. I can only read the occasional name or symbol so it must be in Russian with quite a few of those odd reversed letters. But the graffiti is comforting in a way, the rawness of its expression reminds me that real people with real thoughts and ideas once dwelled here. Someone had been here but whether it was scrawled before or after the accident, I don't know. Why would anyone be here in this place now?

I sneeze twice as I proceed through the lobby and up the stairs, leaving a trail of dusty footprints behind me. If I don't find whoever was moving up there, at least there will be some kind of panoramic view of the city. I wonder what the Sarcophagus will look like from the roof of one of the tallest buildings in Pripyat. Maybe if I can see the whole city in one view there will be other signs of life. That would make the fifteen flights of stairs worth the exertion.

The first apartment that I enter on the top floor is a total mess, but for some reason I expected everything to have been left neatly in place during the evacuation. I'm surprised to see broken chairs and ruined furniture lying scattered amongst the debris in the living room. There's dust on every surface and mould growing on the cracked and peeling walls. The windows are loosely covered by a pair of filthy flowery curtains that gently move in the breeze that enters through broken glass. Anything of value has long since been taken by looters.

My shoes crunch on the broken shards of a mirror as I ghost carefully through the room. I run a finger through the dust on a smashed mahogany sideboard. Kneeling down, I pick up the dried stalks of some long dead flowers but they crumble in my fingers. There is no sign of the vase that once nurtured them.

On the floor by the window I find a couple of faded black and white photographs that must have fallen off the sideboard. I carefully pick them up and see smiling faces looking up at me. There are two Ukrainian boys, maybe sixteen with shaven heads and wearing some kind of military uniforms, trying to look like tough soldiers. Their youthful faces betray them though and they're unable to conceal their smiles at having a picture taken for their proud parents. Perhaps they had returned as Liquidators and were now dead or struggling against the long term effects of radiation exposure. Or maybe they were some of the lucky ones who were a long way away from the Ukraine when disaster struck.

The second picture is badly crumpled and looks like it has been wet at some point in time, showing a couple on their wedding day. The man is overweight but smartly dressed in a suit and tie. He's squinting and holding his hand up to shade his eyes from the sun. His new bride is wearing an old fashioned dress, perhaps once belonging to her mother. She appears to be much younger than him but she looks happy. Their faces and smiles are oblivious to what would one day happen to their home and I wonder where they are now. Maybe they had been lucky enough to flee Pripyat in time and keep the contamination in their bodies to an acceptable level, if there was such a thing. I place the two photos back on the broken sideboard on top of some faded yellow newspaper clippings. It seems disrespectful to just throw them back onto the floor.

'Anyone in here?' I call out, but there is no response.

Perhaps the movement I saw was just a curtain being caressed by the wind. I doubt there are any ghosts here now – even they have left. There is nobody living in this sorry place any more, just faded photos and memories that nobody wanted.

The apartment building is spacious but the corridors feel oddly claustrophobic at the same time. I decide that every apartment will probably be in the same dilapidated state, so I leave them behind and climb the final staircase to the roof. Surprisingly I find a door that opens smoothly without any protest and it's refreshing to find something here that has escaped the decay.

Being inside the building was like being underground so it feels liberating to step out of the stairwell and into the light. The temperature outside has dropped now but the cool breeze on my face and the fading afternoon sunshine are refreshing and almost invigorating. I stride eagerly to the edge of the roof to survey the ruins of Pripyat in their vast expansive glory.

The city is huge, with dozens of accommodation towers surrounded by large areas of greenery and open space. From up here I can barely tell that the streets are cracked and broken, and that weeds and trees grow in places they shouldn't. Pripyat makes for a tranquil, quite beautiful scene but also like a garden that has been left unattended and neglected for years. It must have been a wonderful place to live before the disaster, when it was modern and still buzzing with life and young families.

The view feels almost personal to me as if it's been put here solely for my benefit. I can just about make out the river, twinkling in the distance but wonder what contamination lies in its silty poisonous depths. Most striking of all is how easily I can pick out the Sarcophagus in the distance. It must have been a terrifying but spectacular sight for the city's residents when the reactor was smouldering and the fire was exhaling its toxic death into the sky. It wouldn't be difficult to think of radiation as the embodiment of evil – a silent, slow and deadly killer but nuclear power isn't really our enemy. The radiation here is just an unfortunate bi-product of our insatiable need for energy, released during a terrible accident.

I walk slowly along the roof, admiring the view and enjoying the last of the afternoon sunshine as the breeze strokes my face. Up here on the roof the smell of decay is replaced by the scent of foliage carried in the wind. It feels almost clean up here, as if what had happened below in the city is another world away.

'It's beautiful isn't it?' I ask the doll.

It's a rhetorical question and I don't expect a reply, but she almost seems to smile through plastic cheeks as if the despair and loneliness has been eased in her empty heart.

Bu then my thoughts are brutally and violently interrupted when a large shape suddenly flashes past and almost knocks me over. The unknown beast screams like something out of a horror film as it brushes against me and blazes towards the stairway.

'Shit!' I yell defensively, as if the obscenity will somehow protect me.

All of my senses desperately seek to identify the beast but its movement is too fast. As my chests pounds like thunder I accept that it was probably just a dog or a wolf, or something similar, grey and fast like a wisp of smoke. It disappears instantly through the door to the stairway and the sudden flash of life in this dead place is gone as quickly as it had appeared.

But the sudden impact of its collision sends me sprawling backwards into the metal railings and the impact rips out the decaying bolts holding them to the roof. The precious doll tumbles accidentally from my hand and I snatch desperately for her as the railings collapse. My heart continues pounding in my chest and my stomach leaps, just like when you drive too fast over a big hump on a country lane. No sound escapes from my mouth as my voice is swallowed up by the instant terror and realisation that I'm falling off the roof. There isn't time to think about anything, just an instinctive flailing of hands desperately grabbing at empty space for some connection to the building's roof. But the doll and safety are both beyond my grasp. There is a momentary flash of blue sky, then a sensation of spinning and cold air rushing through my hair as I plunge towards the ground. The last thing I see is the sun near the horizon before my only awareness is the sickening and dull thud of impact in my ear drums.

The first thing I become aware of is a sickly warm, dull taste in my mouth and instinctively I swallow but the taste doesn't go away. There is no pain and I can't see or feel anything. All of my senses seem frozen, except for taste – a taste of what must be blood. But slowly something begins to happen to my vision. First there is just a vague blue blur, closely followed by a grey blur, although neither seems important to me. I swallow again but don't try and move. There doesn't seem to be anything to move or any reason to try. Moving isn't important now, there is only the taste, the silence and the blue and grey blur in my eyes.

My mind can't seem to process time or understand how long I've been experiencing the dull taste and the blurred colours. It feels even colder now though, and so deathly quiet. But the silence is suddenly broken by a muffled voice.

'Fucking hell, he must have fallen!' says the voice.

The voice is unfamiliar but it's a welcome sound and I realise that I would rather not be alone here like the doll.

'Jesus Christ,' follows a second, more panicky reply.

This voice seems vaguely familiar somehow but I can't remember where from. The face of the doll intrudes into my mind and I quickly decide she will be much safer up on the roof than down here.

'Jesus Greg,' shouts the first voice. 'Get Virgil on the radio, quick!'

I hear the crackle of a radio but only the doll seems important to me, the doll I was supposed to be looking after. Why did I have to leave her behind, just like the little girl had? The doll needed protecting, not to be abandoned again.

'Help her,' I gasp desperately, my voice sounding strange in my ears, sort of bubbling but purposeful. I try to spit out the blood but can't seem to get the right movement in my mouth. A large grey shape seems to crouch down beside me.

'D....d...doll,' I say.

'For God's sake take it easy and don't move,' says an urgent voice. 'Where the hell is Virgil?'

The reply is instant. 'On his way. He's on his way right now.'

Those are the last words I hear before the taste in my mouth and the blurred colours suddenly disappear.

2
Mixed Legacy

The meeting room is small and windowless, although it's brightly lit. A long scratch has been gouged into the smooth veneer surface of the meeting table as if something heavy had once been accidentally dragged across it. There are some maps on the walls and a framed photo of a massive engine, possibly from a plane. In one corner by the door are several boxes of leaflets or catalogues stacked under a huge green plant. The leaves look too perfect though, almost certainly plastic and more than a little dusty. As I blink I realise there is a man and a woman sitting opposite me at the table.

'Mr. Charles?' the man says.

He knows my name but what the hell is going on? What am I doing in here? The man speaks again. 'Ewan?'

Yes that's me, but I just fell off a bloody roof! I should be dead. How did I get here? One minute I was dying on a pavement in Pripyat and the next minute I'm sitting at a table in a meeting room!

'Yes...' I reply. 'Sorry?'

'I was asking about your long term ambitions?' the man says.

For a moment I blink rapidly as my mind tries to understand the logic of my new surroundings. The man sitting across the table is in his mid-fifties, almost bald and wearing expensive looking bi-focal glasses. His suit is neatly pressed and inky black like a night sky in the countryside. An uninspiring green paisley tie hangs loosely and informally around his neck, the colour and the pattern reminding me of the vegetation in Pripyat. He steals an uncomfortable glance to his right at the woman sat next to him who is much younger than him and formally dressed in smart business attire. She is a little plain looking but I'm strangely relieved that her hair is nothing like the dolls in Pripyat. It's short and neat with barely a hair out of place while her makeup is understatedly subtle except for around her eyes. Long fake lashes and heavy eye make-up draw my eyes to hers, almost as if that's where she wants people to focus their attention. A business folder and notebook rest open on her lap and she slowly taps a pencil rhythmically on the paper. I wonder if she knows how I got here or why I'm not dead. I should have been killed falling off that roof. Correction, I was killed. My hands involuntarily clutch at my chest but I realise that I can feel my legs under the table and they haven't been smashed and broken by the concrete street.

The man clears his throat to interrupt the momentary silence. 'Are you alright?' he asks.

Jesus, I am alright! I don't know how, but somehow I'm alive! I'm unable to stifle a small laugh so I quickly turn it into a cough and stammer out an apology. 'I... I'm sorry,' I say, 'I was just thinking.'

They'll never believe what's going through my head. The woman frowns at me and writes something down in her notebook, but the man only seems relieved that he's finally regained my attention.

'Are you sure you're alright?' the woman asks me.

My focus returns to her and I suddenly feel a little uncomfortable and embarrassed. No I'm not alright; a few minutes ago I fell off a goddamn roof! Thankfully I don't repeat the thought out loud but I feel a sudden urge to get up and walk away from their questions and this room. Unfortunately I'm unable to think of the social etiquette for doing so. I cough nervously and realise my throat feels dry.

'Yes, I'm sorry,' I say, apologising yet again. 'Really, I'm fine. Can I have some water please?'

They simultaneously slide their chairs backwards and prepare to stand up, but the woman speaks first. 'I'll get it,' she says, making the man sit down and shuffle his chair back under the table. She walks around the table to a water cooler against the far wall and fills me up a plastic cup.

'There you go,' she says, placing the drink in front of me.

I watch her slowly return to her seat and try not to stare too obviously at the lower half of a figure which is well emphasised by her tight skirt and heels. The sight of her body is a welcome distraction from my confused thoughts.

'Thank you,' I say, as she sits back down with knowing eyes and the merest hint of a condescending smirk on her lips. At least I know that I can't be dead if I've noticed her. I swallow a mouthful of the mineral water, although it's lukewarm as if the cooler is perhaps switched off, but it's refreshing all the same. My throat relaxes a little but the memory of tasting blood in my mouth returns. It seems like it happened only minutes ago, but a second, larger gulp of water helps dilute the thought. I have to focus on the present and the situation in front of me.

'Please go on,' I tell her, 'what was your question?'

'Is it a career you're looking for?' asks the woman generically.

This must be an interview! My reply is automatic and equally generic but it seems to satisfy her. 'That's right, I'm looking to stay here and maybe progress in the future.'

The man studies some paperwork in front of him and raises an eyebrow. 'But you have moved around quite a bit in recent years,' he probes, 'are you sure you're ready to settle down?'

'Yes, I'm sure,' I acknowledge automatically.

Two-on-one interviews are always a little more intimidating so I glance down at the table to gather my thoughts. My hands feel damp somehow but there is no blood on them, they are just clammy. There really should be a window in here, but the only glass is a small panel in the door through which I can see desks and people working. There are windows out there, and daylight. Strange, I can't remember interviews ever making me this nervous, but then I don't normally die just before being asked to explain my career goals.

'So you see a long term future here?' asks the man, repeating the same question a little differently. I'm smart enough to know that it suggests my first answer wasn't convincing enough.

'Definitely,' I reply more positively. My hands are flat on the table now, body language at ease as I regain some control. I smile faintly and make eye contact with each of them in turn. 'I really think this is the company for me.'

'Well that's great to hear,' replies the man, leaning back in his chair and relaxing for the first time. 'I think that's really everything we need, unless you have anything else Gemma?'

'No, no,' the woman says, shaking her head and flicking through the pages in her notebook. 'I think I'm done, Virgil.'

Virgil? Why does that name sound familiar? Virgil who? There is a spark of recognition in the back of my mind somewhere but I can't immediately place it.

'Virgil?' I ask.

Virgil nods and raises an eyebrow. 'Yes,' he says, 'Is there anything else you want to ask us?'

The woman offers me a supporting prompt. 'Anything about the job?' she suggests, 'or the company?'

My eyes are drawn one more time to hers before I glance back at Virgil. He is watching me closely through those bi-focals which magnify his eyes, and there is the merest hint of a smile on his face.

'No, no,' I say, slowly shaking my head. 'I think you've covered it all actually. Thank you.'

The interview went as well as could be expected considering that I died just before it started and missed almost all it, so I could forgive myself if I'm unsuccessful. It feels like the most ridiculous thought I've ever had. The whole concept makes no sense, but thankfully the gentle rocking of the crowded London city bus soothes my thoughts like a mother cradling a baby.

The familiar city streets slide past the windows of the bus and a thousand people with expressionless faces jostle past each other. Everyone is trying to move at their own pace, uninterested in the others around them and seemingly oblivious to them. There are so many individuals, but in the social environment of the street no eye contact is made and no words are spoken to strangers. Everyone has their own personal thoughts, all of them private and secret.

It's a blessing to forget my own thoughts for a moment and I'm suddenly far more interested in theirs. I watch the men, women and children, all moving through the crowd at different speeds, some purposeful, some ambling, some being pushed along by the flow. Where are they all going and who are they? What thoughts are preoccupying their minds?

Suddenly the bus judders to a halt as a bell rings somewhere near the front. The street looks familiar and somehow I know this is my stop. The bus doors close behind me with a hiss like a giant mechanical snake, but the sound is quickly swallowed up by the cacophony of the street. An orchestra of vehicle horns, car engines and the sounds of people overload my senses. As the bus pulls back out into the heavy traffic and lumbers away into the distance I notice the street is wet. The rain has already stopped but puddles have formed in the uneven parts of the pavement.

There is a magazine and newspaper stand nearby and its colourful tapestry of enticing magazine covers draws me towards it. The newspapers appear dull and uninteresting though, editors desperately searching for dramatic headlines on a day when there clearly aren't any. 'Recession Confirmed,' reads one, 'Opposition to cut taxes' reads another.

The man running the stand is old, his face wrinkled, but still pink and healthy looking. His meagre patch of greying hair is shiny and damp from the recent rainfall while water still drips from his shabby duffel coat. I hear the musical clink of coins as he moves around the stand adjusting magazines and muttering about the rain. There is something familiar about that sound, and his face for that matter.

'Hello Ewan,' says the elderly man, with a broad smile.

'Hello Eric,' I reply, apparently knowing his name.

'How was the interview?' he asks, 'did it go alright?'

How does he know about that? He knows my name and about as much about my day as I do, but does he understand it any better than me?

'I'm not really sure,' I tell him. 'They seemed to like me, I suppose.'

'Well it's about bloody time someone hired you,' he says, shaking his head. 'I can't afford to lose a regular customer can I?'

I nod my head towards the newspaper headlines. 'I figure you need all the business you can get, looking at those.'

Eric shakes his head disapprovingly. 'Bloody Politicians!' he grumbles, 'they're all the same, bloody useless like the weather. They should come out here and try doing a real days work for once.'

I shrug my shoulders indifferently but in vaguely polite agreement. Politics have never interested me and I haven't bothered to cast my vote since doing it once when I was eighteen. 'Your Grandfather fought for democracy!' my own father used to say. But that was a long time ago and my parents were long gone; both from heart problems, although my memories of them are all happy ones. The thought of them makes me smile. Why can I remember them so vividly but not what happened after my apparent death in Pripyat, or how I ended up in an interview?

'You got my stuff?' asks Eric, interrupting my thoughts.

'What stuff?' I ask, a little bemused, 'I don't understand.'

Eric sighs and punches my shoulder hard but jokingly with his bony fist. 'You're always screwing around,' he says laughing, as he reaches for my coat pocket.

I push his hand away and take a step back, my hands raised at his sudden intrusion. 'What the hell are you doing?' I demand as I rub my sore shoulder where he punched it.

'Take it easy,' he says, 'what's with you? Are you sure that interview went well?'

I lower my hands, surprised at my own defensiveness but I reach instinctively inside my coat pocket and pull something out.

'I knew you would get them!' chuckles Eric, snatching away the small plastic bag that I've removed from my pocket.

He opens the bag and holds up a bottle of pills with a prescription label on it and gives it a little shake before putting it in his pocket. I don't even remember where I got them from.

Eric turns away and retrieves a magazine from his stand.

'Here you go,' he says, cheerfully handing it to me. 'I kept one aside for you.'

It's a National Geographic. The bright yellow border on the cover is unmistakable and familiar, but the picture on the cover makes the blood drain from my face. Images of Pripyat are suddenly forming in my mind. Ruined buildings fill my thoughts and I'm falling from that roof again, clutching at empty air. The doll's face is there too, a single tear sliding down her disappointed plastic face. Suddenly I feel dizzy and my head is hurting. I scrunch my eyes shut and rub my throbbing forehead as the images all come too fast, too clear, too frightening.

'What's the matter?' asks Eric, his voice hauling me back from the Ukraine. Staring up at me from the magazine's front cover is a photograph of the Chernobyl Sarcophagus with trees surrounding it. The headline read 'ANIMALS INHERIT MIXED LEGACY AT CHERNOBYL.'

The waiting room is full with maybe twenty people, most of them old and half of them coughing. Why do people always cough so much in Doctors waiting rooms? Boredom tempts me to pick up a magazine with flowers on the cover. I flick through the mauled and out of date pages at the clichéd collection of stories: 'My Baby Scare,' 'Win a Three Week Cruise,' 'New Diet Horror.' The magazine is quickly discarded back onto the obsolete but well-thumbed pile.

There's a mobile phone in my pocket and I realise there is one missed call on it, but the number is unknown. It must have rung during the interview but appears to have been set to silent mode, another thing I don't recall doing. As far as I remember I was in Pripyat one moment and then in an interview the next. The call can't have been important though because whoever rang didn't leave any message.

How long have I been waiting now? It seems like hours listening to the endless coughing. I'm relieved when a voice finally crackles from a speaker above the reception desk, 'Ewan Charles, Doctor Reed, Room Two.'

Dr. Reed is a prim middle aged female doctor who is dressed conservatively in an uninspiring long plaid skirt. She sits upright in her leather chair with a perfect posture, back straight and motions for me to sit down. I sit in the patient chair facing her and she smiles in welcome. The screensaver fish swimming leisurely around the computer screen on her desk and a half empty coffee mug with a dolphin on it tell me something about her. Her mature face seems friendly and trustworthy, the very mask of professionalism. I sense that her real personality switches off in this room and she becomes a hundred percent doctor. Patients would open up their worries to her.

'So, what can I do for you?' she asks automatically. It sounds like she has asked the same question a million times before, but I wonder where the hell to start.

'I'm not exactly sure,' I reply.

'Alright, well tell me what seems to be the problem,' she says encouragingly.

I force myself to cough, just like the people in the waiting room, as if it might somehow add some credibility to my presence here, or maybe even assist her diagnosis.

'I think there is something wrong up here,' I say, pointing to the side of my head.

Dr. Reed immediately seems interested and a little intrigued now that she has been given some direction. 'You have a headache? A migraine?' she inquires, sitting forward in her chair and leaning a little closer.

'No, no, not really' I reply, shaking my head, 'it's not a pain.'

'Go on,' she says patiently, 'please go on.'

It's difficult to explain something when I can't understand my own symptoms and I'm conscious of sounding ridiculous, but she has such an aura of trustworthiness about her.

'It's not pain,' I explain. 'It's like... I think I've been forgetting things, but also remembering things. But I'm not sure they are things that really happened. For instance, I think I dreamt that I died last night, but...I'm not sure. It felt like I really did die. It's kind of stupid saying this I know, but I feel... confused, you know? Like everything is all wrong and somehow mixed up. I know that doesn't make much sense.'

I'm embarrassed to realise that my body is rocking slightly backwards and forwards as I finish and I even have to stop my left leg from shaking. If my words haven't convinced her that I'm crazy then that probably has.

'Alright, let's just slow down for a moment,' she says, 'can you tell me when all these feelings started?'

That part is clear to me at least. 'Yesterday,' I say with certainty. 'That's when I fell off a building – in the Ukraine.'

'You were in an accident?' she asks while frowning.

Dr. Reed quickly regains her professional facade to hide the first display of doubt I've seen on her face. Suddenly the memory of falling returns to my mind and my hands clutch desperately for something to grab onto. I'm falling and grabbing for the roof and then there is the inevitable and terrifying thud against concrete. I jump in my seat as I remember the impact again, my hands gripping the arm rests of the patient chair.

'It's alright Mr. Charles,' she says soothingly, 'just take your time.'

'Yes, yes. I was in an accident,' I say, nodding with absolute certainty. 'But I think I was killed...'

My words sound ludicrous but it's impossible to doubt an actual memory and while the implausibility of dying yesterday confuses the hell out of me, I clearly remember it happening.

'It doesn't seem like you were killed,' she reassures me, 'were you in a hospital maybe? Where were you treated?'

'I don't know,' I reply.

'Well there's nothing here in your records about any accident,' she says, gesturing to her computer. 'Did you fly back yesterday from the... where did you say again? The Ukraine?'

I have no recollection of any flight in my memory, so maybe I survived the accident and just forgot about being treated and flying back.

'No I didn't fly,' I tell her while shaking my head. 'I had an interview this morning.'

'An interview?' she asks with a baffled look, finally allowing her professional facade to slip totally. I wonder what took her so long.

'I know I'm not making sense,' I acknowledge, clenching my fists in frustration. 'Everything is just so... confusing.'

'Are you on any medication, or seeing any other Doctor?' she asks, digging for clues as to what's wrong with me.

Now we get to the point where she understandably thinks I'm crazy. 'Look, I'm sorry,' I say, suddenly feeling uncomfortable, 'I'm wasting your time here, I should go.'

'No really, its fine,' she says, 'let me take a look at you first. Let's see if we can figure out what's wrong. I want to start by listening to your heart and checking your blood pressure, okay?'

But suddenly I don't want her help any more, this doesn't feel right somehow. Dr. Reed can't help me and I want to go home. Her usual patients are alive, not recently deceased. Being here doesn't make sense anymore, in fact nothing makes any sense, but this time social etiquette won't stop me from leaving abruptly.

'No,' I say firmly, as I stand up quickly. 'Sorry, you can't help me Doctor. I'm fine.'

'You're not fine!' my wife Helen insists.

I'd taken the short taxi ride from the Doctors to the apartment and it truly feels good to be home. I want Pripyat forced out of my thoughts. Perhaps my death was just a daydream, a distant unreality that will fade away with time. It had to be. This was my reality – at home in the apartment with her, not wallowing in confusion and ambiguity.

'Honey?' she asks, interrupting my thoughts and being as persistent as ever.

'What?' I reply.

'I said you're not fine!' she says a little louder, 'you weren't even listening. You're miles away. What were you thinking about?'

The late afternoon sunlight shining through the window of our apartment makes Helen almost a silhouette. She is beautiful, fiery and always persistent – just a few of my many reasons for loving her.

'Jesus Ewan!' she snaps with sudden annoyance, 'talk to me.'

'Alright, alright!' I reply abruptly. 'I am fine. I was just thinking, that's all.'

Helen folds her arms defiantly. 'You come home telling me that you thought you died and were so confused that you went to the Doctors. And then you stand there miles away, barely hearing a word I'm saying. And you haven't even told me about the interview. Then you tell me you're fine. What the hell is going on?'

'Look Helen, I must have had a bad dream last night,' I say as convincingly as I can, 'you know how I sometimes read about that stuff, about Chernobyl.'

But this doesn't feel like a dream. I can remember it as clearly as the taxi journey or Doctor Reed's questions an hour ago. If dying was a dream then why can I picture the trees in Pripyat, almost smell the decay and remember the eerie silence? Why can I feel myself falling, hear 'Virgil' on the radio, taste blood and feel the darkness coming for me. Helen is right – I am a long way from being fine.

'You never go to the doctors Ewan,' she says, placing a hand on my shoulder. 'And no one goes to the Doctor's after a dream, do they?'

That was a statement of fact rather than a question and I can't argue with her logic. But I did go, so does that mean that it wasn't a dream? Or am I losing my mind?

'I don't even know why I went,' I tell her, 'it was stupid.'

'Well what did they say? They must have thought you were insane telling them you died yesterday!' she says.

Helen deserved some kind of reassurance and there is no sense in us both worrying. 'Look, it's alright,' I tell her quickly. 'They checked me out and I'm fine. I'm not insane and I don't need to be locked up. And I don't have a tumour either. It's just been a long week, that's all. Probably a stupid daydream and that's all there is to it.'

Helen puts her hands on her hips and takes up a defiant stance. 'Well no job hunting tomorrow,' she insists. 'You can stay at home where I can keep an eye on you. How about I make us some dinner and you can tell me all about the interview, alright?'

The walls of the dining area of our apartment are painted yellow, the colour of sunflowers at Helen's insistence. Eating at the dining table always makes food taste better and the steak is perfect, well done but not chewy like beef so often is. The thick cut chips and fresh peas taste as good as ever. Helen always cooks my favourite meal perfectly and she smiles at me as she eats her pasta. Since Helen had renounced meat ten years ago and became a vegetarian it was a wonder I ever got steak, but she always cooked two different meals. She was considerate like that, never one to force her diet on others, Jenny or me. Thinking about our daughter banishes Pripyat to the back of my mind.

Helen picks slowly at her pasta, often eating like that to ensure that her meal would last as long as mine. She knows I always take my time over steak because I like to savour every mouthful. It's little wonder we're still together, we are even compatible diners.

'This is good,' I say, breaking the silence now that I'm half way through my meal.

'Thanks, it's your turn to cook tomorrow,' she reminds me, picking up a celery stick from her side plate.

I think about how much I hate celery as I nod in agreement.

'I'll hopefully hear back from them next week,' I tell her. 'They seemed impressed enough.'

'That's good, I'm glad it went alright,' she replies.

I shrug. 'They said I'd moved around a bit much, but I say that gets you experience right?'

'Yeah, I guess so,' agrees Helen. 'Fifteen jobs in the same number of years doesn't look very good on paper though does it!'

Has it really been that many? Jobs just didn't seem to work out for me. Sometimes I didn't like the company, or they closed down, or they didn't like me, or I found something I liked better. That's just the way it usually panned out, but at least it wasn't always for the same reason, and more often than not it was my choice. But the statistics only remind me that I'm unemployed and probably shouldn't have walked out of my last position just before the job market went to hell. The realisation hits me that finding a new job this time might not be so easy.

'So what time is Jenny coming home?' I ask, changing the subject.

'Eh?' says Helen, 'Jenny?'

'Yeah, what time is she back from college?' I ask, wiping some mustard from the side of my mouth.

'Who's Jenny?' asks Helen, smirking in amusement, 'your college bit on the side?'

'Yeah right!' I joke, 'you know I've only got eyes for you.'

The woman in the interview flashes briefly into my mind, walking round the meeting table with my cup of water. Gemma was it?

'I might believe that one day,' laughs Helen, 'maybe when your seventy and too old to do anything about it.'

I laugh too. 'I won't stop at seventy I hope, so what time will she be home?'

'Who?' she asks again.

'Jenny,' I sigh impatiently, 'bloody hell, I thought I was the mad one!'

'You are!' she says, 'Jenny who?'

'Err... Jenny,' I repeat slowly, as if explaining it to a child, 'our daughter.'

Helen begins to laugh and puts her fork down for a moment. She is still chuckling when she picks up a cherry tomato and pops it into her mouth, but when she notices my expression she stops chewing and the colour drains from her face.

'We... haven't got a daughter,' she says cautiously.

What the hell is she talking about? Of course we have – Jenny. She must have gone mad, but her face is anything but that of someone insane.

'Of course we have!' I reply, expecting immediate confirmation from her. But it doesn't come.

'You're winding me up right?' she says, forcing a faint smile. 'One flew over the cuckoo's nest, right?'

My expression tells her otherwise and my fork slips from my hand and clatters onto the dining table. I'm losing grip of my own puzzling reality and suddenly my favourite steak seems to have no taste at all anymore.

The photographs are lying, irrespective of what Helen believes.

'She's got black hair,' I shout in annoyance, 'she's eighteen and beautiful. She goes to fucking college!'

'Calm down!' yells Helen, desperately trying to get through to me.

'How the hell can I calm down?' I demand, flicking through the pages of the next album in frustration, 'our bloody daughter has vanished.'

'Ewan?' she says quietly, 'you're....scaring me.'

Helen's words don't register at all with me. I scour the last album but there isn't a single picture of our daughter Jenny, at any age. Impossibly, there are only pictures of Helen and me.

'For fucks sake Ewan, stop it!' shouts Helen desperately. 'We haven't got a kid!'

I barely hear her outburst as I throw the last album onto the coffee table. It slides along the glass surface and disappears off the edge, taking the pot pourri and two remote controls with it.

'What the hell is going on?' I demand. It wasn't meant to be a question, just a release of frustration. Anger is not my style but without thinking I kick the coffee table and it tips over, the top shattering in a shower of glass fragments onto the carpet. What is happening to me? First there was Pripyat, and now this. I desperately need a glass of water but I slump despondently onto the sofa and put my head in my hands in despair.

The sudden pain is immeasurable and drives away all of my other feelings, thoughts and emotions. I gasp desperately for air as shock rolls through my body, freezing me for a moment in time. The glass of water slips from my hand and smashes on the tiles of the kitchen floor. My legs buckle and I sink to my knees as the knife is yanked roughly from my back. What the hell just happened?

'Helen?' I gasp urgently.

As I look up, I see her silhouetted against the kitchen window with a jagged bread knife in her hand, slick with blood. The knife glints as my blood drips from it to fall seemingly in slow motion towards the kitchen floor. The pain is unbearable but for some reason an image of a water droplet splashing into a pond flashes into my mind, the way it makes a splash and smaller little droplets form a circle around it. That is what my blood will do when it drips onto the tiles.

Helen stands there silently and motionless, just a vision of murderous intent. My loving wife has stabbed me. The back of my shirt feels wet and heavy from the blood that must be streaming out of the deep cut in my back. Our kitchen floor is always so clean, that is the last random thought that enters my mind as I desperately gasp for air. But nothing can help me in my desperate fight for survival against the fatal wound. At least there will be an end to the confusion of the last few days, my thoughts will finally be at peace and I'm almost glad this nightmare is over. If I'd had the time, I might have wondered why she did it but I was gone before my body finally slumped to the floor.

3
Life is no Picnic

The park is beautiful this morning, lush green grass and not a cloud in the perfect blue sky. Sunlight basks down through the tree branches turning the grass into a patchwork of light and shadows. The air smells pure like a summer meadow and somewhere birds are chirping. It's still morning and not too hot yet, but it's bright enough for me to feel grateful for my sunglasses. A large pond reflects the sunlight on its gently rippling surface. The water looks inviting and popular as ever with the ducks and swans that paddle in it or peck away at the grass searching for food. I inhale deeply and enjoy the morning air as my legs feel the tickle of warm grass beneath them where my shorts end. Our picnic is spread out over a red and white check blanket next to an open basket. There are little plates of sandwiches, a sponge cake and an open bottle of Taittinger champagne already poured into two glasses. Sitting opposite me on the blanket is Helen and she is holding a knife in her hand. The glint of the knife blade snaps my attention back to being stabbed as the brutal memory of it hits me like a sledgehammer. Jesus, she just stabbed me and now we're having a picnic!

'Christ!' I yelp as my pulse accelerates and my heart thunders in my chest.

I scramble backwards off the blanket and quickly stand up. Helen jumps in startled surprise at my sudden movement and peers up at me over her sunglasses. I raise my hands defensively although she hasn't moved, but my surprise quickly turns to anger. 'What the hell did you do that for?' I demand, my pulse still racing.

She looks at me with a puzzled expression. 'What? I was just going to cut us some cake,' she says innocently. 'What's the matter with you? Did you see a wasp or something?'

She knows how much I hate buzzing insects and the way they always seem to appear the moment a picnic basket even touches the floor, often before it's even opened.

'Put the knife down!' I demand.

Helen angrily tosses the knife down next to the cake. 'Fine! Happy now?' she snaps. 'You cut the bloody thing then.'

I frantically reach behind me to check my back but my T-shirt is dry, there is no blood and no fatal wound pouring my life away. Without the knife Helen looks harmless enough in her NYC baseball cap and short sleeve top. Her wavy red hair looks much lighter in the sun and her freckled cheeks are lightly tanned, but my eyes still focus on the knife. I won't turn my back on her again, not after she stabbed me in the back for no damn reason. At least that's what she did a minute ago. But then why am I alright now? What the hell does this mean? Wait a minute, I remember! First there was Pripyat and then her. Did I just dream of dying twice? That doesn't make any sense. But it wasn't a dream – it just happened, we were in the kitchen a moment ago and then she stabbed me – it was all over so fast. And suddenly I'm right here having a picnic. I must be losing my mind, you can't die twice.

I scan the park nervously with my eyes, looking for potential dangers, but there doesn't appear to be any, there are just clusters of trees scattered around the grassy parkland and the lovely pond. Four or five other couples are innocently sunning themselves on blankets or enjoying their picnics. One even has a couple of kids with them, kicking a football around and laughing. This is hardly the time and place to quietly murder your husband.

Reluctantly I begin to feel myself relax slightly as I look at Helen. She is staring straight at me with a surprised and expectant look on her face, or is she just waiting for me to drop my guard? Will she plunge that knife into me at her first opportunity?

Sitting back down I avoid taking my eyes off her. I haven't relaxed enough to do that, but my beautiful loving wife seems anything but dangerous now. I can't fathom any reason she could possibly have for wanting to hurt me.

'What the hell was all that about?' she asks.

'You stabbing me!' I say accusingly.

Helen doesn't answer though. She just stares at me with a blank expression on her face.

'I mean you're going to stab me!' I say, 'in the kitchen.'

'What are you on about, stab you?' she says slowly and precisely.

She's right, my words sound crazy. The whole thing is madness but she isn't *going* to stab me – she has already done it! I remember the whole thing clearly. We were in the apartment arguing about the missing photos of Jenny and then I smashed the coffee table. Jesus, our daughter! Nothing seems to make any sense but Jenny's pure and smiling face appears clearly in my mind. Helen looks totally puzzled which only feeds my confusion and frustration.

'Almost stabbed me,' I amend my statement. 'I mean you almost stabbed me – just now.'

'I was nowhere fucking near you,' she snaps angrily, 'I was only cutting the cake.'

Now I feel stupid. 'I know, I'm sorry,' I say apologetically, 'go on and cut it.'

Helen scowls and snatches up the knife, making me flinch, then pulls the sponge cake towards her and cuts two slices. 'What did you mean when you said I was going to stab you in the kitchen?'

Am I seriously suggesting that she will stab me in the future? Were the stabbing and the fall in Pripyat both in my future, like a premonition maybe? But that makes no sense either, you still can't die twice.

'With the kitchen knife,' I say, stumbling over the words, 'I meant stab me with the kitchen knife. You know how clumsy you are.'

'I'm damn sure I can cut a slice of cake without stabbing anyone,' she says, holding out a plate to me. 'See? Once slice of cake and no corpses.'

I take the cake from her and notice that I'm sweating. It must be anxiety because it isn't quite hot enough outside for that yet. Helen is behaving normally, just my loving wife and not like some maniac killer. Maybe everything else is back to normal too. This place seems perfect, almost idyllic and I urge my worries to subside and force myself to sound calm.

'Look at them kids over there,' I say, gesturing with my plate and changing the subject, 'kids are hard work, aren't they?'

'Boys maybe,' she nods, smiling and biting into her slice of her cake, 'we haven't done too badly though.'

'How do you mean?' I ask cautiously.

'Well Jenny hasn't been much problem has she?' she says.

Her response comes as such a blessing after what happened yesterday. A warm feeling of relief washes over me and I stop watching her to gaze up at the blue sky. Is this nightmare finally over? Jenny hasn't vanished and I'm not dead. Helen doesn't even want me dead either and just maybe I've never even been to the bloody Ukraine.

Helen re-fills my champagne glass and I watch the clear sparkling liquid bubble and fizz in the sunlight. I quickly drain the glass in one gulp and the fizzing makes my nose sting. The champagne may have already lost some of its chill but it's still sharp and refreshing. I lay myself down on the blanket, putting down my empty plate as the sun warms my face and I feel myself smile.

'God it's nice out here, isn't it?' I say.

Helen doesn't answer though. She just crawls forward and lies next to me instead. I feel her warmth as puts an arm around me and begins to kiss me. Her close proximity in the sunshine and the fresh air combined with the champagne is an intoxicating combination. She stares piercingly into my eyes and a small grin forms on her smudged lips.

'What do you reckon?' she purrs suggestively.

'What about?' I ask, frowning.

She smiles demurely. 'Shall we do it?'

I'm not completely naive, but am still not quite sure she is serious. 'What here?' I ask doubtfully.

'Why not?' she teases.

I steal a cautious glance either side of me. The other picnickers are not that close, but we aren't exactly concealed either. Helen senses my thoughts and giggles. 'Don't worry Ewan, we can be discrete,' she whispers.

The combination of her kisses, the sunshine and two glasses of champagne is a potent cocktail that dispels any inhibitions I have left. Desire washes away my concerns at being noticed and I return her kisses, only differently now which is all the answer she needs.

Our rental car tears down the uneven country lane, cruising comfortably over the humps in the road. Its early afternoon now and only half an hour's drive back to our apartment in the city. I glance across at Helen in the passenger seat and grin. She smiles knowingly back at me.

'How was lunch?' she asks.

'Not bad, but dessert was better!' I reply.

'We'll definitely have to come out here again another weekend,' she says, and I don't hesitate to agree with her.

This morning has been perfect but my mind refuses to accept normality and drifts back to the moment of being stabbed. My wife killed me in cold blood and yet it seems impossible. I've spent my morning with her and she is as real as I am, and far from murderous. Why do I recall picking up a lost doll in Pripyat and falling from a roof? Why didn't Jenny seem to exist yesterday? I must have lost my mind, it seems the only logical explanation, but surely someone insane doesn't speculate about it. As I glance over at Helen again I just don't feel crazy.

The steering wheel feels solid in my hands and the vibration of it is reassuringly real. I can feel every bump in the road and my foot relaxes on the accelerator slightly, slowing the car down just a little. That's cause and effect isn't it? My thoughts wander back to Chernobyl which must be the ultimate example of cause and effect.

'Helen, I was just thinking about Chernobyl,' I tell her.

'Uh-huh,' she murmurs in vague acknowledgement.

'You know there's something like a 30 kilometre exclusion zone around that place these days,' I explain, repeating what I've learnt from various media sources. 'After the accident they built a massive building around it called the Sarcophagus. You know, to keep all the shit inside.'

Helen seems to be listening but doesn't answer me, and I reach the conclusion that she's probably heard me talk about this before. We often talked to each other during car journeys without really having a conversation. Sometimes I would just recite my frustrations about my week at work and complain about company bureaucracy or she would share details of her week in marketing. Neither of us would comment much on what the one other said or even take much interest, just listening passively to help the journey pass.

'Yeah, they say the Sarcophagus is leaking now,' I continue, 'and they're going to have to build a completely new one around it. Imagine the cost of that fucker. It's amazing really. It'll have to be like that for hundreds of years.'

Helen finally voices some interest. 'Is that how long the radiation will be there then?' she asks.

'Dunno exactly,' I admit, 'but it'll be a bloody long time.'

'Oh,' she replies, quickly losing interest again.

I find it so easy to talk when driving. Maybe it's because you don't need to make any eye contact and can just talk away without the scrutiny of someone staring at you. I know that I'm delaying explaining my real thoughts to her, but realise that this car journey is probably my best opportunity to do it.

'Helen, let me ask you something,' I say.

'Yeah what?' she asks, turning her head to look at me.

'Have you ever had like... déjà vu?' I ask. 'Or daydreams maybe? Only they're really convincing ones, I mean like they were real events?'

I see her nodding out of the corner of my eye. 'Yeah I've had déjà vu before. I think everyone has at some point or other.'

'Well I don't really mean déjà vu,' I reply. 'I mean has something ever happened to you that you think didn't actually happen or that you just dreamed it happened maybe?'

Helen remains silent for a moment, staring at the road ahead in thought while presumably exploring the question in her mind. 'I don't think so,' she says finally, shaking her head, 'only déjà vu occasionally, like that time we were horse riding in Greece. Do you remember that?'

I did remember. Helen was convinced that we had done the whole thing before, but it wasn't very likely as neither of us especially liked horses and that was our only trip to Greece. We had only booked the excursion on the spur of the moment because it sounded like a romantic thing to do while we were on holiday.

'Yeah I remember. You were so bloody convinced!' I say, 'but what about the feeling that something that has already happened then suddenly hasn't happened?'

'Eh?' she says, frowning and trying to wrap her head around the concept. 'Not really, no. Why, have you?'

'You wouldn't believe me if I told you,' I tell her in clichéd fashion.

'Why wouldn't I?' she asks.

Should I try to explain the mad thoughts that I can't get out of my head to her? I know her well enough to conclude that it can't do any harm.

'Well it's weird, and this will sound dumb,' I begin, 'but in my mind, it's like yesterday we were at home and you just stabbed me in the back for no reason and killed me. Next thing I know, we're in the park and you're cutting cake.'

Helen laughs sceptically. 'What are you on about?' she asks.

'I'm serious!' I tell her, emphasising my point by gesturing with one hand. 'It's like that's what really happened. It sounds mad but I can remember it as clear as anything. And the thing that's even weirder is that the day before yesterday I was in Chernobyl and I fell off a roof and died again. As soon as I died it was yesterday and that's when you stabbed me.'

Helen pulls down the visor on the windscreen and looks at her reflection in the little vanity mirror. She reaches for something in her handbag and then begins touching up her lipstick as if my words haven't registered at all.

'That's pretty messed up,' she says finally.

'I mean it Helen,' I stress to her, but not very convincingly. I'm not even sure I can convince myself of what I am saying.

'Oh well,' she says, returning the lipstick to her bag and closing the sun visor. 'I'm not sure whether that's actually a kind of déjà vu or not, but at least you're still alive now.'

Maybe she is wrong to dismiss the idea so readily, but she is definitely right about one thing – I am alive now. I can't expect her to start panicking or taking the whole thing too seriously. I wouldn't if our roles were reversed. Perhaps I should just stop wondering about it or searching for answers that aren't there. It's best just to stop talking and get home.

Driving fast on country lanes in the sun is a liberating experience but as I accelerate out of the next bend a tractor lurches into the road ahead. The red monstrosity suddenly appears from behind the hedge of a field and lumbers straight into the middle of the road. Helen screams out a desperate warning as I slam my foot down hard on the brake, but the agricultural road block is too close. The piercing blast of the car horn, which I don't even remember pressing, joins the sound of Helen's scream in my ears. Our car smashes violently into the side of the tractor with a deafening and sickening bang.

There is an explosion of airbags inside the car, burning my arm during inflation as the whole world becomes a blur. The seatbelt burrows hard into my shoulder and the windscreen explodes as I feel myself upside down and torn at by unseen forces. Everything in my eyesight seems to flash alternatively light and dark and is accompanied by a disorientating feeling of spinning, but it's the rapid sounds of crunching and banging which are most frightening. The whole terrifying experience probably lasts only a few seconds and every sense in my body is overwhelmed in a desperate struggle to interpret what's happening. Everything occurs too rapidly to digest and understand though. As I frantically wonder if Helen is alright, something suddenly smashes hard into the side of my head. For a split second I can feel that the car is still moving, but then everything goes dark and I feel nothing at all.

A woman's voice pervades the depths of my mind. 'Honey?'

I blink slowly but the lights are so bright and intrusive that they sting my eyes. I'm forced to squint because everything seems blurred and out of focus, almost as if I'm under water.

'Ewan it's me,' she says.

There is something white all around me covering my body and I realise it's a bed sheet. My hand is outside it and someone is holding it and squeezing it. I can see her gripping my hand but can't seem to feel the sensation of her touch.

'Oh my god...you're awake,' the woman sobs with relief, 'can you hear me?'

Her face appears above me and it's blurred but familiar.

'Ewan!' she says. 'My God, you've come back.'

As her words begin to register in my mind, questions immediately replace them. What happened to me and where am I? There are more thoughts flooding into my head than I seem to be able to process and my mind feels disorientated. I know that I need help but it's just too bright in here to concentrate properly and the lights are making me dizzy. Sharp pains suddenly fill my head and the room begins to spin. I gasp for breath and start to panic 'Where am I?' I call out.

'Ewan?' she says, 'it's me Helen. I'm here.'

The pain subsides slightly as I recognise the voice of my wife. Thank God she's alright.

Helen is interrupted by a new voice, calmer, deeper and with an insistent tone. 'Let him rest,' the man urges.

I close my eyes defensively for a moment against the bright lights and my consciousness retreats back into the dark, away from my questions and away from the light. The woman is still talking but I can't hear her clearly anymore, her voice is just a fading whisper swallowed by the darkness.

My eyes blink groggily open and I wonder how long I've been asleep. The room isn't quite as bright now and I notice a window covered by the open slats of Venetian blinds, through which I see the late afternoon sun sinking behind some trees. The hospital room only has one bed but it seems huge, either that or I feel small laying in it. I glance furtively around the room but can't seem to move my head properly. There is something stiff around my neck. I hear a faint whirring noise behind me and feel something pressing into my arm, but I'm not sure what it is. Somewhere a hospital machine emits an intermittent beeping sound but it's gentle and oddly reassuring. The purpose of the beep is meaningless to me but I sense that the machine is helping me somehow.

I call out softly but there doesn't seem to be anyone else in the room, although it makes me realise that my mouth feels dry and my tongue awkward when I try to speak. Slowly I move my hands up towards my face. There's a tube in my nose which feels strange and alien when I gingerly touch it. Holding my arm up seems to take a lot of effort so I allow it rest it back down on the bed.

'Hello?' I say croakily, wondering where the man and woman have gone to.

I suddenly feel very alone but the pillows are soft and comfortable, so I try to relax and focus on the reassuring feeling they give me. I'm so groggy and tired that sleep comes quickly.

The car is rolling over, smashing through a hedge and tearing up the surface of the field. Now I'm standing in the field with Helen, and an enormous tractor is driving straight towards us. Suddenly we're both running and desperately stumbling over the rutted ground as the tractor looms down on us, but Helen trips and falls. There is a thunderous crashing sound and I have visions of glass shattering and exploding in slow motion. I hear Helen scream because suddenly there are more tractors now, dozens of them bearing down on us and this time we both fall. The tractors are about to crush us when suddenly a voice magically washes all of the nightmare images away.

'Hello Honey,' says Helen, making my eyes flicker open.

I glance at the window but the slats of the blinds are closed now. My head is throbbing but it doesn't seem quite as painful as earlier. It feels so good to see her face. 'Helen?' I say, trying to form a smile on my face.

'I love you Ewan,' she says.

Her words are familiar, like I've heard them from her thousands of times, but they feel particularly comforting right now. 'What time is it?' I mutter.

She leans over and hugs me carefully as I lift my hands to rest on her waist. 'It's seven o'clock,' she says, 'how do you feel?'

'What happened to me?' I ask.

Helen sits down in the chair beside the bed and holds my hand. I try to turn my head but realise I've got a plastic brace around my neck and can only see her out of the corner of my eyes. There is a smile on her face but also a distant worried look, and for the first time I notice a bandage wrapped around her forearm. I need to look closer and check she's alright but I can't seem to move.

'We were in a car accident,' she explains. 'You were unconscious, don't you remember?'

My memory seems smudged and hazy and I can't seem to access it. I'm determined to remember but concentrating makes the pain in my head worse and I can only visualize hazy images of this room and the brightness of the ceiling lights.

'Accident?' I say, repeating the word slowly as if it might help to trigger my memory.

Helen squeezes my hand and this time I feel it, her fingers warm and her grip tight despite the bandage on her arm.

'Do you want some water?' she asks.

Despite the neck brace I manage a tiny nod and she pours some water into my mouth from a plastic cup. Swallowing feels strange and uncomfortable but the drink is good and I remember someone else giving me water in a plastic cup, a different woman. The water seems to jog my memory and I remember her figure moving round a table. Yes, it was during an interview. The memory is slowly building up in my head like its returning in fragments, but how did I end up in hospital? The interview finished and I took the bus, but then what? I wonder if they've given me some drugs which are blurring my mind and affecting my thoughts. Helen looks pale. 'Are you alright?' I ask her.

'I'm fine,' she says, 'it's only a cut arm.'

'How long have we been here?' I ask.

'Five hours I think,' she replies.

A single tear escapes from of one of her eyes and she wipes it away quickly with the back of her hand in an attempt to conceal her emotions.

'It's OK,' I say, as she blinks a few times to compose herself.

'You've got a head injury,' she explains, 'I told you earlier when you came round the first time. Don't you remember?'

That would explain the uncomfortable neck brace, the headache and my confusion. 'No, I can't remember anything' I reply, 'just the interview.'

'What interview?' she asks, 'Don't you remember the accident?'

Did she just say we were in an accident?

'I'm not sure,' I reply.

Helen looks concerned. 'We crashed into a tractor,' she explains to me. 'Our car rolled over and they had to cut you out of it.'

As I try to take in her explanation, the door to the room opens and a man in a shirt and tie walks in. There is a hospital ID round his neck and a brown folder tucked under his arm. He has a steely, focused look on his face as he strides purposely over to the bed. I sense he is one of those people who always arrives exactly where he needs to be, on time and without rushing. It's like there's an aura of confidence following him that can barely keep up.

'Good! You're awake,' he says, 'My name is Virgil Adams, Head of Neurosurgery.'

The name Virgil is familiar and I ponder where I have heard it before, blocking out his voice as I search my memory. It seems important to know, so important that when he continues talking his words barely register.

'Hello again,' says Helen with a note of concern in her voice.

I need to explain something to you both,' Virgil says. 'Mr. Charles has suffered a serious head trauma, which has unfortunately caused a cerebral haemorrhage.'

Suddenly I place his name, I heard it in Pripyat! That was where I had heard the name Virgil, on the radio after my fall! But it's surely just a coincidence.

The surgeon continues. 'Your CT scan shows some cranial bleeding in the brain that we are going to need to deal with. It's important we take care of it as soon as possible, so I'm going to have to operate immediately.'

His words seem unimportant because memories are flooding back into my mind as if his name is a key that unlocked them. It's not a bloody coincidence! There was a Virgil at that interview too – on the second day that I died. And now this surgeon, three people since this shit started in three different places with the same first name.

I notice Helen rubbing her hands on her neck, remembering how she always does that when she is really worried or concerned. 'I thought you hoped that operating wouldn't be necessary?' she says.

'Mrs. Charles, the bleeding and swelling is extensive,' explains Virgil. 'We have been monitoring it closely, but it's near to some critical nerves and its progressing. I'm sorry but not acting now could potentially be fatal for your husband.'

Helen looks to be fighting back tears in her eyes, but she doesn't succeed. Virgil approaches the bed and addresses me directly. 'Do you understand me Mr. Charles?' he asks.

I stare deeply into the eyes of this confident, assured stranger, Virgil Adams – the neurosurgeon who needs to operate on my head. Five minutes ago I didn't even know him.

'Virgil?' I say, trying out the sound of his name.

'Yes, Mr. Charles?' he replies.

'Who the fuck are you?' I demand.

The surgeon leans over me and smiles calmly, with the knowledge and confidence of an expert who has dedicated his life to a specialist area of health care. 'I'm the Doctor who's going to save your life,' he answers, 'God willing.'

The trolley bed moves swiftly through the corridors of the hospital on soundless, well-oiled wheels. It's a smooth journey to the operating theatre with nothing but the white coats of orderly's and the flash of hospital ceiling lights to see. A huge lift big enough for two beds takes us down to the theatres and Virgil looks down at me on the trolley bed and smiles. 'Don't worry Mr. Charles, you're in expert hands,' he says, smiling reassuringly. 'My team and I will do our best for you. We're one of the best neurosurgical units in the country. And next time we talk, you'll be in recovery.'

His words seem genuine but give me no comfort. He seems so certain, so assured and confident of his own ability but my time on the trolley since Helen signed a consent form on my behalf have given me plenty of time to think. The hypnotic passing of the ceiling lights of the corridor has strangely focused my thoughts.

The poor naive surgeon has no idea that he is either going to botch the operation or that something is going to go seriously wrong. But I do know. He may be sure of his skills and experience but my certainty is stronger than his. In the last two days I have died in Pripyat, then in my kitchen and yet here I lay, still alive. For the first time in two days everything is crystal clear in my mind.

I'm staring at the picture of a cartoon character painted on the ceiling to relax children, wondering why the badly drawn mouse looks sinister. Somehow I know that I'm not going to survive the surgery, but I also know that it doesn't really matter. By the end of the day I'm going to be dead, but as for tomorrow, well, that will be a brand new day for me. An anaesthetist looks down at me and asks me to count backwards from ten. I think I only make it to five before everything goes black.

4
Flight of the Damned

I hate waiting around. Airports are always the same, first you have to queue for check in, and then you have to wait again wait at baggage check and passport control. Then you have to sit and wait in the departure lounge. It's all so tedious and even when you finally reach the lounge there's yet another wait before you can board the plane. Cheap tasting expensively priced coffee and unnecessary travel shopping are your only distractions. Finally you're herded onto the plane, surrounded by passengers who are desperate to get in front of you and board first. And no matter how quickly you take your seat, you're still going to be sat in it for hours. Yet still everybody jostles to try and get through the boarding gate first, almost as if they're worried their seat will be taken. But eventually the waiting is over, you're on the plane and soon you'll be en-route to your destination.

The seat in front of me isn't fully inclined for take-off but the air stewards don't seem to have noticed. It doesn't really bother me though because the angle of the seat is so small that it barely makes any difference. Perhaps that's why they haven't noticed. The safety briefing is well underway and I try to feign interest by glancing occasionally at the stewardess and nodding, pretending as though I'm learning some great secret for the first time. The stewardess has to do it and we have to listen, or at least go through the motions as she performs the well-rehearsed cabaret. But the woman sat next to me is just staring out of the plane window. She isn't paying attention and there is no pretence of interest or polite display of participation from her. The stewardess finishes with a flourishing wave of her oxygen mask and then busies herself putting the well-used samples away in a storage locker, her job done. I tug gently on my seatbelt to tighten it as a voice comes over the cabin audio. 'Cabin crew, seats for departure.'

I feel cold air blowing down on me from above so I reach up and switch off the air conditioning nozzle. The reading light glares down at me like a torch, dazzling me and I wonder why it never seems that powerful when it's shining on a magazine. I decide that it's almost as bright as the lights in the hospital corridor. The sudden flash of memory comes into my mind, instant and clear as if somehow activated by the reading light. Jesus – I've just gone down for a brain operation!

There is no gradual recollection of what happened to me, the memory is just suddenly there. A moment ago I was on a trolley about to go into the operating theatre when the face of neurosurgeon Virgil Adams appeared; assuring me that he would see me in recovery. But now I'm here sitting on this plane waiting for take-off and reliving all of the waiting in my mind. But I don't remember the airport; it's as if I've transferred from the theatre to a plane cabin instantly. The two memories seem to have blended together and I realise that my assumption was correct; the surgeon did mess up the operation. I had to die again, didn't I? I'm dying every bloody day, in some kind of twisted cycle of death, like a time loop where I always end up dead. But not a time loop, more like a 'dead loop.'

I lean forward, looking around the passenger next to me in order to see out of the window and notice the airport fence slowly moving past. The woman in the seat next to me is frail and elderly with silver grey hair and large thick rimmed glasses. I guess she must be well into her eighties at least. She's wearing a pale blue cardigan with a thick gold chain that hangs around her neck. There is a gold locket hanging from the chain that has sprung open but the pictures inside are too small for me to see. She catches my eye and smiles, but I suddenly realise that I have to get off this plane!

I reach up and press the call button on the console above my head but the action feels strange, and I don't recall ever having to press one before. Nothing seems to happen at first so I press it again, harder and this time a small LED light turns orange. I look both ways up the aisle but there is no one coming to assist me and the plane is still taxiing to its designated take-off runaway.

'Are you alright young man?' asks the elderly lady.

I don't think I've ever seen someone so old on a plane before so even at thirty-nine I must seem young to her. Her question spurs me into motion and I fumble to release my belt, feeling my body itch uncomfortably with the tell-tale signs of nervousness.

'I have to get off,' I blurt out to the woman as I rise from my seat and into the aisle.

I'm sat in the middle of the plane, directly over one of the wings but as I stand up I suddenly remember the hospital and Helen at my bedside. Quickly dismissing the thought I stride purposely up the aisle, although moving makes me want to quicken my pace and I have to resist the urge to break into a run. The plane is almost full and everyone seems to be looking at me marching up the aisle while the seatbelt signs are illuminated. Uncomfortable with my own behaviour, my face begins to feel a little flushed but I have an overriding instinct that I have got to get off the plane.

The stewardess rises to her feet at the front of the plane leaving her seatbelt hanging over the edge of her fold down seat. 'Sir, you must be seated for take-off,' she says immediately.

I identify her as Donna from the name badge pinned to her red and blue uniform. Her hair is shaped into a perfectly neat bun and her face is a picture of calmness. For a brief moment, her assuredness slows my heart rate down and eases my feelings of discomfort a little.

'Please return to your seat Sir,' she instructs me.

The sensation of movement from the plane re-ignites awareness of my purpose. 'But I need to get off,' I tell her quickly.

Donna places her hand on my shoulder and steps towards me, gently trying to turn me around and guide me back up the aisle towards the middle of the plane. I take a step backwards from her and begin to feel a little nauseous.

'No! Please I have to get off,' I insist.

I don't relish the thought of a confrontation but this plane is surely going to go down. Can I really be the only one who knows it?

Donna's colleague Rachel rises swiftly from her adjacent seat to assist her. Despite her name she is Mediterranean looking, a little older than Donna and presumably more senior.

'What's the problem Sir?' she asks politely.

I notice the eyes of the passengers sitting in the front few rows staring at me and sense that those behind them are almost certainly doing the same.

'Stop the plane,' I whisper, unable to stop a hint of panic creeping into the tone of my voice. 'Please, I've got to get off, right now.'

Rachel tries to exert her authority. 'That's impossible Sir, you must return to your seat immediately,' she says.

Without waiting for my response she squeezes past Donna and tries to encourage me to go backwards with a gentle push of her hands. I find myself being ushered back a few steps and am unable to bring myself to push past her. I feel the plane beginning a turn and realise that we must be almost near our take-off starting position. Rachel's small victory over me seems to encourage her and she uses her hands to push me more forcefully down the aisle towards my seat.

'You don't understand,' I protest desperately, but she is already guiding me backwards and I sense that I'm too late. Everyone on the plane is staring at us when she finally ushers me into the nearest empty seat. It's not even my original seat, it is a few rows nearer the front but

I sit down, defeated by her authority and automatically buckle up my seatbelt. Rachel's reaction surprises me, completely nonplussed, as if she finds the whole situation normal.

'Thank you Sir,' she says politely and efficiently before striding quickly back down towards the front.

As soon as my seatbelt is fastened I hear the engines roar and feel the familiar force of being pushed backwards into my seat. The plane is taxiing down the runaway now and engaging its full thrust. I see Rachel has sat back down with Donna but she glances back to make sure I'm still in my seat.

'You scared of flying?' the person sat next to me asks.

The plane leaves the ground and climbs at a steep angle as I look at the passenger speaking next to me. He grins at me cheerfully; the kid must only be about twelve years old.

I've been staring at the seatbelt signs for what seems like hours without even registering they are on. The light is just something for me to focus on, a way of channelling my anxieties into a state of calm. An unexpected beep disturbs me as the light goes out and is immediately followed by the sound of half a dozen nearby seatbelts being unclipped. The boy next to me has unclipped his belt, so I follow his lead and release my own.

The cabin audio crackles into life again. It's a man's voice with an Italian accent. 'This is first officer David speaking,' he says. 'We're now cruising at 36,000 feet and the Captain has switched off the seat belt signs, although we recommend that you keep them on for your comfort. Donna is leading the cabin crew today and her team is here to assist you and make you comfortable. Don't hesitate to ask them if there is anything at all you need.'

It appears that I was mistaken to assume that the assertive Rachel was the one in charge. The voice from the flight desk continues. 'Flying time to Singapore is thirteen hours today. Weather on route looks good and we should land around 16:30.'

As soon as the audio finishes I rise from my seat and head towards the back of the plane. A few people look at me as I pass, probably remembering my pre-take-off antics no doubt. I have to shuffle past a man on his way back from the toilet before I reach the back of the plane. He avoids making eye contact with me and I step into the now vacant toilet and lock the door.

My reflection frowns back at me as I face the mirror. My hair is short, neat and dark and I stroke my chin with its usual few day's growth. I never was one for shaving every day. Splashing some lukewarm water on my face is mildly refreshing and seems to sharpen my senses a little. The gentle humming of the engines suddenly seems a little louder and I feel the floor gently vibrating as I run my wet fingers through my hair and take a few deep breaths.

I don't mind taking off or flying, it's just the approach and landing that freaks me out. Jesus, a thirteen hour flight, how disparaging is that? That means I'm probably going to die on board this bloody aeroplane! I can't remember living through a full day since falling in Pripyat, being stabbed in the apartment and then dying in hospital. But am I being paranoid to assume that the plane will crash? That would affect every one of the passengers not just me. But if not then who will cause my death this time? The boy sat next to me? Or will I suffer a freak heart attack in a place where there is insufficient medical expertise? I can imagine the clichéd words in my mind now, 'If there is a Doctor on board please make yourself known to the flight deck.'

Suddenly my thoughts of dying are disturbed by an insistent banging on the toilet door which seems amplified inside the tiny washroom. I dry my hands and face with some tissue and deposit it in the bin before opening the door. It's the stewardess, Donna.

'May I have a word please Sir?' she asks.

There is no sense in freaking her out any further so I cough into my hand and try to appear normal. 'Yes?' I reply.

'I just wanted to check you were alright Sir,' she says politely, but without stepping back to let me out of the washroom. 'You told my colleague that you needed to get off the plane.'

'I'm just not a very good flier,' I reply sheepishly. 'I guess I just... err... panicked a bit.'

'So you have flown before then?' she asks.

'Yes, a few times,' I reply nodding. 'Look I'm alright now, really.'

She backs away slightly so I can step out of the washroom.

'Okay, but you must be in your seat when the seatbelt signs are on, alright?' she says.

'Yeah I know,' I say, holding my hands up in mock surrender. 'I'm sorry about that.'

Donna seems sufficiently pacified for the moment and strangely I also feel a little calmer too. There isn't much I can do about my situation anyway.

'Well if you need anything else, or have any more worries please press the call button,' she advises me.

'I will, I promise,' I reply with a smile.

Donna steps aside to let me out and then follows me back down the aisle. A few people stare at us as we pass, no doubt observing our conversation outside the toilet. As I get nearer to the wing the old lady

I was sitting next to shakes her head and scowls rather obviously in my direction. Her scornful expression convinces me to keep moving and I sit back down next to the boy instead.

'She was a pretty one wasn't she?' he says cheerfully.

He is right I suppose, although I hadn't particularly noticed before. 'Yeah, I guess so,' I agree, watching Donna walk past us towards the front of the plane.

'Was she telling you off for trying to go to the toilet before take-off?' asks the boy.

'What's your name son?' I ask.

The boy smiles and rolls up the comic he is holding. 'Danny,' he says. 'I'm going to see me grandparents for a week while Mum has an operation.'

'That sounds cool,' I reply. 'I'm Ewan by the way. I'm flying for...'

Suddenly I realise that I don't actually know why I'm going to Singapore or why Helen and Jenny aren't with me. I consider standing up but quickly realise that there's nowhere to go, besides after dying three times why should not knowing the reason I'm on a plane surprise me? I'm trapped on a plane and trapped in this 'dead loop'. Is this poor kid Danny going to have to watch me die? Or could this nightmare finally be over now I'm surrounded by lots of other people? The futility of my questions isn't lost on me but it seems unnatural to panic when everything is so calm in the plane cabin. Danny is still staring at me expectantly.

'For a holiday,' I add, finishing my sentence. 'What's your Mum having done?'

Danny fidgets with his comic for a moment and looks down at his lap. 'It's some heart thing,' he says quietly.

'Well I'm sure she'll be fine Danny,' I reassure him. 'My Mum had a heart thing too, and she lived to a ripe old age.'

I'm not sure why I lied to him but am surprised how naturally it came out. He would never know that both of my parents died in their late fifties from heart attacks, but he seemed satisfied enough with my response anyway, even it wasn't true.

We are maybe five hours into the flight when the cabin audio crackles back into life. Small talk with Danny had passed the time surprisingly well even if it was a little pointless to me. I don't know a lot about computer games, football, or secondary school other than bits that Jenny had told me. I politely listened to him and asked questions just like I would with Helen when she was talking in the car. Danny didn't even stop talking during the in-flight meal, but at least he didn't ask me anything about my life. The first five hours of the flight seemed a very long time indeed, and I even resorted to reading Danny's comic, but at least the staring from the other passengers has finally stopped now.

The audio makes me freeze in my seat. 'This is Captain Virgil Barnes speaking. We're making good time with a tail wind behind us and hopefully we should be able to touch down a little earlier, around 16:00 local time. The First Officer will speak to you again when we're starting our final descent. In the mean-time, just sit back and relax and enjoy the rest of the flight.'

For the last few hours I'd begun to wonder if anything much could actually happen to me up here but there he is again – Virgil. His presence can mean only one thing as far as I'm concerned, another death. A different surname and a different guy but why is he here? I'm out of my seat and heading down the aisle towards the front of plane without even considering my actions. Donna watches me coming and can probably see the mask of intensity and determination on my face. She steps behind a dividing screen at the front of the plane and I quickly join her.

'I want to speak to the Captain,' I inform her bluntly.

Rachel and another stewardess are sitting in their seats watching us intently.

'Sir, what's wrong?' asks Donna. 'How can we help?'

Her efficiency and formality are beginning to annoy me. How easily she would lose that facade if she was in my situation.

'Like I said, I want to speak to the captain,' I repeat my demand to her.

'Sir, passengers aren't allowed to speak with the flight crew,' she points out.

I take a step towards her. 'Just let me speak to Virgil,' I demand, anger rising from my sudden panic. 'That's not asking too fucking much is it?'

Rachel stands up swiftly as the third stewardess squirms uncomfortably in her seat. Donna looks horrified at my tone and her reaction makes me cringe so I rub my clammy hands over my eyes for a moment and take a deep breath.

'Look I'm sorry,' I apologise, 'I didn't mean it like that.'

But Donna hasn't regained her composure yet and still looks a little intimidated so it's Rachel that speaks. 'You're out of order Sir,' she says firmly. 'Sit back down, right now.'

I stare at Rachel with her fierce and determined expression as Donna nervously watches our standoff.

'Look, why can't I just speak to the Captain for minute?' I ask. 'Can't you at least get him on the phone for me?'

But this time it is Donna that speaks before Rachel can respond. 'We're not allowed to do that Sir,' she says. 'If you return to your seat then perhaps we can get a message to him.'

The two women seem skilfully adept at defusing situations like this and their combination of firmness and peaceful pacification are difficult to resist. Rachel seems to instinctively sense their proximity to victory.

'Sir, if you continue to disturb the flight you'll be reported to the Singapore authorities in advance of our arrival,' she warns me, adding further pressure.

And once again her words are enough to make me retreat back to down the aisle towards my seat. I glance over my shoulder and see that all three stewardesses are talking together until Donna picks up a phone receiver. At least Danny offers me a friendly face when I sit down.

'Have you managed to get a date yet?' he asks.

'What do you mean?' I reply.

'With the stewardess,' he replies with a big grin on his face. 'You keep going up there. I would too if I was a couple of years older.'

'Not quite yet Danny,' I say, returning his grin and relaxing a little. 'Maybe she isn't into me after all.'

Danny shrugs. 'Don't worry there's still a good few hours left. Maybe I should give it a shot instead.'

Danny seems very sure of himself and just maybe he is a little older than twelve after all, but his matchmaking gives me an idea. 'Will you do me a favour Danny?' I ask.

'Sure,' he replies enthusiastically, eager to help.

I take out a sick bag from the seat pocket, rip it open and borrow Danny's Spiderman pen. My fingers tremble slightly as I write the note:

Captain Virgil, My name is Ewan Charles. You might know me, you might not. I would like to speak to you as a matter of urgency. If you are unable or unwilling to do so, then please at least consider these words. I have reason to believe that I am in imminent danger on this flight but am not sure if this will affect anyone else. Please take this seriously. I don't want to be the cause any problems but would ask that you land this plane as soon as possible, and allow my urgent departure. This is not a joke on my part and I mean no threat to this flight, I just have to get off. Something I did express to the cabin crew before take-off. Thank you.

I have to use both sides of the bag and write pretty small to fit my letter on it. As I proofread it back to myself I contemplate what someone might think reading my bizarre words, but satisfy myself that it isn't threatening in nature. I fold it up as small as possible and wink at Danny.

'One of the stewardesses is called Donna,' I tell him. 'Will you give this to her for me?'

'A love note?' asks Danny, sniggering. 'Are you serious?'

'Yeah it's a bit lame,' I admit, 'but sometimes you have to try everything right?'

I hold my palm out flat and Danny slaps it. 'Okay,' he says with a murmur of laughter. 'Can I read it though, just to pick up some tips?'

'No you bloody can't,' I tell him, 'it's personal!'

Danny stands up and I move aside to let him squeeze past. He trots enthusiastically down the aisle towards the front of the plane. Danny turns around when he is halfway there, waves the note in the air and then sticks up his thumb. He's bloody loving this.

I stare out the window at the clouds below us and listen to the gentle hum of the engines while trying not to think too much about what Donna's reaction may be. She would have to do something with my note, either tell the Captain or at least talk to me again. I go over the letter in my mind. They would definitely have to do something about it; they couldn't just ignore it, not unless they want their passengers to see a man die in flight. How the hell is it going to happen? Not a bomb surely? It's only me that's died before so it must be something other than that, but if it turns out to be a heart attack I'll go down fighting this time.

It's been a good ten minutes now since Danny handed in the note and returned to his seat. He keeps watching the front of the plain and grinning to see if anything is happening. After another five minutes I finally see Donna approaching down the aisle with Rachel right behind her, although someone stops her and asks for something. She leaves Rachel to deal with them so Donna reaches my seat alone and leans down to whisper to me. 'Sir I've given your note to the Captain,' she explains. 'Could I ask you to accompany me to the back of the plane please?'

'What for?' I ask.

'Please Sir, we can talk at the back,' she says, just as Rachel joins her.

'We can talk here,' I say, now whispering like her. 'So what did the Captain say?'

Donna looks agitated. 'He'll consider your note I'm sure,' she says, 'but I must insist you accompany me and take a seat at the back of plane.'

Rachel steps forward and holds my forearm and tries to pull me out of my seat and into the aisle. 'Let's go Sir,' she says.

Reluctantly I get out of my seat and step into the aisle, breaking her grip on my arm. 'Get your hands off me,' I snap.

'Calm down!' says Donna with a sudden abruptness to her voice.

Fear and growing apprehension about my situation fuel an unwelcome anger in me that I can't prevent from manifesting itself. 'Leave me the hell alone,' I say loudly, 'just let me sit down and then tell me what the bloody Captain said.'

I feel a tap on my shoulder and I spin around to be confronted by two male passengers standing in the aisle. 'Just do as she asks,' the first man says. 'Go to the back and don't cause any trouble.'

I move swiftly, unintentionally having to force my way past Donna as I dash towards the front of the plane. Unfortunately I knock Rachel onto the aisle floor as I pass her, but I have to get this plane landed. I'll break the cockpit door down if that's the only way to get an answer from Virgil. But I'm only halfway there when I feel the solid thump of someone's shoulder in my back as the bigger of the two men tackles me to the floor. My head grazes the armrest of a seat as I fall down and the other man grabs my legs. I hear gasps of shock from a few of the nearby passengers as I struggle, but the man's weight keeps me pinned to the ground.

'Get the hell off me,' I shout as loudly as I can with his weight pressing down on me.

'Stop this shit!' the man demands, 'you're freaking everyone out.'

I hear Donna and Rachel discussing moving me to the back of the plane but it's impossible to get up with the two men on top of me so I quickly stop struggling. One of the men restraining me is breathing hard as if the short quick exertion and sudden adrenaline rush are affecting him. I hear Danny's loyal voice from nearby shouting at them to leave me alone.

Someone is approaching from the front of the plane and I lift my head to look up from my position on the floor, stunned to realise that it's my wife Helen.

'You always create a scene don't you?' she says, glaring furiously at me.

'Christ Helen!' I say in surprise, as the man on top of me shifts slightly to let me breathe. 'Where the hell did you come from?'

'From my seat Ewan,' she says bluntly, 'my seat nowhere near you. I want a divorce.'

'What?' I ask, confused. 'What are you talking about?'

'After what you did to me, what did you expect?' she says. 'It's over and you know it.'

What on earth is she talking about? I can't believe this scene is playing out on an aeroplane with me restrained on the floor and being watched by half of the passengers. The whole thing is farcical.

'Did what?' I protest, 'what did I do?'

Helen stands there in silence, hands on her hips but makes no effort to answer the question. Before I can repeat my words I smell something, faintly at first but then a definite smoky smell in the air. I notice a faint misty haze forming around Helen as a few nearby passengers begin to cough and the plane banks slightly to the left. The familiar sound of the seatbelt warning sign activating plays throughout the cabin, closely followed by a loud bang from somewhere outside the plane. The sudden noise is accompanied by a strong juddering sensation that reverberates through the whole cabin.

The man kneeling on top of me stumbles forward, forcing Helen to step backwards as he sprawls onto the floor in front of her. Suddenly Donna begins repeatedly bellowing instructions for everyone to get in their seats. Still prone, I look up to see both male passengers and Helen hastily taking their seats. As soon as they sit down, the plane banks violently to the left and angles its nose downwards. The smoke suddenly seems much thicker now and a few people are beginning to scream out in panic. The aeroplane is sick and there is no doubt in my mind about what is coming next, just a cold stark terrifying realisation that it's going down, fast.

Rachel has regained her footing and is tugging at my arm and shouting furiously. 'Get back in your seat!' she yells, but I won't die following instructions from her. I don't think the brace position will make much difference no matter how loud the stewardesses shout the instruction. There are five long, terrifying minutes before the nose-diving aeroplane smashes into the ground.

5
Rizpah

The sun is descending behind the mountains creating a warm orange glow that reminds me of molten metal. Sparse trees and dry brush move gently in the faint breeze causing their shadows to flicker and dance on the rocky ground. The breeze is sufficient to stir up the dust on the dry ground beneath my feet but the Greek mountainside looks beautiful in the late afternoon sun. Even from up here I can still make out the coast in the distance, glinting and shimmering in peaceful stillness far below me.

Helen is standing next to me wearing a T-shirt and combat trousers while her arms and face glow pink from sun exposure. Wavy red hair flows loosely around her face as the sunshine enhances her natural beauty and brings out the freckles on her cheeks. The countryside always agrees with her complexion.

There are maybe sixteen other people standing nearby us wearing casual clothes and chatting amongst themselves, all of them presumably couples. I can see a large rustic building nearby with only two walls and a huge unlit brick barbecue inside. There is a dusty coach parked outside it on a cracked tarmac road that leads down out of the mountains which kind of spoils the authentically rural scene. Behind the building are what appear to be stables and my instincts suggest that this place is familiar to me.

Helen stands closer to me and clutches my arm tightly.

'This was a great idea of mine,' she says. 'Wasn't it?'

'I guess so,' I reply, as I try to remember exactly what her idea was.

'Don't worry, it'll be fun I promise,' she assures me, 'I told you we should do this again one day.'

Before I can pass comment, a young woman in her early twenties comes bouncing enthusiastically towards us from the building, wearing jodhpurs and a tight white t-shirt. She is fearsomely tanned and looks right at home in the Mediterranean, displaying all the usual boundless energy of a travel rep.

'Hello and welcome everyone,' she says brightly. 'My name is Kitty and I'll be looking after you all this evening. Thank you all for joining us this evening, now have any of you ridden before?'

About half of the group raise their hands, including Helen and myself although I've only been in a saddle once before.

'Okay,' she says. 'Well for those of you who haven't – don't worry. It's a very gentle ride across the countryside and you'll all be fine. And we have champagne and some fabulous food for you afterwards, alright?'

Two of the louder couples cheer enthusiastically and Kitty seems to soak up their encouragement.

'Right!' says Kitty. 'Let's get you all geared up and then we can get underway, follow me everyone.'

She turns on her heels and bounds back towards the building almost as quickly as she had arrived, the heels of her riding boots leaving little puffy clouds of dust behind her. Helen takes my hand and tugs me along after her with the rest of the group also in tow.

As I try to pick a riding helmet that actually fits and doesn't look too battered and dirty, I think about the flight. The last few moments had been probably the most terrifying experience of my life. Initially when the smoke came into the cabin I'd been determined to stay on the floor and ignore the annoying Rachel's commands. There hadn't seemed much point in getting up only to face death in a seat, but that was before the plane seemed to go into some kind of sideways nosedive.

Screaming and sobbing had filled the cabin along with thicker grey smoke, and oxygen masks were swinging violently from the roof of the plane like little orange lampshades. It was the feeling of pure terror that got me off the floor and into a seat, my seatbelt fastened before I even realised I'd moved.

During the confusion I'd lost sight of Helen and Danny and couldn't even tell who was sitting next to me with all the smoke. Rachel, Donna and the other stewardess had continued bravely shouting orders at the passengers, right until the end. Shaking my head, I refuse to continue with the memory of the last few minutes of that flight.

My chosen helmet is a reasonably good fit and at least it looks fairly clean, even if the neck strap is a bit frayed. Helen looks just as silly with her helmet on though, we all do. It occurs to me that riding helmets don't really go with summer clothes, unless your name is Kitty and you're tanned, fit and in your twenties. The frayed strap of mine is so irritating under my chin that I decide to leave it undone.

For some reason the image of Danny's smiling face suddenly comes back into my mind. The poor kid, twelve years old was no age to die and plummeting to his death in an aeroplane was no way to go. My darling wife Helen was there too, but it's impossible to acknowledge the fact because she's right here in front of me. But if I remember the crash, then why doesn't she?

My most recent death seems curiously different this time as there were maybe 150 people killed alongside me. I know that I've died before but why did all those people have to join me? Was the crash my fault just for being there? If only Donna had let me get off, would they have been okay? Maybe it would be better for everyone if I kept to myself in future and stayed away from people so I don't bring death down upon them. I consider the possibility that none of the other passengers are actually dead after all, which is the best I can hope for.

My situation raises more questions every time I die, but there is no one here to answer them and no logic in what's happening to me. I think about Helen's final words to me before the disaster. '*I want a divorce.*' Why did she say that? She is here right now and seems as loving as ever. '*After what you did to me, what did you expect?*' Christ where did that come from? All I've ever done is love her and care for her, other than having an occasionally argument maybe. Anyway, those were usually my fault for being so impatient when she persisted with an idea or opinion that I strongly disagreed with. We've never had any reason to discuss a divorce, we're happy and normal. She knows how much I love her and I'm sure the feeling is still mutual.

So what had gone wrong with our plane? The terrifying sound of the bang outside the fuselage is fresh in my mind and I can almost smell the rapidly increasing smoke inside the cabin. Somehow I force myself not to allow my memory to venture back to the fatal moment of impact. Gratefully, I'm able to shut that memory out and hope that I can keep it that way.

'Helmet comfy?' asks Helen, making me look up as she interrupts my thoughts.

Lost in my own thoughts I don't catch her question, staring at her blankly until she knocks on my helmet with her knuckles.

'Hello, anyone in there?' she asks sarcastically.

'Oh yeah, sorry,' I reply, 'it looks trendy doesn't it?'

'Are you sure you don't mind doing this?' she asks.

'Doing what?' I reply.

'Riding,' she says, 'I know you weren't crazy about the idea of doing it again, but it was romantic last time wasn't it?'

'Déjà Vu,' I reply. 'Have you got déjà vu?'

Helen laughs. 'Yeah, but at least this time I know why!'

'Why?' I ask.

'Because Dummy, this time we *have* done this before,' she says. 'But at least this time, we know to pick a friendly looking horse.'

She was right. The first time we'd ridden, Helen picked a grouchy mare of a horse that kept shaking its head, walking the wrong way and generally snorting at everyone in sight. I'm surprised that she even wanted to get on a horse again after two hours on that bad tempered beast. But here we are again.

Once everyone has adorned helmets and the couples are mingling and chatting again, some Greek men start leading well-groomed horses out of the stables. Kitty walks alongside them smiling, speaking in Greek to them and communicating with enthusiastic gesturing of her hands.

'I caught you!' says Helen, blowing air at the side of my face.

I scratch my face where she blew. 'Caught me what?' I ask.

'Looking at her,' jokes Helen. 'I think she is a bit young Ewan, even by your standards.'

I chuckle in amusement and watch Kitty and the approaching horses. 'Nice arse she has though,' I reply, with a wry grin.

Helen slaps me playfully around the face with her hand.

I may be happily married but I can still appreciate Kitty's athletic appearance, especially in those jodhpurs. Anyway it's not that I'd really thought about it until Helen mentioned her, but she serves as a welcome distraction from my more troubling thoughts. For a brief moment Helen's words on the plane echo in my mind again. *'After what you did to me, what did you expect?'* But I've never cheated on her so that couldn't be what she meant, although I seem to have forgotten this second trip riding with her in Greece so anything is possible. I glance over at Kitty again who is busy assisting each couple in choosing a horse from the Greek men. Perhaps Kitty and I are the reason, or rather will be the reason for Helen's anger but I quickly dismiss the thought as ridiculous. You can't be threatened with a divorce for something that hasn't even happened.

'Hello Ewan?' says Helen, 'you're so bloody obvious!'

'Shut up,' I say, poking her playfully in the ribs as I turn my gaze away from Kitty. 'I bet she's probably even more high maintenance than you are. Come on let's get a horse before all the shit ones are left.'

The ride across the gentle mountain slopes is incredibly scenic if a little uncomfortable on my rear. The mountainous region is even more beautiful than I remember from our first trip. Our horses walk slowly along the mountain track in single file, picking their way past dry bushes and olive trees giving us time to appreciate the view. There are only the odd few farm houses up here but in the valley far below us is a large cluster of alabaster white houses surrounding a lake. The village looks beautiful in the sunset and it's no surprise that people would build a settlement down there. Part of me wishes that I lived among them, enjoying a simple life picking olives, drinking wine and living till I'm 95. The heavenly image is probably unrealistic and a little naive thinking on my part.

My horse is slender, grey and somewhat aptly called Rizpah which according to one of the Greek men means 'hope'. I'm not sure exactly what I'm supposed to be hoping for, but it seems ironic that the particular horse I chose from the six remaining represents a symbol of looking forward. I'm beginning to see only death, fear and paranoia when I look beyond the moment.

I pat Rizpah's neck firmly, feeling the thick muscles beneath my hand and although she barely registers it, I sense that she appreciates it. Helen and I are riding near the back of the line with two of the Greek men who have accompanied the group. One of the others is leading at the front but Kitty remained back at the building to organise the barbecue for our return.

Sitting in my saddle on Rizpah has definitely relaxed me, but paranoid thoughts start creeping into my head as I go over the deaths in my mind. First there was falling in Pripyat and then being stabbed in the back by Helen. I wince at the memory before my mind wanders to the moment where the anaesthetic was administered to me and I awoke with no knowledge of the surgery, only to die again in a plane crash. Is this really happening to me? And what about the name 'Virgil', is my 'dead loop' constant here somewhere? Where is the next 'Virgil' going to appear? I'm sure that Virgil isn't a Greek name but the very thought makes me suspicious of every other man in our group. Is one of these eight male tourists a Virgil somebody? I intend to find out somehow because I expect to die tonight and I anticipate that a 'Virgil' will have to be here for it to happen, so in the absence of any answers to my questions at least I can try to find him.

We stop at the edge of a steep cliff as the lead horse pulls up under the instruction of its Greek rider. All of the other riders begin to dismount as the three Greek men start to tie the horses to a nearby wooden frame. As I climb down from Rizpah and stretch my legs I realise why we have stopped. The stunning view of the Greek sunset over the valley below is truly magnificent.

Once she has dismounted, Helen leads me to a low crumbling stone wall where some of our group are already enjoying the view. The amber sun is setting on the horizon over the sea, bathing the countryside with a dark orange light. It's even more beautiful and spectacular than the view from the Pripyat rooftop. But there is life here too. I squeeze Helen's hand at the thought of the Ukraine and take a little step back from the wall. Although it's not a sheer cliff by any means, I'm keen to avoid another fatal fall.

'It's beautiful,' sighs Helen with awe in her voice.

A couple of the other riders are taking pictures of the panorama and one lady offers to take one of us. Helen hands over her camera and she takes a photograph of us holding hands and standing against the wall with the sunset behind us. Although I assume that I will never get to see it printed, I thank the lady and we return our attention to the view.

The sudden sound of a distant engine comes from somewhere behind us and we all turn to look back along the horse trail. A silver four wheel drive jeep is bouncing along the track towards us and leaving a cloud of dust behind it. It must make a hell of a bumpy journey for whoever is inside. After sounding its horn to announce its arrival, the vehicle finally shudders to a halt, well clear of the horses that seem uninterested anyway. Kitty climbs out of the driver's seat, jumps down from the jeep and waves to us. One of the Greek men unloads a crate from the back of the jeep and soon Kitty is handing around glasses to everyone and pouring out champagne.

Sipping the ice cold but uninspiring champagne in the sunset of a remote Greek hilltop is as romantic and pleasant an experience as Helen suggested it would be. The bubbly is obviously cheap, but cold, fragrant and very plentiful so I'm soon through three glasses of it. The drink seems to go to my head somewhat as I figure incorrectly that our altitude shouldn't make that much difference. Kitty sips at a glass herself and I assume she isn't too worried about getting pulled over and breathalysed up here. I leave Helen chatting with a couple of the women who are around our age and head over to the jeep to get another refill.

'More champagne?' asks Kitty.

She seems sultrier to me than even Helen suggested, especially with the sky's orange glow on one side of her tanned face. I hold out my glass and feel the warming effect of the alcohol in my mind. Kitty smiles as she fills my glass but up this close I estimate her age to be late twenties rather than early twenties. From a distance her suntan and attire give her a much more youthful appearance.

'Thank you Kitty,' I say. 'Don't you like horses then?'

She pats her free hand on her thigh, highlighting the fact she is wearing jodhpurs. 'Yes, I love them,' she says with a hint of amused sarcasm in her voice. 'But I can't get the champagne on one, so it has to be the jeep every time for me.'

'Of course, makes sense,' I reply, 'Well that's good news for the rest of us at least.'

Kitty raises her glass in a mock toast and I bump mine into hers, but a little more heavily than I intend. Our glasses clink together loudly and some of her champagne sloshes onto her hand. Kitty laughs as I awkwardly stumble out an apology.

'That's alright, I probably shouldn't drink a second glass anyway,' she says. 'One is enough and if I total the jeep on the way back down I'll end up working in Corfu.'

She chuckles at her geographically topical joke and wipes her hand on her thigh.

I glance back at Helen who is so busy chatting that she hasn't even noticed that I'm still talking to Kitty. I had better go back anyway. The champagne has done a fantastic job of relaxing me, but it also reminds me of the picnic and the accident with the tractor. Also, the sky highlights to me the significant fact that the day is nearly at an end.

One of the men from our party strolls over and Kitty refills his two glasses before cracking open yet another bottle. The man marches swiftly back to his wife and hands her one of the glasses and she immediately starts laughing about something he says.

'Kitty, can I ask you something?' I whisper, leaning a little closer to her.

'Sure, what's up?' she replies.

'That guy you just topped up, refilled I mean, what was his name again?' I ask.

'Not sure,' Kitty replies with an indifferent shrug. 'Ask him, I can't remember everyone's name.'

'I thought I recognised him,' I explain, 'do you know if there is anyone in our group called Virgil?'

'No, I don't think so' she replies. 'There are only eight guys and I don't remember anyone called Virgil.'

I feel a tinge of disappointment at her revelation but don't understand why. And the news only adds to the uncertainty of my situation, if there is no Virgil then what does that mean for me? Can I afford to feel safe now?

'You'd best go and enjoy the view,' suggests Kitty, 'we'll be riding back for the barbeque soon.'

I re-join Helen who is flitting from couple to couple, as ever the social butterfly. She wraps her arm around mine and drifts away from the people she is talking to, leading me back to the little wall at the edge of the cliff. I drain my champagne and put the glass down on the ground.

'So where have you been hiding?' she asks, with a little smirk on her face.

'Just talking,' I say, 'mingling and getting a drink.'

Helen glances back towards Kitty and the jeep. 'Yeah right!' she says sarcastically, 'I saw you mingling with Little Miss Jilly Cooper.'

'I don't think she is quite as young as you thought,' I inform her, 'not up close anyway.'

'Well don't forget that you're all mine,' Helen says, reminding me by kissing me on the lips.

As I embrace Helen and cuddle her closely I feel safe and reassured by the warmth of her clinch. For a moment my problems seem unimportant, just like at the picnic, but the painful memory of her verbal attack on the plane and her accusing words are still raw in my mind.

'Helen,' I say, releasing her from my arms, 'what's the worst thing I've ever done to you? The one thing that pissed you off the most?'

She looks at me and smirks. 'How long have you got?' she asks drily, 'it's quite a long list you know. Marrying me maybe?'

'No seriously,' I say, 'have I ever done anything that's made you so mad, that you didn't want to be with me?'

'Well' she replies, a little bemused. 'I think you would know if you had.'

'So what about if I slept with that holiday rep?' I suggest, unintentionally forming an intimate image in my mind of Kitty and myself in a comprising position.

Helen laughs. 'You wouldn't do that,' she says confidently, 'I trust you, even if you might want to!'

'So there's nothing then?' I ask.

Helen thinks for a moment and then hugs me again. 'There is one thing,' she says slowly before staring into my eyes. 'You talk too much and ask stupid questions.'

'Maybe you're right,' I agree. 'Just one more question Helen, and then I'll shut up. Do you know anyone called Virgil?'

She looks into my eyes and appears to be thinking for a moment, but then releases her grip on me slightly and glances out over the wall towards the valley. 'I don't think so,' she replies finally, but I sense a spark of recognition on her face.

'Are you sure?' I ask.

She frowns and looks back at me. 'Actually yeah, there is someone called Virgil at work. I think he works on the fourth floor in the International Department maybe. Why?'

'Do you know him?' I ask. 'Have you ever had any dealings with him?'

'No, I hardly ever go up there,' she says. 'Why, you don't know him do you?'

I shake my head but also wonder if Helen is being deceptive. Could she be lying about not knowing him? She has already killed me once and she did seem to act a little oddly at the very mention of his name. But I don't know what to ask her.

'Let's go and get our horses,' I tell her, taking hold of her hand and leading her away from the wall.

Kitty arranges for the Greeks to get everyone mounted back onto their horses and gathered up on the cliff top. She climbs onto the back of the jeep where one of the men is loading up the empty champagne crate. The jeep puts her at perfect eye level to us on our horses. Kitty stands poised on the flat bed of the jeep like a politician about to make a speech and forming a rather shapely silhouette in the fading light.

'I hope you guys all enjoyed the views and the champagne,' she says.

Her words are greeted with resounding cheers of approval from the riders. She seems to enjoy having a captive and slightly inebriated audience hanging on her every word.

'Well there is plenty more drink,' she continues. 'So you'll be riding back down a slightly quicker route to the restaurant where we have our fantastic barbeque waiting. I want to say a big thank you to Pedro for his wonderful horses, and for getting us all up here.'

One of the Greek men, presumably Pedro waves his hand in salute and we all politely applaud him.

'I'll meet you all back down at the barbeque,' Kitty says.

Her speech is a little over the top for the occasion but everyone seems to appreciate it and soon she is back in the jeep, motoring back down the trail. Our horses form up into a neat line and I pat Rizpah's neck again as we trot between two large trees onto the new trail.

The gently sloping path leads us down into the valley, winding its way around mountain rocks and tufts of soft dry grass. At least there is no real riding involved, Rizpah is as calm and placid as his name suggests and more than happy to plod along behind the chestnut horse in front. It's so quiet that all I can hear is Rizpah's hooves, the sound of insects in the grass and the distant murmur of the ocean. It's a hypnotic and relaxing sound that almost lulls me to sleep. Although it's not completely dark yet, the champagne has made me more than a little sleepy and I'm grateful that my saddle is uncomfortable enough to stop me nodding off. Rizpah's gentle sway is enough to make me want to stretch out and go to sleep.

I think Helen is a few horses ahead of me as we got mixed up a bit when we joined the new trail, not that we could talk much in single file anyway. The horse in front of me is a good few lengths away as Rizpah seems content to follow her own meandering pace, even though I'm keen to see what the barbeque has to offer. Maybe the chef's name will be Virgil. I curse my own negativity at having the thought and wonder what it would be like if somehow Helen and I make it back to our hotel. What would I do if I went to bed and woke up on the next day of our Greek holiday? What would it be like for this nightmare to be over? And it is a nightmare of endless uncertainty, the mixed feelings and suspicions I keep having towards people, even my wife. Paranoia keeps gnawing at me and I don't enjoy the sensation. I'm sick of it.

Suddenly and without any warning Rizpah makes a terrifying whinnying sound and rears up on his back legs. I hear myself calling out in shocked surprise, wondering if a snake or something has spooked her. My helmet falls off as I lose my modest grip of the reins and tumble backwards, feeling a sense of falling as I curse my inexperience and lack of alertness. Rizpah bolts away from the trail without me as I land heavily on the ground and something brutally hard and sharp hits my head. It's a savage reminder of my missing helmet but the realisation is short lived. I only feel the pain for an instant before a sensation of numbness spreads rapidly through my body. What little light there is left around me quickly disappears into a permanent darkness.

6
The Law

Helen shakes my shoulder violently and calls out my name. 'Ewan, wake up,' she hisses in my ear.

I roll over onto my front and pull the duvet tighter around me. I'm too tired to be disturbed from my warm and comfortable bed, but Helen is very persistent, trying my arm this time and tugging it hard.

'What is it?' I mumble, desperate for sleep and pulling my arm away.

'I heard something,' she hisses right against my ear, 'I think there's someone in the apartment.'

Groggily I roll over and look at her, squinting as I see that she has already switched on her bedside light. 'It's probably just Jenny,' I reply, but I strain my ears to listen.

And then I hear the sound of soft footsteps and a slight scuffing sound from somewhere in the apartment.

Switching on the light on my side of the bed, I see that our bedroom door is still shut. 'Jenny?' I call out.

The only response is an eerie silence from the apartment and I start to feel the prickle of tension as Helen squeezes my arm, her nails digging into my skin.

'Jenny, is that you?' I call out again as my heart begins to beat a little faster.

This time the response is a loud bang followed by sudden heavy footsteps and a crashing noise. Startled, I jump out of bed instantly and switch on the ceiling light.

'Who's there?' I shout as Helen gets swiftly out of bed.

I hear a door slam shut as I pull open our bedroom door and peer out into the darkened hallway. Helen already has the cordless phone in her hand but is hovering hesitatingly over the buttons with her finger.

'Ring the Police,' I tell her as the door across the hall flings open and Jenny emerges from her bedroom in her silk pyjamas. Even in the gloom her long black hair is in stark contrast to her pale white skin and she still has that familiar moody pout to her mouth. Jenny looks half asleep, just as she does after studying most of the night for a big college exam.

'Dad?' she calls out, running quickly across the hall to our room.

I pull her inside and she puts an arm supportively around Helen who is already speaking to an emergency controller on the phone. It reminds me that at eighteen Jenny's just a bit taller than her mother now.

'It's alright,' I reassure them, 'I think they've gone.'

Heading out of the bedroom, my heart beats furiously as I move cautiously across the hallway and switch on the lights, bathing the hall in bright comforting light. Feeling more confident now I can see, I head for the living room desperately hoping to confirm that we're alone.

'Be careful,' Jenny calls out before Helen instructs her to close the bedroom door.

The front door is shut which accounts for the loud bang I heard, but the living room is a total mess. The drawers of the sideboard have been yanked out and their contents scattered all over the floor. The coffee table is lying on its side and the glass top has fallen out, although amazingly it hasn't broken. Surveying the mess in the living room reminds me of that apartment in Pripyat. I notice our DVD player is missing, leaving a trail of ripped cables underneath the television like an umbilical cord. The clock on the wall displays 3:15 am and the apartment is deathly silent. It's a reassuring contrast to the clamour that the intruder made.

The confusion of being suddenly woken up is short-lived and already dissipating, but as it does I suddenly remember falling from Rizpah. Having just woken up I could almost believe that the equestrian accident was just a dream, but I know that I haven't simply woken up in bed after a good night's sleep. The fall in Greece must have killed me outright when my head struck a rock, so unfortunately old Rizpah hadn't quite lived up to his name. It's crazy that I'm now in my apartment being burgled. The fact that Virgil wasn't present in Greece and that death was relatively painless is no consolation. Why does this keep happening to me?

The sound of the bedroom door slowly opening behind me interrupts my thoughts and I turn to see Helen's face peering around the edge of it.

'Ewan, are you alright?' she calls out softly, but urgently.

'Yeah, I'm fine. They're gone now,' I reply. 'Quickly, go and bolt the door.'

Helen moves swiftly down the hall and pulls the chain across the front door. Seconds later she is in my arms in the lounge.

'You're shaking,' I tell her.

'You are too,' she says, making me realise it for the first time.

'Oh God,' she sobs, noticing the state of the living room.

Neither of us notices that Jenny is at the end of the hall studying the front door until she calls out. 'I think they broke the lock somehow,' she says.

I glance towards her and relax my grip on Helen. 'Are you two both alright?' I ask.

'Yeah I'm fine,' Jenny calls out.

'I've called the Police,' Helen says, quickly regaining her composure. 'They said they're on their way.'

Jenny switches on all the kitchen lights and Helen releases me but as soon as she does, I recall the last time I cuddled her. It was on the cliff side in Greece before getting back onto my ill-fated steed.

'Burgled,' Helen announces, 'I can't believe it.'

'It's happened,' I say, 'let's just establish what's missing,' but I'm suddenly unsure if possessions really mean that much to me now.

In the kitchen Jenny is running the tap and splashing water on her face, probably trying to wake herself up. Helen begins to pick things up off the living room floor where the drawers have been emptied, but then she suddenly stops.

'Wait a minute,' she says, 'we'd better not move anything until the Police get here, just all have a check round instead.'

Jenny joins us in the living room, holding a glass of water and wearing a towel around her neck but has managed to splash water on the arms of her pyjama top. She has an alert look on her naturally pale face.

'That was my DVD player,' she complains, gesturing to the empty space under the television, 'the bastards!'

'It doesn't look like there's much else missing in here,' says Helen, 'they must have heard us wake up.'

'Do you think they knew we were in?' asks Jenny.

I place my hand on her shoulder. 'I expect they assumed we were away Sweetheart,' I reassure her. 'Otherwise they wouldn't have scarpered so quickly. 'Stay here and see if anything else is missing, I'm going to speak to Ali.'

The lock of our front door is hanging off and the handle is loose and next to useless. The intruder must have got through the communal door downstairs somehow as well, unless by some chance we were burgled by someone from another apartment. There are only two large apartments on our floor and the door to the other is firmly shut and undamaged. I'm relieved to flick on the hall light and see that there is no sign of any intruders up here but it feels a little strange knocking on my neighbour's door at half past three in the morning.

After knocking on the door four times, each occasion progressively harder, it finally opens and our Muslim neighbour Shafi Ali peers around it. Nobody calls him Shafi though; all his friends including us just call him Ali. Jenny was dead right when she first said that he looks like a young Will Smith and I think it every time I see him now. I used to wonder how a medical graduate who is only training as an ophthalmologist at the hospital could afford such an expensive apartment in London but Helen says his parents who are both Doctors own it. Ali is bleary eyed and just wearing his shorts, but he soon opens the door fully when he realises it's me.

'Alright Ewan,' he says yawning and surprised, 'what's up?'

'Sorry to wake you,' I tell him, 'we've just had a break in at our place and I thought you should know.'

Ali's eyes widen at the news. 'What? You're joking,' he says. 'Is everyone alright?'

'Yeah, they ran off when we woke up,' I explain, 'luckily I don't think they took much, Helen is checking now.'

'Shit,' Ali says, 'do you need me to do anything?'

'No it's alright,' I reply, 'I've called the police anyway, you go on back to bed. I just wanted to check that they hadn't got into your place too.'

'No, they haven't. Are you sure there's nothing I can do to help?' he asks, repeating his offer while rubbing his eyes. I assure him that there isn't and he wishes me luck before closing the door.

The personal intrusion of the burglary gives me something other than death to focus on, albeit an unpleasant distraction. Although a part of me wants to dismiss the event as unimportant and meaningless, I can't overcome a desire to secure my property and protect and support my family. The thought occurs to me that I might die again before my family has the opportunity to appreciate me. Right now they seem far more important to me than trying to understand what is happening to me.

When I return to our apartment I find Helen sitting at the kitchen table with a notepad and I hear the kettle beginning to boil. She looks a little startled at first when I open the front door, until she realises it's me.

'Ali's place wasn't robbed,' I tell her.

'That's good,' she replies. 'What did he say?'

'Not a lot, just offered to help,' I reply. 'Where's Jenny?'

'Getting dressed,' she replies. 'She's decided to get up. By the way, it looks like they didn't go into the other bedrooms and I've had a quick check everywhere else. I've written a list of what's missing. It's just the

DVD player, my bloody laptop and a few DVD's. Oh, and your iPod is missing from the dock.'

I cringe at the memory of giving away all of my original CD's to charity. 'Fantastic, all my music was on there,' I groan. 'I bet it was drug addicts.'

'I'm more annoyed about my laptop,' says Helen, banging her hand down on the table in frustration, 'thieving bastards. How do you think they got in?'

'They obviously smashed up the lock somehow,' I reply.

'I'm surprised we didn't hear that,' Helen says.

'No, I'm not sure how they did it without waking us up either,' I agree. 'I wonder how they got in downstairs.'

'Perhaps they used to live in the building and still had a key,' she suggests.

Helen gets up and picks up the boiling kettle. 'I'll pour this over the little buggers if they come back,' she threatens. 'Fancy breaking into someone's place while they're asleep.'

'I doubt they'll be back,' I say. 'Not judging by how quickly they took off.'

Helen makes us both a coffee and I stand the table back up, forgetting for a moment that we weren't going to move anything. We sit down together on the living room sofa and I enjoy a sip of the aromatic coffee. Helen leans into me and lifts her feet up under her on the sofa. The two of us share a relaxing moment of silence and calm as we each process the events of the night. I lose track of how long we are cuddled up like that and more than once I nearly fall asleep.

It seems like only minutes ago that Helen woke me up panicking about the intruder, but it also seems only minutes ago that I was thrown off Rizpah. What a stupid way to die, falling off a horse that was plodding calming along a serene path in Greece. Could it really just have been a snake that spooked her or was it something else altogether? If I ever needed a reminder of what I hate about riding, then there it was. Never trust a mode of transport that has a mind of its own. I ponder the chances of hitting my head on a rock and dying from it. It was incredibly convenient that my chin strap wasn't done up and my helmet came off, but if I was destined to die somehow then what would have happened if I'd had the chin strap done up and my helmet hadn't come off? I gingerly press my fingers on the spot at the back my head that hit the rock, but unsurprisingly there is no sign of any injury there.

Helen breaks the silence. 'Once the Police have been, I'd better call the Insurance Company,' she says. 'Can you dig out the policy?'

I nod in reply as her words rouse me from my thoughts.

The living room clock reads 4:42 am as Jenny walks in with a towel round her head and wearing her white dressing gown.

'Are you alright Jen?' asks Helen.

Jenny rubs her hair briskly with the towel. 'Yeah I'm fine Mum,' she says, smiling. 'I thought I might as well have a shower now I'm up.'

I suppose none of us felt like going back to bed, but me in particular as I couldn't be sure how long I had left alive today. I consider having a shower myself but suddenly we're all startled by a loud knock on the front door.

'That'll be the Police,' says Jenny immediately. 'I buzzed them in while you two were sleeping.'

I'm sure that Helen and I had both stayed awake on the sofa and Helen's surprised face confirms that she feels the same.

'The Police?' says Helen, glancing at the clock. 'An hour and a half isn't too bad I suppose.'

I move to the door and undo the chain, hearing Helen yawning in the living room behind me. When I open the door I'm greeted by two uniformed officers outside in the hallway. The male officer has short ginger hair and looks around thirty. He seems very burly for a policeman and is no doubt a valuable asset in a crowd control situation. The female officer is tomboyish and looks ridiculously young so is probably a rookie. She yawns with a hand over her mouth as her partner introduces them as PC Anton Giles and WPC Holly Fortune.

'Excuse me,' says Holly, but she is still yawning as she apologises.

'It's alright,' I assure her, inviting them to come inside and sit down in the living room.

PC Anton Giles crouches down and studies the lock of the front door while Holly follows me straight to the living room. Jenny says hello as she passes through on the way to her bedroom to get dressed and I realise how close they appear in age. Anton concludes his spot of detective work and Helen offers to make them both a coffee. Neither of them refuses and once we are all sat down with drinks Helen takes the lead and explains what happened before giving them a run down on what's missing. The two police officers listen intently and Holly scribbles down notes.

'How do you think they got into the building?' Helen asks.

'Well there's no damage on the doors downstairs,' says Anton. 'We had to use the call button to get in. They could've had a key maybe, or were buzzed in by someone.'

Holly stops writing for a moment. 'There have been a couple of similar burglaries,' she informs us, 'from different apartment buildings.'

'Were those people inside at the time?' asks Helen.

'No, they were out,' Anton says, shaking his head. 'It's most likely they picked your apartment by mistake, thinking it was empty. Now what about your neighbour, is he in?'

'Yes, his name's Ali,' I inform them. 'I woke him up and told him about the break in.'

Anton nods and checks his watch. 'Well, we'll pop round there in a bit and see if he heard anything,' he says. 'I'll try to get the Scene of Crime guys out to you as quickly as possible. It'll probably be at least a couple of hours I'm afraid, so if you could avoid any tidying up until then, that would be helpful.'

Helen sighs at the debris on the floor. 'Of course,' she says, 'if it will help.'

Anton stands up and puts his coffee mug down on the table.

'Are you going to be able to secure your door?' he asks.

'Yes thanks,' Helen replies, 'I'll ring the Insurance Company about it,'

'We can't promise any results but we'll be looking into this alongside the other burglaries,' Holly says.

'Thank you,' I reply, 'I figured these don't often get solved.'

Anton writes down a crime reference number on a page ripped from Holly's notebook and hands it to Helen.

'Holly let's come back later and have a chat with some of the people downstairs,' Anton says.

'Maybe we should check with the building owners for a list of former residents too,' suggests Holly, changing my opinion of her just being a naive rookie. They discuss her suggestion as Helen shows them out.

Once the police officers have gone, Helen and I head to the bedroom to get out of our pyjamas and into some clothes. I watch her remove her nightdress and change her underwear while I pull on a pair of jeans, and the thought occurs to me how sexy she looks naked. Our traumatic morning certainly hasn't dampened my appreciation for her body, but it's hardly an ideal time to demonstrate it.

Outside our bedroom window the early morning sky is already starting to get lighter and as soon as I put on my T-shirt there is another knock at the front door. Helen tells me to get it, probably because she is still fussing over which bra to wear.

Ali is standing at my door, dressed for work in a shirt and tie and looking far more awake than he was earlier on.

'Alright Ewan?' he says. 'The police came round to see me.'

'Hello Ali,' I reply stifling a yawn. 'Yeah, they said they're looking into a couple of similar burglaries. They don't know how they got in downstairs yet though.'

'Did you lose much in the end?' he asks.

I shrug. 'Not really. The worst thing was Helen's laptop. She's pretty pissed about it though. Do you want to come in for a coffee?'

Ali waves his hand dismissively. 'No thanks mate, I've got an old university mate round at mine. We're having a quick breakfast and then I've got to get my arse to the Hospital.'

'Oh yeah, is she nice this university mate?' I tease him, 'just staying the one night is she?'

Ali laughs and pretends to punch me. 'I wish mate, it's just my old university roommate, Virgil. He's come up from Devon for a couple of nights. Maybe we'll get lucky tonight though.'

'What did you say?' I ask.

But I didn't need to hear the name repeated. His buddy was called Virgil. His revelation chills me as I imagine death somehow stalking me and moving in for the kill.

'We might get lucky!' Ali repeats himself, leaning in to whisper jokingly to me. 'Why, are you going to ask Helen for the night off and come to a club with us?'

'Another time maybe,' I reply. 'I'd better get going.'

'Anything I can do to help?' he offers.

'Look sorry Ali, I'll catch you later alright?' I say, slowly closing the door on him.

Jenny makes us all some toast and we eat it quietly at the kitchen table, only interrupted by the occasional obscenity as Helen curses her missing laptop. After breakfast, Helen phones her boss and arranges to take the day off work to wait in for the Scenes of Crime Officers. She wants to get the place in order as soon as they have gone and the locksmith still hasn't been anyway. Jenny goes off to college as if nothing has happened, with only a vague grumble about her DVD player. I tell Helen that I need to go out for some air and she doesn't seem to mind, although my sights are set firmly on a visit to the police station to request some help from the law with a personal problem.

It is unexpectedly quiet in the reception of the police station this morning, with just a few visitors at the front desk. I can't recall ever having a reason to go to a Police Station since we moved into London and I expected it to be chaos for some reason. After explaining to the civilian desk officer that I needed to see someone about harassment, they ask me to take a seat.

The badly worn chairs in the waiting area are desperately in need of upholstering and unlike the Doctors there are no magazines to read. There are a few posters on the walls showing photos of missing people with the date of when they were last seen. My eyes are also drawn to a poster warning against knife crime and the irony isn't lost on me. I've certainly been stabbed before, although Helen seems to have got away with it. I also feel more like a missing person with every passing day, or rather it's my life that is missing. And so it strikes me that it's time to enlist some help, something that's long overdue.

After everything that has happened to me since Pripyat, I'm killed falling from a horse, only to wake up in the middle of a burglary. In the aftermath of that, another stranger called Virgil turns up next door. So where was he in Greece then? Did he have the day off or something? Was he watching and gloating at me from afar? If he was a friend of Ali's then how could he also be a neurosurgeon, or a pilot or a voice on a radio in the Ukraine? None of this makes any sense and I wish I could picture myself on Rizpah, riding away into the sunset with Helen on the back, escaping from my life and away from Virgil.

The police in the station are much quicker than their emergency response team were this morning. I'm called into an interview room after only twenty minutes.

'I'm DC Lee Orton,' says the plain clothes, casually dressed CID officer.

I shake his hand, introduce myself and thank him for seeing me so promptly. Lee Orton is a relaxed and trendy man in his early thirties with what I would call properly styled hair. My first impression is that he is good looking enough for me to safely assume that he's popular with the female officers. As I shake his hand I notice the absence of any rings and expect that he does well with the women on the force. Right now though his focus seems only on assisting me and his professionalism makes me feel comfortable opening up.

'So what can we do for you Mr. Charles?' he asks, sweeping his hair back with his hand.

'I'm being followed,' I reply, getting it straight out into the open.

'Followed?' he repeats. 'Followed by whom?'

I stroke my chin for a second. 'His name is Virgil,' I inform him.

'Okay, now how can you be sure this "Virgil" is following you?' he asks.

'Because everywhere I go, there he is,' I explain. 'And it's pissing me off quite frankly. I'm sorry.'

'That's alright,' says Lee. 'So do you know who this man is or why he might be following you?'

It's a fair question. 'I don't know Lee,' I reply, resting my elbows on the table and leaning forward. 'But every day he seems to be there. He's always around, and now he's staying in my neighbour's apartment.'

Lee picks up his pen and writes down a few lines on a notepad. His forearm obscures the page and I can't see what he is writing but I notice he has some kind of military tattoo on his arm.

'Has he spoken to you or threatened you in any way, or caused you any problems? Other than just sort of being around?' asks Lee, digging a little deeper. 'Can you give me some examples of where he has been following you?'

I can hardly tell him that I've been dying every day and that Virgil is always hanging around in the background. Not only will it sound ridiculous but what crime has this Virgil actually committed? He can hardly be arrested and charged with being a symbol of impending death. Perhaps I haven't fully thought through my quest for assistance.

'Well I was burgled this morning,' I inform him, 'which is kind of strange since this guy has been following me every day. It's kind of a coincidence isn't it? Especially as the main building wasn't broken into, it was just my apartment. And Virgil is staying next door.'

'Your burglary has already been reported?' asks Lee.

I nod. 'Yeah your boys are on it, Holly Fortune and Anton somebody.'

'And you think this neighbour could be involved somehow?' Lee asks.

I don't really, it doesn't make sense. He can't be the same person, but if I'm dying every day then what's so strange about Virgil changing his persona? My thoughts confuse me as I struggle to decide what to tell Lee. Dying every day isn't a crime either, and he isn't likely to solve that.

'He isn't my neighbour, he's just staying there,' I tell him. 'I mean he could be involved I suppose.'

'Let's come back to that, says Lee, scribbling down some more notes, 'And I'll be sure to pass that information on to PC Anton. Let's get back to this following business and if you can think of any reason this man might have to want to follow you.'

'He's like a stalker,' I reply.'

'A stalker?' Lee asks.'

My mobile phone suddenly rings and the number flashes up as Helen's.

'Sorry, can I take this?' I ask Lee, while accepting the call.

'Honey, it's me,' says Helen.

I notice a slight shakiness to her voice. 'What's wrong Helen?' I ask.

'Where are you?' she asks.

'I'm just... out for a bit,' I tell her, as I turn away from Lee. 'Why, what's the matter?'

'I've found something else missing,' she informs me, her voice trembling. 'That photo of Jenny has gone.'

'Which photo?' I ask.

Her voice sharpens into anger. 'The one of her sixth form graduation,' she replies. 'Why would someone take that?'

I picture the photo in my mind, propped up on the living room sideboard in its own frame. Its theft is far more personal than any of the other items. The hairs on my neck tingle with suspicion and Helen's tone stirs my own anger.

'Ring her and get her to come straight home,' I tell her. 'I'm coming back now.'

I close the call and quickly thank Lee for his time.

'Is everything alright Mr. Charles?' he asks, 'I still need some more information...'

But I cut him off mid-sentence. 'It'll have to wait,' I tell him. 'I'm going to find that little bastard.'

I'm halfway out of the interview room, ignoring Lee's protests but I catch the tail end of a few words, something about not doing anything rash.

The only things on my mind now are finding Virgil and protecting Jenny. All of my frustrations and anxieties surrounding my situation have merged into a single emotion – rage. I feel the churning cocktail of anger inside me for which the loss of the photo is the catalyst. For some reason he theft of the photo feels like a threat towards Jenny although I'm not quite sure why. The photo has no monetary value, so why take it? Nobody threatens my daughter. I'm determined now to establish once and for all who Virgil is. I cover the short distance from the police station at a fast jog and half expect to see Lee following me. His absence makes me assume that he either has more pressing matters to attend to or that my abrupt departure and threats are not something he is taking too seriously.

I use my few brief moments in the apartment building lift to regain my breath, but my hands are trembling with anger and adrenaline. Seconds after the lift door opens I'm banging on my neighbour Ali's door. After a short delay he opens it and I push my way straight past him and into his living room.

'Where's Virgil?' I demand.

'Virgil?' says Ali, 'he's not here. What's got into you Ewan?'

I grab Ali's shirt with both hands on his collars and glare at him. 'Where the fuck is that thieving bastard?'

His eyes widen and he raises his hands in protest. 'I don't know what you're talking about. What do you mean, thieving?'

I hesitate for a moment, my fists still clutching his shirt.

'I thought you were working,' I say fiercely, pushing him back against the wall.

'I've come home for lunch,' says Ali, 'Virgil must have gone out. What's this all about?'

Somehow it feels wrong intimidating my friend and neighbour and his innocent protests quickly bring me to my senses. As I release his shirt the door opens and a young white man with blonde hair enters the apartment.

'Here he is now,' says Ali.

I make a sudden lunge for the newcomer. 'Where's that photo?' I demand.

Virgil stumbles backwards into the hallway and without hesitation I throw a punch towards him. My fist skims Ali's front door but still connects hard against the side of Virgil's head. He yells out and pulls away from me, making a dash towards the stairs of the apartment building.

'Come back!' I shout as my own front door opens and Helen suddenly appears in the hallway.

'It was bloody Virgil!' I shout out to her as I pursue the fleeing young man towards the stairs.

'Leave it out!' yells Virgil over his shoulder as he hurtles down the stairs with me in close pursuit.

By now I'm convinced that he is responsible for the break-in and the theft of Jenny's photo. The suspicious nature of his presence on the day of my death is insignificant now compared to this personal intrusion on my family. I'm fully committed to catching him but he has the advantage of youth and his flight down the stairs is frustratingly swifter than my own.

As I turn the last corner of stairs to the second floor, I barrel headlong into two Scenes of Crime Police Officers. One of their hard plastic briefcases smacks hard into my knee as I sprawl headlong into them. One of the officers loses his footing and I fall on top of him, my knee protesting with pain. His partner yells out something, but I'm already scrambling to my feet and limping back down the stairs after Virgil.

Moments later I burst out into the street and see Virgil already fleeing down the pavement. Ignoring the pain in my knee, I resume pursuit as he dashes across the road towards an underground train station. I'm still not fully recovered from the jog from the police station and my knee is still protesting from the fall on the stairs. I frustratingly have to concede that Virgil is pulling away from me.

In desperation, I lunge across the road diagonally to try and regain some ground on him. The sudden blast of a vehicle horn gives me a fleeting memory of a red tractor but I force it out of my mind as my overriding thought is catching Virgil. Somehow I am going to chase him down and get some answers about why I keep dying and find out why he stole Jenny's photo. The second horn is much louder and nearer than the first and I stop dead in panic. My feet are swept clean off the tarmac surface of the road as the impact of the car is bone crunching, and fatal.

7
The Jump

Blistering cold air streams past my face as if an icy tornado has sucked me up. My nostrils are being blasted with air making it a struggle to breathe and blood rushes into my head, making me feel faint. The fierce rush of the air stream deafens me but doesn't seem to be affecting my eyes and it takes me a moment to realise that I have goggles on. As I focus through the tinted glass covering my eyes, I realise that I'm falling head first through the sky at near terminal velocity. My arms feel like lead as they are pulled at by the sheer force of gravity and turbulent air. Involuntarily I gasp in shocked surprise at my predicament, causing fast flowing air to fill my mouth as I plummet down, head first in vertical freefall.

I feel very small in the vast blue void of sky that surrounds me but realise that while the ground may be far below, it's looming rapidly towards me. There are straps covering my shoulders like some kind of rucksack, but something makes me realise it's a parachute harness. Instinctively I reach for the rip cord but my concentration feels numbed and the cold air has weakened my fingers. Quickly I raise my head and arch my back allowing my body to level out, easing the pressure in my head and helping my blood to begin circulating properly again.

Finally I pull hard on the parachutes lifesaving rip cord and feel only a fraction of a second pause before the parachute opens and violently slows my descent. I scream out in a combination of excitement, adrenaline and blessed relief as my head begins to clear and I can celebrate another fantastic skydive. I can barely believe it – I've 'awakened' in the middle of a parachute jump! That's how the dead loop feels to me now – like dying and then re-awakening. But how did I die last time? It's slowly coming back to me but the view spread out below me forces me to postpone my reflections.

A beautiful landscape of rocky desert and sparse trees is laid out before me like a Google Earth image. I see no sign of civilisation, just an expanse of sand, rocks, trees and some hills in the far distance that give me a liberating feeling of being in the great outdoors. There is a beautiful river, twisting and cutting its way across the landscape like some never-ending silver snake. A burning yellow sun blazes in the cloudless blue sky, completing the scene perfectly and somehow I know that I'm slowly descending over Arizona.

I guide my parachute towards a smooth clearing that looks free of bushes and rocks while still being close to the river. The parachute control lines feel natural in my hands and minutes later I'm on the ground after a nearly perfect landing. I disconnect the parachute from my harness and bundle it up. It's been a long time since I've felt so alive and free, a very long time indeed. This isn't my first skydive but it will be a memorable one as it makes such a welcome change from the nightmare of the last few days.

Pausing a moment to allow the adrenaline and my euphoria to ease off, I gaze up and observe a small plane high up in the sky. Removing my goggles, I shield my eyes from the sun and squint up at the plane but it's too small and far away to see any details. I suddenly realise that if I'd awoken a few minutes later, I wouldn't have had time to deploy the parachute and it would have been my quickest death yet, not to mention a very unpleasant one.

My feelings of relief are interrupted by the sound of an engine, making me turn around to see a large yellow off road pickup truck lumbering towards me. It pulls alongside me in a cloud of dust and I find myself coughing as I put my goggles back on and approach the vehicle. There is a bundled parachute on the back of the truck and I hoist mine up alongside it and turn my attention to the occupants. The passenger side window of the big pickup truck slowly opens and Helen's face appears behind it.

'You deployed a bit late,' she says with a grin, 'it looked like you were taking a nosedive!'

I lean through the window and kiss her in response, the vision of her face reigniting my feelings of euphoria. It feels wonderful to see her and to feel so alive.

'Jump in,' yells the driver, leaning across Helen and looking at me through her window.

The man is maybe forty years old, well built and considerably tanned, wearing mirrored sunglasses. He looks like an ex-marine or something with his short shaved hair and rugged appearance. Clipped to his cheesy Arizona State T-shirt is a name badge which reads 'Buzz – SkyBlaze Tours'.

'Fair enough Buzz,' I agree, climbing into the truck and smiling with unintentional amusement at his name.

Soon the truck is thundering across the desert and away from my landing spot before the dust of its arrival has even settled.

'Ready for the next one?' shouts Helen across the roar of the engine. The truck is bouncing us around all over the place as it traverses the uneven desert surface. 'Next one?' I ask.

'Yeah, now we're gonna do 10,000 feet,' she says, her face beaming as she holds my leg to steady herself. 'I told you we would eventually.'

I remember that we had jumped from 8,000 feet before but neither of us has ever broken into five figures.

'Perfect day for it too guys,' yells Buzz in his strong American accent. 'It's as clear as anything up there.'

Helen smiles and gives him the thumbs up as I close my eyes for a moment and allow my body to relax against the buffeting ride. How had I died again? I remember faintly chasing Virgil across the street but I can't picture what hit me. There were horns and then a sudden impact. It hardly seems real but I shudder in my seat, hoping it goes unnoticed by Helen and Buzz with all the other movement of the truck. I must have been hit very hard because I don't remember dying. There was a loud bang and a fierce pain in my side and maybe my back. I remember thinking that my wrist was in agony and then it was suddenly all over. I can almost picture a sudden final flash of pain but then I was in freefall and struggling to right myself in the air.

Did Virgil break into our apartment and steal a photo of Jenny as I suspected? God, where was my daughter now and how can I protect her while I'm out here in the desert? Was it all just in my imagination that the friend of my neighbour Ali is a perverted burglar? There is nothing I can do about it now though.

I open my eyes and see Helen's smiling face looking out of the open window. The chisel-jawed Buzz wrestles with the steering wheel and grits his teeth as he pushes the truck a little over enthusiastically across the desert as if he is racing someone.

'Take it easy Buzz,' I tell him, 'I'm a nervous passenger.'

'Don't worry!' he calls back, 'I'm used to this terrain Buddy.'

We've been skydiving in quite a few places in America but never with 'SkyBlaze Tours' as I recall and I'm sure I would have remembered G.I. Joe 'Buzz'.

Twenty minutes later, Buzz brings the truck to an abrupt halt at the edge of a long dusty airstrip surrounded by small trees. My body feels unwilling to move, as if every bone has been shaken loose by his bouncing truck ride but Helen clambers down enthusiastically out of the truck.

I climb out of the truck more slowly but immediately notice Helen's curves in her skin tight pink and black flight suit, wishing my own figure hugging suit was quite as flattering on me. Buzz climbs out of the driver's seat and takes off his tatty grey baseball cap and wipes his forehead. The sun is absolutely beating down on us and its boiling hot outside without the benefit of the truck's air conditioning. Buzz passes us each a bottle of water from a big cool box on the back seat of the truck and gulps down a whole bottle himself. Helen and I drink greedily from our bottles and they seem to relieve the heat for a moment. Buzz is already pouring a second bottle over his head as we finish.

The glint of a small aeroplane appears on the horizon in the distance. We squint at it as it glides surprisingly quietly onto the dirt airstrip and bounces once before beginning to taxi towards us.

'Last jump of the day,' says Buzz, 'are you guys ready?'

I look over at Helen and she smiles before coming into my arms and cuddling me. 'Damn right we are, Buzz,' she answers for the both of us.

I watch as the approaching plane slows to a stop about a hundred yards away from us and its two propellers begin to slow down. Buzz climbs up onto the flatbed of the truck and passes down two new parachutes marked with our names, hand written on large white labels.

'There you go Guys,' he says.

Helen collects hers up and begins pulling it onto her back as Buzz assists her. I notice one of the pilots climb out of the plane and walk around it, doing spot checks perhaps. I catch the reflection of his sunglasses before he disappears around the other side of the plane. The aeroplane offers me a tantalising opportunity to enjoy a proper jump from the start, rather than appearing half way through, and my mind is immediately made up. As soon as Helen and I are both wearing our new parachutes, Buzz double-checks our harnesses and then we all head across the dusty airstrip towards the plane.

Buzz ushers us up a ladder and into the small twin-propeller plane where one of the two pilots gives us a thumbs up from the cockpit. I'm relieved to find that it's much cooler inside the plane than it is outside. As soon as we're on board, Buzz closes the door from the outside and waves at us through the window.

One of the pilots leaves the cockpit to join us. With a white shirt and tie, the mature man looks almost like a professional airline pilot – the illusion only betrayed by the jeans he is wearing. He smiles warmly and salutes us with a mock army salute.

'Alright,' he says while checking the door. 'You two all set?'

Helen confirms we are, as I glance out the window to see Buzz pulling away in the pickup truck.

'Buckle yourselves in and we'll get under way,' the pilot says.

Helen and I each take a seat and fasten our seatbelts as the pilot returns to the cockpit through a small door, and puts on a headset. He talks briefly to the other pilot who is silver haired and considerably older. I can only see the back of his head but he has the same white collar and I wonder if he has the matching jeans too.

The engines start abruptly and the propellers spin into life. Soon we are turning on the dusty runway and beginning to taxi in the opposite direction they landed from. For some reason I anticipate a bumpy ride but the runway is deceptively smooth and nothing at all like the trail we took to get here in the truck. The plane lifts effortlessly off the ground and enters a steep climb, pushing us back into our seats.

I rest my head back and feel Helen's hand squeezing mine. She isn't a great air passenger either but she should be grateful that she hasn't been in an air crash before. But then I suddenly realise that she has, Helen was there when the airliner went down. But unlike me though, I know she wouldn't remember it so perhaps she hasn't really been in one after all. The whole thing is confusing and reminds me that I can't remember the last time I had a normal night's sleep. It's as if I have somehow been awake for days without becoming exhausted. There is no logic in why this is only happening to me, it just doesn't make sense. What has happened to my normal life?

I try not to think about my situation because skydiving is something that I love doing after all. I always thought it strange that Helen hates flying but is quite happy to jump out of a plane. It was her who had convinced me to try sky diving in the first place. She had done it once as a teenager and although it's an expensive hobby it was worth it, and we could certainly afford it now. We both love the adrenaline rush it gives us, so I try to be grateful and think positively about the experience we're about to have.

'What are their names?' I ask Helen, pointing to the cockpit.

'The pilots?' she replies, 'Oh it was erm... the old boy was Gerry or Garry I think, and the other one is Josh.'

Well at least they aren't called Virgil.

'This will be worth every penny,' says Helen keenly, 'I can't believe we're finally going to jump from 10,000 feet.'

'Me neither,' I tell her. 'Wait till we tell Jenny, maybe you can convince her to try it now.'

'No chance!' Helen replies. 'You know she only likes planes if she's inside them.'

The sky suggests that it's around noon now but I don't have a watch on to confirm it. The afternoon is only just beginning which means there's plenty of time to die once I'm back on solid ground. I hope it doesn't happen up here though, before Helen and I can enjoy one nice thing together before I die. Right here and now it seems a long time ago since she stabbed me in the back and this seems much more like the picnic but with a less intimate conclusion, and a different kind of adrenaline rush.

'I love you,' I tell her.

'I love me too,' she replies sarcastically.

'You doughnut,' I say, pinching her arm and lightly punching her helmet.

I look down out of my window at the desert landscape far below us, shimmering slightly in the early afternoon heat. The engines hum reassuringly loud for such a small plane but the propellers are practically invisible. They will make a hell of a noise when the door is opened for us to jump.

After twenty minutes of the plane climbing and banking, the younger pilot Josh unbuckles his seatbelt and joins us in the cabin.

'We're almost in position,' he says, 'everybody ready?'

'Ready,' we both reply simultaneously.

'Buzz will be waiting for you on the ground,' Josh says, 'just sit tight in your landing zone and he'll come and pick you up again.'

'What kind of name is Buzz?' I ask with amusement. 'Does he want to be an astronaut or something?'

'That's not his real name,' explains Josh. 'His name's Virgil but everyone calls him Buzz. Yeah, at school he swore his uncle was Buzz Aldrin and that's where he got the nickname. So he says anyway.'

A sudden chill runs up my spine at the revelation and I open my mouth in surprise. Here he is again – right on cue and I just had him in my sights too. Still, punching a person of Buzz's formidable build would be far more dangerous than attacking Ali's friend. But could Virgil be in control of my situation somehow? Is he somehow responsible for me being stuck here? Or is he just an innocent part of it? I compare Buzz and Ali's friend's faces in my mind, thousands of miles apart, different nationalities, different ages and completely different people. Neither had acknowledged knowing me or indeed anything about my situation, so perhaps there is no connection between these 'Virgils' after all. They simply can't be the same person.

But a sudden frightening thought occurs to me that this situation is exactly what the dead loop needs, if indeed it does 'need' anything from me. Jumping out of a plane with a fresh parachute is the perfect opportunity for my death to occur. It's the first time that I have considered the possibility that some conscious force is responsible for what's happening to me. Could it be something that I can challenge? The concept brings a new dimension to my thought processes and opens my mind to other intriguing possibilities. Jumping out of the plane might be akin to suicide now, but maybe I can change the tide of what's happening to me just by staying put.

'Helen, I've decided not to jump,' I tell her quickly, 'you go and I'll meet you back on the ground.'

'What do you mean?' she asks. 'You have to jump. We've got to do this together. It's the 10,000.'

'I'll do it next time,' I assure her, 'this one just doesn't feel right for me.'

'Why?' asks Helen, insistently, 'we've done this loads of times and you've never been worried about a jump before.'

'It's just superstition probably,' I reply. 'Jumping again today just gives me a bad vibe.'

'We need to do this now,' Josh interrupts and signals towards the door. 'Our jump window will close soon.'

I know Helen will only persist and argue with me and we don't have the time, so I quickly lie. 'Alright Helen,' I tell her. 'You go first and I'll be right behind you.'

'You bloody better!' she says. 'I'll see your ass on the ground.'

Once she's outside the plane she will never know until she lands that I chose to remain on board. She can berate me all she likes later, but not until I've contradicted the dead loop. Somehow it feels like I'm regaining control of my life and it feels good as I smirk to myself in the face of death.

Helen gives Josh the thumbs up and she takes her position by the plane door. Josh taps the other pilot on the shoulder and then secures himself to the cabin before pulling the door open. Air swirls into the plane around us and the noise of the engines fills the cabin. Adrenaline begins to flow through my veins and my heart races as Helen prepares to jump. She sits on the edge of the doorway, air howling around her and blows me a kiss before leaning forward and falling out. She disappears into the blue sky, falling like a stone and I immediately signal to Josh with my fingers across my throat and shake my head. He points both thumbs down and I nod. Quickly he pulls the door shut and closes the handle, silencing the noise and the wind for good.

'Are you alright?' he asks.

'Yes, but I'm not jumping,' I tell him. 'I don't fancy the 10K today.'

'Are you sure?' he asks.

'Yes,' I tell him. 'I'll meet up with her on the ground.'

Josh unclips himself from the cabin wall but suddenly there is an odd grinding noise outside the plane that seems to come from one of the engines. The sound disappears just as quickly as it started but one engine suddenly starts to splutter. Josh and I look at each other and he points to my seat. I sit down immediately as he retakes his place in the cockpit. As soon as my seatbelt is done up the sound occurs again but for a little longer this time and the engine recognisably loses power. The high pitched whine of the other engine seems louder now as if it's somehow being made to compensate for the other one. A disturbing vibration accompanies the grinding noise and the plane seems to drop violently in the air, losing some altitude. Suddenly the plane begins to shake with increasing turbulence and Josh and Gerry are clearly discussing the situation through their headsets.

Feeling considerable concern, I lean forward and tap Josh on the shoulder. 'What's wrong with the engines?' I ask him.

'Gerry says it's nothing to worry about,' Josh replies. 'It's probably just an air bubble in one of the fuel lines. I'm sure it'll clear itself up in a minute.'

But his words don't reassure me at all, I suddenly realise exactly what's going to happen. It'll be another plane crash that kills me and not the sky dive after all. But this time I know that I'm capable of avoiding it. Finally there is a chance to break my cycle of death but what will happen if I don't die today? Perhaps 'it' hasn't reckoned on my ability to avoid death if I anticipate it coming. All I need to do is reach the ground and avoid this now inevitable, but predictable plane crash. Perhaps then I can regain my life and end this madness once and for all.

'I've changed my mind,' I tell Josh, 'I'm ready to jump.'

Josh shakes his head. 'There's no need, there's really nothing to worry about.'

But in defiance of his assurances, the engine stutters again and the plane loses more altitude. Even though the plane is still flying level it doesn't reassure me.

'No, I paid for a jump and want to go,' I insist.

Gerry turns in his seat and I see his wrinkled veteran face for the first time as he tells me the bad news. 'You can't just jump anywhere,' he yells. 'We're way past our drop point and Buzz will never find you.'

But as the plane vibrates even more and the turbulence intensifies, Gerry is forced to turn his attention back to the controls.

'I'm jumping,' I shout to Josh, 'whether he likes it or not.'

'You can't jump with all this turbulence,' shouts Gerry angrily, but he is too busy fighting against the spluttering engines to reinforce his argument.

I've already seen Josh operate the door and I have no intention of letting death claim me again. They might leave the door open when I've gone but I have to assume that they will be unaffected by my actions. Helen was in the airline crash and now she is here unscathed so nothing bad can happen to them as a result of me. Besides, I won't leave her alone down there with Buzz or Virgil or whatever the hell his name is.

I unbuckle my seatbelt and move towards the door. The plane is shaking even more violently now and I'm certain that it's both engines that are struggling. One of the propellers is even visible now as it spins too slowly. Once at the door I begin to fumble with the handle and prepare myself to open it. Seeing the ground through the window I guess that we have lost maybe 2,000 feet of altitude already since the engine problems began. It looks like there will be no 10K certificate for me then. Josh suddenly turns his head and notices that I'm at the door, but I've already decided that there's no turning back.

'You can't go!' he shouts. 'Sit back down!'

The sound of air rushing into the cabin drowns out his voice as I pull down the handle and open the door. I allow the vortex of air to suck me out of the plane and into the cold sky. I'm free of the doomed plane and falling towards my Helen and I feel a euphoric sense of triumph knowing that I've finally cheated death.

As soon as I leave the plane I crane my head and try to see if Josh has door shut behind me, but the plane is too far away before I can get my bearings. I assume the plane is still descending steadily as the strange spluttering engine noises fade slowly away. It is going down for sure, I'm convinced of that.

I opt to pull the rip cord much sooner than last time so my freefall is shorter. As my chute deploys cleanly and pulls me upwards I take a moment to scan the terrain. The ground looks very similar to my first jump but there is little in the way of recognisable landmarks, except the river. I steer myself towards it, keen to make up some of the distance we have travelled during the flight. Helen and Buzz could be miles away by now, so I scan for any sign of her parachute or maybe a dust trail from the truck. I know there is a small radio in my kit so maybe I can reach Helen on that when I'm on the ground.

The plane is too far away to hear now with the wind in my ears and the flapping of the parachute. There isn't much further to descend now, so I select a clear looking spot fairly close to the river and guide myself towards it. I feel a sense of disappointment that I've spent most of the time searching for Helen, rather than enjoying the view. A few moments later I land smoothly onto the desert floor, disturbing a little cloud of dust.

It feels ten degrees hotter on the ground than it was after the last jump, less than an hour ago. The slow moving calm surface of the river looks inviting and I have to resist the temptation to jump in. I unbuckle my harness to release me from the parachute and abandon the whole lot, with no intention of taking it with me. Given the likelihood that Josh and Gerry have crashed, Buzz will just have to forgive me for leaving it behind, besides I'm not about to do anyone called Virgil any favours anyway. I quickly retrieve the radio from my gear and start walking upstream along the river bank in the direction of the airstrip.

I can't be too sure of the range of the radio or how far away they are, but after twenty minutes of walking all I receive is static. The river meanders quite a bit so I decide to avoid the bank and follow a straight line instead. My biggest problem is the heat and the fact that thirst is prickling at the back of my throat. At least there isn't enough time for me to die of thirst today and with the plane going down I start to believe that I really have outfoxed death. I feel a liberating sense of relief as I take in my surroundings and realise that I've beaten the death trap.

There are enough trees dotted around to offer a welcome break from the sun and I try to walk under them whenever possible. I don't know what kind of trees they are as they all have sharp trunks and jagged branches, but as they give me shade it doesn't matter. It's difficult to estimate how far the landing strip might be and I even try calling Helen's name a few times. I really don't fancy a night out here and Buzz's truck is my only way out. It's a disparaging thought even though I'm grateful to be alive. I think a bottle of water would have been much more use than the radio and at one point I walk to the river bank and splash my face with the lukewarm water. It's incredibly refreshing but I resist any small temptation to try drinking any of the murky stuff. I'm not Bear Grylls, that's for sure.

After maybe another hour walking, struggling with the heat and sweating profusely, I take refuge under a large tree. I spot some small hills in the far distance that look vaguely familiar and decide to head for them after my rest. Sitting down beside some rocks and leaning back against the tree, I wipe my forehead and try to lower my temperature. The dust and sand that are disturbed by the occasional gust of wind make me wish I hadn't tossed the skydiving goggles into the river at the first opportunity.

I decide to try the radio again. 'Helen?' I call, holding down the transmitter button. 'Can you read me?'

The only reply is static so I give the radio a little shake as if it might somehow help. 'Buzz? Virgil? Whatever your name is?' I say into the microphone. There is only static again.

I place the radio onto the ground and sigh. It's too damn hot to go walking across Arizona and I try to imagine myself falling through the cool air on the sky dive again. I wish I was back up there again. Perhaps I should have made a better guess at the direction of the airstrip but I was too absorbed in trying to watch the plane descending. As I wonder how far Gerry and Josh got before they crashed, the radio suddenly crackles faintly into life.

'Ewan?' says a crackly voice.

I pick up the radio and hold it to my ear. 'Ewan?' says the voice again. 'It's Helen.'

I respond ecstatically. 'Helen, it's me!' I reply, quickly turning up the volume to maximum.

Her reply is a little clearer now. 'Where in the hell are you?' she asks. 'We can't find you anywhere.'

'I'm not sure,' I tell her. 'I jumped a bit late but I'm fine. Where are you?'

'I'm in the truck with Buzz,' she says. 'We're looking for you but he didn't even see you coming down.'

'Christ, you're with Buzz?' I ask.

'Of course,' she replies, 'he wants me to ask how late you jumped.'

As much as I detested Virgil, I feel some comfort that Helen has been picked up. At least she has water, transport and air conditioning.

'Follow the river downstream,' I reply. 'I only jumped about five minutes after you. I'm on the East bank.'

'Okay,' Helen replies, 'Buzz heard you too.'

'Tell him the plane went down,' I say, 'that's why I had to jump.'

There is a pause for a moment and then Buzz replies on the radio himself. 'No way,' he says, 'the plane didn't go down. They just had engine problems. They radioed me and said they would have to land on the flats. You never saw them crash did you?'

'No,' I reply, 'but it was going down...'

'They were probably just shaving off altitude,' he replies. 'I'm sure they're fine.'

I feel a slight tickling sensation on my left hand, followed by a small scratching sensation. I snatch my hand away quickly from the ground and see a sandy coloured scorpion fall onto the ground. I scramble up and get well clear of the tree's shade and out into the open. Insects freak me out as it is but a scorpion is in a whole different league of terror. Its tail curls over as it scuttles away and I realise that the bugger has stung me. I shake my arms and feel myself itching all over as I watch it retreat under some rocks. My hand has a bright red mark on it and I've left the radio under the tree. There doesn't seem to be anything like a sting protruding from the mark on my hand my so I hastily retrieve the radio and jog towards the river. I'm not even sure how dangerous scorpion stings are.

'Ewan?' crackles Helen's voice over the radio.

'I've been stung,' I shout, my heart still beating fast from the initial surprise and shock, 'by a bloody scorpion.'

'Jesus, are you alright?' asks Helen.

'It's alright, I got him straight off,' I reply. 'I should've stomped on the little bastard.'

And then a sudden revelation hits me, Buzz was right – the plane didn't crash after all. There wasn't any crash and I didn't die in the jump either, but I haven't avoided death at all. The plane was just a decoy designed to get me down here, however crazy that sounds. But why my sudden paranoia that the dead loop is somehow sentient and determined to kill me? I feel a strange mixture of despondency and annoyance, a bit like being a bad loser I suppose.

'Hold on Helen,' I say before placing the radio down in the hard baked sand and washing my hands in the river.

The red mark already looks angry, red and swollen and I can see a small black hole where the sting pierced my skin. My hand is beginning to go numb and I experience what feels like little jolts of electricity travelling up my arm as I retrieve the radio.

'Damn, it's actually quite painful Helen,' I say.

'Stay by the river,' she says. 'Stay there whatever you do, we're on the way.'

Sitting down on the river bank, I submerge my arm in the water to see if it helps to soothe it. The sun seems stronger than ever since my premature departure from the shade of the tree and sweat drips off my forehead. My arm keeps shaking involuntarily in the river, causing ripples on the surface.

Ten minutes later the pain is excruciatingly intense and I have to lay flat on my back and grit my teeth as I struggle against it. I begin shaking spasmodically as the sun seems to roast my head and I even consider trying to crawl back over to the shade of the tree but I'm already struggling to breathe. I lick my lips but they taste frothy and strange. At some point the pain has spread from my arm into most of my body, making my legs feel weak and my arms immobile. Perhaps I'm allergic to scorpions.

I try and lift the radio to ask Helen to hurry but it slips out of my hand and splashes into the river. Cursing my carelessness I try to sit up but it's impossible, my muscles aren't working.

'Help... me... Helen,' I gasp desperately and for just a second the pain seems to subside. I take a ragged intake of breath and the pain immediately returns with newfound ferocity. Oh God, I can't breathe now, its agony. Where is Buzz? My throat feels swollen and my head is bursting. Never again will I believe that death can be eluded. Someone please help me. I open my mouth to scream in poisoned agony but nothing comes out.

8
Gratitude

My eyes flicker open and I'm staring up at a pale grey ceiling that reminds me of the sky. The double bed feels hard and comfortable but when I reach out for Helen with my arm I realise that I'm sleeping alone. I yawn and rub my itchy eyes to wake myself up before pulling the bed sheets aside and standing up.

The hotel room is pleasantly decorated with pastel painted walls, floral borders and there is also a generous sized television. Against one of the walls is a writing desk with a massive blue vase standing on it that contains some weary looking flowers. Behind the desk are some full length drapes running from the carpeted floor, right up to the ceiling. I switch on a bedside lamp and walk past a small settee into the tiled bathroom to use the toilet. My reflection stares back at me in the bathroom mirror looking tired, drawn and unshaven.

After properly waking myself up with a wash, I dry my face and return to the bedroom. I pull the cord to open the drapes and immediately recognise the view of downtown Paris. It is still early in the morning and I check the time on my watch which shows 7:45 am. The city is already alive though, with cars, taxis and bicycles manoeuvring through the street. I guess my room is on around the tenth floor of the hotel and I can see the river from here, but not the Eiffel Tower as my view is disappointingly obscured by other buildings.

I remember coming to Paris a few times before, but only on business trips and I try to recall why I'm here this time. Opening the wardrobe I survey my clothes, consisting of a smart business suit and three shirts hung up neatly on quality wooden hangers. There are also my smart black shoes, two ties and a smattering of casual clothes. I never travel particularly heavily on business trips but there aren't enough casual clothes for this to be a holiday.

For some reason I can't seem to recall my journey here or even the flight, but what I start to remember clearly is the river, the desert and a sky dive. The scorpion sting comes back into my thoughts and the memory of suffering the intensely painful after effects. Rubbing the back of my hand I decide that it was the worst death so far. The pain went on for what seemed like hours, getting progressively worse and attacking my whole body but I can't actually remember it ending. Odd as it seems, I'm certain that death would have been a welcome relief as I shudder at the memory of what the sting had done to me. I hope that I never have to endure anything quite as slow and painful as that again.

While surveying the clothes I notice a brown leather briefcase at the bottom of the wardrobe which I retrieve and place on the bed, instinctively entering the combination. The case is familiar and opens with a satisfying click that I'm sure I've heard before. The paperwork inside is headed with 'D.G.E.C' and I recognise the name, Dynamic Global Energy Consultants. I work for them as a senior energy consultant – or rather I *used* to work for them. The memory seems blurred as if I can't quite dial into it properly, but as I continue to flick through the documents I recognise the account details of one of D.G.E.C's major French clients. I was one of their key contacts.

The French manufacturer has dozens of sites throughout France, relying on us to support them through the energy procurement and contracting process. Boring stuff, but saving companies money on their sites energy costs was a lucrative business. I remember that their expectations were always unrealistic and our costs saving promises often over exaggerated, leading to a turbulent working relationship. I don't recall a trip to Paris ever being a good sign but at least my memory hasn't completely eluded me this morning.

The thought occurs to me that this time I appear to have been taken into my past. Was it really two years already since I left D.G.E.C because the promises they made to staff were as unreliable as some of those that we made our customers? But I refuse to accept that I'm travelling through time because time travellers wouldn't die every day, not to mention the fact that it's impossible. Shaking my head, I realise that concepts which should sound ludicrous don't seem so strange anymore, but to go on functioning I have to keep some kind of perspective. How else can I maintain my sanity and some grip on reality?

Returning to the bathroom, I pick up my electric razor and start to shave. The bite of the blade is always a little uncomfortable at first, but this morning it feels welcome. The scratching seems insignificant compared to the crippling pain of yesterday. The buzz and hum of the razor sounds like a placid bumble bee hovering around my face, and I leave the bathroom as I continue shaving.

For the first time I notice the smell of the flowers on the writing desk as I enter the bedroom. Despite how tired and old the flowers look, they still smell strongly. I finish shaving and drop the shaver on the bed. Opening the wardrobe again, I start to get dressed in a shirt and trousers, but as I tighten up my belt my stomach rumbles in anticipation of breakfast. My throat also feels dry, reminding me of how thirsty and parched I was under the burning Arizona sun. After pulling on my black slip-on shoes I pick up my mobile phone and a key card from the bedside table and leave the bedroom.

The empty lift must have already been on my floor because the doors open almost immediately when I press the call button. Once inside and with the lift descending, I check my phone. There is a text message from Helen waiting for me to read. *'Good morning Honey. Hope your flight was good, love H. xxx.'*

I remember the sound of vibration on the bedside table and realise that it must have been her text message that had first awoken me. As the lift doors open, I decide to wait for breakfast before replying. The spacious hotel lobby is very quiet this morning, with just one person behind the desk. A cleaning lady is sweeping the marble floor as a couple of guests walk silently past me in the direction of the dining room. I follow them though the double doors into the familiar looking room. I've definitely stayed in this hotel before.

I collect an empty tray and pick up a continental breakfast of croissants, Danish pastry, some cheese and ham with a glass of orange juice. There are quite a few tables occupied so I sit down at the nearest empty one, but I'm only sat down for a few seconds before an efficient waiter is offering me the choice of tea or coffee. It has to be coffee.

The waiter returns with a cafetiere before I've even eaten half a croissant. The food tastes fresh and the coffee looks strong. I thank him and pour some into a slightly chipped cup and smell it. Heaven! Impending death or not, good coffee is still good coffee. I reply to Helen's text message with my best assumption of how my flight went, using a favourable memory of a previous flight to Paris. *'A little bumpy on landing but the stewardesses were fit,'* I type, smiling to myself. *'Hope you're both well. See you when I get back. X.'*

As I press 'send' and the phone flashes, I realise that I'll only see her again after I've died – and that's only assuming that she's wherever I am when I 'awaken'. The thought seems less ridiculous that it would have done a week ago. I suppose by tomorrow my text message will be old news, assuming that she has even received it. Maybe I should text her something unusual and see if she remembers it next time we meet, but which Helen might that be? Will it be my darling wife, the adventure loving thrill seeker or the murderous knife wielding one?

My thoughts are interrupted by a female voice. 'Sending me a text to check that I'm awake?' she asks.

I look up slightly startled, but it's not Helen standing before me.

'Morning Tina,' I reply automatically.

It's short for Christina, my joint consultant at D.G.E.C but it seems strange seeing her so abruptly after all this time. In the seven months that we'd worked together we had developed a professional and mutually respectful relationship, albeit a slightly flirtatious one. At 42, Tina is three years older than me but well-toned, sporty and very youthful looking. She plays a lot of racket sports, everything from squash to badminton to tennis, and is known to be fiercely competitive. Tina always applies makeup subtlety, but very effectively with particular emphasis around her eyes. Her shoulder length waves of raven black hair and pretty face are enough to ensure she always has her fair share of admirers, from colleagues and customers alike, while her exceptional body was just an added bonus.

In the short time I'd known Tina she had a string of failed relationships because most men couldn't keep pace or measure up to her high expectations. I suppose the same thing could be said for D.G.E.C by our customers and I feel no joy to be back with them, even if it is only for one day. I chuckle to myself at the thought of it being such a brief reunion.

Tina pulls up a chair and sets down a tray of ham, cheese and yogurt with a small glass of juice. Unlike me she has dressed casually for breakfast in jeans and a T-shirt.

'You look smart,' she taunts me, as if reading my thoughts. 'You know the meeting is tomorrow right? Or are you just trying to make a good impression with Ninette?'

'Ninette?' I reply, recognising the name of one of our contacts from the French customer. 'No, the shirt is all for your benefit,' I tell her. 'I thought you liked having smart guys for breakfast.'

Tina smiles wryly and I wince uncomfortably at how that sounded. Fortunately I'm saved by my phone beeping and vibrating on the table. I hastily pick it up and read the text from Helen. '*Have a good meeting. X,*' it reads.

'I like smart guys for every meal,' Tina teases, not allowing me to get away with the statement, 'luckily for you not married ones though. Was that Helen?'

'Yes, just checking I got here safely,' I reply, before biting into another croissant.

'You're always safe with me,' says Tina. 'I'll be sure to keep you out of mischief.'

The waiter brings Tina a pot of tea and I assume she must have collared him before sitting down. I watch her pour it out, add some milk and taste it with her full red lips, finding myself grateful and appreciative of her company. She looks as fresh faced and attractive as I remember, and I decide it will be a lucky man who finally succeeds in matching up to her expectations. Tina looks at me curiously as if trying to work out what I'm thinking, and for a moment I have to avert my eyes. 'Let's get down to business Ewan,' she says.

'Alright,' I say, looking her in her the eyes and then pouring myself more coffee.

'Right, well I've rung Ninette and she's kindly offered to meet us here at 12:00 to give us some feedback before the meeting tomorrow,' says Tina. 'You see? Didn't I tell you that keeping her sweet was a good idea? You know, woman-to-woman. Thanks to me, she's willing to give us the low down on what to expect when we meet her bosses.'

'Okay,' I reply, 'you're right that does sound useful.'

Tina puts down her cup. 'Well it's still not going to be an easy ride,' she says. 'According to Ninette, they're pretty peed off with last quarter's results and are going to be demanding some answers. You and I have been stitched up on this trip, as usual.'

For a moment I feel tense at the thought of a meeting with the Directors of a key customer who are dissatisfied with our performance. The energy savings across their network of sites were always far below what we'd promised of course, but then I suddenly realise that tomorrow has a habit of not following today. I'm unable to suppress a large grin appearing on my face at the prospect of a rare positive coming out of my situation.

'What?' asks Tina, swallowing a spoonful of yogurt, 'what's so amusing?'

'Does Ninette still play squash?' I ask.

'Yes, I guess she does,' Tina replies. 'Why do you think watching us in short skirts will help us at all?'

'No, not for me,' I reply, 'you take her out this afternoon. Give her a game and let her win. Do whatever it is you do to keep her sweet, and I will sort out a battle plan for tomorrow.'

'What plan?' asks Tina with a curious frown. 'We plan things together remember? That's why things work out.'

'Don't worry, let me sort this one myself, just this once,' I say reassuringly. 'I guarantee that they will be satisfied tomorrow once I've presented to them. Just leave everything to me.'

'You're kidding right?' she asks.

'No, I'm serious, leave it to me,' I reply. 'You just keep Ninette sweet.'

Tina finishes her yogurt and waves her spoon at me in mock threat. 'Alright you win,' she says, 'but I'll find out from Ninette what their main issues are and get some suggestions, in case you mess things up. She isn't stupid, remember? We can meet for dinner in the restaurant tonight and you can tell me your plan. I'm not going in there blind tomorrow.'

'Alright,' I reply, holding up my hands. 'But don't you worry your pretty little head about a thing darling.'

My intentionally playful words would have been sexist and offensive to most women, but not to her. We both know damn well that she can hold her own in any boardroom, probably better than most men too. I remember her putting a Finance Director from one customer in his place, in a meeting room with fifteen people in it.

Tina finishes her yoghurt and stands up to leave. 'I'll see you later,' she says. 'Please try and do something constructive this afternoon.'

I watch her leave but can't help staring at the sway of her hips as she walks away. When she reaches the exit to the dining room, she turns around and waves at me. I quickly look down at the table as if I haven't noticed her but she is definitely smarter than that.

So I decide to spend my day relaxing in the hotel, perhaps I'll go swimming, drink some more coffee and wait around for death. Actually, swimming might be a bad idea under the circumstances.

Death doesn't show its face and by early evening I'm finishing my dinner and pushing the last piece of veal around my plate. Tina hadn't shown up, having texted me earlier to inform me that Ninette had invited her out for a 'girly meal.' An hour sitting in the hotel restaurant filled primarily with holidaymakers had been a lonely and depressing ordeal. It felt particularly distasteful as I'd anticipated spending more time with Tina. Was I really looking forward to her company that much? There is no doubt that she has an infectious charisma about her that is hard to resist, but I'm also grateful that she has never escalated her flirtations to being anything more than playful. I was grateful, but perhaps a little disappointed if I'm to be honest with myself. It's a safe bet that Tina's advances would be difficult to resist in light of the chemistry between us, and she probably knows it. Fortunately there are some boundaries that she wouldn't cross, and married men were one of them. It's little wonder that most women liked her as well, except for the especially jealous ones of course.

My phone suddenly beeps twice. One of the texts is from Helen to tell me that she's having an early night because she has a headache, and that although Jenny had found her history exam stressful, she still felt confident. Jenny hated exams as much as I did when I was at school, but hopefully she will still get good results like me. The second text gives me a reason to feel brighter. Tina has finished her meal with Ninette and wants to meet me in the bar in half an hour.

My meal was deceptively filling despite looking quite meagre and I'm lounging in a comfortable sofa in the ambient lit hotel lounge with my second pint of Kronenbourg. The cold beer goes down well and looks especially appealing in the low light while the lounge pianist plays out a sleepy French melody that I don't recognise. The music and low lighting blend together, creating an atmosphere that relaxes me and causes me to yawn.

Suddenly someone sits clumsily next to me and knocks into my hand, and although I recover well, I spill a good quarter of the cold beer into my lap. Startled by the sudden cold I'm about to swear at the person but realise that it's Tina. She is wearing a shiny black cocktail dress and has squeezed right up against me on the sofa, giggling at the accidental spill.

'Whoops!' she says,' Sorry about that Ewie.'

I dab at the beer with my handkerchief but Tina snatches it out of my hand and starts trying to mop the beer from my lap herself. I grab it back off her and stuff the damp cotton handkerchief into my trouser pocket before standing the remnants of my beer on the table.

'Had a good time then?' I ask drily.

'You know me and Ninny,' she says, grinning. 'It's always a party when we go out.'

I know from experience that Tina isn't a regular drinker and a couple of glasses of wine would make her tipsy. They must have had a very good time indeed catching up. But with her natural stamina I don't doubt she will be awake and alert for business in the morning. Tina and 'Ninny' as she sometimes calls her have a great working relationship, despite what her bosses thought of D.G.E.C's performance. Any insider knowledge she could obtain from Ninette might help us, even if only a little.

'So what did you find out?' I ask.

'Hold on a second Mr. Business,' she replies. 'Wait a minute while I get you a replacement drink.'

Tina totters over to the bar on high heels that she is definitely not used to wearing, being far more comfortable in tennis shoes. Before she returns I remove my sodden handkerchief from my pocket and drop it on the table next to me. Tina returns with two pints of Kronenbourg and puts them down somewhat heavily on the table with a bang, slightly spilling both of them.

'One for you and one for me,' she says giggling.

A little pool of beer has now formed around the glasses on the table surface but I thank her and take a sip from mine. Tina sits down right up close again and I feel the warmth and firmness of her legs against mine. It's a little more intimate and forward than I am used to from her.

'I thought you didn't like beer?' I remind her.

'I have a pint sometimes,' she says, looking straight at me with a sudden serious expression, 'alright Dad?'

Before I can reply, she begins laughing again and then takes a big mouthful of beer to prove her point.

'You're a nightmare,' I tell her, 'and anyway, you're older than me, Mum!'

'Ouch! You have got your claws out tonight,' she says. 'I better be careful that I don't get scratched, Little Tiger.'

As I drink the beer and feel more relaxed, the feeling of loneliness that I had at dinner washes away. Her words *Little Tiger* and my own alcohol consumption feed my flirtatiousness.

'Well if I did scratch you, then you would know you'd been scratched,' I joke.

'Yeah, you think so?' she replies. 'I'd eat you alive.'

'Dream on,' I tell her,' You wouldn't even beat me at tennis.'

I know it's the ultimate insult.

'I'll play you anytime,' she says, poking me hard in the ribs, 'right now if you want and I'll kick your butt easily.'

I try to fend off her prodding. 'How many bottles of wine did you and Ninny have?' I ask. 'Six?'

Tina leans right into me and grabs my face in both hands as if she is going to kiss me, but then turns my head to one side, allowing her to whisper softly in my air. 'Listen up Ewie,' she says, 'I was doing research, important research.'

I drink more beer and then whisper back. 'Like I said when you first sat down, what did you find out?' I ask.

As I finish the sentence with my mouth close to her ear, intentionally mocking her whispering, I can't help but inhale her perfume. It's a strong, fruity scent but I can't begin to guess what's in it. The combination of the perfume and her body leaning against mine is dangerously arousing and I pull back slightly from her, in a half-hearted attempt to avoid her charismatic, albeit tipsy allure.

Tina presses her finger to my lips and takes another mouthful of beer. 'I found out nothing Silly,' she says. 'I simply told Ninny what you said. That you had a plan and she had absolutely nothing to worry about, so I skipped the research. We know it'll be the same old rubbish anyway.'

Tina's professionalism is notably absent as she would never have missed an opportunity to gather information, and I'm frankly amazed she hadn't made better use of a rare social occasion with a client. Still, it's a relief that she doesn't ask me to explain my great plan, especially as I don't have one.

Tina and I enjoy yet another beer and she still seems to be coping with it, but at the speed she is drinking I suspect that the alcohol in her system will win the battle over sobriety. She continues to be wildly flirtatious, even more than usual but at least her words seem clearer now. She kicks off her high heels after complaining they hurt her feet and curls her feet under her legs on the sofa. Her hair and her dress are still immaculate despite how much she has drunk.

I catch the barman's gaze and he smiles at me knowingly. Although I'm starting to feel the effects of alcohol too, his glance is a gentle reminder of the dangerous path this might lead down. Tina's resolute aversion to playing around with married men is even stronger than my own considerable conscience, but I feel the alcohol breaking down the barriers of my resolve. It doesn't make me proud to think that if Tina's conscience slips that my own might not be strong enough to resist her. There is just something indefinable about this raven haired woman that stirs something deep within me.

'Tina, I think we'd better call it a night.' I tell her, glancing at the barman as if to prove his assumption wrong.

After a pause to finish her beer, Tina grabs my arm and pulls me up out of the sofa. She is remarkably strong for a slim woman and I haven't felt her physical prowess before.

'You're right,' she replies. 'We have some butts to kick tomorrow, right?'

Tina half drags me towards the exit of the lounge before I realise that she's left her shoes by the sofa. I leave her propped up against the wall as I go back and get them. Tina is swaying slightly as I return so I hold the shoes under one arm and then support her with the other. Slowly I guide her carefully out of the piano lounge. Tina stumbles ahead of me towards the lift and presses the call button, but I have to grab her to stop her falling over. She spins around as I wrap my arm around her but accidentally knocks her shoes out of my hand and onto the floor. And suddenly she is in my arms with her body pressed against me, her face inches from mine and her eyes slightly glazed and staring. I picture her in all her business meetings, so assured, so confident, strong and determined. The scent of her perfume seems intoxicating as she clings onto me with a rare trace of vulnerability. Her shoulders feel firm in my hands and I feel a tinge of regret at not seeing her since we worked together. As Tina leans towards me, her scent takes hold of my mind and her raven black hair seems to shimmer. I smile warmly but to her it's as much of an invitation as she needs. It's not exactly the signal I intended but her mouth is suddenly on mine and we're kissing intimately.

The interruption is sudden, intense and shocking but it's enough to convince my conscience that our deep kiss had never happened. An enormous explosion rocks the hotel building and the walls and floor around us began to shake, exactly how I imagine they would during an earthquake. I fall on top of Tina who screams as clouds of dust fill the corridor and a deep fracture appears in the wall next to the lift. From somewhere behind me I hear more screams and the sounds of yelling and banging. The clamour is followed by the high-pitched shrill blast of the hotel fire alarm.

Despite her initial scream, Tina recovers her composure far more quickly than I do and she crouches above me and shakes my shoulders. I feel groggy as if I fell heavily.

'What the hell was that Ewan?' she demands with no trace of alcohol affecting her.

'It must be a bomb!' I reply, the shock realisation seeming to clear my mind. 'A terror attack, it's got to be.'

'Get up!' Tina yells the instruction. 'We have to get out of here, now.'

By now people are fleeing from the bar in terror, most of them screaming and shouting. I see the barman in the piano lounge looking around, seeming dazed and uncertain what to do. Two of the waiters are half dragging an elderly lady out of the bar who appears to have fainted. Her husband limps behind them with a walking stick.

The corridor by the lift is rapidly descending into pandemonium as one of the reception staff appears through the dust. She shouts something about a bomb upstairs and for everyone to head for the fire exits, but unlike the air stewardesses she only shouts it once and then disappears back towards reception.

'Come on!' shouts Tina fiercely, almost pulling my shoulder out of its socket.

As I struggle to my feet, I notice that her black hair is a mess for the first time ever. Her cocktail dress is covered in dust, the strap ripped at one shoulder and her bra is visible. Tina's presence had helped me to forget about my situation, if only for an hour or two and for that I will be forever grateful. But I also realise that she is pulling me towards reception and the fire exit, so I break her grip and stop her.

'Wait!' I shout, trying to be heard over the voices of the other evacuees. 'You go, I'm going back upstairs.'

'Don't be stupid,' she yells back at me. 'There's nothing you can do up there.'

'Go!' I insist, pushing her towards the others.

Despite her protests, the flow of people forces her to go along with them. Soon Tina is lost to me as she disappears towards the emergency exits and safety. As the final few people from the lounge evacuate past me, I notice the lift doors are half open and making a terrible grinding noise.

I needn't be afraid of death anymore because I realise that it is harmless to me. Suddenly I recognise that I have a purpose here – to save these people. Without giving it a second thought, I turn my back on the exit route and I begin to climb the hotel stairs. Pushing past the intermittent flow of people descending the stairs is easy enough as I seem to be the only person going up. After the first few floors, the flow of people stops and I call out periodically down the corridor of each floor, but hear no response. As I hurriedly ascend and presumably get nearer towards the blast, the stairs become littered with broken tiles and bricks, and the air becomes a choking haze of acrid smoke. On the seventh floor I find a terrifying scene of devastation. The stairway ahead is completely gone and no longer continues any higher than the seventh floor. Flames dance violently in the corridor and some of the bedroom doors are on fire. A huge gaping hole in the wall where there were once rooms, reveals a smoky view of the Paris night sky.

I urge myself onwards, choking and fighting against the smoke that stings and burns my eyes, forced to turn left down the corridor because the flames are too intense on my right.

'Anyone here?' I bellow as loudly as I can while stumbling down the ruined corridor.

The cry for help is instant and seems to come from behind a nearby bedroom door which seems badly buckled. The same door that appeared so secure earlier when I'd locked my own takes just two hard kicks to force open. The door bursts open to reveal a vision of destruction far beyond the apartment in Pripyat and a wave of hot air hits me. The devastated room is filled with smoke while black, charred debris litters the floor. The piles of rubble in the centre of the room can only have come from the collapsed ceiling which now has sparks, dust and water falling from it.

From amongst the rubble beside the bed, an elderly woman reaches towards me an outstretched hand, her blue pyjamas covered in grey dust.

'Please!' she cries desperately with a weak coughing voice, 'I think my leg is broken.'

Immediately I grab her and drag her from under the plaster ceiling debris and into the corridor. Her screams of pain are terrifying to hear but I force myself to ignore them and keep moving. By the time I've dragged her to the stairwell my eyes are streaming and painful from the effects of smoke, but the huge hole in the wall makes the air much clearer than in the corridor. I gasp desperately for some relief from the night air and rub my stinging eyes. Blinking, I notice that woman's head is bleeding and her face is almost completely grey with dust. She looks up at me pitifully and rubs her eyes.

'You have to help my husband Virgil,' she pleads. 'He's still in the room.'

For a moment I just hold her in my arms on the floor as my mind processes her husband's name. I'm not sure why, but I want to feel anger and rage towards Virgil but I can't.

'Don't worry,' I tell her, coughing to clear my painful throat. 'I'll be right back.'

I prop the injured woman up against the wall and dash back into the corridor but the fire has spread much quicker than I expected, fuelled by the fresh air coming in through the hole in the wall. I have to save her husband before it's too late. Two or three steps are as far as I make it towards her room before I'm surrounded by searing hot flames that quickly ignite my clothes. The flames scorch my flesh with a sickening smell and a nerve shredding agony.

Mercifully, the corridors ceiling suddenly collapses down on top of me with a sound like thunder. The falling rubble prevents me from having to endure the experience of burning to death and for the second time tonight, I'm grateful.

9
Faith

I'm lying in bed with my eyes closed and feeling too lazy to get up. I already know that there's no hurry. Death will find me at some point today so it can at least allow me a lie in.

Death is one of life's certainties – an inevitable absolution that we all have to accept. It's the instant when life is extinguished and your own personal spark fades away forever. Dying is your last experience and a final door closing on life's journey of existence. It's also supposed to be a permanent affair and for you at least it will be. But dying isn't the end for me. It's only the beginning of another opportunity to experience death again in a different way.

I've lost count of the number of times that I've died and how often my body has surrendered to the darkness. Counting them seemed important at first and it terrified me every time my life ended, but dying has become part of my daily routine now. It seems as normal to me as brushing my teeth or putting on shoes. Sometimes I even find myself smirking at the irony of death's apparent inability to finish me off.

My death feels insignificant now, just as my past has become irrelevant to me. Somewhere along the line dying became my way of life and living became almost meaningless. So I've stopped looking beyond today or thinking about the future, and can only wonder where my next death will come from. I'm trapped in an endless tiresome cycle where every time I die I seem to lose a little bit more of who I am.

I'm not some immortal being, it's just that life and death are both the same to me – there is no distinction between them anymore. This isn't the afterlife or some kind of re-incarnation – it's something that I call the 'dead loop'.

The thoughts echo clearly in my mind as I remember my last death in a hotel in Paris. The bomb had interrupted my unintentional but enjoyable kiss with Tina and stopped me following a more dangerous path with her. Kissing her was undoubtedly a mistake, no matter how pleasant it was at the time but the intimate memory makes me feel both guilty and warm in equal measure.

After we were interrupted, I had saved an old lady from the fire upstairs but I'll never know if she made it out of the hotel alive. Although I feel a sense of curiosity, it seems of little consequence now. All that matters to me is how I felt in those last few moments when I was trying to save people, when I was doing something good and making a difference for once.

My situation affords me the rare opportunity to act without any fear of the consequences. I can act without hesitation and in spite of the risk to myself. How many people could I protect or save while living without any fear of death? But am I really so unafraid of death? The idea of running up the stairs of a bombed out building reminds me of the fire-fighters in New York on 9/11. But they were far different to me because they had acted with bravery and courage – in spite of the risk to themselves, knowing that they might die. I had only climbed those stairs in France because death is irrelevant to me and I knew that it wouldn't be permanent. But nothing I ever do will allow me to justifiably compare myself with those brave souls in New York. But maybe the results could be the same.

I change my mind about lying in and decide to get out of bed, but for some reason find it impossible. My body feels weak and lifeless, and my breathing seems shallow. With a determined effort I slowly manage to raise one arm but recoil in shock at the horrific sight of it. The skin of my forearm is pale, blotchy and my arm is stick thin with a plastic tube running out of it. My eyes pan around the room but everything seems washed out, colourless and bland. What's happened to me? For a moment I consider that I might have survived the bomb but that doesn't make sense because I'm not burnt or bandaged. My legs feel so weak that I can barely even lift them, but I don't seem to have an urge to panic.

This room reminds me of the hospital after the crash I once had with a tractor. It seemed a long time ago that Helen held my hand as Dr. Adams discussed the impending brain surgery that led to my death. But this room was different somehow, less medical and more homely with soft furnishings and devoid of machinery. The walls are painted with peach pastel shades and there are framed pictures of the countryside hanging on them, I think they are Monet or something like that.

The sound of a door opening gets my attention as a nurse enters the room and bustles hurriedly over to my bed. She is middle aged and as generic and stereotypical as I can imagine. Her brown hair is tied in a neat bun and she has a caring but oddly indifferent and detached look on her face. She probably does care but just isn't affected by what she sees. Her white uniform is clean and sharply pressed with a little watch hanging from her breast pocket that swings on its chain as she leans over my bed.

'Mr. Charles?' she says.

'Where am I?' I ask her.

'You're in Saint Thomas Hospice, dear,' she replies.

Hospice, that's where people go to die isn't it? It makes her answer seem kind of ironic, given my situation and I wonder if this could actually be the perfect place for me. But I'm not dying slowly – I'm dying regularly and my condition isn't really terminal.

As if my body is in dispute with my thoughts I suddenly feel a severe pain in my stomach, making me cry out. I feel my eyes roll back in my head as sudden panic hits me. The pain continues to intensify and my body tries to double up into a foetal position but my muscles don't have the strength to achieve the goal. My eyes scrunch closed and I'm unable to suppress a long groan as I fight the agony with muted determination. When I open my eyes again, the nurse calmly picks up a chart from the end of my bed and walks back to my bedside.

'You aren't due any more pain relief for twenty minutes,' she says, 'but I'll see if we can bring that forward.'

She smiles and leaves the room through a set of double doors, but as they close behind her a robed figure walks past in the corridor. Something metal glints on their chest and from my superficial glance it looks like sunlight glinting off a crucifix. The connotation with religion and death make it an evocative image and one that seems to burn itself into my brain. I'm certainly not a man of faith but I can respect a member of the church community.

Still desperately fighting the pain in my stomach and trying to find something to take my mind off it, I wonder why a small private room has double doors. Then I realise it's obviously to get the bed in and out, probably in an emergency.

After laying still and gritting my teeth for a few minutes, my pain slowly but surely begins to subside. I close my eyes and take a few deep breaths, enjoying the respite. But my relief is short lived though because the pain quickly surges back and I try everything to fight it until the nurse returns, but it seems impossible. My body is just too weak to fight, too broken to resist and I barely have the strength to groan. What the hell has happened to me?

The nurse's reappearance is a welcome sight and the pain relief injection she administers is a huge bonus.

'It's morphine,' she says as she delivers the shot, but wherever she put it I don't feel the needle go in.

'Thank you,' I murmur.

The nurse smiles and disposes of the hypodermic into a small yellow box on the bedside table. 'Your wife is here to see you,' she says, smiling.

As she leaves the room I form a picture of Helen in my mind, beautiful and full of life. I don't want her to see me like this, a skinny dying shadow of the man she married. Is this how I am going to die this time, lying on this bed? Am I destined to die weak and frail, unable to use my unique situation in the pursuit of helping others? Frustration begins to boil inside me and I want to kick out in anger, but I can't muster the strength. I'm powerless to move, unable to do much of anything for myself and it's an uncomfortable and embarrassing feeling. Somehow I have to stop Helen from seeing me like this but the door suddenly opens and she walks straight into the room.

Helen approaches my bedside and kisses my forehead before sitting down next to me on the bed. She is as beautiful as ever and her freckles and red hair are a welcome sight, despite my painful discomfort. There is no trace of shock on her face at my condition, just a hint of sadness and I suspect that she is putting on a brave face for my benefit. Her eyes reveal no hint of long suffering anguish or worry at my condition and presumed deterioration.

'What happened to me?' I ask.

'What do you mean?' she replies.

'I mean what's wrong with me?'

Helen strokes my head and my hair feels thin and straggly at her touch. 'You know it's cancer,' she says. 'I'm sorry.'

She merely confirms what I suspected but hearing the 'C' word aloud still generates a chilling feeling of raw terror inside me. 'How long?' I ask.

Helen's eyes begin to show the tell-tale signs of tears welling up in them and her hastened blinking confirms it.

'You know that it's best not to think about it,' she replies, her voice faltering a little.

'Not that,' I reply, shaking my head. 'I meant how long have I been here?'

Helen sighs and squeezes my hand. 'Almost two months Honey,' she tells me. 'God, has it been that long already?'

I consider asking her what kind of cancer I have but a sudden pain in my stomach prevents me from speaking and reminds me that it doesn't really matter. The fact that I'm in a Hospice confirms that much. I try to conceal the intensity of my pain from her, unsure if she has been a witness to it before. I force out a semi convincing smile. 'Yes, I remember now,' I lie. 'So how is Jenny?'

Helen squeezes my hand. 'She has an interview today,' she tells me. 'She wants to come in and see you again, but you know she can't... I mean she struggles... seeing you like this...'

The idea of our daughter seeing me in this condition haunts me even more than having Helen see me. 'She gets upset?' I ask, making the assumption.

Helen opens her ludicrously overpriced Radley handbag, takes out a pale yellow envelope and adeptly changes the subject. 'That woman you used to work with dropped this off at the apartment,' she says, waving the envelope in front of me.

'What woman?' I ask.

'You know, that brunette who plays all the sport,' she replies. 'We haven't seen her since you left D.G.E.C. But she still remembers you obviously. No one else from there has sent you anything.'

I struggle to focus my blurred vision on the envelope as an image of Tina's face floods into my mind. My memory flashes with images of the hotel and the bomb. Tina is laughing after returning from her dinner with our customer Ninette. Then she is kissing me, an illicit and forbidden liaison that is so out of character for her. I notice Helen watching me intently and wonder what she is thinking, but her words interrupt me.

'Do you want me to open it for you Honey,' she asks.

'Yes please, go on,' I reply.

The morphine seems to be working now and my pain subsides considerably as Helen carefully tears open the envelope and looks at front of the card before showing it to me. It reads 'Best Wishes' and I can only presume that a 'Get Well Soon' card would have been inappropriate in here. The picture on the front shows a bizarre orange and black cartoon tiger.

'Ahhh, she got you a Tiger,' Helen teases. 'I'll read it out for you.'

She opens the card and reads Tina's words aloud.

'Dear Ewan, I just heard about your illness. I'm so sorry to hear that you're in St. Thomas. I wanted to make sure you know how much I appreciate everything that I learnt from you. I hope you might have picked up the odd thing from me too! Life at D.G.E.C is still pretty much the same. We lost the French account eventually, even Ninette couldn't stop that. We've lost half the other European accounts too, but they always find new ones to replace them. Anyway I decided that

I had to send my best wishes to you and your family at this time. Keep scratching Tiger! Love Tina XXX.'

Helen shows me the inside of the card and even though it's blurred, I recognize Tina's writing.

'Tiger?' Helen says drily, with a hint of amusement in her voice. 'What's all that about? And three kisses too! I guess she really likes you.'

The nickname causes me a hint of embarrassment even in my terminal condition and I hastily reply. 'We worked together on a lot of accounts,' I explain. 'She always said I was tenacious. Like a Tiger I guess. We were...kind of competitive.'

My voice drifts off as I picture Tina choosing and writing the card. Does she think it's inappropriate to visit a terminally ill married man or is she just too upset?

Could Tina be anything to do with the reason that Helen once stabbed me? Had I crossed some kind of line with her and then been discovered somehow, only to suffer the vengeful spite of a betrayed wife? I think about the kiss with Tina in France but it really was nothing, and Helen couldn't have known about it. I shake my head involuntarily, refusing to accept that I've had an affair when I have no memory of it. A part of me wanted Tina, wholly and completely, but Helen is my life. And she is here at my death.

'Nice words though Tiger!' says Helen teasingly and perhaps to lighten the mood. 'I hope she didn't leave any scratches on my husband though.'

My eyes are fixed on Helen and no other images enter my mind. She is the very picture of trust and love as I squeeze her hand with what little strength I have left.

'I've never cheated on you in my life,' I tell her.

Helen shrugs casually. 'I know that Honey,' she replies.

As much as Helen's presence is comforting now that I don't feel as self-conscious about my appearance, there is something I need to do. The opportunity to speak to someone religious seems too good to miss in light of my situation.

'Helen, I think there may be a Priest or a Bishop or someone like that here,' I say. 'I'd really like to see them.'

Helen looks at me a little surprised. 'You mean a Minister?' she asks.

I cough weakly. 'Yes whatever, anyone like that,' I reply.

Helen clutches my hand firmly and kisses it. 'If that's what you want, then I'll find out,' she replies. 'Now get some rest.'

She kisses my lips and leaves the room but less than five minutes after she has gone, my stomach pain returns fiercer and stronger than ever before. The morphine couldn't have worn off already, it was as if for a moment that her presence had somehow kept the pain at bay. I grit my teeth and try to ignore it.

I'm drifting in and out of sleep when the sound of the door opening disturbs me. A man wearing robes walks into the room with a crucifix around his neck and he speaks my name.

'Yes, I'm Ewan,' I reply as he moves closer to the bed.

I discover that what I thought were robes are actually just a billowing white shirt worn over his black trousers. But a large gold crucifix does indeed hang around his neck and he clutches a bible in one hand. The religious man has grey hair and must be around sixty years old. His face is kind of regal looking with a neatly trimmed ginger-grey moustache and beard. His deeply wrinkled brow gives the impression of wisdom and I suspect in different clothes he could pass as a medieval King. Meeting him like this seems strange but it was my idea after all.

'Hello Father,' I say, guessing at the correct address for him. 'Thank you for seeing me.'

He smiles warmly and nods approvingly. 'You're welcome my son,' he replies. 'I'm glad that you asked to see me.'

He stands before me as a beacon of comfort that seems to do more for me than the morphine injection. My pain seems to almost disappear completely although there is no newfound strength in my body.

'Are you seeking our Lord?' he asks me.

'Yes sort of,' I reply politely, not actually sure that's what I need. 'But can I ask you what you know of death?'

The man places his bible on the table next to the bed and pushes a chair close to my bedside. 'Are you a man of faith, my son?' he asks as he sits down.

'I'm not sure,' I reply honestly, 'I don't understand enough about... God.'

'It's never too late to find God,' he explains. 'God loves all of his children and has a place for us all. God is grace and forgiveness and light. I know that no one needs to die with any regrets or fear or guilt.'

'What do you think happens when we die?' I ask.

'Do not think too much about death,' he replies, placing his hands on one of mine. 'Freedom comes from trusting God and accepting that he has a plan for you. It's God's will that we live on this Earth and find his love again when our spirit passes from this body and into his realm.'

I manage to lift my head slightly and look into his eyes.

'What happens if death doesn't take you into his realm?' I ask.

'All who open themselves to God and ask for his love and forgiveness are welcome in Heaven,' he replies.

'But I've already died before,' I try to explain to him, 'and then I came back.'

'Then it wasn't your time my Son,' he says, apparently unsurprised at my statement. 'God only takes us when he's ready for us.'

For a moment I wonder if it's even possible for me to find any solace in the riddle of religion, but having faced death many times before I suspect it wouldn't have helped me greatly on those occasions. Perhaps finding any comfort through faith is unrealistic, although acceptance of death doesn't require any faith on my part because evidence has demonstrated that death doesn't mean the end for me.

'Surely God won't take me before he is ready, make a mistake and then send me back?' I ask.

For some reason I wish this man did have some answers but instead he just looks at me with a quizzical expression.

'God will summon you to Heaven when he is ready,' he replies, not really answering my question.

'But what if you don't deserve to go to Heaven?' I press him, 'do you get sent back to try again until you accomplish what you're supposed to do?'

'If that is God's will for you,' he replies, smiling.

'How do I know if it's God's will for me?' I ask.

'You must have faith my Son,' he replies. 'And then you will hear and feel God's touch and presence.'

'That's not really what I meant,' I reply, but the man ignores my statement, stands up and places his bible in my hands.

'Will you take this?' he asks, 'A gift for your time here. Let it comfort and guide you as you prepare for God. I hope it will help you find a little faith in your heart my Son.'

I don't quite know how to reply but the Minister accepts my silence as a yes and leaves the room with the bible still clutched in my hands. The thought occurs to me that I didn't even thank him for it which isn't a good start on a road of faith.

The day drags on without any structure. Helen goes home to eat and the nurse periodically administers more of the ineffective pain relief. On one occasion I'm in absolute agony and I squeeze her arm so hard when she injects me that it leaves fingerprints on her forearm.

It doesn't seem to bother her though and she turns on a radio for me to listen to before continuing with her rounds. I lose track of how many times I drift in and out of sleep and the radio is too quiet for me anyway. When I'm awake I feel either pain or nausea before drifting off for a few moments, then I wake up in agony again, and so the cycle goes on. I hold the bible to my chest at one point and make up a prayer, pleading for the pain to go away and minutes later the pain does indeed subside. I chalk it up to coincidence though as it doesn't work the next time the pain returns. Unlike my day in Paris with Tina there will be no excitement or pride in this death, and no dignity either.

The door to my room opens and an impossibly frail elderly man hobbles in, pushing a drip stand in front of him. The legs of his pyjamas flap loosely as if there is nothing inside them as he shuffles towards me. He has a gaunt and saggy wrinkled face but I dread how similar we must look. His frailty and the absence of flesh on his face make his bony nose seem enormous. His eyes are hollow, sunken into his skull and bloodshot but a hint of steel and fire still burns deep in his pupils. Although his arms are skeletal and he is the very image of death itself, this man clearly hasn't yet surrendered. He coughs and splutters his way over to my bed, a coarse, deep and guttural sound and points to the bible clutched to my chest. 'That won't do you any good,' he says with a cynical tone.

I had almost forgotten that the bible was still there but have neither the strength or will to move it. 'This?' I reply, nodding towards the book.

'All a load of old bollocks that,' he replies.

Part of me wants to defend the book although I have no idea why. He drags his drip stand closer with a scraping of metal wheels and peers down at me. 'What are you in for?' he asks drily.

'Cancer,' I reply.

'Well don't let those God fearing folk preach at you while you're at your most vulnerable,' he warns me, pointing a finger accusingly in my direction. 'They do their best recruiting here you know, but the applicants don't stay in the club too long.'

The man wheezes and coughs at his own joke but the sight of him doubling over laughing while struggling to breathe is infectious and I laugh too. The sensation of laughing hurts my stomach though, so it only lasts a few seconds but he continues until he looks like ready to collapse and die. I'm about to ask him if he is alright but he suddenly recovers and sits down in the chair next to the bed.

'How long have you been here?' I ask him.

'Me?' he asks, frowning. 'Damn site longer than you sonny boy,' he says. 'They can't seem to get rid of me. I think it even pisses the nurses off that I'm still taking up a spot. I've seen twenty or thirty like you come and go, but death must be too busy for me. I've seen more pain than a bloody dominatrix.'

Oddly this determined old ruin of a man has a quirky charm about him with his candour and blunt outlook that I find immensely likeable.

'So what have you got?' I ask, wincing at a sudden sharp pain in my gut.

'Me? Oh...heart, liver, bones, kidneys,' he replies. 'I'm as screwed as you can be.'

'I'm sorry,' I reply uncomfortably.

The man claps my shoulder with a bony, long fingered arthritic hand. 'Don't be sorry for me Sonny,' he says. 'I just wish it was over and done with. God, I wish it was over.'

His eyes have a faraway look for a moment and I see a flicker in his pupils suggesting a momentary lapse in his steely long suffering resolve.

'Kick Death in the bollocks for me, if you see him first,' the man says, his steel returning again. 'Right in the family jewels, alright?'

'I will, I promise,' I try and assure him.

The old man smiles, showing me a terrifying grin made up of about four broken yellow teeth like some ghoul from a pirate ghost ship. 'You tell him it's from Virgil,' he says. 'Tell him to come and fucking get me if he thinks he can.'

Hearing the name of my stalker comes of no great surprise. So Virgil is here as usual, and right on cue this time. But on this occasion I feel no anger towards him, just like I hadn't towards the Virgil in the hotel room who I couldn't save. How can I be angry with this man anyway, someone who is dying of Cancer? I'm baffled how the old man could have retained his sanity for such a long period of time while suffering his decline. I know that I'm facing the end but at least I've have been fortunate enough to miss what was presumably a long and painful deterioration in my condition.

One day in the Hospice has been too much for me but I can only presume that a person would gradually become used to the symptoms of a terminal illness. Perhaps they would even develop some kind of coping mechanism. Although I have no experience dealing with this terminal illness or developing such a coping mechanism, at least I have missed the slow harrowing decline. I think they call that taking the rough with the smooth.

A few hours after I make my promise to Virgil about Death my pain returns with a fearsome vengeance. My breathing is so shallow and weak that I feel frighteningly powerless and I immediately wish Helen was back. I'm sure that I can sense death stalking me like a vile predator but I also welcome it because it will bring an end to my suffering.

I realise that death will be especially cruel to me this time and I groan in agony as the nurse's latest injection has no effect. She leans over me and looks closely into my eyes. 'Don't worry Mr. Charles,' she says soothingly. 'We've sent for your wife.'

I don't know if Helen made it in time or if death beat her to me, but I suddenly wish that Jenny and Tina were both here too. My eyes close for the last time and the pain finally stops.

PART 2

DARK TIMES

10

Mercy

The singing is raucous and out of tune but it takes me a few seconds to realise that I'm the only one who isn't joining in. I quickly find my voice and sing along.

'*Happy Birthday dear Jenny... Happy Birthday to you.*' Everyone starts cheering and applauding but at least this time I'm involved from the outset. As the applause fades I recognise the 'Happy Steakhouse' restaurant as the one that's near our apartment. It's one of Jenny's favourite places to eat and we appear to have a long private table for around twenty people. Jenny loves steaks almost as much as I do although she eats hers rare which is something I couldn't do.

Helen is sat on my left, smiling and toasting the birthday girl but Jenny is sat at the opposite end of the table. I recognise her three best friends Kirsty, Annabelle and Shelley, but not the two young men sitting beside them. Most of the guests are familiar to me but I'm surprised to see Helen's brother Bill here and his two sons Dale and Albert. Helen only vaguely keeps in touch with her brother, exchanging birthday cards and the occasional phone call so it's a real surprise to see them. Bill is maybe fifteen years older than his sister Helen but his wife is unsurprisingly absent. If I remember correctly I think Helen told me they had separated. His son Albert has bought his wife with him though. I'm pretty sure that Dale was single when I last saw him and he still appears to be on his own. Jenny can't have seen her uncle and cousins for at least five years so I assume her eighteenth birthday must have inspired them to make the effort.

Our neighbour Ali is here with an attractive Asian girl and together they sip champagne while toasting Jenny. For a moment a flash of anger rises inside me as I see Ali, but he raises his glass to me and nods. I automatically raise my own glass back to him and the Asian girl smiles. My flash of anger subsides as quickly as it had arisen.

The majority of the other guests are probably Jenny's work colleagues and their partners. At least that's what I assume from their colourful urban clothes. She only works part time in what she says is the trendiest shop in Carnaby Street and these look like just the kind of young Londoners I would expect to find working there.

Our table has an elegant arrangement of flowers in the centre of it with the number eighteen formed from pink and white petals. I don't know what kind of flowers they are but they look and smell nice enough. There are also a dozen tacky foil birthday balloons with '18' printed on them, haplessly spread around our table while Jenny has a pile of open cards and ripped envelopes stacked up in front of her.

Our table takes up almost one entire side wall and the remainder of the restaurant looks fully booked too. The other diners who aren't in our party have stopped eating their meals to applaud Jenny. It gives me an overriding feeling of satisfaction quite unlike anything I have experienced before to see a roomful of strangers suddenly participate in our celebration. I feel warm inside to see my daughter so vibrant and surrounded by her friends on such a special day.

Although I find myself smiling, I also feel a growing sense of confusion at the party because I already have memories of Jenny's eighteenth birthday. We paid for her to go on a Mediterranean cruise and she took one of her best friends Annabelle with her. As far as I recall, on the day of her birthday we didn't arrange a big gathering like this, Helen and I took her out for a quiet family lunch in Knightsbridge. That evening Jenny had gone into Central London with her college friends. She didn't come home until 3:00 AM and I found it hard to sleep until she was back. I'm baffled as to whether today should supersede my previous memories or merge them all together into one event.

One of the young men sitting next to Jenny sets off a party popper and the bang disturbs my thoughts. I glance at Jenny who is laughing as the paper contents land in her hair and she starts to pick them out with Kirsty's help. Before they finish, the other man and two girls unload their poppers too and all six of them are laughing now as the streamers rain down on her, some even landing in her wine glass.

There is a window behind them and I notice that it's daytime but I realise that we have already eaten lunch because I can still taste the steak in my mouth. I feel a twang of disappointment that ironically I hadn't 'awakened' thirty minutes earlier and am already full.

The thought of awakening from death reminds me of Virgil, the old man in the hospital and his wheezing and coughing. And then there was his laughing too, his near toothless grin and the staring of those hollow but piercing eyes. I shudder involuntarily at the memory but I'm unsure whether it's his frightening appearance or my day of suffering that causes my discomfort. I decide it's probably both and try to forget about it because it's time that I focused on what's important now, on how I'm going to die today and who I can help before it happens.

Everyone is smiling and enjoying the last of their meal so there is nobody here in any danger. In fact there appears to be no immediate danger to me either but at least one of us must be in jeopardy – me. I drain the last mouthful of wine from my glass and stand up.

'I'm just nipping to the toilet,' I tell Helen.

'Alright,' she replies before turning back to the conversation with her brother.

As I leave the table I hear her mention something to Bill about catching up more often but it's drowned out by the noise of the restaurant. One of the waitresses smiles as I stand aside to let her pass me with a tray full of desserts bound for our table. I wonder if Helen and I are paying for the whole meal, and what the bill might be but however much it is it'll be worth it for Jenny's birthday. Not to mention the fact that the money won't even matter to me tomorrow.

Once inside the men's washroom, I splash some cold water on my face. The bright blue and orange tiles around the sink remind me of a beach, and as my reflection stares back at me from the mirror I run my damp fingers through my short dark hair. I breathe a sigh of relief that I'm clean shaven and there is no trace of the terrible illness that reduced me to a dishevelled wraith only moments ago.

'See what a steak can do for you?' I ask my reflection.

I hear a flush behind me and the sound of a cubicle lock being opened. A young man wearing an un-tucked bright yellow shirt appears from the toilet cubicle. He glances at me for a second and then immediately looks away. The man runs his fingers under a tap without even stopping walking in a meagre display of personal cleanliness and then leaves the washroom. I watch him depart while still drying his hands on the back of his jeans and I shake my head.

My reflection looks back at me as I smile to see if my teeth have any steak stuck between them. They don't but I take a handful of water from the tap and swish it round my mouth like mouthwash just in case. After spitting it out and drying my hands on the warm air dryer, I give my reflection a wink and return to the restaurant. I look good.

Helen and everyone else are already tucking into their desserts, making the table strangely silent. A thick wedge of chocolate gateau is parked in my place setting and I sit down and begin eating it. Helen has the same but is already halfway through hers.

'This is lovely,' she mumbles with her mouth full.

She isn't wrong and I almost manage to catch up before she finishes her gateau. Helen dabs away at the sides of her mouth, removing the chocolate from her pink lips and puffing out her cheeks. Most of the other guests have finished their desserts too and begin chatting loudly again.

As soon as everyone has finished, I tap my empty wine glass with a spoon and silence gradually falls over the table. The effect is greater than I anticipate though and the waitresses around the restaurant freeze in their tracks as silence falls over all the other tables in the room too. When I stand up Jenny puts her head in her hands in what I presume is mock horror.

'Sorry for interrupting everyone,' I begin, directing my words mainly to the diners around the room who aren't even in our party. 'I'll be very brief I promise.'

Helen tugs gently at my arm to encourage me to sit down. 'Oh God Dad, no speech please!' says Jenny from behind her hands, 'how embarrassing.'

But I'm quite sober and I realise that I've never had the chance to do this properly. Now that I have a second chance, I won't waste the opportunity to say something special about someone I love.

'I just wanted to thank you all for coming,' I say, gesturing to the people at our table, 'and for making our daughter Jenny's eighteenth birthday so special. It only seems like yesterday that she was starting to walk.'

The whole room breaks into applause and a few people cheer. Jenny smiles but stares down at the table and shakes her head as her friend Shelley whispers something to her.

Ali looks over at me. 'Go on Ewan,' he says encouragingly.

'I just want to take this opportunity to congratulate Jenny for being such a wonderful daughter,' I continue, 'a beautiful person and a credit to Helen and me.'

Helen stops tugging at my arm and is smiling now.

'A credit to her exceptional parents of course,' I joke and gratefully receive a ripple of laughter, along with a shout of 'Yeah right!' from one of Jenny's work friends.

'I'm watching you,' I say, pointing at him with the pretence of threat. 'But most importantly to say how proud Helen and I are of you.'

Helen squeezes my hand and nods in agreement as Jenny smiles at us from the other end of the table.

'Now if you have anything left in your glass then I want you to join me in a toast to Jenny,' I ask everyone. 'And if you haven't got a drink, then steal one from the person next to you.'

I wait a moment for everyone to raise their glasses. 'To Jenny!' I say.

Everyone repeats her name including the guests at the other tables and even the waitresses pretend to toast her with their invisible glasses.

'I'm grateful for the opportunity to do that,' I say closing my speech. 'We love you sweetheart.'

I retake my seat to the sound of 'Ahhhh' from the room and a couple of people from other tables come over and clap me on the shoulder and congratulate me. The room quickly erupts back into noise, driving away the temporary silence as if it had never happened.

Two waitresses begin to clear away the dessert dishes as another distributes pre-cut slices of birthday cake to everyone.

'That was sweet,' Helen whispers in my ear but still loud enough for her brother Bill to overhear.

'Yeah, well done Ewan,' he says. 'I never spoke at my two's eighteenth, but good on you. Nice words.'

'Thanks Helen,' I reply and nod politely in Bill's direction.

Helen kisses my cheek. She then starts talking to Ali's girlfriend who is sat opposite her and asking what she does for a living. I don't pay much attention to their conversation once I hear something about tax accountancy and soon I'm lost in my own thoughts, wondering how my day might end. But I soon find myself going over the speech again in my head, analysing it, deciding what worked and which parts I didn't like. But I realise that the audience's positive reaction should be the ultimate assessment of how it went down, even if they were a little biased due to the occasion. Being self-critical was just human nature for me, but on this occasion I felt I performed well.

'Dad?' says Jenny, appearing suddenly beside me and interrupting my thoughts.

'Yes Jen?' I reply.

She crouches down and hugs me tightly. 'Thank you for lunch and for what you said,' she says. 'It sounds like you meant it, and it meant a lot to me.'

'Of course I meant it sweetheart,' I say a little guiltily. 'Perhaps I should have said something like that before.'

Jenny smiles and squeezes my arm affectionately. 'Don't get all sentimental,' she says. 'This is a party, remember? I know what you and Mum think of me so you don't need to say it.'

She was wrong, it did need to be said but I decide not to risk upsetting her by reiterating how important it was to me. I should have said more the first time around but death has made me realise how much time I have wasted and what opportunities I've missed. She was right though – this was supposed to be a celebration and not a time to dwell on regrets so I fake a smile instead.

'Are you all off into the West End tonight?' I ask.

'Of course!' she says brightly. 'Shelley has got us tickets to a club opening. Her brother is part owner so we've got VIP tickets.'

'That's great,' I reply.

Jenny's friend Kirsty appears behind her and pulls her away from me. 'Come on you,' she says in a posh accent. 'Dean is at the bar getting more drinks.'

Jenny kisses my cheek and I watch the two girls enthusiastically join their friends at the restaurant bar. Her departure from the table makes me realise that other than paying, most of my role in this celebration is complete. As much as my time here feels precious, I feel an overwhelming sense of urge to find out if Virgil is a real person at the hospice. Jenny is with her friends, and Helen is busy catching up with her long lost brother so I feel like a bit of a spare part anyway.

'Helen?' I say, tugging at her arm to draw her attention away from Bill. I hadn't even noticed her finish talking to Ali's girlfriend about corporation tax.

'Yes, what's up?' she asks.

'I need to disappear for an hour,' I tell her.

Helen frowns. 'You can't, we're all going to walk to Hyde Park,' she reminds me.

'There's something I need to do,' I tell her. 'Pay on the credit card and I'll meet up with you later alright?'

'It's Jenny's eighteenth!' says Helen with more than a vague hint of annoyance in her voice.

'Oh, she's alright,' I tell her, gesturing towards Jenny at the bar. Helen glances towards the bar but scowls at me.

'Look, the truth is my heads killing me,' I lie, but know it's justified. 'I just need to take some pills and lay down for an hour.'

'Fine,' snaps Helen. 'I'll just stay here and entertain everyone while you're gone.'

'Don't be like that,' I urge her, but she has already turned her back on me and resumed her conversation with Bill.

'Just go if you need to,' she mutters without turning around. 'It's fine.'

I consider saying farewell to Jenny but she is surrounded by her friends at the bar, along with a handful of people from other tables offering their congratulations. So without another word I slip out of the restaurant and into the quiet London street.

The taxi to St. Thomas Hospice is slow and expensive but money doesn't matter to me. It's the time loss that annoys me because I don't arrive until official visiting time has almost finished. The woman at the reception desk is polite but insistent that visitors have to leave by four o'clock. It's already 15:55 and she informs me that it's too late for her to admit anyone.

The receptionist looks fairly mature and wears a lot of thick gold costume jewellery including a massive brooch in the shape of a scorpion, the sight of which makes me shudder. Huge tacky plastic earrings hang from her ear lobes and she has lots of rings on her fingers too. Her facial expression is intensely blunt and she is no doubt a stickler for the rules.

'I just want to put my head in for five minutes,' I explain to her. 'I've come half way across London and I got stuck in traffic. Please?'

She sighs and looks at her watch again. 'What's the patient's name,' she asks.

'It's Virgil,' I reply.

She looks up from her computer screen. 'Surname?' she asks.

'I can't remember,' I reply. 'He has cancer of... well he has cancer of quite a few things. He's been here a long time.'

The woman looks a tiny bit more sympathetic now. 'Are you a relative?' she asks.

'Not exactly,' I tell her. 'But we go way back and I only found out he was in here yesterday.'

'But you don't have his surname?' she reminds me.

I look up at the wall clock. 'Look please, its two minutes to four and I just want to pop in and wish him the best. I'll be in and out in five minutes, I promise.'

The receptionist takes off her glasses, then leans back from her keyboard and studies me for a moment. She starts to speak but then hesitates.

'Please?' I urge her. 'I haven't seen him for years. I can't remember his surname and have only just found out about his illness. It's important because he doesn't have long left, plus I know exactly which room he's in.'

The receptionist sighs and begrudgingly nods her head.

'Alright go on,' she says, conceding defeat, 'just this once. But you had better be back here by quarter past or I'll send security in to find you.'

After making me sign my name in the visitor's log, she puts the 'in' time down as 15:45, to cover herself no doubt.

Before she can change her mind I hurry through the door leading into the residential area and begin to explore the surprisingly complex maze of corridors. Finding the right ward isn't as easy as I expected, having never seen the outside of my room or even got out of bed during my one day here. I remember Helen telling me yesterday that I was in the Joanne Simons ward, whoever she is. After rushing around aimlessly for far too long, I turn a corner and stumble upon a sign for 'JS ward' and follow it. The signs direct me up a flight of stairs and down a brightly painted yellow corridor. The door at the end is marked with 'Joanne Simons Ward.' I hesitate for a moment before pushing the door open and entering the ward.

The open plan reception area has a few artificial plants and a couple of drab sofas clustered around a coffee table. At the main nursing station two nurses are standing behind a desk and looking though files while deeply engaged in conversation. The wall clock behind them tells me that it's almost ten past four already so I decide not to rouse their attention. Instead I stride down one of the wide corridors where I anticipate the private rooms will be. The individual bedrooms seem to be situated off this central corridor.

Peering through the glass panel of a door that I think was my room, I quickly realise that the curtains are different and the bed is vacant and unmade. All of the similar looking rooms in the ward are occupied by somebody dying. Finally after checking four more bedrooms I see him, the unmistakable sight of the aging man lying in a bed just as I was. He has a drip in each arm and an oxygen mask over his face but at least he is alone. I take a deep breath, certain of what I must do and enter the room.

I lean over the bed and stare down at the pitiful wretch. The thought suddenly crosses my mind that this man might not even be Virgil after all. If he keeps appearing in different guises then maybe this old man is no longer him. The thought also occurs to me that this is the first time I have consciously sought to find him. But who is he? Why is he always here, and where was he hiding when I was in Greece? He certainly looks to be the identical man I saw yesterday. Tentatively I shake the man's bony shoulder to wake him up.

'Virgil?' I call out his name softly.

He appears to be sound asleep and doesn't respond, but I realise that my extended visiting time is rapidly running out.

I shake him again, as hard as I dare with his fragile looking frame and speak louder.

'Virgil, wake up!' I say close to his ear.

This time he does stir, but immediately begins coughing and spluttering as his eyes flicker open. I recoil slightly in surprise and suddenly he sits bolt upright in the bed, deceptively fast given his condition. As his blankets slip down I notice he has no pyjama top on. His whole torso looks blue as if it is bruised and his chest is sunken in.

He is impossibly frail, almost like a holocaust survivor, but he still has thin patches of silver hair on his chest. The man pulls off his oxygen mask and glares angrily at me. I don't think he is actually the same person after all.

'What do you want? Who are you?' he demands.

'It's me Ewan, don't you remember?' I ask. 'You're Virgil aren't you?'

'Ewan bloody who?' he demands, scrutinising me with the same sunken but steely eyes that I remember from yesterday.

For some reason I'm reluctant to give him my full name and I just stare blankly at his weak body. His failure to immediately recognise me makes me step back from the bed and closer to the door.

'You wait there!' he snaps. 'I do remember you. You're the bugger with stomach cancer and the pretty wife. I saw her yesterday checking up on you.'

I immediately step forwards and he pulls his blankets defensively over his body with his bony hands. 'You remember me?' I ask. 'Virgil, do you remember me?'

He frowns at me although it's barely noticeable through the permanent deep grooves in his forehead. 'Of course I do,' he snaps impatiently. 'But what the hell happened to you? You're not the same man.'

I look down at myself, fit, strong and healthy, now a visitor here instead of a patient. 'It's a bit difficult to explain,' I tell him.

'Fuck me!' Virgil swears, slowly and precisely forming the words. 'You still got that Bible?'

This man genuinely remembers me from yesterday. For a moment, I am too stunned to speak as I realise that he is the first sign of continuity between one death and another.

'No I haven't got it,' I tell him. 'But do you know what this means?'

I'm not even sure myself though. Virgil coughs again and draws a huge gulp of oxygen from his mask. 'Yeah, it means that the power of prayer isn't all a load of old bollocks,' he says sarcastically. 'How did you get better?'

'I didn't get better Virgil,' I correct him. 'I died. But now I'm back.'

'Impossible,' he spits out the word.

'No it's not impossible,' I tell him. 'I've died a lot of times, but every time I come back again.'

The clock in Virgil's room reads 16:20 and I hope the receptionist doesn't make good on her threat to have me thrown out. I need to know what this means and why he can still remember me after I have died. Virgil lays back down, rolls onto his side and lets out a mournful howl of pain like the sound of a dying animal. The sound chills every nerve in my body and I plead in my mind for him to stop.

Virgil seems unable to speak and it takes a couple of minutes before his pain subsides, but the time reinforces in my mind what I must do. I crouch down beside the bed and place my hand on his forehead. His eyes are clenched shut and his head is burning hot and feverish. Sweat runs down his temple and onto his face.

'I think I can help you Virgil,' I tell him. 'I understand your suffering because I've experienced it first-hand.'

'Leave me alone,' he groans, 'get me the bloody nurse.'

I shake his shoulder and his eyes flicker open. 'Virgil listen, I think I can help you. That's why I'm here, to help people. It's my path.'

Virgil snarls at me like an animal, a bestial and fierce sound. 'All I want is to fucking die,' he growls.

'That's what I meant,' I explain, a slight quiver in my voice at what I know I'm suggesting.

Virgil opens his eyes wider and the intensity in his eyes is as fierce as it was yesterday. 'You can end it?' he asks, his hands suddenly gripping mine, 'End this shit?'

'Yes,' I say as a tear slides down my face which I quickly wipe away with my free hand. 'If that's what you want. God can't give you mercy, but I can.'

Virgil squeezes my hands with a grip harder than the firmest handshake. 'I want you to end it,' he groans. 'Now, please?'

I stand back from the bed and survey the poor suffering old man and wonder how many weeks or months he has been here. How much pain and suffering has he experienced? It's certainly far more than all of my suffering since falling in Pripyat. I know I will die today and that knowledge gives me freedom of action, freedom to grant mercy and help the needy. This particular Virgil may be my only link to any continuity but he needs to die.

Half in a daze, I carefully remove one of his pillows from behind his head and lower it towards his pained face. Turning my face away I place my hands in the middle of the pillow and lean my weight onto it. My legs are shaking and I close my eyes but I continue to push. His hands lock around my wrists but he isn't fighting me. Virgil is not fighting for his life – he is embracing mercy and death. My eyes start to water as I try to extinguish his life but suddenly I'm interrupted as the door to the room bursts open. I spin around, instinctively removing the pillow to see a furious, red faced nurse bellowing at me.

'What the hell are you doing?' she yells at me, causing me drop the pillow.

Virgil is writhing on the bed behind me and I hear him coughing weakly. Panicking, I run towards the nurse, forcing her back against the wall and she screams, but I'm already sprinting out of the door and heading towards the stairs. My eyes are streaming from the fear and shock of my actions, but also in frustration that I failed to complete the task. I was unable to use my situation to benefit others. Virgil wanted to die.

I run down the corridors and through reception like a tornado, tears blurring my eyes. Behind me I hear the receptionist shout 'Security!' but I don't stop. I dart straight out of the Hospice and into the busy London street, fleeing across the road with tears streaming down my face.

My ears don't register the sound of any vehicle horns but I feel a crunching pain in my legs as I'm hurled through the air like a broken doll. I scream and spread my hands out to protect myself, unsure of where I will land. Somewhere I hear the sound of a police siren wailing. There is a second impact as my head hits what must be tarmac and I yell out in painful terror. For a split second my chest feels like a sledgehammer has been driven through it and out of the other side.

11
The Birthday Girl

The toilet floor is freezing cold and uncomfortable. I lift my head and see daylight coming through a frosted window partly covered by a floral blind. My forehead is pounding and throbbing and lifting it causes me to wince. The toilet is open and there is vomit in the bowl. I pull myself up off the floor and use the toilet, pressing the flush afterwards. My head is spinning and my mouth is as dry as sandpaper. Zipping up my jeans, I notice they are filthy and I still have my coat on. I must have slept on this bathroom floor.

My head throbs even worse as I dizzily stagger over to the sink and switch on the tap. I place my mouth below the water stream and begin greedily swallowing the tepid fluid. Quickly it begins to warm up and I suddenly realise that it's the hot tap. Water splashes onto my jacket and jeans as I switch on the cold tap instead and drink as much as I can. To try and ease my pain, I splash cold water over my head. The water streams down my face and neck, and onto the floor, but at least the cold relieves a little of the throbbing. I know that I'm fiercely hung-over and dehydrated but this is far worse than any hangover I've experienced before.

My stomach begins to churn and involuntarily I kneel down and open the toilet lid. Without much warning I'm forced to empty the contents of my stomach again. Nothing but water comes out and the retching at the end makes my head immediately throb with a newfound level of pain. I lie back down on the floor and place my hands over my eyes to shield them from the light coming through the window.

A sudden banging on the bathroom door wakes me up. The noise is constant and persistent.

'Ewan?' someone yells. 'Ewan, open up.'

I raise my hand to my eyes again to shield them from the light. 'Hold on,' I groan, 'I just need a minute.'

I stagger to my feet and flush the toilet but notice the mirror above the sink for the first time. My reflection is unrecognisable. My hair is a long matted, unwashed mop and my eyes look bloodshot and puffy. It looks like I haven't shaved for weeks and my teeth are yellow and dirty. I splash some cold water on my face and scruffy beard but it makes little difference to my appearance, although the pain in my head at least seems bearable now. It seems odd feeling hair on my face and I dread tackling it without some proper beard clippers.

The towel rail is empty and I notice a towel on the floor, near to where I slept so I pick it up and shake it before hanging it back up. I fumble in my pocket for something and I pull out a small bottle of Gordon's Gin. I hate neat liquor but find myself unscrewing the cap and raising the half empty bottle to my lips. The banging on the door suddenly resumes, causing me to hesitate. What the hell am I doing? I pour the repulsive gin down the sink and drink some more water from the cold tap, filling my stomach with as much as possible. At least this time I don't throw up.

Washing my face with cold water again is a relief and I soak my hair more thoroughly this time, sweeping it back and flattening it, feeling the cooling effect on my head. My appearance is still terrible and the terracotta bathroom floor tiles have pools of tap water on them, but at least I can face opening the door now.

I'm surprised when I unlock the door to find the slim figure of Tina standing outside, hand raised and about to bang on the door again. She is wearing a thin white dressing gown and pink slippers.

'Jesus Christ Ewan,' she says. 'You've got to stop doing this.'

Unsure of how to answer her and with my memory all jumbled up, I scratch my head where the water has made my scalp itch.

'You look fucking terrible,' she says.

It's an easy one to answer this time. 'Thanks,' I reply.

'You can't keep doing this to yourself, you need some help,' she says.

I stare at the floor and breathe deeply to try and control my nausea, not wanting to lose all the precious water from my stomach again. What did she mean by '*keep doing this to yourself?*'

'Listen, do you think you can stomach a coffee?' she asks.

'Yes please,' I reply, unsure if I can but eager to be compliant considering the state of what I presume is her bathroom. I step forward and close the door behind me before she can notice all the water on the floor. Tina must realise I'm swaying on my feet because she takes my arm and leads me to the living room and deposits me on a large chocolate brown sofa.

The room is dark, although I know from the bathroom window that it must be morning but then I notice thick heavy curtains covering what looks like double patio doors. I realise that the only window is also blocked by curtains and I'm grateful that only a thin swathe of light escapes from the sides of them. Raising my hands to my head, I try massaging my temples which appears to help with the pain, although my thirst is already returning.

'Don't throw up in my lounge,' Tina warns me, 'Stay there, I'll go and put the coffee on.'

As she leaves the room I search my memory for answers to my situation. Yesterday seems to be a complete blank but I try to piece something together. I'm married and I have a daughter, Helen and Jenny, but I work with Tina and she is good to me. No, that's not right – I only *used* to work with her but that was in the past. So why am I drunk and at her house and where is my wife Helen? This isn't my apartment and I'm sure that Tina lives in North West London somewhere. So what am I doing here? Have Helen and I had a fight or has she thrown me out? She can't have done, I don't remember anything like that and it seems implausible.

Tina re-enters the room with a mug of coffee that is barely half full. 'Try and drink this while I get dressed' she says.

'Okay,' I reply, taking the mug from her.

She hesitates before leaving. 'Are you alright Ewan?' she asks, a note of genuine concern in her voice.

I stare into the black coffee and watch the steam rising in pretty spirals from the surface. 'I don't know,' I reply.

She places a hand on my shoulder. 'Look I'm sorry about earlier,' she says. 'I didn't mean to have a go, but I'm worried about you. Every time you go off the deep end – you turn up here in the middle of the night. And you look worse every time you come. You have to get some help.'

She is giving me too much information for my mind to absorb so I close my eyes, try not to listen and blow on the coffee to cool it down.

'Let me get dressed,' she says. 'And then we can talk.'

Tina leaves the darkened lounge and I sip my coffee. The aroma is good and the warm taste begins to breathe some life into my aching body and limbs. Unlike the water, the coffee begins to replace the stale taste in my mouth and its warmth soothes my aching throat. The coffee perks me up but makes my stomach churn uneasily. I manage to keep it down by taking small intermittent sips and not pushing my stomach too hard. My back and neck seem to revel in reminding me of how uncomfortable a night on a bathroom floor must have been.

Tina pokes her head around the living room door in a nightdress but with no dressing gown now. 'Do you want some toast?' she asks.

'No thanks,' I mumble and she disappears again.

The last thing I can stomach right now is any food or even the sight of her shapely figure in a shiny sensual nightdress. The word toast stirs something in my memory though, I remember proposing a toast to Jenny on her eighteenth birthday. That was yesterday though, so how much must I have drunk to leave her party and end up at Tina's in the middle of the night? But more importantly why did I come here? What the hell will Helen think about me not coming home? I've never even been to Tina's house before. More blanks are slowly being filled in as I sip the coffee and try to shake off my headache.

When did I leave the restaurant? That's right, I left on my own, but Helen wasn't pleased about it. Then I took a taxi across London. Instantly all of the pieces seem to fall into place and my memories flood back into my mind. The sensation of sudden recall makes my head hurt as I remember some of my deaths, staring with Chernobyl and Pripyat. There was a scorpion bite too, Helen stabbing me and the burglary when Jenny's photograph was taken before I was hit by a car. It's as if the door that was blocking my memories has literally been blown open, but one memory surfaces above all others -smothering Virgil with a pillow in the hospice.

I begin to feel queasy, retching and quickly holding my mug under my mouth in sudden panic. I'm just able to grit my teeth and thankfully avoid emptying my stomach again. Christ I actually smothered an old man even if that was what he wanted. Is that the reason I was drinking – to forget? I remember him coughing as I fled the room after being disturbed by a nurse. But the mercy killing was the right thing to do, I was sure of it at the time. So why did I fail? Maybe Virgil wasn't supposed to die at my hands and it wasn't my purpose to take his life. Am I a fugitive now or has being run over erased all responsibility for my actions? Virgil was present on two consecutive days and it was the same Virgil too. So just maybe my actions stand too. Even if he has survived, it would still be attempted murder wouldn't it?

Tina enters the lounge again, fully dressed now in black jeans and a red checked shirt. She walks towards me while brushing her hair but it seems odd to see her wearing glasses. She wears contact lenses all the time and I didn't even realise she sometimes wore glasses. They make her look different, possibly even smarter than usual.

'You look a bit better,' she says, inspecting my mug to see if I drank the coffee.

'So do you Tina,' I reply with a wink, glancing at her tight jeans.

'At least you still have your sense of humour,' she replies with a faint smile. 'So what happened?'

It wouldn't be right to burden her with all my problems, particularly as she had already been kind enough to give me shelter in my hour of need. 'I'd rather not talk about it,' I tell her.

'Well you have to talk to someone,' she says, suddenly producing the empty bottle that I left in the bathroom and holding it up like a piece of evidence. 'Gin Ewan?'

'Most of that went in the sink,' I reply defensively.

'But who carries this shit around?' she demands, sounding unconvinced. 'You're an alcoholic Ewan.'

I shake my head at her misunderstanding. 'I just had a bad night and drank too much,' I tell her. 'You've got it all wrong.'

'No! Someone has to tell you, and you have to accept it,' she says adamantly. 'You're drinking all the time Ewan, you've even lost your job.'

'I've lost a lot of jobs,' I reply shrugging my shoulders, 'it's no big deal.'

I have far more important tasks to perform than working now, and anyway Tina will never understand my situation or the insignificance of employment.

'Listen Ewan, I'm only saying this because I care,' she tells me. 'But every time things get too much and you drink yourself half to death, you come right back here and I have to pick up the pieces. So don't forget that it's *you* that keeps coming to me.'

Her words don't make any sense because this is the only time that I've ever been here. She's trying to confuse me and complicate things, but why? All I need to know is if the old man in the hospice had benefited from my actions. No one will understand what I did, because they haven't experienced the suffering involved with a terminal illness like cancer right through to its deadly conclusion and still been in a position to reflect upon it. Virgil's suffering had to end, he needed an absolution and I know it was right for me to assist him. If I have truly succeeded in helping him die then that affirms what my purpose in life is, even if it most rational people would never understand the justification for my actions.

'You wouldn't understand,' I tell Tina.

'Of course not,' she says impatiently, 'because you're the only one that's ever had problems right?'

'It's... complicated,' I reply.

'Well bloody talk about it then,' she says with anger rising in her voice.

'Look I'm sorry Tina, I can't' I tell her regretfully. 'I just need some painkillers and a taxi alright?'

'Fine,' she snaps angrily and snatches up her mobile phone from the coffee table. 'I'll call you one, but if you ever come to my house in that state again and ask for my help, you can forget it. Until you go and get some fucking help.'

Tina storms out of the room with her phone pressed to her ear, but I won't need to come back again. And at least the next time I see her she won't even remember this conversation, hell it might not even have happened for all I know.

A moment later she returns and places three tablets and a glass of water on the table in front of me. The anger on her face seems to have faded just a little. 'Ten minutes for the taxi,' she says a little bluntly.

I swallow the three painkillers and drain half of the water.

'Thank you,' I say, a little sheepishly.

Tina leaves the room and I use the time to rest my head and drink the rest of the water until the doorbell rings.

I climb out of my chair and head straight for the front door, eager to get away from here. As I exit the front door of Tina's house, she suddenly places a hand on my arm to stop me. Her tone has softened little now. 'Have a shave Ewan,' she says. 'And please take more care of yourself, alright?'

'Don't worry about me,' I tell her. 'I'll be just fine, I promise.'

Hangover or not, death has given me a purpose and I finally understand it now. I walk away from the house, chuckling despite my headache and climb into the back of the London taxi. 'St. Thomas Hospice please,' I instruct the driver.

I'm relieved to find that the hospice reception looks quiet from across the street, with no sign of police cars. My head is a lot clearer now and the pain has subsided a little. I pick up a cheap pair of sunglasses and a bottle of water from a street vendor near the car park. The glasses are a welcome relief for my eyes and I can see the spot where I think I was run down yesterday. There is no sign of any accident or any blood on the road, almost like it never happened but I cross the road cautiously, watching for cars as I head towards the Hospice building.

The same woman as yesterday is on reception and she doesn't appear to recognise me, although I can't be sure that it's not down to my dishevelled appearance. A quick wash, a coffee, three painkillers and a bottle of water have done little to improve the state of my creased clothes. At least on this occasion visiting time hasn't finished.

'I'm here to visit Virgil,' I tell the receptionist.

She looks up from her computer screen and is unable to suppress a scowl at my unkempt, scruffy appearance.

'Surname?' she asks.

This is déjà vu all over again. 'I'm not sure,' I reply. 'He is in Joanne Simons Ward.'

The receptionist scans her computer screen for a moment and removes her glasses. 'Sorry, we don't have a patient called Virgil,' she replies, a little too pleased about it for my liking.

'That's impossible,' I reply, 'he must be here. Can you check again please?'

The woman complies but I sense that she is just going through the motions and not actually checking anything. 'There is no one here by that name,' she says. 'Do you know when he was first admitted?'

'At least a month ago,' I reply. 'Are you sure he hasn't recently passed away maybe?'

She shakes her head. 'No this shows everyone from the last three years,' she replies. 'That includes patients who've died. There is no one listed called Virgil, but if you had a surname I could try searching that.'

'No, it doesn't matter,' I reply, my voice trailing off.

Virgil isn't here, I feel it. The only continuity in my life has gone. What are the implications of that though? Did I succeed in giving him the merciful death he wanted? Has his existence been erased now or is there something else going on? There is nothing for me to do here.

I suddenly realise that I've walked out of the building, lost in my thoughts and I'm about to step into the road. Fortunately I stop myself this time and avoid a second death in the same location. It takes maybe twenty minutes to flag down a taxi and I'm sure my appearance has something to do with it. My bottle of water just lasts until I climb aboard the taxi. It's time to go home to Helen and Jenny although explaining my absence last night and the condition I'm in to my wife won't be straightforward. 'Hi Helen, I murdered, no, I mean mercy killed an old man who has been stalking me. Then I was killed in a hit and run accident and drank myself nearly to death. Don't worry though because I slept it off in Tina's bathroom. So what's for dinner?'

The whole thing sounds ludicrous but this is what my life has become. I wonder how I'll die today, but more importantly what good deed can I perform before the day ends?

The taxi ride through London seems to take forever and it makes me regret that I didn't buy a second bottle of water. It's mid-afternoon before I finally open my front door and enter the apartment. Inside, I find that the lights are off and the place is in darkness, but the air also smells kind of stale. The blinds are still shut so I turn on the lights and massage my forehead as I walk to the kitchen for a desperately needed glass of water.

'Helen? Jenny?' I call out as I flick on the kitchen light switch.

The kitchen is a total shambles and the units are littered with empty beer cans, wine bottles and assorted liquor bottles. There are pizza boxes strewn all over the floor and the surfaces look dusty. I also realise that the cold tap is still running into the sink so I turn it off, wondering if Jenny has had some kind of coming of age house party.

'Jenny?' I shout out, but there is no reply.

There are no clean glasses in the cupboard, just lots of used ones near the sink so I rinse one out and take a large gulp of tap water.

Entering the lounge reveals much the same picture of disorder as the kitchen. I open the blinds to let in some light which shows the true extent of the squalor in the room. The duvet from our bed is draped across the sofa, the television is still on and empty gin bottles litter the coffee table. There are even a couple lying on their sides on the carpet. Staring in disbelief, I notice that the bin is overflowing with empty crisp packets and the room hasn't been cleaned for what looks like weeks. I walk to Jenny's room and knock on the door. 'Jenny?' I call out through the door, but there is no response.

I open the door and peer inside the bedroom. Her bed is neatly made and the room is as tidy as usual, but there is no sign of her. Mine and Helen's bedroom also proves to be empty and the bed looks bare without a duvet. Maybe Helen is at work. I pull out my phone and ring her mobile but it comes up unobtainable. I try Jenny's number too but the call is rejected after a couple of rings. What the hell is going on?

My nerves are frayed and I feel the urge for a drink so I return to the lounge and pick up one of the bottles of gin from the floor which still has a few drops in the bottom. I pour the warm, sour, stale liquid into my mouth and swallow. As I do so I'm startled as it dawns on me that the bottles are not from some eighteenth birthday party Jenny may have had, they are mine. I throw the distasteful bottle across the room and it bounces into the kitchen.

Tina's words echo in my head as I realise she was right, I am an alcoholic. The realisation is such a shock that I almost throw up. Why am I? What the hell happened? I look through my phone and find Tina's mobile number stored in it. I start to ring her but I'm distracted by a pile of cards laying flat on the sideboard, Jenny's birthday cards I guess. One of them has fallen onto the floor next to an empty gin bottle so I pick it up. The front shows a pastel painting of a bunch of flowers and the slogan '*Deepest Sympathies*.' I flick open the card and read the message.

'*So sorry for your loss. My darling sister Helen will forever be in our thoughts, as will you and Jenny. Keep strong. Bill and Susan.*'

The words make no sense so I grab the pile of cards and read a second one. It's from Ali, my next door neighbour and it reads: '*Sorry about Helen. If there is ever anything I can do, don't hesitate to knock or ring. Ali + Kim.*'

The cards fall from my hands like giant confetti to scatter amongst the empty bottles on the dirty carpet. Helen can't be dead, that's impossible – she isn't any older than me. Please not my darling wife. But the cards silently confirm it and I know she would never allow the apartment to get into this state, even if it meant nagging me to clean it.

An intense empty pain grips my heart, worse than anything the dead loop has thrown at me so far. I kneel down on the floor, curl up into a ball and sob her name despairingly into the carpet.

Some time later, I don't know how long, the beeping and vibration of my mobile phone in my pocket interrupts my grief. I squint through sore eyes and rub them before reading the text message. It's brief, blunt and very worrying.

'*I'm on the roof, don't ring me again. J.*'

But Jenny never goes up there. A second later, I'm stumbling over empty bottles and bursting out of the apartment, not even bothering to close the front door behind me. I don't wait for the lift either, sensing that I just have to keep moving. Soon I'm charging up the stairway towards the roof taking two steps at a time, but the climb makes my head begin to throb in protest. A sense of panic tells me that I have to reach Jenny urgently.

My eyes are still stinging from the shocking news that Helen is dead as I charge onto the apartment roof. There is a small roof garden and a few garden chairs up here but this afternoon they no longer seem inviting. Immediately I see Jenny on the far side of the roof, standing on the wrong side of the surrounding wall and holding onto the metal railings. Can she really be doing what I think she is? The situation of being on a rooftop reminds me of Pripyat and I desperately call out her name as I run towards her. 'Jenny!' I shout, 'get down from there!'

She turns at the sound of my voice but doesn't reply or attempt to climb back over the railings to safety. The wind is blowing around her pyjamas and she looks so vulnerable and lost. My heart sinks with the frozen chill of terror to see her bare-footed in her pyjamas and so close to falling. Why isn't she wearing shoes?

'Jesus, sweetheart get down off there,' I shout, extending a hand out towards her. 'Grab my hand.'

'No!' she yells as the wind whips at her long black hair, 'Stay back! I don't want you up here.'

'Jenny please,' I plead with her, 'just tell me what the hell's going on.'

Jenny scowls down at me angrily and I notice her mobile phone clutched in one of her hands. 'Look at the state of you,' she snaps. 'As if you don't know what's going on.'

In this moment Jenny is all that matters, my daughter, my little birthday girl. I feel panic and nausea spreading through me. Please don't let her fall.

'Just please come down,' I say, desperately trying to persuade her with my hand outstretched. 'I've lost Mum too. I can't lose you as well.'

'You took her,' she yells accusingly, pointing a finger at me. 'You took her from us.'

Jenny sways dangerously with only one hand on the railing and the wind seems to make a renewed effort to dislodge her. My heart is in my mouth and I panic as I try to grab her hand but can't quite reach. She screams and suddenly grabs on with both hands, accidentally dropping her mobile phone off the roof in the process.

'Hold on sweetheart, please hold on,' I yell. 'I'm coming up.'

'Don't!' she shrieks, 'just go away!'

I ignore her protests as my instincts to protect her take over my actions. I climb over the railings and the sudden power of the wind surprises me. Although shocked at its strength, it instantly clears my head of any remaining effects of my hangover. What did she mean by '*I took her from us?*' My hands feel cold and I glance with worry at Jenny's, her knuckles bone white as she grips the railings. She must be freezing up here in only her pyjamas and I wonder how long she's been here. I edge towards her and reach out with my hand. 'Stay calm, I'm coming to you,' I tell her.

'Stay the fuck away from me!' she yells but her voice is almost drowned out by the wind.

I've never heard her use that obscenity before but it's impossible to feel any more shocked than I do right now.

'I love you Jenny,' I tell her, desperately trying a softer approach in an attempt to calm her down. 'Whatever's happened, I still love you.'

She leans over the edge of the railing and looks down. Her beautiful long hair is whipping all over the place like a flag and her face looks as white as paper.

'Don't do it,' I scream, but I'm frozen to the spot, too petrified to approach her in case she panics.

'You touch me and I'll jump,' she threatens.

'Alright, please! I'll stay right here,' I assure her.

'The accident was your fault,' screams Jenny accusingly before beginning to sob, 'you killed Mum!'

Tears are streaming down her face now but the wind blows them away as quick as they appear. Why is Helen's death my fault? The magnitude of the accusation is soul destroying and rips into the depths of my heart but Jenny truly believes it. But what does she mean? I can't remember even her death but the mere concept is painful enough in itself. Desperately I search for answers in my mind but there are none, just the overriding terror that I'm about to lose my precious daughter too.

'We can talk about it,' I urge her. 'Please I'll do anything, just give me your hand.'

Jenny is sobbing and crying like a baby now and her strength seems to be faltering. 'Mum has gone and you're a drunk,' she sobs while shaking her head from side to side. 'I can't carry on like this without her.'

'Please Jenny. I'm begging you,' I implore her, 'climb down. I'll sober up. Even if you hate me forever, don't let your life end like this.'

I realise that I'm crying too now and slowly shuffling along the railings towards her, desperate to stop her from killing herself. The wind is howling across the rooftop like a messenger of evil and pulling at me. As I almost reach her she shuffles back away from me and wipes her face with one hand.

'Hold the railings,' I press her, 'please!'

I raise my hands out to my sides, releasing the railings to show her that I won't come any closer. 'I love you, please don't do this,' I say.

'You bought us here,' Jenny says, her tone suddenly cold. 'You took her from me.'

I shake my head in denial. 'I don't want you up here,' I say. 'I love your mother and I love you too. Helen is my world. I wouldn't take her away from you.'

My words only seem only to infuriate her further and she takes a step closer to me with an angry look in her eyes. I make a desperate lunge for her wrist but she shoves both hands into my chest. The force of her hands causes my foot to slip off the edge of the roof. Before I can quite believe what's happened I scream out in surprise and I fall backwards. I briefly see Jenny clinging to the railings again but my view is only like that for a split second.

I can't tell if she is safe because I'm spinning and falling from the roof just like in Pripyat, only this time the doll on the roof is my daughter. But unlike Pripyat there is no lying on the ground waiting for death or any time to listen to the voices on a radio. I think death is too quick for me to even register it this time. The concrete below ends all of my unanswered questions.

12
The Confession

The sun's rays feel nice on my back as I lay face down with no shirt on. My legs are warm where my shorts finish and my eyes are closed. Bathed in gentle sunlight I feel as comfortable and relaxed as I can remember, with no desire to move and I'm practically asleep. The breeze tickles the hairs of my legs and gently caresses my back. It's a blissful state to experience.

As I slowly become more aware of my surroundings I hear the intermittent sounds of people chatting nearby and notice a very slight movement, or maybe just a vibration. Without opening my eyes I think about the feeling and how it's helping me to relax and inducing me to sleep. But before I fall asleep the sound of children noisily running past stirs me. Opening my eyes I realise that I'm lying face down on a sun lounger, not a bed after all, with a rolled up black towel serving as a pillow.

I roll over onto my side, catching sight of the clear blue sky and the unmistakeable white railings and wooden decking boards of a cruise ship surrounding me. The sun is already climbing into the morning sky and there are dozens of other sun beds scattered around an appealing but small swimming pool. Half of the sun beds are already occupied or have towels draped over them by people staking their claim.

Sitting up, I look towards the side of the ship and although I'm high up I can still see the tranquil and still ocean below the horizon. In the distance I can just make out the tell-tale dark yellow stripe of land. It's regrettable that we've only been on a couple of cruises before. Helen much prefers adventure holidays and doing things like sky diving, jeep safaris or scuba diving.

I'm a little surprised to see Helen sitting up on the adjacent sun bed, in white shorts and blue bikini top reading a book. The vision of her is like a wakeup call for my memory and a sudden thought overwhelms me. She's alive! That's why I'm surprised. I remember throwing up in Tina's bathroom, the sympathy cards and the empty liquor bottles. I quickly stroke my chin and realise that I'm clean shaven rather than in a dishevelled state of mourning. My face has the tell-tale oiliness of sun lotion on its smooth surface. Helen really is alive!

'Helen!' I call out her name.

She lowers her book for a moment and looks at me over her sunglasses.

'Yes?' she asks.

I stand up and snatch the book out of her hands and drop it on her sun bed.

'Hey, what are you doing?' she asks.

She looks startled as I pull her up onto her feet and hug her. Her body feels so warm and reassuring against mine as I rest my chin on her shoulder and squeeze her tightly. Despite her possible annoyance she hugs me back, and for a few moments I can't bear to let go of her. It's ultimately her who releases me first, long before I'm willing to allow my grip on her to relax.

'What was that about you fool?' she asks.

'Nothing,' I reply, 'it was just because I love you.'

'I love you too,' she says, 'now do you mind if I read my book in peace?'

Helen sits back down on her sun bed and I realise how fabulously sexy she looks in her bikini and shorts, her legs and arms lightly tanned. The sun has brought out the freckles on her face, albeit quite subtly and her red wavy hair is unkempt and a little more wild than usual.

Rather than sit back down I walk over to the side of the ship to gather my thoughts. I'm greeted by an elderly couple who wish me a friendly good morning as they walk past. I smile as they pass and the ship's railings feel warm to my touch as I peer down over the side at the sea far below. The railings remind me of something though, my apartment building and Jenny up on the roof. I squeeze the metal a little harder and begin to feel dizzy. The dark blue ocean is sliding past in contrast to the white bow wave that fans out from the hull. I fight the urge to step back, telling myself that the railings are what's supporting me.

Jenny's teary face suddenly forms a powerful image in my mind as the memory of her pushing me off the roof returns. My own daughter sent me to my death! But if Helen isn't really dead then does that mean that everything on the rooftop never happened? Did Helen not die in an accident after all? Jenny's words haunt my mind, her accusing tone clear in my head.

'You took her from me... I can't carry on like this without her.'

The memory of Jenny's anger is too painful to bear, the thought of her suicidal despair on the rooftop and the fact that she blamed me for it all. I can't bear to picture such venom from my daughter and my eyes begin to water with the first sign of tears. The sea air stings them and I quickly wipe my eyes with my hands and blink rapidly. My situation can be merciless and cruel in its torment but I've never felt anything quite like this. I want to be free of it all, free of Virgil and my continual experiences of death. I want my life to be normal again, just a man living one day after another and not dying. I need to be with Helen and have the love of my daughter back.

Suddenly I realise how tightly I am gripping the railings and my knuckles have turned white. The sensation reminds me of Jenny's hands on the rooftop and I snatch my hands away from the railings and walk towards the swimming pool. A young couple are splashing around in the water and laughing. The water looks clear, pure and inviting as sunlight dances on its rippling surface. With only the briefest moment of hesitation I jump straight in and sink to the bottom of the pool, exhaling through my nose. I feel only a slight shock as the water rapidly cools my hot skin but the feeling is gone almost immediately. I allow the water to surround me, enveloping my body and face, caressing my skin and washing me clean of the last few nightmare days. I need it all to go away, the hospice, Virgil, Tina and all the suffering. Please let me forget the alcoholism and the deaths, but most of all Jenny's tears. I stay under the water as long as I possibly can, allowing it to wash away my despair. As I finally exhaust the air in my lungs I surface from the pool. Water runs down my face removing any trace of tears. My hair and body feel clean and refreshed even if the pool fails to rinse my memory and soul of darkness.

I tried my best to use my situation for good and help Virgil, twice, and I'm repaid with Helen's death and Jenny despising me. Holding onto the side of the pool, I look over at Helen as she turns over a page in her book. She suddenly notices me and stops reading to smile and wave at me. I wave back and then lean back to rest my head in the cool water. My eyes stare up into the clear blue sky and I promise myself never to help Virgil again.

The deck is beginning to get busier as more couples and children walk past and occupy the remaining sun beds. I climb out of the pool and feel slightly chilly as the sea breeze meets the water on my body. Looking up towards the ship's control room high above I realise the enormity of the vessel and its stark white livery dazzles me as it reflects the sun. I return to my sun bed and towel myself down with the makeshift pillow as Helen smiles at me.

'That was a quick dip,' she says, before returning her attention back to her book. 'Was it too cold for you?'

It may have been quick but it was sufficient to help me realise that my attempted good deeds had gone unrewarded, maybe even punished.

'No, it's lovely and warm,' I reply.

'How come you got out then?' she asks without looking up from her J.D. Robb novel, ironically with 'Death' in the title.

'I was missing you too much,' I reply sarcastically, but after what happened yesterday – quite truthfully.

'Awww... that's so sweet honey,' she says a little patronisingly. 'And I was hoping for some peace with my book.'

'Helen?' I say.

She finally lowers her book for a moment to look at me.

'I'm hoping this will be a great holiday,' I tell her.

'It already is,' she says, rubbing her hand on my leg.

I lie back down on my sun bed and allow the sun to re-warm my body as I close my eyes. If only I could awaken here on this ship every time I die, that would be bliss. But the thought isn't that soothing though, because I find myself wondering where death will await me this time. But somehow the sun drenched cruise slowly begins to drive such negative thoughts away, as if they have been tossed overboard and left behind.

The sun's warm caress is a welcome companion once again and I feel myself drifting off with the barely noticeable movement of the ship. In my mind I begin to picture Helen on her sun bed in just the two piece bikini but without the shorts. The image is immediately arousing and I try to focus on something else while we are out here by the pool in such a public area.

My memory drifts randomly back to a time when Helen was pregnant with Jenny and she was a week overdue. Her waters had finally broken one Tuesday morning while she was coming down the stairs in our house. I remember driving her to hospital, my hands shaking on the wheel with my urgency to get her there though the Watford rush hour. At least Helen's labour was problem free although the nine hours had seemed to last a lifetime. I sometimes thought that Jenny would never arrive, but after being overdue and the long labour, she grew up to be a stickler for punctuality which was in contrast to her mother.

If the drive to the hospital was scary, then the return trip with Helen and our baby girl was petrifying. Every car seemed like a threat to the precious tiny life we had inside and I was forever checking my mirrors and over my shoulders for dangerous drivers. I'll always remember how damp my shirt was when we finally got home. Jumping out of planes was less frightening.

Both of us had always agreed that we only wanted one child to love and spoil and so Jenny's arrival was everything we hoped for. As soon as she was home and we were a family, we both knew that we didn't need another child. Helen's parents had flown over from Australia a week after Jenny was born to visit their new granddaughter. They had emigrated there just after we got married.

Jenny was five before we moved into London to avoid us having to commute every day, and to fulfil our dreams of living in the city. Raising our daughter in the city was our perfect life and we never regretted having to give up adventure holidays for sixteen or so years.

'Ewan?' says Helen, prodding me gently in the ribs.

My eyes flicker open and look at her. 'Yes,' I say, stifling a yawn.

'You were asleep,' she says. 'And you haven't put more cream on since you came out the pool. I don't want you to get burnt.'

Sitting up on the sun bed, I stretch my arms and yawn. The pool is almost full of people now, mainly kids and every sun bed is occupied. The sun is high in the sky now and my skin feels a little tender and hot, not burnt but the warning signs are there. She was right, but sunburn would be nothing compared to being set alight in a bombed hotel in France.

'Do you fancy getting changed for lunch?' she asks.

Feeling hungry myself, I immediately agree. Helen closes her book and marks her place with a gold bookmark that I bought for her about five years ago in Harrods.

'Let's go,' I say, taking Helen's hand.

Even with having missed all of the holiday so far, somehow I seem to know where our cabin is. Nothing much surprises me these days, but strangely when I enter the cabin it's like I'm doing it for the first time. It's an outside cabin and a lot bigger than ones I remember staying in on previous cruises. There is much more floor space and a long narrow window that's much larger than a basic round porthole.

Helen goes into the bathroom and I look at my reflection in the wardrobe mirror. I look healthy with clean shaven, pinkish skin that looks almost brown in the light of the bedroom. I open the wardrobe and take out a Hawaiian shirt and as I close the wardrobe door and toss the shirt on the bed I hear the toilet flush. While looking at my reflection and trying to decide if I could do with losing a couple of inches on my waist I just catch a flash of movement behind me in the wardrobe mirror. Helen cuddles into the back of me and wraps her arms around my chest. I first sense, but then immediately feel that she is naked, her body warm but slightly oily from sun cream. Her body is pressing hard against me and she cranes her head up to kiss the back of my neck. My hands reach behind me and rest on the outside of her thighs as I turn my neck to welcome the soft feel of her lips behind my ear. Slowly her hands begin to inch down the contours of my chest and I breathe deeper, becoming aroused. With her body pressed against mine her hand slowly inches its way into the front of my shorts and any negative thoughts of life or dying that I have are forgotten.

Washing away the sun cream and chlorine in the warm shower is invigorating and even more refreshing than the pool. I almost feel like a new person. Stepping out of the shower I pull on the complimentary cruise dressing gown and stretch my arms. Helen is already dressed in clean shorts and a T-shirt, sitting on the bed brushing her damp hair. I wink at her as I enter the room and she smiles but continues brushing. She looks so beautiful, so youthful and yet elegant.

I wonder if I should tell her about my situation and see if she can help me make any sense of it, but decide it might spoil a perfect day. The memory of the last time I tried to tell her is still raw and how that ended with her stabbing me in the back. I'm sure you're supposed to share your problems with your partner though aren't you? Maybe I could try it if there were no sharp objects around, but my situation seems far beyond any problem that a little friendly advice can help with.

I towel myself off and pull on some light trousers and the Hawaiian shirt, then slip on my sandals and look out of the window. The sea is a long way down and is as calm as ever. A large expanse of deserted beach and lush green jungle are visible on an island in the distance. It looks like an island paradise or a picture of the Maldives from a magazine.

I allow myself a contented smile at the memory of our time in the cabin. Sex with her is incredible when it is so spontaneous and she instigates it, especially on the rare occasions where I'm not shrewd enough to have already anticipated her intentions. I can often guess when she is thinking of surprising me, but not this time.

'Ready?' asks Helen. 'Let's go get some lunch.'

The fish restaurant is way back at the stern of the ship and two decks down but Helen suggests it because it's quieter and already the peak of lunch time. She is proved to be right because somehow we are fortunate enough to still get a table next to a window. Not only is there an amazing view of the sea but the sun bathes our table with light too. It occurs to me just how relaxing a cruise is compared to a holiday spent jumping out of planes. Maybe I can persuade her to take less adventure holidays in future and steer her towards more relaxing ones with fewer opportunities for an adrenaline rush.

Helen picks slowly at her sea bass. Even as a vegetarian, she has never considered fish to be meat which I didn't really understand. My lemon sole is delicious and I squeeze every remaining drop of juice from the lemon over the last few forkfuls.

'Shall we go ashore tomorrow?' asks Helen.

'If you like,' I murmur, figuring that's what I should say. If only she knew that there won't be a tomorrow in this place. There is no harm in playing along though, because I can't be certain that there won't be for her, irrespective of where I awaken. I can't begin to accept the foolish notion of some kind of parallel universe.

'Remember the Captain's dinner is tonight,' says Helen.'

That would be as good a place as any to die when the whole ship would be celebrating and dining.

'How about we give it a miss it and have a quiet night in?' I suggest.

'We've just had a quiet morning,' Helen replies with a wry grin. 'I can't manage a quiet evening as well...'

'But it's not like we will see much of the Captain anyway,' I point out.

'It's a Gala evening you doughnut,' she replies, 'the cream of on-board society will be there. Oh! And us of course.'

'Helen I'm serious, can't we just stay in and get our dinner delivered to the cabin?' I ask.

There are lifejackets in the cabin, no cars, minimal sharp objects and definitely no careless neurosurgeons or angry unprovoked scorpions. Helen finishes the last mouthful of her fish and takes a sip of her white wine.

'No,' she says firmly, shaking her head, 'we have to go. And we only need to stay a couple of hours anyway.'

I take her hands and pull them towards me across the table.

'Helen listen a minute,' I tell her, staring at her seriously. 'I want to tell you something important and I swear that every word of it is true. You need to trust me and then believe it, however crazy it sounds. Promise me?'

'Promise what?' asks Helen, frowning. 'What are you on about?'

I look her in the eyes. 'Promise to believe what I'm about to tell you,' I persist.

Helen nods and her eyes are fixed on me, but there is the merest hint of amusement on her face. She must think I'm playing one of my silly games.

Slowly and precisely I begin to explain my situation to her, starting with the fall in Pripyat, awakening in the interview and dying every day only to find myself in a new situation. I don't tell her about every death and can't bring myself to include the part about Jenny pushing me off the roof. I tell her about the plane crash even though she was on the plane too, and about how she asked me for a divorce but I leave out Virgil and some of my darker moments. The bare bones of my story are sufficient to explain that basically every day I die and then awaken somewhere else.

Helen's reaction barely changes other than to lose the amusement on her face as if she is intrigued by an interesting story that someone is telling her. I finish by explaining that I expect to die and that's why I want to stay in the cabin this evening. After a brief pause Helen finally speaks.

'You want me to promise to believe all that?' she asks.

I sit back, sigh deeply and release her hands but when I speak there is deep frustration in my voice. 'I knew you wouldn't believe it,' I tell her, folding my arms. 'I don't want to believe it myself but I have to live though this shit every day.'

Helen seems to sense my despondent mood and she leans forward and pats my hand. 'Honey, I listened to every word,' she says. 'The whole thing sounds ridiculous of course but I do think that you believe it. I also think I can prove to you that it's not true.'

My mood softens slightly. 'Alright, I'm listening,' I say. 'How?'

'Look Ewan, suppose you are right,' she says. 'How about we do what you suggest and miss the Captain's dinner? We'll eat in our cabin tonight, and even lock the door if you like. We'll stay together all day and night, and if there's any sign of death coming for you I'll kick him in the bollocks. Then in the morning when you haven't died of illness or a car crash or anything else, we can get on with our holiday. Deal?'

Part of what she says about kicking death reminds me of something that Virgil said and I don't truly think she believes any of what I said. It's more likely that she just fancies a quiet evening in the cabin after all, but for the first time since Pripyat I don't feel alone. A problem shared isn't quite a problem halved, but an evening locked in a cabin with Helen is far from unappealing. And just maybe she can help me avoid death, and the implications of that are staggering.

'Okay, agreed,' I say.

'We'll face death together,' she says, 'and I'm telling you this, I guarantee I won't let anything happen to you.'

She sounds truly serious but I figure she is just entering into the spirit of what I'm asking. 'I love you Helen,' I say.

She smiles, and we leave the restaurant holding hands on the return trip to our cabin and an appointment with death.

The first few hours in the cabin are quiet, dull and uneventful which is just what I need and hoped for. Helen falls asleep and I resort to taking the opportunity to search the cabin for anything deadly and toss it out of our window which only opens a sliver at the top. I find only a pair of scissors, a hairdryer cable and a glass nail file which amount to a pretty meagre arsenal of death. Short of the cruise ship sinking which doesn't seem likely, it's impossible to anticipate how this day could ever end with my death. Although I feel healthy, I wonder about the possibility of a surprise heart attack but I've already exerted myself today as much as I plan to. It's a fond memory too.

As I watch Helen, my guardian angel for the night sleeping, I make a mental note of exactly where the life jackets are stowed and plan the quickest route to a muster station in my head. I even contemplate wearing the orange life preserve but decide that's a little too overcautious. Have I covered every angle possible? My death is still irrelevant but deep down I want Helen to prove me wrong and to somehow interrupt my cycle of death, although I would never hear the end of it.

Helen has ordered us a room service dinner of steak for me and pasta for her, with jam scones, cream and tea. The thought of it is a mouth-watering prospect even though it sounds a bit too much like a last meal for the condemned man for my liking. She looks so peaceful that I decide not to wake her until it arrives, especially as she will be on the late shift of my death watch. I sit down in one of the armchairs and stretch out my legs.

At 7:00 PM there is a knock on our cabin door and I realise that dinner has arrived. Helen rolls over slightly but doesn't wake up, so I answer the door myself. The steward is maybe thirty years old, European looking with short blonde hair and a square jaw. His uniform is bone white just like the ship with a red flag embroidered on each collar. Steam is rising from underneath one of the cloches on his trolley but then I notice the name badge on his chest – Virgil.

I immediately lunge for him, clattering into the trolley and forcing him against the wall with my forearm pinned against his chest. The trolley rolls down the corridor a little way and I hear the clang of a cloche landing on the corridor floor.

'You!' I snarl, almost spitting in his face. 'Why? What the fuck do you want?'

He is a little taller than me, heavier built, younger and probably fitter, but it's his reaction that stuns me. A broad smile fills his face.

'Who did you expect?' he asks, arms by his side, palms facing upwards. 'Did you really expect anyone else, Old Man? You didn't do a very good job with that pillow by the way.'

My stunned surprise causes me to relax my grip slightly as Helen appears at the door behind me, rubbing her eyes.

'Ewan?' she asks, 'what was that bang?'

Virgil exploits the distraction and uses the opportunity to shove me backwards towards my cabin door. He runs off down the corridor laughing but not before intentionally tipping over the trolley in the process.

'Stay there!' I shout to Helen as I jump over the trolley and charge off down the corridor in pursuit.

Virgil is easily quicker than me and I sense that he is deliberately slowing his place to allow me to keep up. It's not easy running with only socks on my feet, but he has finally confirmed any doubts I had about whether Virgil is the one continuity of my situation. Anger at his appearance has possessed me and I barge past everyone in the corridors that gets in my way including another steward. My pursuit of Virgil leads me outside to the stern of the ship on one of the lower decks, but I'm never able to quite catch up with him.

The air is cool this evening and the sea looks an oily dark colour in the fading light. Virgil clambers up a small ladder and climbs over a railing onto the roof of a small building holding life rafts. As he turns I can see that his white uniform is dirty where his chest has touched the railings. I start to climb the ladder after him while gasping to catch my breath, realising that he is cornered.

'Who, the hell are you?' I demand.

Virgil seems to have no trouble breathing and stands there with his hands on his hips, smiling. 'You asked me that before the surgery,' he says, chuckling aloud. 'That was a long time ago, do you still remember that? I had a spot of trouble with the scalpel while I was poking around in your head I'm afraid.'

Angrily I climb the remaining rungs but remain on the opposite side of the railings. He has no way down other than through me although I figure he is capable of doing just that if he wants. I won't make it easy for him though.

'You know what's happening to me don't you?' I point at him threateningly. 'This dead loop is something to do with you isn't it?'

'The dead loop?' he smirks with amusement. 'Is that what you call it? Of course I know what's happening, but it's nothing to do with me.'

I climb over the railings and face him, eager for answers but furious enough to try and smash the smug look from his face.

'Tell me!' I demand.

He shakes his head. 'I don't think I will,' he taunts. 'Maybe I should go back and see that pretty wife of yours instead?'

His threat is too much to stomach and I charge towards him, intent on using violence not words now. He easily sidesteps my charge and shoves me off the edge of the roof. There is nothing on the other side but a drop, although I realise that he has chosen to follow me for some strange reason. We are both plummeting down the side of the ship and I yell out in horror before we plunge into the black seawater.

The shock of the impact and the freezing cold water drive any immediate thoughts of Virgil's whereabouts from my mind. I desperately kick out in a bid to try to reach the surface. Gasping for breath in the dark, almost hyperventilating, I find the surface but there is no sign of Virgil or the cruise ship. The sky and water are both black. Waves jostle me in the water as I shiver and kick my legs to keep afloat, making me regret not wearing the life jacket. The feeling of being in the ocean in the dark, with nothing to reach out to or hold onto is utterly terrifying.

I soon learn that it's impossible for a human being to accept drowning. Even though I want to welcome the embrace of death, my body fights every second to stay above water and keep breathing air. Every time I swallow the bitter salty sea water and cough as it enters my lungs, the feeling of terror fights to overwhelm me. But only for a second though, as the instinct for survival keeps taking over again. It's a continuous cycle of desperation and terror.

I suppose it won't be long until the cold weakens me sufficiently to become unconsciousness and I slip beneath the water one final time. By then I will probably be unaware that my body has fought an impossible life and death struggle to its bitter end. Drowning forces you to use every last atom of energy and determination in what must be the ultimate discharge of human endurance. At least the cold water helps to accelerate the process.

13
A Danger to Others

The vast window is almost as long as the wall and so clean that it gives the impression of there being no glass. I reach out with my bare foot to try and touch the surface which dispels the illusion and confirms that there definitely is glass after all. The window still feels cold as if not yet warmed up by the early morning sunshine.

The view through the window is of a beautiful landscaped garden with lush green lawns split over different levels. There's a large central pond with a fountain that sends twinkling drops of water into the air which are then carried in the breeze before falling back and splashing onto a surface of lily pads. A handful of trees have been selectively planted to break the garden up, along with several well cultivated hedges that separate the lawns into neat sections. An abundance of flowers in every colour are planted in generous beds and they make me want to inhale their scent. Although it may be a beautiful morning outside, the air in this room smells stale and sour.

My armchair faces the window but judging by its dirty and worn armrests, its upholstery is desperately in need of refurbishment however comfortable it is. After touching the window with my foot I suddenly realise that I can't move my arms. I try to sit forward but discover that my arms are crossed over themselves in the vice like hug of a white straitjacket. The archaic symbol of madness is uncomfortable, constricting and frighteningly effective. I struggle against its straps for a moment but succeed in little more than shrugging my shoulders and rolling from side to side in my chair as I wonder where I am. It's the only thing I'm wearing other than a pair of blue and white striped pyjamas.

Turning my head to look around I realise that I'm one of around ten 'patients' sitting in similarly battered armchairs staring into the garden. We're lined up like a grotesque but orderly row of restrained spectators waiting for something to happen. Almost all of the others have straitjackets on too, there's just one or two who are fortunate enough to enjoy the freedom of all their limbs.

The patients are a broad range from maybe twenty years old to fifty, including both men and women but while they may be youthful, every single one of them seems to be staring vacantly of the window as if their soul has been emptied of life. The woman immediately to my right is wearing dirty yellow pyjamas beneath her straitjacket and I notice unblinking eyes above a line of dribble that leaks from her mouth and into her lap. The sight of her is an image of despair and indignity that urges me to close my eyes and imagine that I'm somewhere else.

It feels awkward standing up with my arms restrained while trying to maintain my balance but I somehow manage it. As soon as I'm on my feet I feel someone touch my shoulder and push me gently but purposefully back into my chair. For the first time I notice the calming sound of classical music playing from two old fashioned, wood-effect speakers positioned near the ceiling of the garden room. The woman that encourages me back to my chair is mature, stocky and brutish looking, wearing pale blue overalls and a name badge. I decide that she doesn't look much like an Amanda because her face looks too blunt and mean for the image that her name conjures up.

'Sit down Mr. Charles,' she says. 'There's nowhere you need to be right now, so just enjoy the view.'

I shuffle uncomfortably in the chair and make a half-hearted attempt to get up again but she holds my shoulder firmly this time and a hypodermic needle appears in her other hand.

'Please, no drugs!' I insist as I try more determinedly to stand up again.

None of the other patients so much as glances around or stirs from their stupor as the needle pierces my leg though the pyjamas and almost immediately my vision begins to blur.

'It's just something to help you stay calm,' Amanda whispers. 'Nothing to worry about, just enjoy the view.'

I feel my muscles begin to relax and my lower jaw to hang open slightly. The image of my drooling neighbour springs to mind and I clamp my jaw shut, shaking my head defiantly but it's no use – the drug is already taking effect. All I can see is the garden but it looks different now, almost as if it's clouded. The pretty flowers seem to merge with the green of the grass forming a soup of colour as the shapes of the trees seem to blend into the sky. For some reason the idea of trying to focus more clearly feels unimportant. The detail of the garden is no longer relevant to me as I moisten my lips and lean back in the chair.

Lunch time is a humiliating experience. The effects of the drugs are only just beginning to wear off and somehow I know I should be questioning my situation and fighting it, but for some reason I'm overwhelmed by a powerful desire to conform and to demonstrate compliance.

The armchairs have now been wheeled into a semi-circle in the middle of the room and three more sturdy looking women that I assume to be nurses are spoon feeding some of the patients. The radio has been switched off and cartoons are playing on two large televisions suspended from the ceiling but there is no volume, just the colourful moving pictures.

Not all of the 'inmates', as I choose to think of them now, are being fed like oversized babies. Some of them are no longer wearing straitjackets and are feeding themselves with some kind of porridge using large plastic spoons. Everyone is wearing some kind of towel, tied loosely around their necks but it still amounts to a bib.

The woman who was drooling earlier no longer has a straitjacket on but has managed to cover herself in porridge while one of the staff makes a vague effort to spoon some of it off her pyjamas and into her mouth. My mind struggles to resist the indignity of the situation as I too monotonously spoon feed myself with the warm, bland, lumpy porridge. Hadn't I asked for steak and scones? The thought seems out of place and strange.

As soon as everyone has finished eating, the television is switched off and where necessary the inmates are wiped clean by the staff, each nurse using just a single white towel. As we are pushed back into a line by the window I'm grateful that I don't need any cleaning up.

As soon as I'm locked back into the straitjacket and staring out of the window again, I feel a sudden change in me. The garden ceases to be a blur and the shapes of flower beds and lawns begin to sharpen and reform. And as my vision clears up, so does my mind.

Wait, I did order steak and scones! It was in my cabin, on the cruise with Helen. Virgil delivered the dinner! The recollection causes me to begin shuffling angrily in my chair and gritting my teeth. Could this be his doing somehow? Is this part of some sick twisted game perhaps? I struggle against the straitjacket and bare my teeth as if about to snarl when one of the nurses approaches with a clipboard under her arm. As she glances at it and frowns, I force myself to stop struggling.

'Do you need another shot Mr. Charles?' she asks, with the vague hint of threat in her voice.

Instinctively I turn my face towards the window and stare silently at one of the trees with as vacant a look as I can muster on my face.

'You're not due yet anyway,' she says, flicking over a page on her clipboard. 'Nice and calm please, okay?'

I don't dignify her with an answer but behind my vacant stare there is a simmering anger and my mind is furiously at work.

I can't recall ever having stronger feelings of hatred for someone than those directed towards Virgil since he confessed to being aware of my situation and refusing to explain it. I need to get out of here, to see Jenny and find Helen, wondering if she will even remember the conversation we had on the ship. She was wrong about me being able to survive the night in seclusion in our cabin. But what if I had slammed the door on Virgil and locked it, rather than chasing him onto the deck? Would I have eluded death as planned or would the ship have conveniently sank? Every question has no answer and only seems to lead to another. Why did he follow me overboard to his own death?

The vivid memory of fighting against the inky black seawater returns, and I remember swimming in circles once I'd recovered from the initial shock of the water temperature. I desperately searched for somewhere to go, any logical direction to swim or a sighting of the ship. Once, when a wave had lifted me a little higher in the water I thought I caught sight of some distant lights that might have been our ship. But after that one occasion I never saw the lights again.

Did Helen follow me and Virgil down the corridor? He certainly led me a merry chase through the ship and even though he slowed down just enough for me to keep up I doubt Helen would have seen which way we went. Why didn't someone see us fall overboard and sound the alarm?

There was nowhere to swim to in the darkness, no hope of rescue and no land. How long had it taken me to finally succumb to the cold and drown? I feel the urge to vomit and expel sea water from my lungs, making me shiver in my chair. The futile struggle with the straitjacket suddenly reminds me of my relentless battle with the ocean. I can't swim in the straitjacket and I try desperately to move my arms, but it's a wasted effort. My forehead is hot and sweaty and I feel the onset of claustrophobic panic, making me gasp for breath and struggle harder against my restraints. But the man to my left isn't panicking in his straitjacket, he stares calmly out of the window so I close my eyes and try to stop fighting. I must somehow replicate his blank, stony-faced image of calm. Concentration gradually helps to dissipate my feelings of panic and my breathing slows down as I try to accept that I'm just immobilised and not drowning. Trying to stand up again will only get me another injection.

One of the nurses comes into the room and I recognise her as the mean faced Amanda. 'Toilet anyone?' she calls.

One of the two patients without a straitjacket raises his hand and two of the women to my left stand up. The drooling woman starts nodding continuously but doesn't get to her feet. Two of the nurses escort the volunteer who raised his hand out of the room through a pair of double doors. Amanda comes over to the drooling woman and whispers something to her, but I catch her words. 'Beth you're in nappies,' she says. 'You don't need to nod.'

When everyone that needed to go has been escorted one at a time to the toilet, Amanda comes to me and places a hand on my shoulder. 'Ewan,' she says, using my first name now, 'it's time for you to see the doctor.'

Grateful for the opportunity to be out of the chair, I stand up and she leads me through the double doors and into a plain corridor. My mind is fully clear now and my thoughts focused, but I maintain a veneer of compliance to avoid the risk of another injection. Amanda knocks on a door leading off the corridor, opening it immediately and then ushering me into a small empty office. The room contains little more than a plain wooden desk and two chairs and she guides me into one. One is brown leather but mine is more like an arm chair with restraints on it. Amanda buckles the straps around my legs, waist and chest securing me to the chair. Logic tells me to resist, but I decide against it.

'There we go,' she says, pleased as much with her work as my lack of resistance.

The whole scenario is playing out like a humiliating nightmare but it gets worse as a man of around thirty walks in carrying a document file in his hand. He is European looking with blonde hair, a square jaw and wearing a smart shirt and trousers, but he doesn't need a name badge this time. It's the cruise ship steward who delivered the food to our cabin, the identical man – it's Virgil. Instinctively I try to move but immediately realise that it's pointless as I am strapped into the chair.

The man offers his thanks to Amanda who smiles then leaves the room, closing the door behind her. The man sits behind the desk in the leather chair opposite me and opens up the file he was carrying. I decide not to speak as he flicks through the paper contents while glancing occasionally at me. Finally he speaks in the same voice that I recognise from our heated discussion on the cruise ship.

'Hello Mr. Charles,' he says slowly. 'I'm Doctor Addison. How are you feeling?'

'I know who you are Virgil,' I snap, 'so quit with all the bullshit.'

He carefully closes the file and places it on the desk.

'I suppose you're right,' he concedes. 'But you can't hold it against me for trying though, can you Old Man?'

'I hope you fucking drowned badly,' I sneer at him.

Virgil opens a drawer under his side of the desk, removes a hypodermic and waves it menacingly at me while raising an eyebrow. 'Don't make me have to use this,' he warns me.

I consider his threat carefully, the words of the man stalking me through my deaths. But he seems more than just a stalker, it's like he is some kind of nemesis who seems to hold all the cards. At the very least he is an uncannily accurate omen of death.

'What do you want?' I demand, as he places the needle down on the desk in front of me.

'I'm just here to help with your treatment of course,' he says, smiling.

'I don't need any treatment,' I say coldly. 'There's fuck all wrong with me. I just need to know what's happening to me and why.'

'No treatment?' he scoffs with an incredulous look on his face. 'But you smothered me with a pillow back at the home of our good Lady St. Thomas. That's no way to treat a friend now is it?'

'A friend? But I don't even know you,' I remind him, 'besides that wasn't even you, it was someone else. An old man with your name and he was suffering.'

'No, no, that was me,' he says. 'I might have looked a little different then, but it was me alright. You did a lousy job of it by the way although it was pretty inconvenient timing from that nurse wasn't it?'

His memory of my situation and my experiences is undeniably accurate. 'You asked me to do it,' I point out. 'They should have let me finish you off.'

'Oh, don't feel too bad,' he replies. 'I'm sure they aren't allowed to do that. All they can do is make us comfortable and let death take its own sweet time. But you know all about death don't you?'

'Yes I do,' I acknowledge. 'But back on the ship you said... no you admitted that you know what's happening to me.'

Virgil leans back in his chair smiling to himself, the same smug grin that I remember from the ship just before we went overboard. But this time I can't reach him, I can't wipe it from his face and I'm forced to grit my teeth and bite my lip to control my rising anger.

'You know a little bit about death but you're still so naive,' he says. 'Just a little of what did you call it again, the dead loop? It's an amusing name.'

'Well, fucking enlighten me then,' I reply, while trying to imagine that I'm no longer restrained and somehow on an equal footing with him.

'Do you ever wonder if you probably shouldn't have fucked Christina from work?' he suddenly asks.

His question catches me off guard and surprises me because I have no memory of what he is accusing me of. The idea isn't completely unfeasible in my mind, even if it is wrong but how dare he of all people question me about Tina?

'I'm erring on the side that you shouldn't have,' he says with an amused tone to his voice. 'Wouldn't you agree?'

'What is that shit your bulldog nurse injects?' I ask, ignoring his question.

Virgil looks amused. 'You mean Amanda?' he asks. 'Oh that's just some rather effective cocktail of anti-psychotic medication. You're a danger to others you know.'

'Oh, I doubt that,' I contradict him.

An antipsychotic would explain the potency of her suppressant and my earlier stupor.

'Don't doubt it,' he replies, 'you're psychotic alright, bloody mental, you're a head case, you're a *one flew over the cuckoo's nest and landed in a funny farm and laid a fucking egg.*'

For some reason our verbal engagement is becoming oddly appealing to me but I know that I'm not psychotic, if anyone is, it's Virgil. It occurs to me that if he truly does understand my situation better than me, or is part of it then he might also represent a way out. Either way I intend to find out and perhaps then I can bring about an end to the dead loop itself. I focus my mind on trying to solve the conundrum, but I need more information, some clue of his purpose and to what holds me in this endless spiral of death.

'I know what you're thinking Ewan,' he says, interrupting my thoughts.

I wonder if he really does. 'Does that scare you?' I ask him.

'No, it bores me,' he says, absentmindedly playing with the finger nails on one hand and feigning disinterest. 'You know I haven't forgotten that you tried to throw me overboard on that cruise ship and never had the decency to apologise. Perhaps I should do something like that to one of your family, maybe Helen perhaps?'

His threat is more than enough to shatter any tolerance I've been exercising for him and it forces my rage to boil over uncontrollably.

'Stay away from her you sick bastard!' I shout, furiously shaking my arms inside my straitjacket. I try to kick out at the desk, but my legs are strapped to the chair and moving is impossible.

Virgil picks up the hypodermic needle from the desk and I snarl at him like an animal as he silently walks towards me with it. 'This should calm you down Old Man,' he says, lowering the needle towards my leg, 'maybe I better call Helen and tell her that you're deteriorating.'

I struggle relentlessly against the straps holding my legs while cursing him with every obscenity that I can muster. None of my words prevent the needle from sliding soundlessly into my leg and the injection being administered. After that my struggles only last for about ten seconds.

The view of the garden has reached a new level of blurriness and now swirls of colour circle in my mind. My head feels like it's spinning just like the girl from the Exorcist and I'm certain that if I was able to stand I would just fall over. I blink my eyes a few times and feel saliva dribbling from my mouth into my lap. My chin feels soaking wet but for some reason I have no urge to try and wipe it. The large blurred shape of a nurse walks past and kindly wipes my chin with some tissue but I'm drooling again before she even leaves my eye line. I close my eyes and try to sleep.

When my eyes finally open again, my chair is back in the circle and the silent cartoons are back on. My arms ache and I notice the curtains are closed and are obscuring the garden. Gratefully I realise that my arms are free and see two nurses busy feeding the inmates that still wear straitjackets. There is an untouched bowl of some kind of stew on my lap with one of the familiar plastic spoons sticking out of it. The food looks starkly unappetising but it does improve the stale, soiled odour of the room. Either the nurses haven't noticed that I was asleep and not feeding myself or they're unconcerned as to whether I eat or not. But I can't bring myself to despise them, irrespective of their apparent indifference to human dignity. All of my hatred is reserved for Virgil and I'm determined not to allow him the satisfaction of seeing me die in this place.

When the two nurses are farthest away from the doors, I haul my lethargic body out of the chair and rise to my feet. The lingering effects of the anti-psychotic seem locked in a battle against adrenaline for control of my body. As my heart pumps blood into my aching limbs, I run towards the doors in a desperate bid for freedom. Appearing from nowhere, Amanda suddenly blocks my path like a rugby player preparing for a tackle. As best as I can manage, I turn my side towards her and duck my head as I charge, trying to ram my shoulder into her. Any damage would be unintended but I doubt a soft approach will work against this formidable looking woman.

Taking my eyes off her proves to be a mistake as she sidesteps me just as easily as Virgil did on the ship. Using my error to her advantage, she grabs me around my chest and arms with a grip like a bear and allows my momentum to carry us both to the floor. I kick out at her with my feet and although they only connect with the wall it's enough to prevent her from interlocking her fingers together.

As we struggle on the hard floor I feel my head bump hard against hers causing her to cry out in pain, breaking the grip she has around my chest and allowing me to scramble free. I hear her cursing at me as I hastily stagger to my feet before crashing into the double doors and flinging them open.

Seconds later I'm running down the seemingly endless grey corridor hearing Amanda's shouts behind me. My head is still spinning but I don't stop for anything until eventually I turn a corner in the corridor, stumbling and breathing heavily. Unfortunately I realise that the way forwards is blocked by a wall of solid bars across the corridor with a locked metal door in the centre. The futility of trying to get through it is obvious, but there is a plain green door on my side of the barrier. I try pushing the handle down only to find it locked. I try barging the door open instead but the impact is ineffective and only brutalises my shoulder. Sensing the urgency of my situation I try again, harder this time but end up cursing in the pain of my defeat. As I look back down the corridor I see Amanda scurry around the corner with two men in black uniforms closely behind her.

Blood is streaming heavily from a cut in the side of her face while the shirt of her uniform is flapping and un-tucked on one side. The men overtake her and without warning grab my shoulders and arms fiercely. They begin frog marching me back around the corner towards the garden room, with Amanda leading the way. Their strength is phenomenal and no amount of struggling is enough to break free.

Halfway down the corridor Amanda produces a large bundle of jangling keys and unlocks a side door that I didn't notice in my escape attempt. They man-handle me onto a plain metal bed with only a wafer thin mattress covering it, and Amanda tightens thick leather straps over my chest, arms and legs. She doesn't stop fastening up buckles until I'm sufficiently restrained for the men to release me. Finally she handcuffs my wrists to two metal bars running along the sides of the bed. She is breathing heavily from the exertion and she pauses for a moment to regain her breath.

'You shouldn't have done that,' she snaps at me, now holding a large white bundle of tissue to her bleeding face.

'I shouldn't be here!' I yell back. 'I don't belong here.'

Amanda takes one last annoyed look at me before the three of them leave the room. I try to slow down my breathing and force myself to relax my tense muscles in spite of the fact there is no pillow and the mattress feels as hard as a concrete floor.

A few minutes later, Virgil enters the room holding a hypodermic needle in his hand and he slowly shakes his head.

'You should play nicely with the staff Ewan,' he says. 'That's quite a nasty cut you gave Mandy.'

I ignore his statement, forced to accept that he has won this round. 'Like I said earlier,' I reply, 'enlighten me.'

'I told you that you were a danger to others didn't I?' he replies sarcastically.

'Fuck you Virgil,' I reply, determined to antagonise him and demonstrate my defiance. 'Just give me the drool shot and then I won't have to listen to your bullshit anymore.'

He walks over to me silently while still shaking his head and slowly administers the injection into my shoulder.

'Sorry Old Man,' he says. 'But that's not a regular anti-psychotic, it's more of a lethal injection I'm afraid.'

For a moment his words don't register, but even when they finally do I don't believe him. Within a few seconds I realise from bitter experience that I don't feel the same effects as the previous injections. This is something different entirely. Surprisingly I don't feel any pain although I sense my eyes beginning to close as if I've just had a general anaesthetic. As I try to force my eyes to remain open, my instincts tell me that I only have a few seconds left. Gritting my teeth as I fight the desire to close my eyes, I just catch sight of Virgil's smug face looking down at me.

'I'll see you in the next life you bastard,' I murmur with my final breath.

14
Sand

The blistering heat is phenomenal and like nothing I have ever experienced before. I squint up at a white hot sun that seems to scorch the very sky around it. I try desperately to shield my eyes from the intense light but it seems to be coming from everywhere around me. Closing my eyes tightly and keeping them shut is the only thing that seems to help.

My throat has gone far beyond parched and my mouth has no moisture in it. There seems to be no feeling in my tongue as I lick my cracked and burnt lips, tasting only gritty sand. I swallow painfully and without any saliva in my mouth but there seems to be none available. Although my shirt and trousers offer little in the way of protection from the unbearable heat at least they keep the sun from my skin. My face already feels raw with the effects of sunburn and it stings as I gently touch it.

I expect my shirt to be soaking wet but I'm so dehydrated that I've even run out of sweat and assume that whatever has soaked into my clothes has long since evaporated. Unable to continue standing I fall to my knees and feel my body slump forwards into the soft sand. The heat of the surface burns my hands and arms as they sink into it. But immediately I feel the sand move as my body slides through it and its fluidic surface carries me down a steep slope. I find myself rolling over and over, getting sand in my hair and under my clothes before the slope deposits me at the bottom of a steep sand dune. My eyes are still closed but I realise that I'm face down after inadvertently inhaling some of the fine sand. Using what little reserves of strength I can muster, I rise onto all fours and immediately begin to cough and splutter. The hoarse rasping sound emanating from my dry throat seems pitifully weak as I try to clear my airway.

I open my eyes but have to shield them as I squint up at a clear sky that seems almost white due to the intense light of the sun. I'm hopeful to see clouds or anything that might offer a moments respite from the tormenting heat, but there are none. There is just the merciless and burning sun.

With fingers that barely seem able to work properly, I fumble at the buttons of my shirt. Unable to find the dexterity to undo them, I yank the shirt apart until one by one the buttons rip off. After my shirt opens I'm able to pull it up a little to cover my head before I collapse back down in the sand, exhausted by my efforts.

I'm too weak to walk now and can't even face trying to stand up. My mind identifies no solutions or options and I feel delirious, confused and unable to focus my thoughts. My head throbs in time with my heartbeat, each beat causing a deep thump in the front of my head that makes me grit my teeth as the painful rhythm overwhelms me and I black out.

When I open my eyes the desert around me seems barren and empty. The air is still fiercely hot and it's difficult to breathe as if the oxygen has somehow been boiled away. The rolling dunes look exactly how I imagine the Sahara Desert or the Qatar Depression to be. The film *Ice cold in Alex* comes into my mind, along with a tormenting black and white image of condensation forming on a glass of Carlsberg lager. My mouth begins to water at the haunting thought of the beer and it's a blessed relief to feel saliva in my mouth again which I immediately swallow.

Time seems to have no meaning anymore, there is just a faint understanding that the time of the sun will eventually end and the heat will disappear. But nothing will speed up that transition and until then there is just the intense heat until my desperate longing for a merciful end to the bright sunshine is answered.

I hear a voice calling out to me, faintly at first but then it repeats itself a little louder. Straining my ears to listen, the words come even louder as I slowly lift my head from the sand and squint.

'Come on Ewan get up,' says Helen, holding out her hand to me.

I feel no surprise at seeing Helen, but her skin looks paler than usual and devoid of any freckles. The sun has lightened her wavy red hair which seems to move, even though there is no breeze to stir it. Her long flowing white summer dress is covered in a pattern of red flowers and that also seems to move. As I look up at her from my position on the ground she appears much taller than usual, even without any shoes. Her toenails are painted bright red and the glint of a silver toe ring dazzles me, but her bare feet seem unaffected by the heat of the sand as it fills the gaps between her toes. Mercifully her body blocks the sun and casts some welcome shade to where I'm lying.

'Take my hand,' she urges me, with one arm outstretched and her hand open.

Weakly I reach out to her and she grips my hand tightly and starts to pull me up. With her help I force myself onto my feet, drawing energy from her strength but losing the shade that her body was affording me. The moment in the shade seems to have recharged a tiny bit of my strength but losing it reminds me of the sun's relentless intensity. The sand feels hotter than ever on the soles of my feet and I wonder where my shoes have gone. Helen releases my hand and I march weakly on the spot for a few moments but my efforts are futile as every footstep is equally as hot, not to mention exhausting.

'That way Ewan,' Helen says, placing her hand in the small of my back and nudging me forwards.

My shirt is flapping open and no longer over my head as I slowly stumble forwards one painful step at a time. Now and again I fall to my knees but the thought of her behind me willing me to continue, inspires me to keep moving. Pushing myself into repeating one determined step after another is all that I can think of right now. Somewhere there has to be shelter.

'We must keep going,' I croak as loudly as my throat allows but without wasting any energy turning around.

Slowly I plod forwards through the unchanging relentless landscape of dunes, avoiding the steepest climbs wherever I can. I try and keep my back to the sun to protect my eyes but it's so high up in the sky that I quickly lose what little sense of direction I had. My only hope is to stumble determinedly onwards in what I think is a constant direction until I find some shade.

After what seems like hours I slide down a small sand dune and come to rest at the bottom without falling over for once. A narrow branch protrudes from the ground with a few flat brown leaves on it, the remnants of some desert plant struggling to survive in the arid landscape just like me. My fingers touch the branch and it feels smooth so I give it a pull but it's firmly rooted into the ground.

I turn to see if Helen has noticed it too but my heart sinks as I realise that she has vanished. Suddenly alone, I squint back the way we came for any sign of her but all I see is the endless sand. Calling her name seems to use what little energy I have left and my voice is swallowed up in the vast desert. But then I realise there is only a single ragged trail of footsteps from the direction we came. I must have lost her some time ago. My beautiful wife, we should have stayed together.

The sand around my feet seems to be moving unless my eyes or mind are deceiving me. There seems to be sand everywhere and even the very air around me seems to be turning to sand. Something in my mind convinces me that I can no longer stand and I sink to my knees again as the debilitating pounding in my head returns, although it probably never even left. As I close my eyes in response to the pain, my face feels on fire and my back is now burnt from when a bare patch of skin was exposed when the shirt was over my head. My hands are the only part of me that's unaffected by the heat.

A desert wind begins stirring up the sand around me, whipping it up into an orange misty cloud. My button-less shirt begins to flap in the gust and I'm forced to keep my eyes closed against the growing pace of the wind. Instinctively I turn my back towards the wind but now it seems to be coming at me from every direction and blasting me with a cloud of fine sand particles. I call out urgently for Helen to take cover, forgetting for a moment that she is missing. As I call out her name, sand enters my mouth and chokes me. Gasping for breath I try to spit out the grainy dust from my mouth, rubbing my leathery tongue with the back of my hand. The air around me has now become a cloud of sand and its intensity makes me drop to my knees to reduce my size.

Visibility is practically zero now as I pull my shirt up and around my head to protect my face, mouth and nose from the whirling sand. The sound becomes deafening in my ears after the eerie silence of the desert, but thankfully the sun seems to be obstructed. I lie down in the sand with my shirt around my head, hoping that Helen has the sense to use her dress for cover against the tempestuous onslaught of the sudden sandstorm.

When the storm finally abates I discover that I'm semi buried by sand. My legs appear from under a covering of sand as I roll onto my side but unfortunately the sun has returned. It now seems to blast down with a greater and renewed effort as if it were making up for its temporary absence. I call out Helen's name again but there is no response and even my own footprints have been wiped clean from the desert surface. Any hope of retracing my steps to find her swiftly disappears and I have lost all sense of direction.

I try to regain my footing but although my legs find the strength, I don't have the balance. As soon as I stand up I keel over backwards and land flat on my back in the soft sand. My head spins in a wave of dizziness as I weakly hold my hands up in front of my face. The enormous sun looms in front of my eyes like a huge white hot ball and it seems to be falling from the sky towards me. As it approaches, it swirls around in a big circle and seems to get even brighter. It's going to crash right into the earth and crush and burn me but I don't have the energy to scream. There is no hope so I just close my eyes and wait for the fire to sear me out of existence.

Someone starts pulling at my hand and shouting. 'Wake up! Wake up!' shouts the voice urgently.

I open my eyes and feel as if I'm drunk and almost blind. Jenny kneels next to me and tugs desperately at my hand. I try to smile but suddenly there are three of her, circling and swimming around me in front of my eyes and each of them is holding an umbrella. The shade they offer gives me blessed relief from the sun and I know immediately that Jenny is my saviour. Together we can find Helen and there will be one umbrella for each of us.

'Dad you have to get up and find shelter,' Jenny says.

The appearance of my daughter and her insistent encouragement gives me a newfound strength, but it's still only enough to get me onto my feet. She hands me an open umbrella and I close my fingers around the handle. Although the shade is a welcome relief, the umbrella has no impact on the desert heat but it does give me a psychological boost that feels priceless. I hold Jenny's hand tightly, determined not to lose her like I'd lost Helen.

Slowly I take one initial unstable step and then begin to stumble forwards, using Jenny's presence to spur me on. This time I don't think about direction, I just follow the easiest path, changing direction only to avoid the slightest hill or incline in the desert surface. There is nothing but burning yellow sand as far as the eye can see but I have long since stopped scanning for shelter. I resort to staring straight down at my feet which gives me something real to focus on.

Holding the umbrella aloft in one hand and squeezing Jenny's hand with the other makes it easier to retain my balance. The shade makes my dizziness seem more manageable despite the throbbing pain in my head. I would commit murder for a thimble full of water now. How can Jenny cope so well with the heat? Maybe it is her age but I only wish I had her strength. I can't stop wondering why she is here with me but then I'm unclear on why I'm even here.

'Where's Mum?' I ask her.

Jenny stops walking and smiles at me. I lower the umbrella for a moment to rest my arm and she begins to laugh, quietly at first, but then a raucous laughter that seems bizarrely out of place and so out of character.

'What's funny?' I croak.

But she doesn't seem to hear me and offers no response. My head suddenly spins wildly in a wave of dizziness and I almost black out which causes the umbrella to slip from my grasp. As Jenny's laughter continues I drop to one knee and my forehead burns with a sudden feverous heat. Dizziness completely envelops my mind and my throat seems to close up before I faint head first into the sand.

This time it's Eric who wakes me up, the newsstand vendor shaking me awake with both of his hands on my shoulders.

'About time you bloody woke up,' he says, 'you won't get a job if you keep falling asleep. Anyway, I've got your National Geographic.'

My throat feels so dry that I can barely move my mouth to reply and it feels as if my whole body has shrivelled up into a dry piece of leather. I manage to rise to my knees as Eric hands me the magazine. The cover reads 'ANIMALS INHERIT MIXED LEGACY AT CHERNOBYL.'

Dazed and confused, I open the magazine with my weakened trembling fingers and thumb through the pages. The pictures are blurred and the words are meaningless, almost as if they are printed in a foreign language. Lifting the magazine up, I place it half open on top of my head as a shade. It has no effect on my temperature and is painfully inadequate in comparison to the umbrella that I once had. Where is Jenny now and what was she laughing about? The realisation of losing her in the desert panics me but my fear turns into a faint escape of anger as I throw the magazine at Eric. But he is no longer there and the magazine flutters down harmlessly into the sand.

'I love you Ewan,' says a woman's voice.

I turn around on my knees and see Tina standing before me in an identical blue bikini to one that Helen owns. She doesn't have any shade to offer me and her words seem strange and alien, but she offers me her hand. While I'm kneeling, her hand is out of reach but I don't have the will to try and stand up, however good she looks.

Desperately I stretch out my arm but she doesn't move forward to take my hand. It would be much easier for her to come to me so why doesn't she just come closer? I shield my eyes against the sun and look down at the sand for a moment, breathing the arid hot air which seems to prevent my lungs from functioning at full capacity. I try desperately to control my breathing but realise that there are now two Tina's, both wearing the same colour bikini. I blink in disbelief but after a closer look I realise that one of them is Helen and that I've finally found her again. Or rather Tina has found her for me.

'I love you Ewan,' Helen says, repeating Tina's words exactly and in the same tone.

Tina turns towards Helen and they shake hands as if making a business deal, but all I can think about is my desperate need for water. Both women smile as I begin to crawl slowly towards them, desperate for their help. I'm not sure how long I'm crawling for but I must have covered ten times the distance required to reach them. When

I can crawl no further I glance up, but they have both disappeared. Despairingly, I lay face down in the sand and prepare myself for death.

Nobody else comes to see me or to offer any help as I lay there hoping for death and eager to embrace the mercy it will bring. I just want this burning, searing, dehydrating torture to be over. I realise that I no longer care if I die, because all that matters to me is that the suffering will finally be over.

The desert is too great an enemy and I have nothing more in reserve to face the challenge with. I'm sure that Helen and Eric will both be fine. Tina will help Jenny get out of here and someone will pick up my National Geographic. My suffering will soon end and it's a relief to know that death is bringing its merciful comfort.

I find myself in semi darkness when I wake up again, but this time I'm roused by a tiny splash of something on my face. My eyes flicker open painfully as if my sore eyelids have been burnt. Another tiny splash hits my face and the tepid water is completely unexpected but I immediately recognise its priceless life giving potential. My hands instinctively reach up and touch my face but the water has already run off my dry burnt skin.

I'm sick of the desert and I imagine that even my tongue has turned into sand. I can barely see through my stinging eyes now, as my thumping headache resumes but I refuse to allow the pain to defeat me. I force myself to sit up in the darkness which is a painful task as my hands and feet are blistered. At least the sun has finally ended its relentless cooking of the desert and the sand feels preciously cool now to my touch.

As I blink my eyes a few times and fully comprehend the strange absence of light, I see a shadowy figure standing over me. He is holding something in his hand, it's a water bottle! I feebly stretch out my arm in desperation, my throat burning as my fingers desperately seek the precious life giving liquid. Despite my urgent need, I don't have the strength to hold out my arm for long and I'm forced to lower it. I'm too weak to stand up or do anything, but somehow I'm still alive.

'Dear oh dear,' says the figure, 'We do get into some scrapes don't we?'

His words don't really register as I sit in silence, running my fingers through the cool sand around me. The grains are no longer scorching hot but my fingers are sore as I caress the loose sand. My shoulders are itching and my head feels like its glowing and radiating the sun's heat back out into the desert night.

'This is the worst state I've ever seen you in Ewan,' the man says.

I lift my head slightly and blink a few times.

'Water,' I manage to croak.

He hands me the bottle and I slowly raise it to my lips but it's almost empty. No more than a couple of drops fall uselessly but tauntingly onto my tongue and seem to be immediately seared away before I can swallow them. My fingers relax their feeble grip on the bottle and it falls to the ground and lands in the sand while my hand remains where it is near my mouth.

'Sorry Old Man,' says the figure. 'That was the last of it I'm afraid.'

'Who are you?' I murmur faintly.

'I'm just a man,' he replies, 'a man not unlike you in fact. You know I read something once that might interest you. This Roman philosopher called Seneca once said '*It is uncertain where death may await thee, therefore expect it everywhere.*'

The man's words vaguely sink into my mind but I close my eyes, lacking the mental acumen to fully process thought, let alone engage in conversation. He continues in spite of my failure to respond although it's closer to a lecture than a conversation anyway.

'Kind of prophetic words those, wouldn't you say?' he asks, 'and uniquely accurate to our situation. You see I guess what I'm saying is that we have a lot of history you and me. Granted I said some things I shouldn't have, you smothered me with a pillow and tried to throw me off a ship... We could go on right?'

For some reason I nod, merely recognising that his words sound like some kind of question.

'But we have to get past all that,' he continues. 'Let bygones be bygones I say. How about we just forget all this everyman for himself routine? I've been watching you I admit it, and following you. The truth is that I'm intrigued. You know your life is actually quite interesting Ewan.'

The man pauses for a moment and laughs as my head sags down and my eyes focus on the empty bottle. Absentmindedly I check it again to make sure it's definitely empty. It is.

When the man stops laughing, he continues. 'I'm not sure why you dragged me all the way to Chernobyl and then jumped off a roof though,' he says in a bemused tone. 'Hell I don't even know whether you fucked Tina or not, but I know that I would have done if I'd had the opportunity. But the important thing is that we can help each other out. A mutually beneficial relationship I think they call that. Do you see?'

And suddenly some of his words begin to register in my tormented delirious mind. Virgil, that's who he is, my sick, evil stalker with his taunts, threats and misdirection. I know him and I fear him, but above all I hate him and must destroy him.

'Where... is... Helen?' I demand, forcing out one word at a time from my dry throat.

'Ewan Old Man,' he says, 'she won't be here, not in the Sahara Desert. Do you really think she's that stupid? If you saw her here then she must have been a hallucination, a mirage. It's handy that you bring her up though, because like I said, I know I said some things and maybe even made some threats, but they were empty ones. That's not really me. I wouldn't do anything to hurt your family or even you for that matter. At least I won't now that you understand.'

I can't begin to ascertain if his words make sense, or even hope to understand what they mean. The core of my being just wants to end this intense suffering, but there is no way to end my long slow decline towards dehydration and death.

'I'm your friend,' Virgil continues, 'and the only person who understands you. And understands your situation, which makes me solid gold right? I'm worth infinitely more to you than what was in that bottle. You need me.'

'I... need... water,' I gasp as my brain begins to fail.

'I could do with a drop myself,' he says, laughing. 'I admit it would be quite refreshing about now, what with all this talking I'm doing but I actually think we would just be delaying the inevitable. You are way too far gone for water and we both know it. I just want you to remember these words when we meet again tomorrow. Stick with me Ewan! You might even trust me eventually. Damn it, you might even fucking like me one day if you keep an open mind.'

'No,' I murmur faintly.

'Let's close the door on all the unpleasantness,' he says, 'Leave it all behind us in the desert. All you have to do is hurry up and die, and then we can be friends and get on with our lives alright?'

'Lives?' I croak, repeating the strange word.

My brain is too fried to process the concept. I haven't thought of my life for a long time. I haven't thought of much. What have I been thinking about?

'You just remember this,' says Virgil, his voice echoing in my ears. 'You've splintered away from the real world and left on a tangent from reality. Nothing is as it seems and rules do not apply, consequences do not apply. Nothing applies except what you and I say. That's the only rule you need to remember in what you call the dead loop.'

I have no idea if Virgil continued talking any longer. Finally and mercifully I black out from the effects of dehydration and presumably this time, I will die.

15
The Apprentice

The car steering wheel jerks slightly in my hands as my eyes blink open and register the country lane in front of me through the windscreen. My attention switches instantly to driving and I hastily depress the brake pedal to slow the car down. The sudden responsibility of awakening in control of a moving vehicle has made my heart beat rapidly, but within a few seconds I'm back in control. I begin accelerating again as my pulse begins to slow down.

Out of the corner of my eye, I see Helen nod. 'Yeah I've had déjà vu before,' she says, 'I think everyone has at some point or other.'

Her answer seems familiar, tickling at the recesses of my memory almost like déjà vu itself, although this feels like something slightly different.

'I've had déjà vu before,' she continues, 'like that time we were horse riding in Greece. Remember that?'

I did remember. Helen was convinced that we had done the whole thing before, but it wasn't very likely as neither of us especially liked horses and that was our only trip to Greece. We had only booked the excursion on the spur of the moment because it sounded like a romantic thing to do while we were on holiday.

'Yeah I remember. You were so bloody convinced!' I say, scratching my head and trying to concentrate.

I feel like I'm halfway through a conversation that I've had once with her before. So maybe that's why we're talking about déjà vu. But getting feelings of déjà vu about talking about déjà vu is an oddly disconcerting and confusing feeling.

I glance over at Helen and her appearance gives me an odd sense of relief as if somehow I expected to find something wrong. She looks so beautiful that I feel an urge to reach out and touch her hair and to make sure she's real. But such a thought is bizarre – of course she's bloody real.

As I guide the car onwards down the country lane my thoughts seem strange and my memory is fractured. Everything in my head seems to be a jumble of confusing information, all bundled together without any focus or clarity.

'Well we've definitely been here before,' I say. 'And I'm sure we've had this conversation before, but maybe it was in another life.'

Helen pulls down the visor on the windscreen and looks at her reflection in the little vanity mirror. She reaches for something in her handbag and then begins touching up her lipstick as if my words haven't registered at all.

'That's pretty messed up,' she says finally.

'I mean it Helen,' I stress to her, but not very convincingly. I'm not even sure I can convince myself of what I am saying.

'Oh well,' she says, returning the lipstick to her bag and closing the visor. 'Well that's definitely déjà vu then.'

Driving fast on country lanes in the sun is a liberating experience but as I accelerate out of a bend, a tractor lurches into the road ahead. The red monstrosity suddenly appears from behind the hedge of a field and lumbers straight into the middle of the road. Helen screams out a desperate warning as I slam my foot down hard on the brake, but the agricultural road block is too close. The piercing blast of the car horn which I don't even remember pressing, joins the sound of Helen's scream in my ears. The car skews to a screeching halt as the brake lights of the tractor light up like two demonic red eyes in the windscreen.

'Fucking idiot,' I scream, banging my fist angrily on the dashboard, but the tractor is already reversing back jerkily into the field.

'Jesus!' shouts Helen, gesturing at the driver as his face comes into view. The rather embarrassed farmer raises his hand by way of an apology as my heart pounds fiercely in my chest.

'That was bloody close,' I gasp with relief, as I slowly regain my composure and remove my foot from the brake pedal. I release my hands from their white knuckle grip of the steering wheel and notice my fingers trembling from shock.

'Are you alright?' Helen asks.

'Just about Helen,' I reply, puffing out my cheeks, 'I'm just about good.'

When I'm certain the tractor is off the road, I turn the key in the ignition to restart the stalled engine and slowly pull away from where the car has stopped.

It's mid-afternoon before we arrive back in the apartment and I'm sitting on the sofa enjoying a cup of coffee. Helen had a quick shower while I sorted out the kitchen and made the drinks. Jenny is out with friends so we have the place to ourselves, something which happens a lot more often these days. Helen is ironing some clothes, a job we take in turns because we both hate it passionately. The near miss with the tractor is still in my mind and something keeps telling me that we should've had no chance of stopping in time. I force myself to concede that it must have just been our lucky day, pure blind luck, that's all.

Suddenly my phone beeps and vibrates in my pocket with the notification of a text message. I take it out and open the message but it's from an unknown number. *Ewan meet me at 15:00 in the Weary Monk. It's really important. Tina.*

Tina? The only Tina I can think of is the woman I used to work with at D.G.E.C but what could she possibly want? I haven't spoken to her for months, not since I resigned and was put on garden leave. She never was too happy about my departure and breaking up our partnership but why contact me now? I begin to type a reply. *'Hello stranger. What's this about?'*

Helen glances over from her ironing and gives me a look that suggests she wishes it was my turn this week. 'Who is texting you then?' she asks, putting the iron down for a moment to take a sip of her coffee.

'Just someone I used to work with,' I reply. There's no point telling her it was Tina until I know what she wants. 'Helen, why don't you leave the ironing,' I suggest.

'Because it needs doing,' she replies, 'and it won't do its bloody self.'

'Tell you what,' I reply, with a secretive grin, 'if you leave it now, I promise to do it all tomorrow.'

'Yeah right,' she replies with a sceptical tone, 'now I'm half way through you mean. And then it'll still be my turn next week I suppose?'

'No, it'll still be my turn,' I tell her, 'even after I finish all the rest for you tomorrow.'

Helen pauses with her drink for a moment and gives me a quizzical look, trying to work out what's in this deal for me or what I could possibly be after. It would be worth her stopping if it helps me persuade her to get intimate while we have the place to ourselves. Maybe she reads my mind correctly because she doesn't take the bait and carries on ironing. I didn't really expect that to work, she is too perceptive.

I lean back in the sofa and switch the television over to a different music channel. The 'Black Eyed Peas' seem to be on all the time, so I search for an alternative but Helen stops me as soon as I switch on to a Bryan Adams video.

'Leave this one on,' she instructs me, still somehow controlling the television even without the remote control in her hand. I sigh as I toss the remote onto the coffee table and close my eyes.

Slowly I rotate and massage my neck where it feels a little stiff from our severe braking to avoid the tractor. I suggested to Helen that we make a report in case of whiplash later but she insisted it would be a waste of time. My shoulder also hurts a little from where the seatbelt jerked into it. *'Summer of 69'* blares out from the television and I open my eyes to see Helen with the remote in her hand, turning the volume up. She starts to sing along as she resumes ironing and my phone beeps again.

'It's life or death,' the text message reads. *'Just come please. Can you be there at 3?'*

I form a picture of Tina in my mind. She always had a powerful feminine charisma about her and a strong sexual appeal, but above all we had a good working chemistry. It was very disappointing to end our working relationship but I couldn't stay at D.G.E.C any more with their unrealistic expectations and empty promises. It would definitely be good to see her again and if she needs something then I owe her enough to at least hear her out. She was a good work friend even if that's not what my preferred relationship with her might have been in another life. And I kind of miss her in my own way.

Life or death, what does she mean by that? My own near death experience earlier makes me think that if something is that important then there's no question that I should meet her. I watch Helen who is still singing along to the last few lines of Bryan Adams. 'Helen they want me to meet them at 3 o'clock for a drink,' I say. 'Is that alright?'

Helen doesn't look up from the television and stands there with the iron motionless in her hand, steam rising from it.

'Yeah okay,' she replies. 'But don't forget we're ordering Chinese at seven though.'

After agreeing with her schedule and then finishing my coffee, I decide to get changed and freshen up a bit. As I haven't seen Tina for ages, a little effort and maybe a splash of aftershave would be the least I could do. Besides, she is the kind of woman that most people would instinctively make some effort for. I send a brief text confirming that I'll be there and then brush my teeth.

The bar of the Weary Monk is fairly quiet this afternoon so I choose an empty table by the window and sit down. I take a long sip from my pint of their special 'Weary Monk' ale which I've never tried before. Real ale isn't my favourite tipple and this particular brew tastes strong and fruity but it seemed rude not to accept the barman's suggestion to try their speciality. It's well past 3 o'clock and there is still no sign of Tina. I wonder why she suggested meeting in a pub that is in walking distance of my apartment and decide it can only be to ensure that I would come. She must be travelling half way across London to meet me so perhaps that's the reason she's late. Being married to Helen has made me used to waiting for women to arrive, although I probably have a lot more faults than her.

I look down at my watch and then take another deep gulp of the ale, finally conceding that my second pint will have to be something else. The street outside is very quiet this afternoon with only the occasional bus or taxi driving past. The red London bus reminds me of the tractor that pulled out in front of me earlier and I involuntarily shudder as I remember it.

Suddenly someone pulls up a chair and sits down opposite me, standing a pint of ale in front of him on the table. The man has blonde hair, a square jaw and is maybe thirty. As he smiles to reveal his shiny white teeth, his face tickles at my memory but I can't immediately place him. His smile disappears and he gestures to my pint of ale. 'I bet you really needed that drink after the desert,' he says.

The statement brings memories crashing back like waves onto a beach, each one washing away a layer of confusion and clarifying my thoughts. I know his name is Virgil. For some reason I remember a terrible thirst and Helen jumping from a plane. An image of the Chernobyl Sarcophagus flashes across my mind before the painfully emotive recollection of Jenny pushing me off a roof. I blink my eyes and shake my head but the waves of memory continue to flood my mind. Rapidly the memories of dying reform and organise themselves into a neat structure in my mind. They leave behind one overriding thought, one focus of clarity as I realise the situation that I am in – I'm dying every day.

'Welcome back Old Man,' Virgil says, taking a long sip of his own pint of Weary Monk.

'Hello Virgil,' I reply coldly, barely resisting a shocking urge to drive my glass into his face. An image of the potential damage that a glass could do to someone's face comes into my mind. Although my anger at him is sufficient to go through with it, it's a level of violence that is beyond my capability. The best I can do is to squeeze my glass as hard as I can and try to relax as I feel compelled to restrain myself.

'Calm down Old Man,' he says, perhaps sensing my anger, 'we're just two old friends having a quiet drink together.'

'What are you doing here?' I demand. 'Where are your threats and needles and empty water bottles?'

'Why were you expecting someone else?' he asks, leaning forward and sniffing. 'Nice aftershave Ewan, was it Tina you were expecting maybe?'

I lean backwards, eluding his proximity and consider just getting out of my chair and walking away from him, but I sense that he is somehow the key to my situation. Just maybe I need him.

'The text was from you,' I mumble in realisation. 'Wasn't it?'

'Afraid so Old Man,' he replies smugly. 'Don't feel too bad though, part of it was true. It is life or death after all isn't it? Have you thought about what I said in the desert?'

His words begin to reform in my memory but I have to make a concerted effort to extract them out and filter them from the memories of dying of thirst. *I'm your friend. You might even trust me eventually. You've splintered away from the real world. Consequences do not apply.*

'You said a lot of things,' I reply, 'but none of them made much sense.'

'Why don't you take a leap of faith?' Virgil suggests.

It's one of the rare occasions that I remember him using my name without also adding '*Old Man*' and somehow it helps dilute my feelings of anger towards him into something close to cynicism.

'A leap of faith from you?' I scoff. 'You couldn't even be honest to get me here. You had to impersonate a woman.'

Virgil holds up his hands. 'I'm sorry about that,' he says, 'I have to admit that you've got me on that one. But I didn't think you would appreciate me just knocking on your apartment door. Last time I did something like that you threw me off a cruise ship, remember? Besides I had to make sure you would come and I was certain you would for Tina. And it looks like I was right.'

'It was you that threw *me* off that ship,' I remind him. 'Anyway, what the hell do you want with me? What's so important that its life and death?'

'Everything is life and death Ewan,' he replies. 'Haven't you realised that yet? Didn't you listen to anything I told you in the desert? Take a leap of faith, come with me and let me show you something.'

I finish my pint in one long gulp and stare at Virgil who isn't smiling any more. His face bears a mask of seriousness and he almost looks a little desperate. Maybe I can learn something about my situation from him after all.

'Alright,' I say, nodding in agreement. 'Enlighten me.'

The taxi drops Virgil and me at Hyde Park corner where the trees look glorious with their golden autumn colour. He pays the driver with a fifty pound note and tells him to keep the change. The driver can't quite believe the huge tip as Virgil strides nonplussed into the park and beckons me to follow him. I hesitate for a moment but decide that having come this far, I may as well proceed. What could he possibly want to show me here? Is he really a friend as he claims or just a scheming psychopathic lunatic and a danger to everyone around him? I'm not sure I can trust a single word he says but that must surely give me an advantage over him. Thus far his deceptions have run so deep and his stalking of me has felt so intense that he can't possibly fool me again. Deception was his power but now he has confessed to being aware of my situation I have to consider the possibility that he might actually be the cause of it.

'Hyde Park,' I say, striding to catch up with him. 'It's very pretty, so what?'

'Be a little patient,' he replies. 'I want you to meet someone. Just bear with me.'

Virgil leads me silently through the historic park until we arrive at the Diana Princess of Wales Memorial Playground and the huge wooden pirate ship surrounded by trees. The sun is beginning to sink a little towards the horizon and it occurs to me that I might not make it back for Chinese take away in time. But will I even be alive at 7 o'clock?

The pirate ship is bigger than I expect, having never really seen it up close. Dozens of children are playing on it, climbing on its decks and jumping off into the sand. Others chase each other around it while their parents look on or chat idly amongst themselves. The park is noisy, colourful and alive with motion.

'I see the life part,' I say quietly, 'but what about death?'

Virgil laughs. 'Not so morbid, Old Man,' he says. 'Follow me and I'll introduce you.'

Virgil leads me over to a few wooden benches and he calls out as he approaches. A beautiful sun-kissed Mediterranean looking woman with dark hair and olive skin gets up from a bench and embraces him. After they finish hugging, Virgil leans over her pram and reaches in and touches whoever is inside. I move closer and Virgil stands upright up and grins, pulling the woman towards him by the hand.

'Ewan,' he says, 'I'd like you to meet my wife Adriana.'

She smiles and extends her hand, so I shake it while feeling slightly dumbfounded. Her hand is warm and she smells of flowers.

'Hello Ewan, it's nice to meet you,' she replies with a pretty smile.

Her English is perfect but her accent is exotically Spanish.

'Hi,' I murmur, a little confused as I glance at Virgil who seems less sinister than usual.

'Oh!' he says suddenly, pushing the pram closer to me, 'And these are our two perfect little boys, Joshua and Marco.'

I look into the pram at the two babies, maybe six months old and with the same olive coloured skin as Adriana. They're both sound asleep and tucked under a single pale blue blanket which rises up slightly as they breathe.

'They're identical twins,' says Adriana, proudly stroking one of the babies' dark hair. 'This one is Marco.'

'They're beautiful,' I concede, even allowing myself to smile. 'Congratulations.'

'So how do you two know each other?' she asks us.

I start to say that we work together but Virgil interrupts me. 'Oh, we go way back,' he says. 'We're old friends and Ewan and I have a lot in common.'

He puts an arm around Adriana's shoulder and smiles at me. The four of them make a perfect little family but it doesn't fit with what I know of him.

'Are you married Ewan?' asks Adriana.

'Yes,' I reply. 'We have a daughter, she's just turned eighteen.'

I think of Jenny when she was still a baby in a pushchair and recall taking her to a park in Watford. It was a happy memory even though it wasn't anything quite like the impressive Hyde Park. She had a wonderful childhood though.

'Maybe we could all meet up some time?' Adriana suggests, glancing at Virgil.

'Perhaps,' says Virgil, 'but right now Ewan and me are going to have a quick drink. I'll be back home later, okay?'

'Alright,' she agrees, standing on tip toes and kissing him.

'Well it was nice to meet you Ewan,' she says.

Virgil leans into the pram and kisses the two baby boys on the forehead, one at a time. 'Ready for that drink?' he asks me.

The Starbucks coffee mug is enormous and although the place is busy we find an empty table with two chairs in the back of the shop. I had switched my phone off as soon as we left Hyde Park because Helen sent me a text message to remind me about dinner, and would probably ring soon as I haven't replied.

'I'm surprised to see you're married Virgil,' I say, sipping my coffee. 'She seems... lovely.'

'I appreciate that,' he replies staring distantly and almost sombrely into his caramel macchiato. 'Adriana and the boys are the best thing that's happened in my life.'

The concept of Virgil in a loving family situation contradicts my venomous thoughts of him but I do share and understand the depth of love one has for your own children. I'm forced to empathise, even though I think I hate him. Empathy is a powerful feeling and I don't try and fight it.

'But why did you want me to meet them?' I ask. 'You and I didn't exactly part under the best of circumstances.'

'To help you understand that we're alike,' he replies, his sombre mood seeming to improve. 'We're both married. We both have kids. And now you see that we've got some common ground. I'm not the person you think I am Ewan.'

I frown in thought, remembering his actions on our previous encounters. 'But some of the things you've done...' I say sceptically, my voice trailing off.

Virgil shrugs indifferently like a teenager who feels unaccountable for their behaviour, exactly like Jenny used to when she was about fourteen.

'Don't you see that I had to?' asks Virgil. 'I had to destroy your opinion of me so I could start again from the lowest foundation. It was the only way to make you understand and to gain your trust.'

'But I don't understand anything,' I point out. 'And I don't trust a fucking word you say.'

Virgil puts down his mug and stares right at me, a guarded look in his eyes as he lowers his voice to an audible whisper. 'Let me explain something to you,' he whispers. 'I'll be absolutely clear on this. I'm exactly like you, dying every day, stuck in random situations with no way out. I'm trapped. Do you see now? I'm in the *dead loop* too Ewan.'

His words are impossible for me to accept and I glance nervously around the room, but no one else has heard him. Everyone is too busy drinking coffee and talking about sport or the weather, just normal things. Could it really be that I'm no longer alone? After misleading and deceiving me all this time, is everything that Virgil tells me over a coffee now plausible?

I reach in my pocket and touch my mobile phone, comforted by its presence. Even though it's still switched off it remains my only immediate contact with my real life – with Helen.

'I know you believe me,' Virgil says assuredly.

'Maybe,' I reply, shrugging noncommittally, 'but why tell me? Are there others like us?'

The idea opens up curious possibilities in my mind.

Virgil taps the table with his fingers and begins speaking at a normal volume again. I think he realises that the coffee shop is actually too noisy for anyone to pay much attention to our conversation anyway.

'Not as far as I can tell,' he says. 'It's just you and me. I've been following you ever since I suspected we were alike – back in Pripyat after you fell.'

Following? That was his word for stalking. 'But why?' I ask.

'Our world is a lonely place Ewan,' he says. 'A place where no one understands us and no one can help. You've seen my family and know that I've lost as much as you. I do still see them sometimes but I've also accepted that they're gone. They're no longer a part of my life, just an occasional distraction.'

I picture his twins in my mind, beautiful, sleeping and innocent. 'A distraction?' I repeat the distasteful word.

'Look I've been doing this much longer than you,' Virgil continues. 'I must have died over a hundred times now, but you're the only person whose path I keep crossing. The only person who sees what I see and knows what I know.'

'But why aren't you always the same person?' I question him, picturing the many faces of Virgil I'd seen before he took this guise.

'Look I don't have all the answers,' he admits. 'But I know that by now you've probably been through an emotional meat grinder. You've felt angry, been terrified, sceptical and scared. I bet you even told Helen about it and tried to save the world. You have looked for someone to help you and tried to stop it from happening, but I've been there and done it Ewan. Nothing you do makes any difference.'

'If that's true then what do you do now?' I ask.

Virgil leans back in his chair, holds out his hands and smiles broadly. 'Anything I bloody want of course,' he replies. 'Tell me Ewan, do you know how to shoot?'

Wooden stairs creak as we descend them into the gloom, the filthy carpet crunching like grit beneath our shoes with every step. The musty basement of the boarded up London townhouse is large, dirty and faintly illuminated by a single light bulb. Boxes of junk litter the floor and piles of old newspapers are stacked against one of the un-plastered brick walls. There is an enormous broken cabinet in one corner and an empty wine rack covered in thick grey cobwebs, both looking unloved and forgotten.

'Is this is your place?' I ask Virgil sarcastically.

'Very funny,' he replies, shaking his head, 'No. It's just a place that's up for rent. And I just happen to know that they leave a spare key in that hanging basket.'

I dust off the top of a large wooden crate but immediately wish I hadn't. As I rub my now filthy hands on my trousers I wonder if I should've just sat straight down without trying to clean a space. This basement reminds me of the apartments in Pripyat – they were just like being underground.

'Why are we here?' I ask.

Virgil pulls out a broken drawer from a filthy teak cabinet and removes a shoe box from inside it. He flicks the lid onto the pile of empty newspapers and shows me the inside of the box. I see the unmistakeable shape of a firearm but I don't know what type it is. The handgun is all black, military looking and about the only clean thing down here.

'Beretta,' says Virgil, winking and picking up the weapon, 'here take it.'

He holds out the alien object to me by its barrel and I'm intrigued enough to cautiously close my hand around the grip. Keeping my finger well away from the trigger, I bring the handgun closer to my eyes to study it. It's far heavier than I anticipated and not as pristine as I first thought. The barrel is scratched and the gun looks well-travelled. I'm worried for a moment about having my fingerprints on it but I can't bring myself to put it down.

As I study the weapon, Virgil opens another drawer and removes a bundle made from what looks like a filthy old bar towel. He unfolds the towel on his lap and grins at me from the gloom.

'And this is mine,' he announces, proudly holding aloft a similar handgun only his has a brown grip, not black. He presses something near the bottom and a magazine slides out of the hand-grip into his palm. He inspects it before snapping it firmly back into place with a loud click.

'You ever fired a gun?' he asks me.

'Only an air pistol,' I reply.

'Same principle,' he replies, 'just a bit more deadly. Let me show you.'

'What for?' I ask, contemplating the relevance of receiving firearm arm advice. 'I'm not shooting anybody.'

'Haven't you been listening?' asks Virgil. 'It's just so you can load it and at least point. You don't need to fire it or worry about hitting the target. All we need to do is make sure you don't come across as a total fucking amateur.'

I point the gun towards the far wall, close one eye and squint down the barrel, lining up the two sights.

'That's the spirit,' says Virgil. 'I'm going to show you what I do in the dead loop. How you can have a great time and start living again, just like me. Being armed is an important part of that.'

I lower my weapon and watch him grinning in the gloom, holding his pistol across his collarbone like James Bond. He looks back at me and smiles. 'It's just like having an apprentice,' he says, winking.

For the next half an hour Virgil teaches me how to load the handgun by pushing the golden rounds of ammunition into the magazine. He demonstrates how to cock the weapon and use the safety. In fact he shows me how to do everything except pull the trigger. The weapon soon begins to feel comfortable in my hand and he warns me about how loud it would be if I pull the trigger. The lesson finishes with me taking aim at one of the backing singers of a forgotten pop group on a ripped poster stuck on the farthest wall.

'Ewan,' says Virgil quietly.

I turn around and am stunned to find him with one hand raised and his gun pointing at my face. Stepping back, I hold out my other hand in defence with my gun pointing at the floor.

'What are you doing?' I demand.

'Do you trust me?' he asks.

My eyes are focused on the small dark opening at the end of his gun barrel. 'What do you think?' I say, 'you have a fucking gun pointed at me.'

'Ewan, Ewan, you've learnt enough now,' he says. 'It's time to start taking control of your situation and enjoying yourself, experiencing life's potential.'

'What do you mean?' I ask. 'Lower your gun!'

Virgil shakes his head. 'When was the last time you chose the moment of your own death, rather than it choosing you?'

I slowly back further away towards the wall and instinctively raise my own weapon to point at him.

'Put it down!' I demand angrily.

'We've done everything we need to do today,' he replies. 'We might as well make this death quick, because life begins again tomorrow.'

'Stop!' I urge him.

'After the count of three I want you to shoot me in the head,' he says matter-of-factly.

'No way!' I yell.

'And I'll shoot you at exactly the same time,' he adds.

'You're fucking crazy,' I shout.

'One,' he says.

'Put it down,' I yell, gesturing at him with my gun. 'I fucking mean it!'

'Two,' he says. 'Trust me Ewan, just this once.'

I stare at him in the darkness and my eyes flick between his gun and his intense stare. My hands are shaking, the gun is wobbling in my grip but I feel the sliver of metal that is the trigger beneath my forefinger. Slowly I shake my head in disbelief but I see his mouth begin to move.

'Thr...' he says.

As soon as his mouth opens to complete the count, I shut my eyes tightly and squeeze the trigger.

16
The Heist

The car engine is running and I feel the vibration in my hands as they rest on the steering wheel. Dreary rain is falling between the buildings and the grey sky is visible through the windscreen. Our car is parked in a quiet street at the mouth of an alleyway strewn with cardboard boxes and litter. Badly worn wiper blades intermittently swish noisily at the rain.

'Good shot Old Man!' says Virgil triumphantly from the passenger seat, leaning over and clapping my left shoulder. 'I knew you had it in you!'

I turn to look at him in his black leather jacket with his smiling face and blonde hair all brushed back.

'You're a maniac,' I reply, shaking my head but that only turns Virgil's smile into laughter.

But for some strange reason his laughter is infectious and although I don't join in, I'm forced to smile at the bizarre realisation that we may have just killed each other.

'Wait here,' he tells me while opening the passenger door, 'and keep the engine running.'

Virgil steps out into the rain but leans back in through the open door. 'Don't worry,' he says, grinning. 'I've done this plenty of times before.'

He strides purposefully into the alley, rain assaulting him as he kicks an empty box up into the air. I move the gearstick from neutral into first but keep my foot on the clutch and gently rev the engine. The car's interior is old and shabby and there's no air conditioning but I turn the heat up and put the fan on maximum. The windows have misted up a little but the airflow is starting to clear them.

At the farthest end of the alley I see Virgil conversing with two figures in long coats and something changes hands between the two parties. The lights of a car appear in my rear view mirror dazzling me for a second but it manoeuvres around me and the driver glares at me as he passes. I switch on my hazard lights as the passenger door is suddenly yanked open and Virgil re-takes his seat. Water drips from his jacket as he fastens his seatbelt.

'Drive!' he says urgently, so I switch off the hazard lights but release the clutch somewhat abruptly. The car lurches forward and we pull out into the road, almost stalling the tired engine. Virgil removes a bundle of cloth from under his jacket and grins at me. 'Starbucks?' he suggests.

Virgil greedily sips his caramel macchiato, his blond hair seeming much darker when it's damp and still flattened by the rain. He brushes his fingers through his hair to restore some of its volume. Starbucks is very busy this morning with London shoppers who are probably keen to get out of the rain.

'I'll never get tired of this stuff,' Virgil says, gesturing to the coffee. 'You know I never set foot in this place before I died Ewan? But I reckoned that was probably a good time to start trying out new things.'

Trying new things after death doesn't seem so ludicrous anymore. Personally I never had much time for anything other than plain regular filter coffee. They could keep their frothy lattes, caramel, ice cream and all the other fancy bollocks.

'Want to try it?' asks Virgil, sliding his mug towards me on the table.

I shake my head and push it back towards him. 'Did you really shoot me?' I ask.

'You shot me,' he says accusingly. 'Kind of cool though, huh? I think you got me right in the face by the way. You must have done because I didn't feel a bloody thing.'

The memory of my finger on the trigger of the handgun forms vividly in my mind. I recall my hand snapping back with the powerful recoil and a deafening bang but nothing more.

'Did we actually kill each other?' I ask.

Virgil shrugs. 'That's one in the eye for your dead loop isn't it?' he says, laughing. 'We beat it to the fucking punch for once!'

'Did it hurt?' I ask him.

Virgil shakes his head and slurps his coffee, sighing at the weather outside. His reaction makes me realise that it wasn't just me that didn't feel a thing.

It's still raining hard and I wonder what Helen and Jenny are doing today. Does Virgil have the same thoughts about Adriana and his twin boys? I wonder why a family man like him would spend all of his time following me.

'Virgil, when I was in Greece,' I say, 'I fell off a horse and died, right?'

'That's nice,' he replies in an amused tone.

'But I didn't see you,' I tell him. 'I think that's the only time that I haven't. Where were you?'

Virgil laughs. 'I just fucking hate horses,' he reveals. 'I figured I would catch up with you later, but I was there alright.'

'So who were you?' I ask, 'were you one of the Greeks? Or were you cooking the barbeque that I never made it to?'

'It's really not important,' he says, but he glances away as if he wants to change the subject. That only heightens my curiosity.

'No, go on,' I urge him, with a slightly mocking tone, 'you weren't one of the horses were you? Oh my God, you weren't a girl were you? Not the one in the jodhpurs maybe? Not Kitty!'

Virgil looks at me and grins. 'Alright, since you insist on knowing,' he says. 'I wasn't her, no, but let's just say that while I might not like riding horses, the same doesn't go for travel reps! Once she got back from delivering your champagne she got the ride of her life in the stables.'

The thought of him with Kitty in the Greek sunset brings lewd thoughts into my mind and maybe even a tinge of jealousy. My response is unintentionally crude. 'You lucky bastard!' I reply, the fact that he is married slipping my mind completely.

Virgil shrugs but has a proud look on his face and I smile in amusement. 'How did we get to this Virgil?' I ask. 'How did we end up in this situation? This can't be real.'

Virgil runs both hands through his hair and rubs his wet fingers together. 'You know Ewan, I used to ask myself that a lot,' he says. 'I asked plenty of other people too, anyone that would listen to me as a matter of fact.'

'And what did you establish?' I ask him.

Virgil reaches behind him and grabs his jacket from the back of the chair, putting it on without bothering to stand up.

'Sweet fuck all,' he says. 'I found out sweet f-a. Now do you want to know what I really do? How I live every day and life to the full, in between deaths that is.'

I lift my mug and finish my coffee. 'Alright enlighten me,' I reply.

Maybe I'm actually beginning to like Virgil, perhaps recognising him as a guide and the only person who understands my situation. We seem to be almost like old comrades but I'm a long way from trusting him. At least I was until I met Adriana because she seems to make it easier somehow. It wasn't so long ago that I hated him, but now I'm close to believing his words.

Virgil takes the car keys out of his jacket pocket and tosses them across the table towards me. They slide the last few inches across the surface with a jangling scraping sound and I snatch them up before they fall off the table edge.

'You can drive again,' says Virgil.

The London street is soaking wet and puddles are forming everywhere. We have parked on a yellow line outside a small bank and a row of shops. I look out of the window at the passing people who stir up memories of a bus ride I'd taken once after an interview. The people without umbrellas duck under shop canopies wherever possible or scurry past as quickly as they can, dodging puddles on the way to their destination. Those with umbrellas move more leisurely as they try to avoid hitting people with them. Its late morning and the streets are already busy as the rain does little to deter these shoppers.

'So where are we?' I ask Virgil.

He simply points to the bank and smiles. 'Let's rob that fucker,' he says.

His words make me laugh. 'You what,' I reply, 'rob a bank?'

But Virgil isn't laughing. 'That's right,' he says seriously, opening the glove compartment and removing the bundle that he got from the men in the alleyway. He opens one end of the bundle and I see the unmistakeable sight of a gun barrel. Leaning over, I quickly flick the cloth back over to hide the weapon. 'You're crazy,' I tell him. 'I'm not robbing a bloody bank.'

'Why not?' Virgil replies as if bemused. 'You want to rob something else instead?'

'I don't want to fucking rob anything,' I tell him in disbelief. 'Besides I've got plenty of money in the bank. Who do you think we are Butch Cassidy and the bloody Sundance Kid?'

Virgil unclips his seatbelt and turns to face me. 'Think about it Ewan,' he says. 'Remember our situation? You're stuck in it and I'm stuck in it. I've been here a lot longer than you and I've tried all the shit you're thinking of. Imagine a life where you can do anything you like, everything you ever wanted to do or saw in the movies. There are no consequences here Ewan. You could shoot everyone in the bank and they would be right back there tomorrow, smiling and without a scratch. We deserve to make the most of it, who else has been through the shit we have? Nothing we do matters anymore and you haven't lived until you've robbed a bank! I've done things and lived more in the last few weeks than most people live in a lifetime. I've experienced shit that adrenaline junkies wouldn't even dream of.'

Virgil's passionate and enthusiastic speech is oddly convincing and strangely compelling after everything I've been through. When nothing truly makes sense, just maybe his crazy ideas could be right. I lift open the cloth in his lap and recognise the two handguns from yesterday. Mine feels natural in my hand and I automatically open the magazine and check that it's loaded, just like he showed me yesterday. I'm almost oblivious to anyone walking past in the street and feel a strange sense of excitement and a pang of anticipation in my stomach.

'That's what I'm talking about,' says Virgil, slapping his hand on the dashboard and picking up his own gun.

His enthusiasm is infectious and I slap the steering wheel and start to open the driver door.

'Hold on Superstar!' says Virgil, laughing. 'We need a fucking plan first!'

As I queue at the bank counter and watch the old lady in front of me with her shopping bags, I have a moment to reflect on how easily Virgil has talked me into this. I'm stunned to think that since our very first meeting and through all his stalking, he could have been building up to this moment when he would introduce me into his world. My heart is pumping hard in my chest and my hand feels clammy as it grips the gun beneath my jacket.

Virgil is idly flicking through the leaflets on a nearby stand. He looks at me, peering over a current account brochure and signals me with a tiny nod. The bulge of his hand under his jacket seems so obvious to me and I expect him to be challenged at any moment, although he looks perfectly calm.

The old lady shuffles forward as one of the three cashiers becomes available meaning I will be next. The clock reads 11:43 but the bank is still fairly quiet. This is an insane idea! After hearing a beep I look up to see a big red '3' flashing above one of the cashier's windows. I move forward to approach the counter and the youngish Indian cashier smiles and looks at me expectantly. I smile back at her and hear Virgil coughing somewhere to my left.

'How can I help you today Sir?' she asks.

I feel a bead of sweat trailing down my forehead and I resist the urge to scratch it as I shuffle nervously on the spot. I've never felt more uncomfortable in my life.

'Sir?' she asks.

'Erm...' I mumble, glancing down at my feet, 'I want to erm...'

'Yes?' she says.

Pulling out my wallet from my trouser pocket, I fumble for one of my cards. They aren't even from this bank. 'Check something on my accou...' I begin to say.

Suddenly I feel someone shove into me and I slide sideways along the counter knocking into the man next to me.

'Sorry,' I mumble out the apology, as I see Virgil take my place at the cashier window and everything explodes into chaos. Virgil's gun is in his hand pointed straight at the cashier through the narrow gap in the glass.

'Get out the cash!' he yells the demand at her.

One of the other cashier staff screams behind the counter and my gun is suddenly out from underneath my coat. I'm waving it at the man who I knocked into.

'Get down!' I yell, as loud as I can, mimicking Virgil's tone.

The man sits down and backs away towards a cash machine against the wall with his hands raised. I quickly turn through 360 degrees and wave my gun madly around the bank.

'Nobody move!' I yell, the adrenaline pulsing through me with the intensity of the situation.

The feeling is fiercely addictive, almost like a narcotic but terrifying at the same time. Three other customers who were inside the bank are now sitting against the wall and cowering with their hands over their heads. I catch sight of the old lady scuttling through the sliding doors, dropping her shopping bag and scattering tomatoes, onions and assorted fruit across the floor as she flees the bank. I wave my gun in her direction and then back at the people against the wall.

Virgil is screaming threats at the cashier and I toss him an empty plastic bag from under my coat.

'Nobody moves!' he yells. 'Get over here Ewan!'

I back into the counter and see a messy pile of bank notes that the amazingly calm cashier is hastily adding to from her cash drawer. The other two women behind the counter are cowering under their stools with their hands over their faces in a display of submission. The image of them horrifies and panics me at the same time but there is no turning back now.

Suddenly the piercing shrill sound of an alarm freezes me in my tracks for a moment, chilling my blood. My panic increases as I hurriedly help Virgil stuff bank notes into a second plastic bag. He merely sniggers at the look on my face.

'That's only the bloody fire alarm,' he yells over the noise.

Half of the bank notes still remain on the cashier's shelf when I grab Virgil's arm and try to haul him away. 'Let's go!' I shout.

We exit the bank together, using our hands to force the automatic doors to open more quickly as Virgil stumbles over one of the old lady's onions. I shove him towards the car which is still parked illegally by the kerb, keys still in the ignition and with the engine running. Half a dozen bystanders have stopped to stare at the bank with its fire alarm still screeching. I spot the old woman who had escaped the bank, further down the street with a couple of people supporting her. Another woman screams at the sight of us with our weapons drawn.

'Get in the car,' yells Virgil, heading for the driver's side.

I climb into the passenger seat and Virgil drives away immediately while my door is still open. It bangs into a road sign as Virgil accelerates and the door slams shut, knocking into my hand and making the gun slip from my fingers. The car careers off down the road with a screech of squealing tyres as adrenaline pumps through me. Virgil turns the car into a side street and blazes straight through a junction and onto a main road, leaving the bank far behind us.

'That was insane!' yells Virgil, punching the roof as he finally slows the car down to match the speed of the rest of the London traffic.

'You're insane,' I reply, gradually calming down and picking up the plastic bags from the foot well of the car. I rub my hand where the door knocked into it as I notice a few stray bank notes have fallen onto the floor by my feet.

'You don't realise how much more fun that was with two people,' Virgil says. 'Amazing!'

Pulling the bank notes from the bag and sorting them into a neat pile is made easier by the fact that many of them are brand new and still in neat bundles with a paper strip around them. It's a considerable sum of money but a meagre haul for the chaos and terror our raid no doubt caused. I put the thick wedge of bank notes into the glove compartment once I'm done sorting through them.

'I dropped my bloody gun when you hit that sign,' I inform Virgil.

He overtakes a stationary bus and glances over at me. 'Well that was a bit careless Old Man,' he replies. 'But don't worry, we'll be long gone and long dead before they start checking for your fingerprints.'

The full realisation of being a wanted armed robber suddenly hits me as the last of the adrenaline wears off. It's even more shocking than knowing that I'm going to die today.

'Pull over a minute,' I say.

Virgil indicates before pulling in between two parked cars and I open the door, vomiting uncontrollably onto the pavement. A few car horns sound behind us and I cough and splutter as I wipe my mouth on the back of my hand. Virgil quickly grabs my shoulder and pulls me back inside the car. Being sick has settled my stomach and I spot my gun wedged down the side of the seat as I close the door. Holding it up to Virgil, I give him a sour look. 'Looks like I didn't lose it after all,' I say.

'Well done Old Man,' he replies, 'because you might need it yet.'

Virgil guides the car back out into the traffic and accelerates to overtake another stationery bus. He turns on the car radio and begins to scan for a station. *'Moves like Jagger'* by Maroon 5 blasts out of the speakers and Virgil turns the volume up to full.

'Where are we going?' I shout.

'Where do you fucking think?' he shouts back over the music, 'Shopping!'

Virgil manoeuvres the car into an empty parking space of an indoor shopping malls multi story car park and switches off the engine. He rubs his neck wearily and relaxes for a moment in his seat.

'That was intense,' he says taking a deep breath. 'Do you fancy some lunch Ewan? I'm buying!'

Remembering vomiting on the pavement does nothing for my appetite. 'Not yet,' I reply, shaking my head.

'Well let's ditch the car here and get a coffee,' Virgil says. 'By the way, bring your gun.'

'What for?' I ask.

'They might catch up with us,' he replies. 'It might come in handy.'

We both get out of the car and I stuff the gun into my belt and cover it with my T-shirt. When I close the car door I realise that the dent in it is considerable and I'm glad it's not my car. Virgil leaves the car keys in the ignition and we walk towards the shopping centre entrance without even locking the doors.

We take the lift into the mall, our pockets stuffed with bank notes and head for a small open coffee area underneath one of the escalators on the ground floor. Every security guard makes me freeze in my tracks and Virgil pokes me in the ribs on each occasion and hisses at me to relax. I'm just not the experienced fugitive that he appears to be. My pockets are stuffed with stolen banknotes and I have a gun under my coat in a busy shopping centre. It's hard to relax.

I take a seat in the coffee area as Virgil fetches two cardboard cups steaming with tea.

'I hope you like Earl Grey,' he says, handing me one of the cups. 'I find bergamot very relaxing after a heist.'

The tea is black, steaming and probably close to boiling so I stand it on the table to cool down.

'How many times have you done this?' I ask.

Virgil shrugs. 'Four or five maybe,' he replies. 'There are much better things to do though, other ways to enjoy yourself besides committing robberies. I just wanted to demonstrate the principle.'

I try a sip of the scolding hot tea and although Earl Grey is a completely new taste to me, I find it delicious and relaxing. 'Principle?' I pose the question.

'Yeah I don't tend to do robberies these days,' Virgil continues, 'but to be fair, it's a whole new experience with a partner on board.'

'I imagine it is,' I reply, wondering how even more terrifying it must be to commit a bank robbery on your own.

Virgil pats his coat where we both know his gun is concealed.

'Do you know what this is?' he asks me. 'It's power. Think about how you feel with an instrument of death with you and how it stands you apart from all these shoppers in here. I always carry one these days, even if I'm not doing a robbery.'

'Have you ever shot anyone?' I ask.

'Yeah I shot you in the face, remember?' he replies with an amused tone to his voice.

'What about anyone else?' I press him further.

Virgil sips his tea. 'How many English people know what it's like to carry a gun around?' he asks, his eyes intense and staring, 'to know that you have that power available if you need it?'

I repeat my question. 'Have you shot anyone else Virgil?'

Virgil suddenly motions towards one of the entrances to the mall and motions furtively for me to look. There are two security guards in close communication with four police officers in black armoured uniforms, all carrying small machine guns. 'Shit they've found us Old Man,' he says rather calmly. 'Let's move.'

I freeze in panic as one of the security guards points in our direction. Virgil leaps from his chair, knocking the table over and spilling what's left of our tea. The officers react instantly, advancing towards us as Virgil hauls me away from the table and towards the nearest store while drawing his handgun from under his coat.

Behind us one of the police officers shouts something but his voice is drowned out by the noise of the mall and the screams of people in the sports shop that Virgil has dragged me into. Customers and staff alike scatter at the sight of Virgil's gun and he shoves me behind the sales counter where I fall onto the floor. He crouches beside me and glances up over the counter as I hastily scramble to my knees and do the same, ignoring my grazed knee.

The officers are still outside the shop, peering around the sides of the door, but not entering. One of them is actually crouching behind a child's fire engine ride which would be comical if I wasn't so terrified. The remaining customers and staff have already fled the shop and we're alone now, trapped behind the counter with at least four weapons trained in our direction. My heart feels like it's about to burst.

'That was fucking quick,' says Virgil, sounding genuinely surprised, 'didn't even give us a chance to finish our tea!'

'We need to give it up Virgil,' I tell him insistently. 'Better surrender before this gets out of hand.'

He looks at me with a wild look in his eyes, his face suddenly determined and unyielding. 'No fucking way,' he snaps, raising his gun and suddenly firing towards the police. I throw myself onto the floor and cover my ears as the deafening blast of the weapon right next to me batters my ear drums. Empty cartridges bounce on the floor around me and somewhere I hear glass shattering. Desperately I begin crawling towards the back of the shop as the police respond in kind to Virgil's gunfire.

The explosion of return fire is deafening and even more terrifying, tearing the shop around me to shreds. Virgil bellows in pain and I hear him crash into the counter and hit the floor. Somehow I'm on my feet, charging out of the back door of the shop and into a store room. I run down an aisle, knocking into shelving and sending tennis rackets clattering to the floor. But I don't stop; I just stumble over them, my heart thumping as I reach a fire exit. I slam down hard on the metal bar and quickly look behind me but there is no pursuit.

The door flies open and I fall into some kind of elevated service yard where the store must receive deliveries. Colliding with a wheelie bin, I slip and fall onto the slimy wet tarmac floor as the bin rolls away and bangs into a row of empty crates. It's raining hard as I hastily pick myself up and run along the service road. What the hell am I doing here? I can see the mall below me through the shopping centres glass walls. There are people running down there, obviously a result of the gunfire but they are scattering in all different directions as if confused as to where the danger is.

Both knees are now grazed from my fall and my jeans are soaking wet, but I run on to where a small van is parked in the yard of a shop further along the road. I try the handle and it opens but there doesn't seem to be any sign of the driver. I fumble at the ignition but there are no keys. Thumping the dashboard in frustration, I suddenly catch movement in the passenger side door mirror.

Two police officers in black armour and helmets emerge from the storeroom door and have short stubby machine guns in their hands. They are cautiously scanning the yard in both directions and I freeze in the driver seat, realising that the van door is still open and resting against my knee. It feels as if the door isn't quite motionless and I desperately try to control my breathing, convinced that they will spot the door moving. One of the officers seems to notice something about the van and crouches down behind a wheelie bin, making hand gestures to his colleague who also takes cover. The first officer shouts down the yard. 'Drop your weapon,' he barks. 'Step out of the vehicle with your hands on your head.'

Rain is drizzling down on the windscreen and I realise that leaving the vehicle now would surely be suicide after Virgil's unprovoked firing. I move my knee and pull the door closed, carefully watching both door mirrors. An officer is clearly visible in each mirror, one still crouching down and the other leaning against a wall, both with their weapons trained on the van.

Two more police officers emerge from the shop storeroom and take cover alongside their colleagues. They surely can't safely approach the van but I'm still trapped here. Suddenly a police SWAT van appears further down the yard and turns sideways to block the service road ahead. Its blue lights are flashing as five officers emerge from it and take cover outside the vehicle.

The gun begins to feels hot in my hand, my heart pumping as adrenaline boils through my system. I duck my head down under the dashboard, fearing being seen through the windscreen or maybe even shot without warning. As my head goes down I notice a small shelf under the glove compartment and there's a set of keys there! I reach under and grab them, testing the vehicle key in the van's ignition while still keeping my head as low as possible.

The key fits and I hear the heating fans purr into life inside the van. Switching the key to the off position, the fan dies and I place my gun on the passenger seat and peer over the dashboard. If I had more time I might stop to wonder how I ended up here but terror of this armed conflict is beginning to overtake me. The officers by the SWAT van have spread out now and two are lying prone on the wet service road. All five of them are aiming weapons in my direction. The blue flashing lights of the van pulse brightly against the grey sky, blurred by the rain on the windscreen.

Now I can only see two officers in the side mirrors, the other two are out of sight. I hear distant shouts from behind me, something like the original surrender request but it's muffled by the sound of the rain. It occurs to me that Virgil is probably dead but his last words echo in my mind as my heartbeat thumps in my ears. '*No fucking way.*'

The three SWAT officers who didn't go prone are walking slowly towards my van, one measured step at a time and evenly spaced out in some kind of tactical formation with weapons raised. Their identical uniforms and tinted helmets give no clue as to their individual personalities or identity and they could be almost anybody. I need to get out of here.

Turning the van key fully, I switch on the engine and sit up in the driver's seat. Changing into gear, I press my foot down on the accelerator and release the clutch. The sound of the engine is surprisingly comforting and a symbol of possible escape. For some reason I don't understand it feels wrong to allow myself to be apprehended but the road is too narrow to turn around in without reversing. Such a manoeuvre would take far too long, so going straight past the SWAT van is the only viable escape route.

At the sound of the engine the three officers stop walking and crouch down immediately, raising their weapons and taking aim. I put my foot down and accelerate into second gear down the service road straight towards them. The three officers hastily back away towards their SWAT van as I change into third gear and aim for the gap between the rear of their vehicle and the service road railings. I know it's too narrow but I can only rely on the van's momentum to punch its way through.

Seconds later my van collides hard with the back of the SWAT van and skews violently into the railings with a deafening crunch of grinding metal. The impact throws me brutally into the passenger seat as the van spins and I suddenly realise that I don't have a seatbelt on. I hear the engine die and the sound of glass shattering but I'm already climbing back into the driver's seat, opening the door and falling into the rainy service road. I see a blur of moving black uniforms and hear warning shouts but their voices all mix together and their words are unintelligible.

Their threat to me is very real and I raise my handgun as I scramble behind the crumpled front of my van and I pull the trigger. My shot flies harmlessly up into the rainy sky, merely a wildly futile and ineffective gesture. Immediately I hear the deafening explosion of return fire and feel multiple searing shards of pain erupting in my chest. The impact sends me sprawling backwards into the railings like a discarded crisp packet in the wind. I feel another piercing jolt of pain in my shoulder and neck as I fall into the railings and my gun flies out of my hand to clatter uselessly onto the road. The cacophony of gunfire is suddenly silent as I slump onto the damp tarmac.

17
Guilt

The noise of the alarm clock rudely wakes me up and I reach over and fumble for the snooze button, but find nothing. The noise is becoming annoying so I open my eyes to see where the clock is hiding. It's not on my side of the bed as normal and my bedside table looks antique and unfamiliar. Helen is already awake and switching off the alarm clock which appears to be on her side of the bed.

'Breakfast time,' she says, patting my shoulder and yawning.

My wife gets out of bed but I pull the blankets over my head and immerse myself in the comforting warmth and darkness. The sound of her footsteps padding softly away leaves me cocooned in a welcome and undisturbed silence.

'Get up!' she shouts encouragingly from somewhere distant, before I hear the sound of a shower coming to life.

The feeling of waking up with her is seductively relaxing and I roll onto my front and stretch my legs out towards the end of the bed. The blankets are heavy, constricting and safe but as I relax a flash of recollection crosses my memory. The antique bedside table is from the bedroom of a French chateau in Bordeaux. I remember its peaceful and unspoilt location.

Peering out from under the blankets for a moment confirms my recollection. The bedroom is large, high ceilinged and old with expensive antique furniture. Our bed is an enormous four poster in deep brown mahogany with thick embroidered blankets. The drapes covering the leaded windows are multi layered and heavy and the ceiling is ornately carved and painted. I remember without looking that the floor is marble and the rest of the furniture is also ornate and extravagant including the sofa, writing desk and ornaments. Even one night here is an expensive luxury but it's a special and unique experience.

Retreating back under the blankets, I indulge myself in the pleasure of just being here and look forward to the continental breakfast and dark aromatic coffee that I know will be served. The thought gives me an incentive to get out of bed and taste that coffee and to see the French countryside. My stomach rumbles slightly and I realise how hungry I am, but the warmth of the bed is too alluring at the moment.

After a while I hear soft footsteps approaching as Helen returns from her shower and demands that I get out of bed. The added encouragement of the blankets being pulled off me is sufficient persuasion so I wearily get off the bed. Helen is wrapped up in a thick white dressing gown and courtesy chateau slippers, busy towel drying her hair while walking towards one of the windows. She pulls a cord to open one pair of drapes and allow some light into the room.

It's a grey and overcast morning outside but the natural daylight brings the room to life, highlighting the furniture and subtly lighting the ornaments and vases. Even the medieval looking paintings hanging boldly on the wood panelled walls seem somehow more alive. A large crystal chandelier hangs from the centre of the ceiling but however extravagant and beautiful, it looks a little out of place. I open the drapes on the other window as Helen continues drying her hair while staring out of the window into the French countryside. Our room must be four or five floors up and at the back of the chateau.

Suddenly I notice how cold the marble floor is without any slippers on so I step onto a thick rug that's an accurate imitation of the Bayeux tapestry. The lure of the chateau coffee entices me to get ready so I head for the bathroom for a wash, pinching Helen's bottom through the dressing gown as I pass.

The antique dining room is authentically rural and a true representative flavour of historic France. I inhale the aroma of my coffee before adding a little cream and savouring a first exquisite taste. Breakfast is even better than I remember it to be, with a vast selection of fresh croissants, Danish pastries and a dozen high quality cheeses to accompany the locally produced ham. Freshly squeezed orange or grapefruit juice is on offer with a choice of white wines, but most importantly their perfect coffee, individually served in a caffetiere.

The dining room is almost empty this morning with only three other couples already at breakfast. They all look French and they pick at their food slowly and precisely. Two waitresses in black and white uniforms move carefully around the room offering more tea to people whose cups are already full. Most of the twenty or so unoccupied tables are laid out with silver cutlery on pristine white tablecloths with a small vase of flowers as a centrepiece. The room has a kind of haze to it and occasionally a beam of sunlight penetrates the overcast skies and shines in through the wide bay windows at the back of the room.

Helen and Jenny are sat at the dining table with me, enjoying their breakfast and both sipping tea. Helen looks immaculate as natural daylight from the tall windows emphasises her defined features and elegant face. The waves of her clean red hair give her a timeless beauty.

Jenny yawns and still looks half asleep, without her usual makeup and with her long black hair pulled back into a hasty ponytail. I smile as I realise that she would never look like that at home or anywhere that her friends might see her. But it's good to see her innocent pale faced natural purity for once. Half asleep and without a shred of naivety in her, my formidable and intelligent daughter could still take on the world and probably win. She looks up and notices me staring.

'What Dad?' she asks.

'Just glad you're enjoying your breakfast,' I reply as she takes a large bite from a croissant smeared with French butter.

Jenny shrugs. 'I am, and thanks for bringing me here,' she says, also directing her words to her mother.

'Well we promised we would,' says Helen, 'as soon as you finished your exams.'

Jenny puffs out her cheeks in apparent memory of her end of school exams. 'It was worth it then,' she says. 'But I'm still glad they're over and done with it.'

From what I remember Jenny had done much better in her exams than she had expected, but I've already asked her that question at home, not here. We didn't even bring her to France after her exams as far as I recall.

'So how do you think you did?' I ask.

Jenny frowns and drinks some tea. 'I told you last week,' she replies curtly.

'Leave it alone Ewan,' says Helen, 'we're on holiday. Let her just wait for her results.'

Helen reaches over and touches Jenny's hand. 'I'm sure you did just fine,' she says.

But I somehow already know for a fact that she did do well.

Jenny smiles at her mother and cuts a croissant in half. It reminds me how hungry I am so I drop the subject, press on with eating my ham and cheese and allow my thoughts to wander. From the outside this place looks like a castle, or at least that's what I would call it. The chateau has high stone walls that are cream coloured with four conical, grey roofed towers like something from a fairy tale. The main roof is steeply inclined with two strikingly higher towers than the four in the corners of the building. Every window is tall and slender and the whole place is surrounded by immaculate green lawns and landscaped gardens. It's no surprise to me that we have come here again. Perhaps the idea was just to celebrate Jenny finishing her exams in a more extravagant way.

'What are we gonna do today?' asks Jenny on cue with my own thoughts.

'How about we all walk into the village?' Helen suggests.

I picture the village in my head with its narrow streets, quaint little houses and old church. There's also a small row of farm shops and a shallow stream running through the village green.

'Yeah definitely, let's go into the village' says Jenny enthusiastically. 'Maybe I can pick up some souvenirs.'

'Alright,' I agree, 'but I'm not going anywhere till I've had some more of this coffee.'

'Well I need to get changed anyway,' says Jenny. 'I'll meet you two downstairs at what? Is half past nine alright?'

Helen checks her slender gold watch and it makes me remember the day I gave it to her for her thirtieth birthday.

'Alright,' says Helen, half nine, bring a coat in case it rains.'

'Really Mum?' says Jenny sarcastically.

'And shoes in case your feet get wet sweetheart,' I joke.

Helen sticks her tongue out at me and wrinkles her nose up. Jenny dabs her mouth with a serviette and leaves the table grinning.

'Why did you bring her exams up again?' Helen asks me with a hint of annoyance in her voice.

'To see how she thinks she did,' I reply. 'What's wrong with that?'

Helen puts down her cup of tea, clinking it onto the china saucer. 'Because she's on holiday now Ewan,' she replies. 'There's nothing she can do about them now. She's supposed to be relaxing – and you know how touchy she gets if we push her.'

'It was only a question,' I say, shrugging innocently.

'Well leave it alone,' she replies, 'let her wait for her results, and don't put her under any more pressure.'

'Alright, alright,' I reply, holding up my hands. 'I won't ask her again. Jesus.'

The rain has held off so far but the overcast skies have managed to convincingly defeat the sun this morning. Walking in the fresh breeze is a perfect complement to a large breakfast and I feel refreshed and awake. Jenny is walking in front of us having not bothered to bring a coat after all, something Helen takes great delight in reminding me as she gestures to the grey skies above. Hopefully the rain will wait until we return to the chateau or Jenny and I will never hear the end of it. Holding Helen's hand as we walk, the country lane soon leads us into the village.

'It's beautiful,' Jenny says, as she sees the little stream and the village green.

I agree with her sentiment as I realise that it's every bit as pretty as I remember.

The first shop we pass is a butchers but it's closed. I notice a light on in the back of the shop above the counter as Jenny peers in through the window. Helen lets go of my hand and pushes open the door of a farm and wine shop next door, disappearing inside. Jenny notices and hurries to join her. I remember the shop well, how it sells locally produced food, a few French souvenirs and an excellent selection of cheap local wines and branded champagne.

Glancing at the sky rewards me with disappointment that the sun still isn't shining and that the clouds are only becoming ominously greyer. The countryside around the village looks lush, green and beautiful all the same and is only slightly spoilt by a long scar of electrical pylons crossing the fields. A large forested hill overlooks the village but there is a small church in a clearing near the top of it. I strain my eyes to make out any detail but it's too far to see anything clearly.

From out of nowhere a car pulls up alongside me on the empty lane and the driver beeps the horn. It's a dirty brown Renault with an engine that sounds badly in need of a service. The driver's side window slides down silently and a man's face appears, leaning through the window. 'Get in Ewan,' he says.

His face is familiar but stirs mixed emotions for me. I frown as I try to recognise him but he stares at me with an expectant look as if he wants me to work out his identity for myself. As I fix my eyes on the French beret partly covering his blond hair, he shakes his head and sighs.

'Dead loop,' he says flatly, with a hint of impatience.

The two words bring everything crashing back instantly into my memory. The thoughts come barrelling into my head at such a rate that I feel dizzy as I try to deal with the intense range of emotions that the images stir up. Instinctively I reach into my jacket pocket for a gun, but it's not there. Quickly I check my belt but there's no gun there either, then I pad down my jacket without even realising before finally accepting that I'm unarmed. My sudden emotional tempest begins to fade as I realise my unique situation and remember the bank robbery.

'You took some bloody finding,' the man says, disturbing my thoughts.

'Hello Virgil,' I reply with an indifferent tone.

'Sorry Old Man,' he says. 'Had you forgotten about everything for a moment?'

I think back to waking up in the chateau, having breakfast and asking Jenny's about her exams. Why had I awoken from death without remembering my real situation? I'm confused about whether to be grateful for knowing that death is stalking me or dejected for suddenly having the illusion of this holiday shattered. The mixture of gratitude and disappointment are a difficult emotional cocktail to deal with but the taste of truth is even stronger. It's better to know that death awaits you, just like Seneca said. Virgil has probably done me a favour even if his timing could have been a thousand percent better.

The breeze feels a little colder now and the countryside seems less beautiful.

'It happens sometimes,' Virgil explains, 'especially with the better awakenings. I'm sorry to break up your little holiday.'

'It's not your fault,' I tell him blandly.

Looking backing into the shop, I spot Helen and Jenny discussing a bottle of wine that Jenny is studying. Helen is laughing at something and Jenny is smiling. It's a beautiful picture and I wish I had a camera.

'Oh don't worry about them,' says Virgil comfortingly. 'They'll be fine on their own. You'll see them again soon anyway. In fact you'll always see them like that now, at that age I mean.'

I look back at him and he pats the passenger seat with his hand. 'Come on get in,' he urges me.

Death is on its way and the idea of being with Helen and Jenny feels too uncomfortable now I realise my situation. I sigh disappointedly as I accept reality and reject the illusion of this holiday. Pulling open the car door, I sit down in the passenger seat.

'I promise no bank robberies today,' says Virgil, obviously sensing my mood.

'Alright,' I mutter distantly.

'Besides,' says Virgil, chuckling, 'I doubt we'd find a fucking bank round here anyway!'

The car pulls away leaving the village and my family behind and I close my eyes against the moist sting of emotion.

Virgil guides the car through the empty winding country lanes at a moderate pace. It feels odd not being at the wheel and for some reason I half expect a tractor to suddenly appear in front of us from nowhere. But it was a much sunnier day when that happened.

I keep going over in my head whether I should be annoyed with Virgil for shattering the false reality of my holiday or to thank him for making me see the truth. It doesn't help that he seems indifferent to anything other than finding me. All he seems interested in is acting as my guide and living life to the full. Maybe he actually needs me more than I need him. If I had been alone in this twisted existence as long as him would I be desperate for a companion too? It's true that sharing my thoughts with someone who understands this situation and not having to explain it again every day is comforting.

'How did they take you down?' Virgil asks, breaking the silence.

I remember stupidly crashing the van into the SWAT vehicle.

'Roadblock and about fifteen SWAT guys,' I exaggerate a little. 'I almost got away though.'

'You got out of the shop?' Virgil replies, sounding impressed. 'I guess my cover fire helped though didn't it?'

Virgil manically discharging his gun without any warning had not been something I expected but it probably contributed to my initial escape. 'Why did you fire?' I ask.

'Oh come on Ewan, we were fucking dead as soon as we sat down and ordered a cup of tea,' he says. 'We were never getting out of that shopping centre alive.'

'Well I got out,' I correct him.

Virgil chuckles. 'Yeah and look what happened to you,' he reminds me.

My mind flashes back to the deafening sounds of machine gun fire followed by the searing pain of the gunshot wounds and my overwhelming terror. It was something akin to a suicidal escape attempt.

'So what would have happened if we had just surrendered like I suggested?' I ask him.

Virgil shrugs and increases the car's speed as we reach an unusually straight part of the country lane. 'What do you think?' he replies. 'We can't last more than a day can we? I never have. Some trigger happy copper maybe, a car crash perhaps. Who knows? Maybe a fucking meteorite would hit us.'

I look over at him with the stupid looking French beret still perched on his head. 'Have you never survived the day?' I ask.

Virgil shakes his head and curls up his lip as if my question was stupid.

'Can you remember what happened the day before you first died?' I ask him, 'how this all started for you?'

'Can you?' he replies.

The truth is I couldn't remember the day before Pripyat, however much I still seemed to know about my earlier life.

'I thought not,' says Virgil, taking my silence as an answer as he slows the car down and turns up a narrow track. 'Anyway, we're here now.'

The track leads to a small farmhouse surrounded by a little copse of trees. The building looks old and shabby but far from abandoned. There are curtains in the windows and a thin wisp of smoke drifting up from the single chimney to be dispersed by the breeze into the dark grey sky. There's still no rain though.

'Sorry about this Old Man,' says Virgil as I peer through the windscreen and study the house. 'Not quite a castle I'm afraid, but at least there's wine in there. Oh, and a fire.'

We get out of the car and Virgil opens the back door of the Renault and takes a handgun off the seat.

'Sorry Old Man,' he says, holding it up, 'couldn't get you one today, but I have got a surprise for you.'

I look at him curiously. 'Surprise?'

Virgil grins and moves to the back of the car and pops open the boot. 'Check it out,' he says.

Nothing prepares me for the contents of the Renault's boot. A woman is curled up inside, wearing a long floral dress that's all creased. Shockingly her hands are tied behind her back with thin cord. There is a hessian bag over her head and she struggles and wriggles against the bonds around her wrists while shaking her head against the hood. My mouth drops open in shock and I'm frozen in horror to the spot.

'Virgil,' I stammer out his name, 'What the hell?'

Virgil shoves his gun under his belt before hauling the woman out of the boot and onto her feet. She struggles and breaks free of his grip then starts to run. With the bag over her head she only gets a few steps before stumbling over a small log and falling onto the soft ground. As she lies on her side with her hands tied behind her I realise that she has no shoes on. Virgil hauls her to her feet and laughs as I stare dumbstruck and trying to imagine that this scene isn't really happening.

'Don't worry Ewan,' he says, 'she's just fine.'

The unnatural scene is hard to absorb as Virgil leads her towards the house via a gravel path. He warns her not to run again and I blindly follow them, half dazed and unsure how to react to what's going on. Virgil seems like a different person in some way and his actions are unlike anything I've experienced before.

He produces a key, unlocks the door to the farmhouse and leads the woman inside. I follow them into the typically rural farmhouse which has wooden floorboards, stone walls and is sparsely furnished with rustic furniture and a few rugs. Virgil leads the woman into another room and I remain by the front door, surveying the place, still in shock.

There is an aged kitchen with thick oak surfaces, a sink and a simple log stove but it's devoid of any appliances. The kitchen adjoins the lounge which has a couple of old fashioned settees, a sturdy wooden bookcase full of dusty books and a small table and chairs. There is no television and nothing electrical, just a few candles burning in little holders on the wall for light. The dying embers of a small fire glow under an oversize stone fireplace with a cracked mantle.

Virgil silently appears behind me and jostles me into the living room. 'Just make yourself at home,' he says, grabbing a bottle of wine at random from a battered old wine rack before inspecting the label.

I slump down onto one of the settees and rub my eyes which are finally growing accustomed to the low light. There isn't a single window in the lounge. Virgil is in the kitchen with the bottle of wine between his knees, pulling the cork out with a muffled pop. He sits down next to me and places two wine glasses on a sturdy looking oak coffee table and sniffs the open bottle. When he blows into the wine glasses I see little particles of dust escape into the air like glitter as they float in the candle light. He fills up the two glasses with blood red wine and hands me one. The glass feels heavy in my hand and the aroma of the wine is strong but I'm not inclined to drink it.

'Who is she Virgil?' I ask him.

'Try the wine,' he suggests. 'That's Mouton Rothschild 1874. It's rarer than rocking horse shit.'

I sniff the wine closely as Virgil takes a long drink from his glass and sighs. I'm no wine connoisseur and as I stare into the inky dark liquid it brings back memories of plunging into the ocean from a cruise liner with Virgil. He looks far less menacing now though, sipping his wine with his eyes closed and savouring the taste.

'Virgil,' I repeat, nudging him to make him open his eyes. 'Who is the woman?'

'Alright, alright, I suppose you would have to ask eventually,' he says. 'She's nobody, or rather to put it another way, she is ours.'

'Ours?' I reply, the concept sounding sinister. 'What do you mean ours?'

'I don't always rob banks,' replies Virgil, unzipping his jacket and placing his gun on the table next to the wine bottle. 'There are other pleasures in the dead loop. I do love that name you came up with by the way.'

His words swim around in my mind as my gaze switches between the gun and the candlelight that dances on the blood red surface of my wine. Virgil drains his glass of rare wine and reaches for the bottle to pour himself another, also topping mine up slightly even though I haven't drunk any.

'Nothing special is it?' he comments, gesturing with the wine bottle before placing it down.

'What do you mean?' I ask uncomfortably, 'other pleasures?'

'Oh come on,' says Virgil. 'Do I have to spell it out? I mean women.'

'You mean her?' I ask, pointing towards the lounge door.

'Of course,' he says matter-of-factly, his eyes taking on a darkly sinister look. 'I'll tell you what Ewan, you can have this one. She isn't really my type anyway.'

If there ever was any doubt in my mind about what he is suggesting, it's now dispelled. Her bonds, the hood over her head and the attempted escape all come back into my mind and I shudder as my breakfast churns in my stomach.

'You're joking,' is all I can say.

Virgil holds out his hands, palms up. 'What are friends for?' he asks.

I shake my head slowly at first but then more firmly. 'This isn't right,' I tell him.

Virgil slaps his palm against the side of his head a few times in an agitated way. 'Ewan, she isn't real,' he says. 'We aren't real any more. Haven't you realised that? We can't harm anybody, not in the dead loop.'

'We're... not raping someone,' I say forcefully, pointing my finger at him.

'Slow down Old Man,' shouts Virgil angrily. 'Who said anything about rape? It's not rape so don't even use that word.'

'What the fuck would you call it?' I demand.

'Showing her a good time,' he snaps, 'enjoying yourself and trying out a little of life's wild side. I'm speeding you along the process here Ewan, so you don't have the same long bullshit battle as I did. I'm trying to do you a goddamn favour here.'

I stand up angrily, feeling disgusted and back away from the settee, away from Virgil.

'Fine, if you don't want her,' says Virgil, 'then I'll have her.'

'No you won't,' I warn him. 'Nobody is having anybody. We're going to let her go before this shit gets out of hand.'

Virgil laughs manically and stands up with his wine in his hand and toasts me mockingly with the glass. 'Out of hand?' he snorts. 'Out of hand? Jesus Ewan, you just robbed a fucking bank!'

'That's not the same,' I shout.

'Rules don't apply,' he shouts back. 'We make the fucking rules, remember?'

I begin moving towards the lounge door but Virgil snatches up his gun, knocking my glass off the table in the process. The inky liquid spills onto the wooden floorboards and drips between the gaps like oozing dark blood. I immediately freeze as Virgil aims the gun towards me.

'Don't you leave,' he warns. 'You need me. We need each other.'

I raise my hands. 'Put it down Virgil,' I tell him carefully.

He hesitates for a moment but does slowly lower the weapon. 'There's no point shooting you anyway is there?' he says.

'I don't want any part of this,' I tell him, turning my back on him and heading towards the front door.

Virgil doesn't reply though. I half expect him to pursue me or to hear the sound of a gunshot and feel a bullet enter my back, but it doesn't come. Soon I'm outside and running towards the Renault.

The keys are not in the car or I would drive off just to get away from Virgil, the psychotic deranged maniac and his rape shack. My hands are shaking on the steering wheel through shock and rage but I realise that my anger isn't directed at Virgil, it's towards myself for my own cowardice and inability to act. As I stare vacantly into the countryside through the trees I see the electricity lines and pylons passing right behind the farmhouse and my thoughts go back to the woman in the shack. What is Virgil doing to her and why can't I stop him? It's not even because he has the gun and is psychotic and capable of anything, it's my revulsion that drives me away. But then my mind remembers something he said before, about riding. I almost empty my stomach as I remember what Virgil had said to me about Kitty, the travel rep in Greece. That sick animal has done this before? How many women has he... raped?

I'm paralysed in the car, relaying the events of the morning in my mind, my pride and dignity crippling me as I think of Helen and Jenny, the most important women in my life. This woman who hasn't even got shoes on was kidnapped and bought here in the boot of a car and shamefully I'm an accomplice. As the thought goes through my head, revulsion overcomes my cowardice and I open the car door and step outside. My eyes are focused and staring at the farmhouse and I know that no matter what happens I won't let Virgil do this. I begin to walk towards the farmhouse, determined to make sure that Virgil never harms anyone again. He is wrong – there are consequences and there are rules.

Bang! The deafening sound of a single gunshot stops me in my tracks and freezes me to the spot. Oh God, what has he done? I'm too late to help and I'm party to murder. I quickly come to my senses and begin sprinting towards the farmhouse, yanking open the front door and approaching the room where Virgil took the woman. I hesitate for just a moment and take a deep breath before pushing the door open.

The sight inside the room cripples me and I sink to my knees in horror. There is only a single bed in the room and a tiny window with a dirty curtain covering it. The woman's discarded dress is on the floor and she is face down on the bed naked, her pale body barely covered by a dirty yellow blanket. Her head is turned to one side, a tangled black mess of tissue and blood in her hair. The woman's blood has splattered against the peeling walls and onto the pale skin on her back. There is no sign of Virgil and I look away from her body and close my eyes as my stomach begins to heave.

After a few moments I dare to open my eyes, hoping that the scene will have changed somehow and that the woman will be gone or that I'm somewhere else. But nothing has changed and I edge towards the bed on my knees, noticing an empty wine glass on the floor. The woman's face is partly covered by a pillow and I try to avoid looking at the bloody mess at the back of her head. With a shaking hand I remove the pillow and see most of her face. Her eyes are open and staring in a mask of death. My stomach concedes defeat and I vomit violently onto the floor as I realise that it's Tina.

I'm crashing through the trees and stumbling past bushes with vomit down the front of my shirt. I have to get away from the farmhouse, from death, from the blood and Tina's lifeless corpse. Tears stream down my face, blurring my eyes as I trip over a branch and fall face down into a patch of mud. Scrambling on my hands and knees for a moment, I rise to my feet, barely aware of the cold mud on my face. I should have stopped that animal. The realisation of my failure tortures me and feelings of guilt overwhelm me. Climbing over a wooden fence and falling to the floor I catch hold of something smooth and metal, gripping it tightly and gasping for breath. It's an electricity pylon.

Without hesitation I begin to climb up it to get away from the ground and from Virgil and my shame. The metal frame cuts into my cold muddy fingers as I ascend the pylon, but I don't care. Climbing as fast as I can, something snags my trousers like barb wire but I wrench my leg free and ignore the pain of my skin tearing. I see some red ceramic discs a few feet from me and their colour reminds me of the wine and Tina's blood. Her face smiles at me from one of the discs and she blows me a kiss. But then she is screaming. Her head explodes and smoke fills the disc as she falls onto the bed.

Helen suddenly appears in the disc with Jenny next to her, holding up a bottle of wine but it's all too much for my tormented mind to accept. There is a loud humming sound coming from the pylon and I feel an overwhelming need to submit to my guilt and shame. I reach out with my hand towards the disc with Helen on it and touch it.

18
Rock Bottom

Ali offers me a bottle of Budweiser and foam begins to escape from the neck as I accept it. Quickly I put the bottle to my lips and tilt it backwards, the dull taste of the cold beer sliding easily down my throat. The flashing lights of the nightclub surround me and the loud thump of bass music is almost deafening. The whole room seems to be vibrating but I don't recognise the music or the terrible song.

With the throng of so many people gyrating around me I can't tell where the dance floor starts and the rest of the night club begins. Somebody jostles past and bumps into me as I feel the softness of carpet under my shoes that suggests that I'm not on the dance floor. A trio of young women grinding their hips and waving their arms beside me would suggest otherwise though.

The crowd of revellers makes me feel old even though I spot a token mature man or woman mimicking the younger ones and my memory drifts to an almost forgotten time when I would be in nightclubs.

'Cheers!' yells Ali, banging his beer into mine and causing a shower of condensation from the side of the bottle. I barely hear his toast through the deafening music. His action causes more beer to froth out of the top of the bottle and I cover it with my mouth as it fizzes up. My head is spinning from alcohol consumption already so I knock my bottle back into his. Ali defensively holds his bottle out to one side, narrowly avoiding getting fizzing beer onto his clothes or the people around him. His striped Ralph Lauren shirt is un-tucked and loose over his trousers and his shoes are black and white. The toes go into a point like some kind of dancing shoes and remind me a bit of my old golf shoes, but it seems hard to focus on them as he moves his feet in time with the music.

Clinging to Ali's arm and holding a bottle of water is a skinny Asian woman in a tiny yellow top and tight blue skirt. There is hardly anything of her and her boyish figure has little in the way of curves, despite the fact that she looks almost thirty. Her smiling face is heart shaped and pretty though and she has a look of kindness about her. Ali puts his arm around her waist and grins at me as he catches my eye. He leans forward, continuing to move his feet as the woman dances seductively against his leg. 'Where's Helen tonight?' he yells close to my ear.

I can't immediately think where she is but Helen wouldn't be seen dead in a nightclub these days. We had outgrown this sort of nightlife when we were in our late twenties. By then we both had good jobs, plenty of money and preferred fine restaurants and quiet nights in to being jostled and deafened in a club.

'At home,' I yell back while beginning to move my feet and arms a little to blend in better with the crowd. Dancing seems like a forgotten skill and I feel robotic and rhythmless so I bring the beer back to my lips and keep it there until the bottle is empty, burning my throat slightly with the cold.

'It's your round!' yells Ali, taking another gulp of his own beer.

Slowly I push my way towards the bar, edging around the writhing girls who seem to outnumber the men by two to one, something that I would have appreciated when I used to come to nightclubs. The display of semi clad girls gyrating under flashing lights is a blurred jumble of hypnotic suggestion and it becomes harder to focus clearly, especially with the alcohol in my system. Making apologies that nobody can possibly hear, I finally muscle my way to one side of the packed bar in search of some presumably overpriced drinks.

There must be close to ten staff working behind the bar, all of them young and wearing black and red shirts. With flurrying hands they rapidly open bottles and hand out drinks, each selecting their next customer by making positive eye contact with only one person at a time. I place my empty bottle on the bar and almost immediately I'm paying a curly haired and efficient Australian barman for three more bottles of Budweiser.

The struggle to fight my way back to Ali and his girlfriend seems much easier this time, as if the path I had cut through the dancers still somehow remains. It hadn't though, so perhaps I was just a little more forceful and confident this time. After handing one of the bottles to Ali, I offer one to his lady friend but she declines it with a dismissive wave of her water bottle. I shrug and sip from both bottles and feel the alcohol beginning to make me feel more comfortable despite my gulf in age with the other revellers.

After a little more shuffling around in a vague display of dancing I finish one beer and place it on a nearby table already jammed with empty glasses and bottles that are probably impossible to collect in here. There is a man standing at the table chatting to a woman much younger than him and her long floral skirt looks vaguely familiar. It stirs my memory and tickles at my thought processes as I drink from the other bottle. The beer suddenly loses its taste and sharpness as I realise that the skirt reminds me of the woman in the boot of Virgil's car.

The thought hits me like a slap in the face, freezing my feet to the spot as the beating music seems to quieten. The people around me that are smiling and dancing now seem to be moving in slow motion. But the woman standing at the table isn't Tina. Evil memories flood into my mind of Virgil and the farmhouse, of wine and blood and guilt. A woman brushes past me in slow motion wearing a mock wedding dress and an 'L' plate stuck to her back. The girls following her cheer as a little plastic tiara falls off her head and one of them has to bend down to pick it up.

I feel nauseous as I look back at the woman in the floral skirt and my stomach twists into a knot as guilt floods into my system. My fingers relax and the beer bottle slips from my hand and hits my shoe before bouncing onto the carpet. I sense someone reacting to the splashing beer but their voice is swallowed up in the music which seems to be getting louder.

The man talking with the woman in the floral dress notices me watching them and glares at me while arrogantly standing more upright in a masculine display of threat. I look away and reach for the table with my hands because my head is spinning wildly. I'd left Tina alone with that perverted animal Virgil until it was too late to save her. I have to force myself not to imagine her final sickening moments.

Holding the table brings back memories of the Renault's steering wheel and my minutes of impotent hesitation before returning to the farmhouse. My hands shake just as much on the table as they did in the car and a glass falls onto the floor, splashing my leg with something cold. The people around the table are dancing in their own world, seemingly oblivious to my existence and unaware of my thoughts or painful torment. Guilt and shame are fiercely powerful emotions and I shakily reach for a glass from the table that has ice and some orange fluid in it. The drink isn't mine but it smells of whisky so I pour it into my mouth, allowing the ice cubes to remain in the glass and bounce against my top lip. The warm sting of whisky burns my throat as I swallow and put the glass down.

Glancing over my shoulder I realise that Ali and his girlfriend have edged their way off the carpet and closer towards the dance floor to join the boiling mass of dancers. I don't belong here and I need to get out of this place.

Stumbling back towards the bar, now oblivious about whether or not I bump into people I spot a neon green exit sign, but I need another drink before leaving. The wait to be served seems far longer this time and my head spins with incoherent thoughts as I shut the nightclub out of my mind and wait for service. Shock fills my mind about what Virgil has become and a stark feeling of terror that it may have been dying every day that drove him to that madness. Is the same thing going to happen to me?

Soon I have another beer to help me stop thinking and I stumble towards the exit sign where the music is a little quieter and the crowd is a little thinner. A slow moving line of people are still entering the main part of the nightclub through some double doors and I squeeze past a group of young men and into the brightly lit lobby. More people are handing in coats or awaiting the inspection of two suited doormen, before paying their entrance fee to a stunning long haired woman sitting inside a kiosk.

After stepping over a small rope barrier I begin to push the exit door open but one of the doormen stops me by placing his hand on my shoulder.

'You can't take the bottle,' he says, gesturing to the full Budweiser still in my hand.

I remain by the exit door for a moment and tip the bottle back, drinking it as smoothly as I can but spilling quite a bit of it down my shirt. Gasping for breath, I hand the empty bottle to the doormen and he removes his hand from my shoulder allowing me to push my way through the final door and into the cold night air.

It is dark and raining outside but the combination of streetlights and the clubs huge neon sign light up the pavement. The sign is blurred and I can't seem to read it so I stumble along the pavement following a long queue of people still waiting to get into the club.

There is an Indian restaurant next to the nightclub and the queue reaches all the way back to it. I stumble through the entrance and am immediately accosted by a mature Indian man. He seems nonplussed by my swaying and offers me a table, so I accept and he leads me to one in the corner of the restaurant. There is a clock on the wall and it reads 23:30, probably explaining why there are only a couple of tables occupied.

'Anything to drink?' asks the man, offering me a menu.

I take the menu but don't look up. 'Kingfisher please,' I mumble, 'and a whisky.'

The Indian man moves away and I place the menu flat on the table and stifle a yawn. The beer I'd drunk quickly at the nightclub exit has gone to my head but I still can't escape her, I can't escape Tina's face in my head. I imagine running through the countryside again, my hands cut and bleeding as I climb the pylon, desperate to get away from the nightmare scene in the farmhouse, a scene I should have prevented. My hand reaches out and touches the ceramic disc but finds only an icy coldness and no lethal electric shock. My eyelids flutter open and find a bottle of Kingfisher beer in my hand, beckoning me with its offer of relief and escape. The waiter has gone so I lift the beer and gulp greedily on it.

Suddenly I realise that there is a woman sitting opposite me at my table which startles me for a moment. I blink my eyes in surprise but have to accept that she is real. Despite my blurred vision, her close proximity seems somehow to focus my eyes and I'm drawn to her face as if it's the only thing in the world. Her hair is short and very dark with a wiry fringe hanging down in thin strands over her forehead like a long toothed comb. She looks around fifty with the tell-tale lines of maturity around her mouth and eyes and a slight ageing to her skin. Her eyes are quite far apart and almost black, peering at me from behind round thick rimmed glasses. The woman wears no makeup at all apart from a faint rouge on the lips of a mouth that turns down slightly at the corners giving her an almost cruel and sour look.

Why is it so easy to focus on her face while everything else in the room is spinning? I place my beer down on the table and notice the waiter out of the corner of my eye, standing behind the restaurant's reception counter and fussing disinterestedly over empty glasses.

There is a glass of whisky on my table with one solitary ice cube slowly melting in it. The woman is staring straight at me but her face begins to blur a little now. I don't know who the hell she is but wonder if she somehow knows about Tina and the murder in the farmhouse. The banging beat from the club still rings noisily in my ears and I swear that I can hear the gunfire from the bank robbery repeating its terrifying roar in my head.

'Hello Ewan,' the woman speaks in a bland voice and I notice her fringe move slightly as she speaks.

'I need the toilet,' I inform her, climbing to my feet and staggering away from the table and towards the bar.

The waiter seems to reads my thoughts as I stumble past him because he points to a door and nods. The door swings open silently and I move awkwardly down some carpeted stairs to a dimly lit hall where there is a lone floral armchair. After leaning on the arm of the chair for support I move through a door and into the brightly lit Gents. I ignore the urinals and enter the single cubicle, locking the door behind me and fumbling at my belt buckle.

Urinating is a welcome relief and I flush the toilet and pull my shorts and trousers back up. After flicking the toilet seat down and closed with a loud bang, I sit down on it and lean forwards, resting my spinning head on the closed cubicle door. Pulling up my sleeve I look at my watch to find the digital display unreadable and I struggle to focus on the analogue hands.

I'm not sure of anything for certain now. There is guilt in my mind, confusing blurred images of female bodies twisting in motion and Ali's girlfriend with her tight clothes. Then a bottle of beer hits my foot and I squeeze my eyes closed and rub my forehead with only the knowledge that I mustn't stay here too long overriding all my other thoughts. But sitting on the closed toilet I realise that I'm failing to regain my concentration as the alcohol concentration still increases in my blood stream. I shake my head but fail to clear my mind before rising to my feet and opening the door.

I stumble out of the cubicle and into the bathroom to wash my hands in a sink with push on taps, splashing cold water onto my face as my reflection stares back at me. My face is a wild blur of swirling pink skin and smudged dark hair. I smile at my reflection before rubbing my hands under the hand drier, enjoying the warm sensation before crouching down to hold my face underneath the air stream. Unfortunately it keeps switching itself off so I wipe my hands on my face and brush the dampness through my hair.

Staggering back up the stairs seems hard work but I feel renewed determination to walk a little straighter into the restaurant. Somehow I manage to give the pretence of sobriety and toss a ten pound note on the bar forgetting all about my whisky and leaving the restaurant. I'm not even hungry anyway.

It's still cold outside but at least it isn't raining any more. I wave at a passing taxi with its lights blazing but it drives past without stopping. Every footstep is now a weary one and I notice the queue at the nightclub is a little shorter because it no longer reaches the restaurant. A couple of the women at the back of the queue are shivering in their short skirts despite having jackets on. One of them stamps her high heels in a futile bid to keep herself warm as I turn my back and walk the other way down the street.

Turning a corner onto the main road I hear the tell-tale thump of music coming from somewhere nearby and assume it's probably another nightclub. I've lost control of my thought processes now and one image after another flood into my mind but I'm unable to distinguish between the good memories and the bad ones. Where are Ali and his girlfriend? It doesn't seem to matter now.

The cold air and exercise do little to improve my blurred vision and more uncomfortable thoughts creep back into my mind. Tina's face appears again with the back of her head blasted open but this time I just can't make the image stay away, it keeps coming back and invading my mind. Only sheer persistence and determination eventually allow me to force Tina out of my mind. But her face morphs into someone else as her hair changes colour and her expression curls into a warm smile. Her face has changed into that of Helen, smiling in the sunshine with her sunglasses. *'Shall we do it?'* she asks suggestively but the image washes away before I can answer. Helen is looking down at me with a cold expression and a kitchen knife dripping with blood held up in front of her face.

A bell rings as I unexpectedly push my way inside a shop and bright lights and vibrant colours overawe my eyes. My hand clutches a bottle and I stumble to the counter and put it down. The man behind the counter asks if I want anything else as I blink at his old, blurred face and notice a line of clear glass bottles behind him.

'Vodka,' I mumble, making him turn around and reach for a bottle from the shelf. I realise his cardigan is all grey and oddly saggy as I hand him some bank notes, but they aren't mine though they're stolen ones I think. I'm unarmed and don't have a gun so I won't be robbing this place.

'Hold on Superstar! We need a fucking plan first!' I hear the words in my head.

Grabbing the vodka bottle and turning away, the cap is off before I even leave the shop and I'm taking a gulp of the raw clear spirit. The taste stings my tongue for a second but swallowing doesn't seem to burn my throat at all. I quickly take another mouthful and stumble away from the shop.

There is a bench sheltered underneath a fume choked tree on the pavement and I sit down and lean back against the cold metal backrest. I gaze around the blurred city pavement and sip vodka and feel as though my head is in constant rotation. Opposite me are some huge display windows and behind them some clothed mannequins are watching me intently. One of them is wearing lingerie and dancing like the girls in the nightclub as she grinds herself against the shop window. Another one, a man poses with a pair of skis making me I wish I had his polar hooded coat on, but then I bet he wishes he had my vodka. I raise the bottle in his direction as a toast and then have another mouthful.

Suddenly I feel a hand on my shoulder and the presence of someone next to me on the bench.

'Hello Ewan,' the woman says.

I turn my head to look at her and she seems a little familiar with her wiry fringe and glasses, short black hair and turned down mouth. It's the woman from the Indian restaurant.

'Hello,' I slur back at her, wishing she would keep still so I can focus on her.

Is she interested in me, I wonder? She looks a little older than me and stony faced, but as she smiles her face seems to take on a warmer look. I gulp down some more vodka but this time it does sting my throat and my head spins violently as I try again to refocus on her face.

'Who are you?' I mumble.

'You already know who I am, Ewan,' she replies.

Her face is actually quite forgettable and only the stringy wire fringe stands out about her, but I'm certain that I don't know her.

'Lily,' she adds.

I shake my head and take a smaller, more measured sip of vodka before offering her a drink.

'I'm here to help you,' she says, declining the bottle with a shake of her head.

Her words are ludicrous and go far beyond amusing, causing me to splutter with laughter and look down at my lap as I spill a little of the vodka.

'Help me?' I reply incredulously. 'Can you get me a taxi? That would help.'

Lily places a hand on mine, the one holding the bottle and leans closer. 'Where do you want to go Ewan,' she asks me. She has a subtle smell of mild, bland and uninteresting perfume with a hint of cheap hair conditioner.

'Home?' I mumble, almost a question.

'Where do you really want to go?' she asks me.

The question vexes me for a moment. Maybe to see Virgil I wonder? Or back to the chateau and somewhere safe? But every fibre of thought tells me that I need to be at home now and I begin to get to my feet but Lily stops me, gently pushing me back down onto the bench. She crouches down on the pavement in front of me with her hands on my knees and looks up at me. As I lift my head and notice her strange position the vodka fuels my confusion and distorts my memories.

'What do you want?' I ask in an emotionless voice.

'To help you,' she says again. 'But first you have to help yourself.'

I would love to pull myself together but there is no help for me, there is only the vodka and its powerful relief from guilt.

'How?' I ask, quite baffled.

'You need to get rid of Virgil,' she says slowly and precisely.

His name causes distaste in my mouth and I wash it away with another slug of vodka as my other hand trembles.

'I don't know where he is,' I reply, slurring my words.

'But you must face him,' she says.

Her hands squeeze my knees as if to highlight her words but they make no sense. When I try to stand up again, she doesn't stop me this time.

'Leave me alone,' I tell her, walking away down the street, but she is immediately alongside me and somehow the bottle of vodka is now in her hand.

'Listen to me,' she says. 'Try to focus on my voice.'

But I can't focus on anything now; she can keep the fucking vodka. My mind is suddenly filled with Tina's face again and her cold staring dead eyes. I stagger away from Lily, unable to force Tina out of my head without the vodka and I rub my eyes, wishing the guilt was gone. Why can't this just be over with?

There are lights coming down the road, a lone pair of car headlights. I hear the vodka bottle smash on the ground behind me but the sound only distracts me for a second before Tina's face appears again. The two blurred white smudges of the headlights blaze at me like Tina's eyes and as the sound of the car approaches my doubts wash away about what to do. With my mind consumed by unassailable guilt I stumble forward deliberately into the road as the car approaches me. My timing is intentionally perfect and the car slams into my legs as I step in front of it. Tina closes her eyes and her face finally disappears from my mind once and for all. It felt good to die.

PART 3

DELIVERANCE

19
Two Sides to Every Story

I'm sitting down and staring straight ahead at a high green wall that seems to curve itself around me. The hard wooden bench situated under a tree is very uncomfortable and all of my joints seem to be aching. One of my knees seems to be bouncing as my toes spring involuntarily up and down. I try pressing down on it but my toes continue to move by themselves despite my efforts. But at least it feels safe here on this bench.

I shiver with the sudden realisation that my pyjamas are too thin and inadequate for the cold temperature. In an attempt to get warm I hug myself, pulling my elbows into my side and sliding my hands under my armpits. The involuntary movement of my toes and leg seem to be soothing me in some way and I lean slowly to one side until my body eventually tips over onto the bench. I rest my head on the wooden slats and curl up into a ball which makes me feel considerably warmer and a little sleepy.

When I open my eyes the green wall in front of me seems to be a little closer than I remember. I also notice tree branches above me, full of small gold leaves that curl up at their edges and tremble slightly in the breeze. I'm grateful that my leg has stopped shaking for the moment as I look up through the gaps in the branches at a dark grey sky. The tell-tale white signature scar of a jet trail highlights to me that an aeroplane has recently passed overhead. The white stripe is already starting to expand as it fans out and gradually begins to dissipate. I wonder where the people on the plane are going and if they think about me down here when they pass over my head.

Closing my eyes again I suddenly feel the comforting sensation of a heavy blanket being placed over my body. The warmth of the blanket assures me that there is nothing to worry about and no reason for me to be preoccupied with thought. Everything is quiet and peaceful here, there is no one to harm me and sleep washes over me like a second protective blanket.

When I awaken and sit up on the bench, a purple blanket falls onto the floor at my feet. It looks extremely thick and feels velvety as I rub my bare feet on it. The blanket still has my warmth in its fibres but my body feels considerably warmer now under my jeans and jumper. My pyjamas have been replaced.

The green wall curves even more dramatically than I initially realised and forms a complete circle around me like my own private little sanctuary. I notice that the aeroplane trail has gone now and the sky is a little lighter. My leg has begun shaking again although the involuntary movement stops when I stand up and walk towards the wall. My legs feel slow, mechanical and weak as if I haven't used them for far too long. My arms also feel feeble and weak making me wonder how long I was lying on that bench.

I stretch out one arm and touch the wall but immediately have to draw my hand back. The surface feels rough and my fingers seem to sink into it. It's a curious sensation and for a moment I hesitate before touching it again, but this time the wall feels a little softer even though the sensation is accompanied by a gentle scratching on my fingers. I realise that it's not a solid surface after all, its foliage. The green wall is actually a hedge! I peer at it closely, it's thick, tightly woven branches and leaves look almost impenetrable while there seems to be only darkness between them. No matter how closely I look it's too thick to see through to what's on the other side. I delve my arm deeper inside the hedge which starts to snag my jumper and scratch my hand. I'm sufficiently deterred by the thorns and decide to slowly withdraw my hand.

My legs are beginning to ache again and I start to feel a little cold so I return to the bench and pick up the blanket. I feel the benefit immediately when I wrap it around my legs but as soon as I sit down my knee begins to bounce again. At least I feel comfortable now with the blanket warming my legs and the jumper keeping my upper body warm.

After some considerable time passes with me staring at the hedge I realise that there aren't any sounds here at all. The silence is complete and total but it also feels slightly oppressive and I begin to feel lonely. For a moment I contemplate calling out but find myself reluctant to break the fragile silence, as if perhaps I might damage or pollute it somehow with my voice.

I tilt my head backwards but the back of the bench is too low to afford me any comfortable support so I curl up on the bench instead, pulling my legs into my chest. My knee continues to shake while I'm lying down on my side but as I spend some time watching the sky through the tree branches it begins to slow down.

I'm not sure if I actually fell asleep or not but my leg has stopped moving completely now and I find myself sitting up again, only this time I'm not alone. There is a man and woman here, both of them standing up facing me. The woman is dressed all in white with dark hair and a wiry fringe. She has her hands cupped in front of her and is rotating her thumbs in little circles. The man is dressed purely in black clothes which are in stark contrast to his blonde hair. His arms are folded as he stands there with a deep frown on his square jawed face.

'I'm disappointed in you,' the man says, his eyes fixed intently on me, but the woman doesn't speak.

His voice shatters the unnatural silence around us but it's a welcome disturbance. 'Why?' I ask him curiously.

'Suicide is so boring,' he replies.

My knee begins bouncing again as I glance at the woman and expect her to speak too, but she seems content to just watch me. I stare almost straight through the odd couple with my eyes fixed on the hedge, ignoring his strange comment about suicide.

'Thank you,' I say, offering them both my gratitude.

'What for?' the man asks, losing his frown and raising an eyebrow.

'It was too quiet here,' I say, my voice immediately swallowed by the silence. 'So thank you both for coming.'

'Well let's go somewhere louder Ewan,' the man suggests.

'But where?' I ask him. 'And how?'

As far as I understand the tall circular hedge that surrounds us makes going anywhere impossible and anyway my legs feel too weak to carry me very far. The man simply holds his arms out wide and grins.

'Vegas!' he says excitedly. 'How about going to Las Vegas? That's much better than jumping in front of a car.'

The place name is familiar to me, conjuring up images of bright lights and huge noisy casino hotels surrounded by an arid and barren desert. But it's the sounds that are the most important thing in Las Vegas and I can almost imagine them in my head, coins falling, loud music, joyful laughter, splashing water and thousands of people. This place is deathly quiet and lifeless compared to the pulsing heart of Las Vegas.

'Yeah, I'd like that,' I reply in agreement.

The man takes my arm and helps me to rise awkwardly to my feet as I allow the blanket to fall to the ground. He guides me towards the hedge wall and I notice an opening that I could have sworn wasn't there before. It's not a doorway though; it's just a rectangular cut out in the hedge, although I see other hedge walls beyond the opening that form some kind of passageway. Could this be the way out maybe?

The man releases my arm and gestures towards the opening with his hand.

'There you go,' he says, sounding very pleased with himself, 'Vegas is that way.'

I shuffle slowly forwards and I'm about to step through the opening when a hand on my shoulder stops me. Turning my head makes me realise that the woman in white has come alongside me.

'Don't go with him,' she warns me, slowly shaking her head.

I glance at the blonde man who is now pointing at the opening.

'Oh, don't listen to her Ewan,' he says. 'You and I are going to Vegas, remember?'

But the woman's warning still echoes in my thoughts and I turn my attention back to her. 'Why not?' I ask.

'Because that's Virgil,' she replies. 'And you have to reject him.'

'Hold on a minute!' snaps Virgil, with a sudden release of anger directed towards the woman.

He places his hand on my shoulder and looks at me closely.

'I've guided him this far, what the hell have you done for him?' he demands.

The woman squeezes my other shoulder gently. 'He isn't real Ewan,' she whispers into my ear.

'I'm talking to you Lily,' growls the man that she referred to as Virgil. 'You could at least have the courtesy to answer.'

But she doesn't answer him or even try to explain what she has 'done for me.'

Standing still is beginning to make my legs ache so I take a step backwards towards the bench, making both of their hands slide off my shoulders. I feel less pressure on my legs without their hands on me but I sway slightly, surprised at how much I must have been relying on them to balance me.

'I want to go to Vegas,' I advise them both.

'You see?' says Virgil triumphantly, looking directly at the woman. 'He just said that he wants to leave.'

Lily speaks quietly into my ear. 'Ewan, why do you want to go there?' she asks.

'Noise,' I reply, 'for the sounds and the noise.'

'Which sounds?' she asks probingly.

I shake my head, uncertain for a moment as the woman's question confuses me.

'Don't listen to her,' Virgil urges me. 'You don't have to answer her bullshit questions.'

He loops his arm around mine and pulls me towards the opening in the hedge wall.

'Resist him!' commands Lily, her voice raised for the first time.

But my legs are already moving under the guidance of Virgil's gentle pull and I step through the opening into a corridor made from tall hedges. Virgil's grip on my arm relaxes and I begin to walk unaided, one tentative weak footstep at a time. After only a dozen steps I reach a crossroads with multiple pathways available to me. It's like some kind of hedge maze but I don't know which pathway leads to Las Vegas.

'Which way Virgil?' I ask, but there is no reply.

I turn my head to discover that he isn't with me anymore and bizarrely there's now a T-junction behind me instead of the tree and the bench. I'm lost in the maze with nothing but hedge passageways around me and the plain empty sky above me. I call out Lily and Virgil's names but there is no reply from either of them and no sign of them in the silent maze.

Each path leading from the crossroads looks identical so I pick a direction at random and shuffle slowly down the passageway. I discover numerous other junctions and turnings in the maze but all the paths look identical and there are no landmarks to navigate by. Three of four times I try jumping up to see if I can see the layout of the maze. Not only does it hurt my legs but frustratingly the hedges are a fraction taller than I can see over, even when I'm jumping.

My legs are aching quite badly now so I decide to sit down on the soft grassy floor and immediately the toes of one foot begin moving involuntarily again. All of this standing and walking have been tiring so I lie down and stretch out on my back. The sky is almost white now but for some reason I find its vast raw plainness of colour mesmerising and sufficiently intriguing to occupy my mind. The absence of anything specific to focus on in the sky only makes my gaze wander in curious exploration of it. The silence in the maze seems so perfect and peaceful now that it no longer feels oppressive. I close my eyes and soon drift off to sleep.

When I wake up I'm lying on the bench under the tree once more, surrounded by the circular hedge. The sky is pale grey, almost white and somewhere I hear the chirp of two or three birds. Perhaps they are nesting somewhere in the hedge. The birds sound cheerful but my ears can't locate where they are as the welcoming sound seems to be coming from every direction at once.

My knee is still bouncing as I swing my legs over the bench and sit up, pressing my hand down onto my knee. This time it seems to help me keep my toes still and my leg stops moving. The hedge circle still looks the same but there is an opening behind me. Didn't I go through there and into a maze? I stand up and approach the opening, whistling to myself as I feel more comfortable making noise because of the bird sounds. My legs and arms still feel weak and I seem to have no strength because even getting up from the bench was difficult. That makes no sense as I'm sure that I'd been resting for some time.

As I continue to whistle the birds fall silent as if they are listening to my tune. But once I reach the hedge opening I stop whistling and the birds quickly start up their own chirping again. It sounds like there are a lot more of them now though.

Moving through the opening and into the hedge maze seems to loosen up my legs and I regain a little of my strength. It feels strangely energising to be on the move and I run my fingers along each side of the hedge as I traverse the passageway. The hedges tickle my fingers but gradually the way seems to get a little narrower, forcing me to lower my arms closer to my body. Soon I reach a T-Junction where I'm surprised to find Virgil and Lily waiting for me and both of them smiling.

'Well done Ewan,' says Lily, speaking first for once.

'What for?' I ask doubtfully.

'For staying,' she replies. 'The maze is a safe place. Being here helps you to control and order your thoughts.'

'I don't understand,' I reply.

Virgil is silent but watches our engagement with keen interest. Lily moves a step towards me and takes one of my hands in hers, squeezing it gently. 'Virgil isn't real,' she informs me. 'He's just in your mind. But he can't influence you here in the centre of the maze.'

Her words confuse me further and I glance over at Virgil who seems just as real as she does. 'Influence me?' I ask.

'Bring yourself back to the maze whenever you need to focus your mind and control your thoughts,' she tells me. 'Then Virgil will leave you alone.'

'I still don't understand about this maze,' I reply

But even as I speak the hedges seem to close in a little more and the passageway gets even narrower, overpowering me with an urge to raise my arms and make sure the walls stay back. Virgil steps forwards and stands right in front of Lily abruptly breaking her warm hold on my hand.

'Remember the dead loop?' he asks. 'Ewan, try to remember who you are. She isn't one of us. She isn't like us, so don't listen to her nonsense. We make our own rules, shape our own lives and control our own deaths. You and me are partners Ewan, don't you remember?'

The dead loop? I search my mind but the chattering birds make it difficult to concentrate. Virgil does seem familiar somehow and I feel an element of trust towards him. But I can't remember clearly who he is or what this 'dead loop' is. I don't know what I'm doing in this maze with these two people or even who I am. Is there a path somewhere to Vegas or should I stay here like Lily says? Nothing makes any sense so how do I decide what to do?

'See what she's done to you?' asks Virgil, stepping aside and pointing his finger accusingly at Lily. 'She's messed up your head and broken your mind with her psycho-babble bullshit. The stupid bitch is trying to come between us.'

Lily's steely but indifferent face has a faintly cruel look to her mouth and I struggle to read her emotions even when she offers me a reassuring smile. Virgil plainly looks desperate, but his eyes and face appear more trustworthy and I sense that he is trying to help me somehow.

'So what do I do?' I ask him.

'Get out of the maze,' he says simply. 'Find a way out and back to me, because this is her domain. She can't touch you once you're outside.'

'But I don't know the way out,' I reply.

'You don't need to find a way out Ewan,' Lily interjects. 'You can leave anytime you want, but it's your mind that's keeping you here Ewan, not me. It's keeping you in the maze because it's safe here even if you don't understand that yet. Virgil is out there, that's true enough but you must reject him and follow your own choices.'

Their rhetoric confuses me with their strange and conflicting advice. Their statements swirl around in my mind and seem to mix together while allowing other thoughts to flood in, thoughts that I don't understand. Faces appear in my head of people that I vaguely recognise but they disappear and reappear so fast that I can't identify them. I close my eyes and press my hands over my ears but the thoughts won't go away. Please, someone silence their voices and stop the birds chattering so loudly. There are too many faces and thoughts which are beginning to torment my mind. I fall to the floor as darkness and confusion begin to overwhelm my brain.

'Stop it! Stop it!' I scream. 'Leave me alone, all of you!'

My eyes flicker slowly open and I'm forced to squint against the bright lights on the ceiling. The room is small and windowless with pale yellow walls and just two chairs in it. There is a single plain brown door on one wall and an air conditioner vent hums quietly from the white ceiling. The temperature is almost perfect for me, even in my plain blue pyjamas. My chair is soft and comfortable although my knee bounces slightly as my toes move up and down involuntarily on the soft carpet. There is a smiling woman sat in the chair opposite me with short dark hair and a wiry fringe.

'How are you feeling Ewan?' she asks.

As she speaks, the smile leaves her face and the corners of her mouth turn down a little giving her a slightly sour look.

'I feel tired,' I reply, 'And weak.'

'Well I'm pleased that you're finally talking to me,' she says, smiling again. 'My name is Lily and I've had quite a long wait.'

'That's alright,' I reply.

'Do you know where you are?' she asks.

I look around the room for a moment, yellow and featureless but my eyes focus on the brass handle of the door. It seems to shine at me brightly as it reflects the ceiling lights.

'I'm not sure,' I say, turning back to her.

'What is the last thing you remember?' she probes.

My hair feels dry and dense as I scratch my head, hurting my scalp slightly as I pull at the roots. My temple also throbs intermittently, the warning signs of an impending headache.

'A maze,' I reply simply. 'I was in a big hedge maze.'

Lily nods. 'Were you alone?'

'Yes,' I reply. 'I was trying to find a way out I think.'

'And did you find a way out?' she asks.

I close my eyes and try to remember, eager to answer her questions. 'No wait! I wasn't alone,' I tell her. 'There was a man there, and a woman.'

'Do you know who they were?' she asks.

'The man was called Virgil. He wanted to help me leave and I think he showed me the way out,' I explain.

'And what about the woman, who was she?' Lily asks.

'I don't know,' I reply, shaking my head.

My knee is bouncing a little faster now as I blink my eyes and try to remember.

'You're doing well, so take your time,' Lily says encouragingly. 'Don't try and force yourself to remember. I'm here to help you.'

'Okay,' I reply, relaxing a little and taking a few slow deep breaths.

'Is that better?' Lily asks.

'Yes thanks,' I reply. 'Virgil was wearing black, he wanted to help me out of the maze. But I think the woman wanted me to stay for some reason.'

'And what happened after that?' she asks. 'What did you decide to do?'

'That's all I remember,' I say. 'And then suddenly I was here.'

'That's fine,' she replies. 'You're doing really well Ewan.'

But suddenly a spark of recognition ignites a memory in my mind. 'Wait! I do know who she was,' I exclaim. 'It was you! You were the lady in the maze.'

'Really?' she asks with a heightened tone of interest in her voice. 'Then I must have really gotten through to you. That's fantastic.'

'It was... lonely there,' I murmur, 'and too quiet.'

'Do you remember anything else?' she asks, 'anything that I said to you perhaps?'

'You said something about being safe I think,' I tell her, scratching and fidgeting at my itching scalp again. 'You said it was safe somewhere, in the maze maybe?'

'Well you're safe here now Ewan,' she tries to assure me. 'Do you understand that?'

I nod in reply.

'Good, well it's fantastic that you're talking to me now,' she says, 'just don't push yourself too hard to remember things, alright? It'll start to come back with time.'

'Okay,' I reply, a little puzzled.

'You look tired Ewan,' she says. 'Would you like to have a lie down?'

'Yes please, I do feel tired,' I reply.

Lily stands up and guides me towards the door and out of the room into a green corridor. It reminds me a bit of the hedge maze, only these walls really are solid. She guides me slowly along the corridor, her hand holding my arm until she steers me through another door and into a small bedroom. The walls are painted half in dark blue and half in light blue and there is a single window covered by closed curtains. The furniture consists of a single bed, a wardrobe and a bedside table. It's rather plain looking but a simple and efficiently designed place to rest and it looks comfortable all the same.

Lily helps me into bed and I notice there are framed pictures of the countryside hanging on the walls. The pillows feel soft against my head as she pulls the purple blankets over me, but doesn't go quite so far as tucking me in. I roll onto my side as Lily switches off the bedside lamp, plunging the room into semi-darkness.

'We'll have another chat in the morning, okay?' she says.

I don't answer but she says goodnight and leaves the room, closing the door behind her.

The bed feels safe, the blankets comforting and my toes and leg are no longer moving. I think about the hedge maze, wondering why I was there and how I found a way out but there doesn't seem to be any answers. I remember Lily's advice about not trying too hard but it's so frustrating to realise that I'm not sure who I am, or how I got here to this place.

Before I fall asleep the bedroom door opens and I see the silhouette of a figure in the doorway. I look up, assuming that Lily has come back but as the person closes the door and walks nearer I realise that it's actually the man from the maze. It's the man that was all dressed in black – Virgil.

'You've really done it now Ewan,' he says, shaking his head disdainfully as he approaches.

'Done what?' I ask.

'I told you not to listen to that bitch,' he replies. 'You don't belong here Old Man. You belong in the dead loop, not in some hospital.'

'Dead loop?' I repeat. 'But I don't understand.'

'Of course you don't understand,' he says, sighing. 'She's still fucking with your mind. Listen to me, you can't die Ewan, neither of us can. Well not permanently anyway.'

'I don't want to die.' I tell him.

Virgil places a hand on my shoulder and leans over the bed.

'You die every day,' he says. 'But just like me you don't stay dead. Can't you remember any of it?'

I shake my head and try to roll back over but his hand on my shoulder prevents me. His words are confusing me and all of his talk about death is disturbing.

Suddenly Virgil yanks my pillow out from under me and my head falls flat on the bed.

'Remember this?' he asks, waving the pillow at me. 'Jog any memories, stuffing this over my face?'

'I don't know what you mean,' I say, trying to grab the pillow, but he holds it well out of my reach.

'You will,' he says, dropping the pillow on the floor. 'You just see. You'll be dead by the morning and then you'll understand everything. You won't be in this shithole; you'll be partying with me again and far away from that bitch Lily.'

'Why am I in hospital?' I ask urgently. 'Why will I die?'

Virgil kicks the pillow in frustration and walks towards the door but before leaving he turns to speak to me one last time.

'I'll see you tomorrow Old Man,' he says.

Virgil closes the door and I'm forced to close my eyes as weariness tugs at the corners of my mind. My knee is shaking again and I don't have the energy to get out of bed and pick up the pillow. I just need to sleep.

20
Trust

There is a knock on my bedroom door and a nurse walks in and opens the curtains, flooding the room with early morning daylight. My eyes blink rapidly as I squint and look at the woman in her blue and white uniform. Her short hair is auburn and quite frizzy as it frames her spectacled face but she turns to leave the room before I can estimate her age.

I begin rubbing my eyes in reaction to the light from window and the woman re-enters the room, wheeling a trolley in front of her. One of the wheels squeaks slightly as she brings it nearer to the bed and I read the name badge on her uniform. She looks around forty years old, her name is Brenda.

'Good morning Mr. Charles,' she says, 'I'm glad you're awake, I've bought you some breakfast.'

The thought occurs to me that I probably wasn't actually awake until she opened the curtains but the idea of breakfast makes up for her intrusion. I sit up in bed yawning and rubbing my eyes again before arranging the purple blanket neatly around my legs. The headboard of the bed is soft and I lean back as the woman switches on the ceiling light which flickers into life. With the curtains already open and the bright blue sky visible, the ceiling light makes little difference and I wonder why she bothered with it.

'I hope you're hungry,' Brenda says cheerfully, lifting up a padded tray from the trolley and placing it over my legs, 'you have cereal and toast this morning.'

She pushes the trolley right up close to the side of the bed and into my reach. 'There's a cup of coffee and some orange juice there too,' she says as I glance at the tray, wondering why she needed to explain everything.

'Thank you Brenda,' I reply.

'How do you feel this morning?' she asks.

My head feels a little groggy as if I've slept too long and then been woken up suddenly. I also feel weak but the fact that my appetite stirs at the thought of breakfast is encouraging, even though my leg is quivering slightly. The involuntarily twitching of my leg is sufficient to make the breakfast tray vibrate.

'I feel alright thanks Brenda,' I inform her. 'What's wrong with me?'

She puts her hands on her hips and smiles. 'Oh don't worry you're just fine Honey,' she tries to reassure me. 'Lily will be in to see you after breakfast, alright?'

'Okay,' I say, shrugging as she pours some milk from a little jug into my coffee.

'Just a little milk as usual,' she says. 'Enjoy your breakfast.'

Brenda leaves the room and I see two other nurses walk past in the corridor, one of whom glances in. I'm unable to catch a look at either of their faces before the door closes automatically.

The toast is dry and undercooked and the little sachets of butter are barely enough to cover even one slice. I like my toast well buttered but make do with what's available, thinly spreading the three slices with a blunt plastic butter knife. There are a few sachets of jam on offer but I don't fancy them. The butter tastes salty in my mouth as I lick the knife clean but the toast seems dry and tasteless. Glancing at the jam again, I peel open one of the sachets of blackberry jam but it looks greasy and unpalatable. I fold the seal back over it and toss it onto the trolley, continuing to eat the toast as it is. Eating feels strange.

The bowl of dry cereal is some kind of muesli and there is a jug of cold milk on the trolley but after the second slice of toast I no longer feel very hungry and my stomach doesn't feel right. I reach over and put the tray back on the trolley and pick up the jug of milk. There is condensation on it and it feels cold and wet in my hand but I realise how thirsty I was before I even ate the toast. Tipping the milk jug back against my lips I slowly drain it all in one steady flow, sighing with satisfaction as the cold milk soothes my throat and fills my stomach. I decide to leave the coffee and juice for the time being to enjoy the refreshing aftertaste of the milk.

Resting my head back against the headboard I close my eyes and relax. My mind feels calm but I wonder what I'm doing here. And then I suddenly recall Virgil, the man at my bedside and his words come back into my thoughts. *'You'll be dead by the morning and then you'll understand everything.'*

But he was wrong, I'm not dead and I don't understand anything. I wonder where he is now. *'You won't be in this shithole; you'll be partying with me again and far away from that bitch Lily,'* he had said.

Lily, her name is familiar too. Brenda mentioned her when she delivered my breakfast and I think she helped me get out of a maze. But what maze? An image of hedges creeps into my mind but the thought is confusing and the concept of being lost there seems strange. At least the images come into my mind slowly though, one at a time and allowing me to consider them before being replaced by something else.

I open my eyes and reach out for the cup of coffee. There is a little paper cup next to it with three red and yellow tablets in it. I pick up the cup and automatically pour the tablets into my mouth like I have done it before, swallowing them down with a sip of the coffee. The coffee is surprisingly nice in comparison to the toast. It tastes rich, dark and aromatic and I take a long sip, soothing my throat where the tablets went down.

I stay in bed until my coffee is finished and then swing my legs over the side of the bed and stand up. My head feels a little dizzy as if I've got up too quickly and I find myself having to hold onto the bed for a moment until the feeling passes. The coffee and the jug of milk have added to my urge for the toilet so I walk across the room and push open a door to the en-suite bathroom.

The bathroom is small but functional, with a toilet and shower but no bath tub and although the thought of being able to soak in a hot bath is appealing the shower also looks inviting. After using the toilet I strip off my pyjamas and step inside the cubicle and turn on the shower. The hot jets spray down all over my body, invigorating and massaging me as I close my eyes. The force of the water in my hair is very refreshing and it streams down my face, neck and back as I slowly rotate my head and welcome it. As soon as I'm accustomed to the temperature I turn the heat up a little and steam envelops me in the glass cubicle. I remain in the shower for a long time and my legs even begin to feel stronger as if the warm water is revitalising them and empowering my body.

Once I reluctantly step out of the shower I retrieve a large white towel from where it hangs on a heated radiator and wrap it around my waist. There is a large mirror above the sink and my torso looks bright pink from the hot water. But my body also looks a little thin. I squeeze my arms and rub my chest but the flesh feels soft as if the muscles have relaxed a little. As I open my mouth wide my reflection copies me and I stare into the darkness of my mouth, running my tongue over my teeth and tasting coffee. There is a toothbrush on the shelf above the sink and I squeeze on some paste and brush my teeth. My wrist aches a little with the effort but after rinsing out my mouth I run my tongue over the smooth surface of my teeth to check that they feel clean. Finally I run my fingers through my hair, sweeping the damp strands backwards until they are neat enough to meet my approval.

Leaving the bathroom I begin to rub myself dry with the towel and I notice that the breakfast trolley has been taken away while I was in the shower. After drying off I return to the bathroom and pick up my pyjamas from the floor and toss them onto the bed. With the wet towel tied around my waist I open the wardrobe and sift through familiar clothes hanging on cheap plastic hangers. Slowly I begin to get dressed, feeling my back ache as I bend down to pull on some trousers before buttoning up a blue shirt. There are some slippers in the wardrobe and they fit me perfectly. After the shower and the food I appreciate how good it feels to be alive. The sensation of being clean and awake is comforting. I decide to leave the bedroom and stretch my legs, encouraged by my newfound energy generated by the revitalising shower.

I open the door of my room and peer curiously into the corridor but there doesn't seem to be anyone around. Taking a stroll down the corridor I notice a large plant growing just outside my room, its dark green colour seeming vibrant against the plainer green of the corridor. I touch its long natural looking leaves only to discover that they are actually plastic. I lean over and smell the leaves but feel disappointed and a little cheated that they have no odour. They are a poor comparison to the real thing.

'Ah, there you are,' says a woman's voice behind me.

I look up from the plant, feeling a little silly for smelling it as Lily walks towards. She has uninspiring flat shoes on, green trousers and a black cardigan. A pair of glasses hang around her neck on a cord and they bounce on her cardigan as she approaches me.

'Good morning Ewan,' she says brightly. 'It's great to see you up and about.'

'Hello Lily,' I reply.

'Were you admiring our shrubbery?' she asks with an amused smile.

I glance a little sheepishly at the artificial plant. 'Just checking they didn't need any water.' I reply.

'Oh I watered them yesterday,' she jokes.

'Okay,' I say, smiling at her a little uncomfortably.

She stands there for a moment studying me as if she is wondering what I'm thinking and it makes me feel a little self-conscious. I break eye contact with her and glance around at the plant and the walls until she finally speaks.

'Let's have a chat shall we Ewan?' she suggests. 'Come on, follow me.'

Lily turns and walks back down the corridor, gesturing at me to follow. Without answering I begin to walk after her.

Lily leads me to a small room with little more than two chairs in it and motions for me to sit in one. The room looks very familiar and I experience feelings of safety as I sit down. Lily sits in the chair opposite me and waits a moment for me to get comfortable. At least my leg is behaving this morning and not causing my knee to bounce up and down.

'So did you sleep well Ewan?' Lily asks finally.

'Yes, thank you,' I reply.

'That's good,' she replies, smiling again. 'You're in the hospital Ewan, do you understand that?'

I had made that assumption this morning or maybe even yesterday but for some reason hadn't given much thought as to why, until she confirms the fact now. Maybe I wasn't even interested why until now.

'Yes, I know,' I reply. 'But what's wrong with me?'

Lily cups her hands on the table in front of her and looks at me closely, her staring eyes fixed on me again. She studies me carefully for a moment but this time I look straight back at her, waiting for her to speak and no longer needing to glance away from her intense studying eyes.

'Ewan,' she says slowly, 'You have been in a state of catatonia.'

'Catatonia?' I reply, repeating the unfamiliar word.

'But you don't need to worry,' she says reassuringly, 'because you've come out of it now.'

'But what is it I ask?' unable to hide the concern from my voice, perhaps because an illness beginning with 'Ca' sounds too much like it could be like Cancer.

'It's a state of motor inability,' she explains, 'like a stupor where you remain in place for some time and don't react to any external stimuli. But we have managed to get you out of it now.'

'But why was I like that?' I ask her, suddenly feeling embarrassed and ashamed that there is something wrong with me. 'I don't remember anything like that, like not moving.'

'That's perfectly normal,' she assures me. 'Don't struggle to remember things, just let them come back to you gradually. The important thing is that you're talking now and reacting so you're going to get better. I'm going to help you.'

Her words are frightening and confusing, no matter how much she tries to reassure me and my knee has begun moving again. It feels very unnerving to apparently have an illness but not remember getting through it but I try to close my mind to those feelings and listen to her.

'So what's wrong with me?' I ask. 'Why does my leg keep shaking? Why do I feel so weak?'

'Your leg is nothing to worry about Ewan,' she says, glancing at it as she talks. 'The shaking is just a side effect of your psychosis medication.'

'Psychosis?' I repeat. 'Are you saying I'm psychotic?'

'Don't be alarmed Ewan,' she replies. 'Psychosis is just a condition of the mind and I'm here to help you understand it. It's a kind of chain reaction in your mind where one extreme thought gives rise to another but it doesn't mean that you go off attacking people.'

This all sounds too much to take in, but I need to know.

'What does it mean?' I ask.

'It's just a problem with your mind that talking to me and taking your medication will help us sort out,' she explains.

Her words seem less reassuring now and the implications of what she is telling me so frightening. Have I lost my mind? Does it have something to do with the maze I was trapped in? Why am I even in this place and what happened to me? I remember someone came to visit me last night – a man and he said I was going to die. His name was Virgil and he told me not to trust her.

'Who is Virgil, a doctor?' I ask. 'He said I was going to die.'

Lily's expression doesn't change but she appears to scrutinise me even closer with those dark eyes, analysing me like a hawk watching its prey.

'You've told me about him before, when you first came out of your stupor,' she says. 'But I don't think he's a real person Ewan. I think he is just someone in your mind, just a part of your condition, that's all. He could be a part of your psychosis but we have talked about helping you to dismiss him from your mind and to help control your thoughts.'

How could he not be a real person? I remember him in the maze and last night by my bedside, as clearly and vividly as this woman in front of me. Should I tell her she is mistaken? The memory of his words, his face and mannerisms are all so real, so believable.

I frown and scratch at my face, feeling quite a few day's growth under my fingers. It feels wrong as I normally shave at least every two days. I will tell her she is wrong.

'But that's impossible, he spoke to me Lily,' I explain. 'I remember his words, as clear as you talking to me now.'

'I'm sure that he seems real to you Ewan,' she says. 'That's perfectly normal for someone with your condition. It's very common to interact with people while in psychosis, people that often seem perfectly real. Hearing voices, seeing people, feeling sensations, it all happens in the mind especially for people who have been in catatonia.'

But I can't accept that explanation.

'Virgil,' I say his name slowly as I picture his face.

He is more than a memory because I remember the touch of his hand on my shoulder, his personality and his insistence that I should listen to him. Could he really just be a hallucination or a figment of my own mind?

Lily is very good at pausing in conversation to allow me time to think about what she is telling me. This is one of those moments where she judges perfectly how much time I need before she continues.

'Everything you've told me about Virgil has negative connotations Ewan,' she says. 'His influence on your mind is something that you need to dismiss. Try to stop thinking about him. Ignore his voice and his presence and you should be able to dispel his influence over you. Doing that will help you get better, do you understand that?'

'Not really,' I reply, shaking my head.

'I understand, don't worry. What was the last thing you remember him saying to you,' Lily asks.

'He was at my bedside last night,' I say.

'Well I can assure you that there is no one called Virgil in the department,' she replies. 'Go on, what did he say?'

'It was something like, "*you won't be in this shithole tomorrow, you'll be with me again,*"' I tell her, but then I hesitate for a moment. 'He also said "*you'll be away from that bitch Lily.*"'

But my words don't offend her. 'Charming!' she says, with an amused smile, 'but you are still here aren't you Ewan?'

I nod slowly, unable to dispute the fact.

'Ewan, when you came out of catatonia, you were very confused and withdrawn. It's taken quite a lot of medication and a number of days for us to break through to you,' she explains. 'I did a lot of talking at first, explaining things to you and it took a long time before you responded. But you did respond eventually. It was just a few words at first but it meant that your mind wanted to get better.'

The resonance of her voice does sound familiar and I feel like it's very normal listening to her speak without me offering much in response. I no longer feel uncomfortable holding permanent eye contact with her.

'Yes,' she continues, 'you started to open up, slowly at first but gradually you let me into your mind. You spoke a lot about Virgil and a lot about death and the things that Virgil wanted you to do. But you are fighting him Ewan, closing your mind to him and shutting out his negative influence. Do you remember?'

I think about her words and about the fact that Virgil was wrong – I'm not away from this place. Lily genuinely appears to be trying to help me but my mind feels so empty, devoid of answers while unaware of the right questions to ask. It feels as if she is re-layering my mind, one level at a time but the picture is empty like a jigsaw with only the outside pieces put together. I don't remember much else of what Virgil told me.

'I can't really remember much,' I tell her disappointedly.

'That's alright, you're making really good progress,' she assures me. 'Now I want you to have a nice relaxing day today okay? Just sit in the common room and rest. Try to let your mind settle and take in what I have told you. I don't want to rush you. We'll talk again tomorrow morning, okay?'

I have to trust that she knows what is best for me and the idea of a relaxing day without too much thinking is an appealing one, so I readily agree with her advice.

My bed is a welcoming sight as I climb beneath the blankets in my pyjamas and accept the warmth of its sanctuary. I rest my head back on the pillow and think about my lazy afternoon. Lunch this afternoon had been much better than the toast I had for breakfast. It was a full roast chicken dinner with all the trimmings, eaten in the common room with the other patients. Most of them didn't speak much except for one or two who commented on the taste of the food, something I couldn't blame them in breaking their silence for.

Lily was right about the day being relaxing, I'd spent most of it in an armchair gazing out of a window into the lush hospital gardens. Later on when the doors were opened we were allowed to walk around the little grassy paths, looking at the flowers and enjoying the fresh air. It was a warm sunny afternoon, the sky was blue and the garden was a tranquil haven, nothing at all like a hospital really. My time in the garden had given me plenty of time to think and it was a perfect environment in which to do it in but I heeded her advice about not exerting my mind and just relaxing.

One thing I did think about though was her allegations about Virgil and his negative influence on me. Somehow I knew she was right about that and every fibre of belief in my heart told me that Virgil is somehow part of my condition. I think I trust Lily now because she doesn't seem to put any pressure on me while she is guiding me through the maze of thoughts that are in my mind. I anticipate our next discussion and her comforting voice with a fresh enthusiasm. Her treatment feels ironically infectious.

After a pleasant and quiet supper one of the other patients had latched onto me, a man called Graham who was probably about my age. He didn't ask me any questions about myself but was keen to tell me all about his condition, his life story and his family. He is the youngest of three brothers and the other two have a history of mental illness which he feared would one day affect him too. Apparently in the last six months, he had lost his job and become depressed when he was unable to find work. He began to have doubts about himself, to lose his self-esteem and believe he was going to end up like his brothers. Counselling and medication had proven ineffective in treating him and eventually he was committed to an institution for smashing up a shop and harming himself in the process.

He was in the institution for a month before being released full time into Lily's care but now he returns here voluntarily just one day a week, apparently to help him focus his thoughts and discuss his anxieties. It seems obvious even to me that Lily was largely responsible for his recovery. Graham is now well on the road to restoring full mental health although he still seems a bit strange to me, continually talking but not really looking at me as his pupils dart around the room.

At times I felt like he could almost be talking to anybody but I was grateful that he didn't ask me anything about myself as I wouldn't be too sure what to tell him. Anyway he was more entertaining than the film they were showing in the common room, but by late evening we were all ushered back to our rooms by the efficient Brenda who seems to work here from morning till night.

I pull the blankets closer around my body, roll onto my side and close my eyes before reaching out to switch off the bedside light. My thoughts turn to tomorrow and I yawn as I think about Virgil and Lily. I drift easily off to sleep, finally knowing exactly which one of them to trust. Thanks to Graham, strange as he may be, I now trust Lily completely.

21
Family

A car pulls up alongside me and sounds its horn twice. It's a filthy brown Renault with an engine that sounds badly in need of a service. The driver's side window slides down and a man's face appears, leaning through the window and grinning at me.

'Get in Ewan,' he says.

His face seems familiar but it stirs mixed emotions in me. I frown as I struggle to identify him but he stares at me with an expectant look as if he wants me to work out his identity for myself. As I fix my eyes on the French beret partly covering his blonde hair, he shakes his head and sighs.

'Dead loop,' he says, flatly with a hint of impatience.

'Sorry?' I reply.

His words are strange to me but his blonde hair is so familiar and I find myself taking a step towards the car.

'You took some bloody finding,' he says.

I continue to stare at the man; my eyes locked on him as he removes his French beret and tosses it out of the window.

'Your hat,' he says.

I react instinctively to catch the beret and it feels warm and soft in my hands as I place it on my head.

'Perfect fit,' the man says, before laughing out loud.

'You're Virgil,' I say, suddenly able to remember his name. 'Sorry but I'm not supposed to see you.'

At least that's what my mind seems to be telling me.

'Sorry Old Man,' he says. 'Had you forgotten about everything for a moment?'

Someone told me to be wary of this man, I'm sure of it. And I think they insisted that I have nothing to do with him.

'Sorry, it happens sometimes,' Virgil explains, 'especially with the better awakenings. I'm sorry to break up your little holiday.'

Am I on holiday? As I look around I see rolling countrywide and I'm in a small village that looks possibly French. There is a row of shops nearby and I spot two women through the window of the nearest shop, discussing a bottle of wine. The older woman is laughing and the younger one is smiling.

'Oh don't worry about them,' says Virgil. 'They'll be fine on their own. You'll see them again soon anyway. In fact you'll always see them like that now, at that age I mean.'

I look back at him and he pats the passenger seat with his hand. 'Come on get in,' he urges me.

I pull open the door but then hesitate about getting in.

'I promise no bank robberies today,' he says.

What does he mean, bank robbery?

'Besides,' says Virgil, chuckling, 'I doubt we'd find a fucking bank round here anyway!'

I lean into the car and dismiss his comment. 'Who are they?' I ask, 'that woman and girl?'

He frowns. 'Helen and Jenny,' he says after a brief pause, 'your wife and daughter. And if you don't mind me saying so, Helen is looking pretty damn hot this morning, no offence. You're a lucky man Ewan.'

Helen and Jenny, my family! I close the car door and take a step towards the shop, cupping my hands against the glass as I peer through the window. It's my beautiful wife Helen and my daughter Jenny. Virgil sounds the car horn again and I hear his voice calling. 'Hurry up and get in,' he says.

The sound of the horn causes the two women in the shop to look around in my direction but for some reason I'm terrified of being seen. Before I realise it I'm running down the pavement with the unexpected and sudden sting of tears beginning to pool in my eyes.

'Wait!' yells Virgil.

But I have to get away from him and away from them.

The narrow pavement feels hard on my feet and I stumble over something obstructive and fall heavily to the ground. As I look up and rub my knee I see my daughter Jenny looking down at me with tears in her eyes and her face a mask of sorrow.

Her face radiates disappointment and blame, all of it directed towards me and it fills my mind with guilt. Tears begin to stream from my eyes with the emotional distress of my daughter's apparent disappointment. Her pained expression seems to contain hatred and the venomous look she has now is simply too much pressure to bear. Painful emotions begin to overwhelm me and her hatred burns into my soul. I'm forced to look down at the ground and then cover my eyes. Pathetically I curl up into a ball, hugging my knees to my chest and begin sobbing, but her face continues to haunt my mind until I scream out in anguished sorrow without understanding why.

I wake up abruptly and sit up in bed in a state of panic, the bedroom still dark and silent. My pyjamas are soaked in sweat, sticking them to my chest and I feel the dampness under my arms and around my groin. I kick away the blankets, gasping to control my breathing and welcoming the cooler air as it surrounds me.

My body heat begins to escape from under the blankets and dissipate as I fumble for the bedside lamp, my hands shaking. I'm still breathing rapidly, almost panting and my heart races as the lamp illuminates the room, chasing away darkness but leaving shadows in its place. The closed bedroom door seems far away and somehow entrapping, giving me a claustrophobic feeling.

As my breathing begins to slow and my body cools down I lower my legs over the side of the bed and loosen the buttons of my pyjama top, allowing the welcome caress of cooler air to reach my chest. Where are my family Helen and Jenny? I can still picture Jenny's face, staring at me from the nightmare with her eyes raining tears, and that cold harsh look of hatred and disappointment she gave me. It was definitely directed at me and I feel the sting of tears in my eyes, the trickle of one escaping from my left eye and onto my burning cheek. Wiping it away on my pyjama sleeve I blink and try to calm down and make sense of the madness of the nightmare images.

I'm thirsty and feel dehydrated from sweating so much but all I can think about is why Helen didn't leave the shop when she saw me. My head hurts. What was the reason for Jenny's feelings towards me? And Virgil's words confuse me too, *'They'll be fine on their own. You'll see them again soon anyway.'*

I want to trust his statement about seeing them, but my instincts tell me that Virgil can't be trusted. Lily told me that and I believe her. Virgil's voice comes into my mind again. *'Dead loop?'* Why does he refer to death so much? What does he mean by dead loop? But now I know more than ever that I want nothing to do with him. He wanted me to get in his car and to take me away from my family. Is that why Jenny was disappointed? But I won't go with him ever again, whoever he is.

My thirst begins to torment me but the bathroom door seems too far away and the floor of shadows is unwelcoming so I lay back down on the bed sheet. My eyes sting but I've regained enough control to prevent tears. Wiping the corners of my eyes I pull my knees up to my chest and lay on my side, kicking the blankets further to the bottom of the bed. I badly need more sleep after the nightmare.

The experience reminds me that I have a family and highlights to me that I haven't even been thinking about them. In a strange way it feels like I hadn't really forgotten about them at all, the reminder of their existence in the nightmare has simply replaced their absence from my mind. I don't feel that I've suddenly just remembered them; they were just absent from my thoughts until now.

One thing is clear in my mind – I want to see them as soon as possible and to feel Helen's arms around me. As soon as I'm better and get out of here we'll all be together again and can maybe take a holiday, somewhere warm like Greece. I wonder how Jenny is doing in her exams.

Trying to ignore my thirst I picture Helen's face in my mind but she seems blurred and undefined, nothing like she was through the shop window. But at least she doesn't share Jenny's tears and disappointment. Helen is actually smiling at me, despite the blurred appearance of her face but I still can't focus on what she looks like. I struggle to try and make her image clearer in my mind, taking long slow breaths as I try to rest. I'm so exhausted and my mind over stimulated but Helen's smiling face lulls me to sleep.

Virgil slurps his coffee and looks at me, smiling innocently.

'Don't you see that I had to?' he asks. 'I had to destroy your opinion of me so I could start again from the lowest foundation. It was the only way to make you understand and to gain your trust.'

'But I don't understand anything,' I emphasise to him. 'And I don't trust a fucking word you say either.'

Virgil puts down his mug and stares right at me, a guarded look in his eyes as he lowers his voice to an audible whisper.

'Let me explain something to you,' he whispers. 'I'll be absolutely clear. I'm dying every day *exactly* like you, stuck in random situations with no way out. I'm trapped. Don't you see? I'm in the dead loop too Ewan.'

'What is the dead loop?' I demand angrily. 'You keep saying that to me. I don't know what this is all about or what you're talking about. And you tried to take me from my family.'

'Every day you die Ewan,' he says firmly. 'I've told you that already, but then just like me you awaken somewhere else on another day. You must remember. I'm not taking you away from anybody. It's the dying that takes you away from your family.'

He is deadly serious about it, but that can't really be happening to me. I don't want to listen to him but somehow I begin to sense that he is right. I can remember my death. I was killed in a plane crash. But there was another time too, being hit by a car and another – being stabbed by someone. It's all starting to come back to me, like a bathroom mirror slowly clearing after a bath is emptied. It's the most bizarre revelation that I've ever experienced but I suddenly feel very uncomfortable. Virgil's words are laced with truths that are embedded deep in my memory.

'Are there others like us?' I ask finally.

'Not as far as I can tell,' he says. 'It's just you and me. I've been following you ever since I suspected back in Pripyat after you fell.'

'Following me? But why?' I ask.

'Our world is a lonely place Ewan,' he explains. 'A place where no one understands us and no one can help. You've seen my family, I've lost as much as you. I mean I do still see them sometimes but I've also accepted that they're gone. They're no longer a part of my life, just an occasional distraction.'

'Your family...' I say, seemingly unable to recall them.

'Look I've been doing this much longer than you,' he explains. 'I must have died over a hundred times already by now, but you're the only person whose path I keep crossing. The only person who sees what I see and knows what I know.'

Virgil's words are really confusing me now, at odds with what I have been told by someone else. It was Lily, she told me not to listen to him and to avoid him. Dying again does scare me and being near him scares me. Right now I need to be with my family, to hold them, and to receive comfort from them.

'I can't help you Virgil,' I tell him.

'We can help each other Ewan,' he says. 'Trust me.'

'No!' I reply firmly. 'You stay away from me.'

Virgil's face turns pale and he slams down his mug on the table, his knuckles white on the handle. 'You need me,' he growls. 'Where were you without me? Stumbling blind from death to death with no purpose and no direction, no fucking idea what was happening to you. Nowhere! That's where you were.'

But I won't be coerced by him. 'Leave me alone!' I snap.

'You'll regret this,' he says threateningly, a sinister look in his eyes. 'You'll come looking for me when you're alone and lost in the dead loop. And I'll remember this conversation.'

A few of the customers are looking round and peering at us over their coffee, stealing sideways glances at our sudden raised voices. But I don't feel any embarrassment or tinge of self-consciousness. I lean forward and stare at Virgil, my thoughts clear and focused.

'Get out!' I shout at him. 'Just leave!'

Virgil slowly stands up and glares at me, most of the customers watching him. 'Fuck you Ewan,' he says bluntly with a voice of finality before marching through the coffee shop exit.

As the door closes behind him I finish the last mouthful of my coffee and close my eyes.

My leg is moving involuntarily again as my calf flexes and my toes make my knee bounce. I had a long shower this morning to wash the night sweat from my body although it seemed to take forever. The soothing water jets had relaxed and soothed my body but failed to wash the nightmares away. Lily now faces me from the other chair and my head hurts a little.

'I had nightmares last night,' I tell her shakily, 'bad ones.'

'Would you like to tell me about them?' she asks.

I'm surprised to find myself nod, despite being consciously aware how sharing my thoughts with her is so effective in helping me to organise my mind.

'Helen and Jenny were there,' I tell her. 'Jenny was upset with me, she was sad and crying but I don't know why. And Virgil, he was there too hassling me to go with him.'

'And did you go with him?' asks Lily.

She has her glasses on today and they make her eyes look bigger but the excess cord seems odd hanging either side of her face.

'No, I refused to go with Virgil I tell her. 'But Jenny was crying so much and she just kept staring at me, like she was angry and hated me.'

'It's good that you didn't go with him,' Lily says encouragingly. 'You're gaining control of your thoughts Ewan and rejecting his influence.'

'But then I did go with him afterwards,' I confess. 'We were having coffee somewhere and he was pushing me again. Hassling me.'

'Hassling you about what?' she asks.

The dream is so clear in my mind, so vivid that it seems like it really happened. It was like one of those dreams you never have to struggle to remember and once you cement it in your head it becomes more like a memory. Only this was different, it wasn't a dream – it was a memory, I'm sure of it.

'The dead loop,' I say, the words still sounding strange to me. 'He kept telling me about dying, us both dying, over and over again. But I can remember it. I can actually remember dying Lily. That makes no sense I know.'

'Dying?' she says, 'You've talked about this before, please go on.'

'I remember a plane crash and that I was killed in it, but then someone stabbed me and killed me too,' I tell her. 'I've died lots of times Lily, I'm sure of it. But every time I wake up and then I'm somewhere else, still alive and starting again. But I always die, I keep dying over and over again.'

'In the dream?' she asks.

I shake my head. 'No, it's not a dream, it's really happening. At least it *was* happening. Virgil knew about it too because he was following me. He witnessed it sometimes and it's in my memory, it's not something in a dream. I remember feeling the knife going in when I was stabbed. And I wanted to get off that plane, because I knew what would happen.'

My words fade away as I suddenly feel cold inside and it makes me shiver. I'm shaking slightly as I pause for thought, but at least my leg has stopped moving.

'Ewan sometimes people with psychosis remember unusual things,' Lily explains. 'Thought disorder can make you experience many things that aren't real. These 'deaths' almost certainly happened in your mind while you were in catatonia and while your mind and senses were blocked from reality. It's quite common to believe you're experiencing things with your condition but you have to understand that they weren't real events. I'm here to help you focus on what is real and help you structure and reorder your mind. I think Virgil could be a link to your guilt, a tie to your psychosis that you are gradually severing. Do you see?'

'But it was all so real,' I tell her, shaking my head sceptically. 'How did I get like this, in this psychosis?'

Lily studies me for a moment with her eyes fixated on me, analysing and almost boring into me with her scrutiny.

'Do you remember what happened before you came to the hospital?' she asks finally.

I concentrate for a moment but there is nothing obvious in my memory, just Helen cooking me steak in our apartment. Jenny had finished her exams and we had a meal in London for her eighteenth birthday, just the three of us. We bought her two cruise tickets so she could take a friend with her, a girl preferably. Jenny had no hatred or blame in her eyes then and no sorrow either. Then I remember having an interview and being offered a new job. I took Helen to a park and we made love discreetly on a blanket under a sunny sky, it was my idea. The day after that picnic was when I found out that my old boss Derek had sadly been diagnosed with cancer. None of that explains anything.

'Well I can't remember how I got here,' I tell her.

Lily places her hand gently on mine and looks me in the eyes.

'Ewan you were in a car accident,' she explains. 'Your car was very badly damaged and you received a head injury. It was a major accident and you had to have neurosurgery. Ewan you were in a coma for six weeks.'

'An accident?' I reply, shaking my head because it's all too much to take in at once. 'And coma? I don't remember any accident or any surgery.'

'That's not unusual Ewan. When you regained consciousness you were in catatonia,' she continues, 'you're physically quite well now so please don't worry, but we are still treating your psychosis and helping you to repair your mind.'

'But... I don't...remember,' I say dejectedly.

'You've probably blocked a lot of it out Ewan,' she replies. 'I assure you that's not unusual and certainly nothing to worry about. Don't try too hard to remember, it may come back over time. The important thing is you're making good progress and you're going to get better.'

She releases my hand and sits back in her chair. 'If you keep working with me you have every chance of making a full recovery.'

'I would really like to see my wife,' I inform her.

Lily looks surprised for a moment but hides it smoothly. She stands up and comes alongside my chair, placing one hand on my shoulder. Her face seems to soften a little from her usual cruel look but she looks a little ashen as she takes off her glasses.

'I'm really sorry to have to tell you this Ewan,' she says quietly, 'but I'm afraid that your wife is dead.'

22

The Visitor

Dead? The thought is inconceivable. I'm the one that's been dying and enduring the reality of my life coming to an abrupt end, not my Helen. My wife can't be dead, it's impossible.

'What do you mean she's dead?' I demand with my brow furrowed in disbelief.

Lily pauses for a moment then squeezes my hand a little harder. 'Your wife was killed in an accident Ewan,' she says sombrely, 'I'm so sorry, can't you remember?'

The words don't seem real and my mind churns with confusion and doubt. My feelings can't seem to focus and I'm uncertain how to respond.

'But she can't be dead,' I reply. 'What accident, do you mean my car crash?'

'No, no, you were the only person in the car,' Lily says, hesitating for what seems like a full minute before continuing. 'Your wife died in February, about four months before your car accident and head injury. Don't you remember her funeral?'

I stare blankly at Lily, her eyes watching me intently from behind that strange fringe of hair but her question is unanswerable. A picture of Helen's face at the picnic forms in my mind and then I hear her laughter as she rides a horse through the Greek countryside. I'm too stunned to formulate any emotion, subconsciously confused about whether or not I should be distraught and sobbing. I begin to wonder if I have maybe already accepted Helen's death and dealt with it or if I still don't even believe it's true. Whichever it is I feel a hollow emptiness in my heart, stemming from the fact that she isn't here with me now.

'I don't remember any of it Lily,' I say. 'How is that possible?'

She retakes her seat opposite me, making me feel a slight sense of loss at the removal of her touch on my hand. 'You were in a very serious accident Ewan,' she reminds me. 'With what your mind has been through, the coma, the catatonia and psychosis, you've probably shut out a lot of your bad memories. It happens in a lot of cases of extreme stress. Have you heard of posttraumatic stress disorder?'

'But that's something to do with soldiers isn't it?' I ask.

'No, it doesn't just affect service people,' she informs me, 'it can happen to anyone who has undergone a stressful life experience. Memory loss is quite common for people in your situation.'

'Are you trying to tell me that I've forgotten my wife's death?' I ask incredulously, but the horrific question makes me feel nauseous not angry. 'That's impossible, she can't be dead.'

But deep down I sense that Lily is telling me the truth. I trust her completely and know that she wouldn't deceive me, unlike Virgil. Her eyes force me to turn away for a moment and I stare at the wall as she remains silent, allowing me to contemplate my thoughts. I can still feel her eyes watching me though as I bite the inside of my cheek and my eyes begin to blink a little faster. My loving wife Helen who I share my life with has gone? Then I am truly alone. She may not have been perfect, nobody truly is but she was my soul mate, if there is such a thing. Helen completed me, enhancing my strengths while complementing my weaknesses. It's unbearable to even dare to contemplate a life without her to share it with. I need to see her flowing red hair again and experience the way she fuels my adrenaline and shares my dreams. My rapid blinking is no longer sufficient and my eyes sting as I begin to lose my struggle to fight back tears.

Lily still hasn't spoken a word, expertly waiting for me to process and deal with my feelings but I see her out of the corner of one eye, watching me. I don't want anyone to see me like this, suffering with my sudden bleak realisation of loss and my exponential release of sorrow. The loss is just too incomprehensible to bear. My distress is too personal for it to be witnessed or shared with anybody.

'I'm so sorry to bring it up like that,' Lily says apologetically, as if reading my thoughts.

I can only shake my head, worried about the weakness of my voice if I were to try and respond. I'm forced to keep my face turned away from her, hiding it as I slowly rub my eyes and feel the warm moisture of tears on the back of my hand.

'I'll give you a little time Ewan,' Lily says, her voice sounding a little further away as she moves towards the door. The instant she leaves the room and the door closes I lose any reason to hide or fight my emotions anymore. I lean forward in the chair, my hands over my eyes and begin to sob uncontrollably.

The room is silent and I'm alone with my thoughts, still struggling to believe that I should be grieving. The last loved one that died was my mother but this feels nothing like that. Her heart problems were sudden and unexpected but she soldiered on for two more years and never gave up hope. She changed her lifestyle by eating healthier and exercising but her heart progressively grew weaker, just like my father's had. Soon she was too ill and weak to cope on her own. My mother had moved in with me and Helen for the remainder of her days but she never stopped enjoying life or ever became a burden to us, living every moment in full as if it were her last.

I'll never forget her saying goodbye at Christmas because it was the only time during the illness that she had been upset. Before she passed away peacefully in her sleep, she made sure to say her personal farewells to everyone, not expecting to see another Christmas she told us. Somehow, preparing for death made it easier for her and allowed her to accomplish her goals. But her only regret was not having enough time to see her only grandchild come of age and maybe get married one day. She said that was the one thing that death was unfairly and cruelly robbing her of, but at least she had the chance to say goodbye to Jenny.

My mother never quite got on with Helen as I would have liked, perhaps not thinking she was good enough for her only son, but that Christmas she told me that there was never anyone she would rather have left me with than Helen. That was the truth of it and I knew in my heart that she meant every word, but Helen was gone too now and I was alone. It was criminal and I want to reject the notion of grieving her death because it shouldn't be like this. My mother died with the knowledge that her only child was safe but this was different and felt very wrong. Helen never had a chance to say goodbye and see her daughter's life complete. Things will never be the same again but I swear that Jenny will have my total love and support until she too is happily married, if that's what she wants.

The door opens and the nurse Brenda walks into the room, her face warm and sympathetic as she moves slowly towards the bed as if treading on egg shells. She obviously knows of my tormented pain and doesn't want to exacerbate it.

'I've bought you your medicine Mr. Charles,' she says quietly, offering me a tiny paper cup and a glass of water.

My hand trembles as I tip the tablets into my mouth and take a mouthful of the water before swallowing. Realising how thirsty I am I finish the rest of the cold soothing water and hand the glass back to her.

'Thank you,' I reply, forcing out a weak smile if only to relax her.

'And by the way, you've got a visitor,' she says. 'If you'd like to follow me I'll take you to the visitor's room.'

Her announcement news surprises me. 'Who is it?' I ask her.

She looks back at me from the doorway and smiles. 'It's your brother in law,' she says.

Helen's brother Bill moves slowly through the visiting room, avoiding eye contact with me and looking down at the floor as he approaches. I stand up to greet him and immediately remember how little he looks like Helen. Bill is maybe fifteen years older than my wife but also of much heavier build. Although we haven't met that many times before the familiarity of his face is a welcome sight and his link to Helen is a comfort to me.

'Hello Ewan,' he says a little uncomfortably but with his hand extended in greeting.

I grasp his palm and shake it, welcoming the strength of his grip even if I don't quite have the energy to reciprocate it. The warmth and value of a firm honest handshake have always seemed important to me and I feel a curious need to demonstrate it to him now.

'Hello Bill,' I say, gesturing to my table in the visitor's room. 'Have a seat, please.'

I sit down and he follows my lead, taking the seat opposite as he hands me a magazine that unrolls as I accept it. It's my favourite, a National Geographic which I place on the table in front of me.

'A bit of light reading,' Bill says. 'I know you like that one and there is an article on New Zealand in there.'

I smile vacantly and thank him for the magazine but he seems embarrassed, as if his kindness is somehow insufficient. But his gesture is far from lost on me. The magazine reminds me of home and is another welcome link to my life even if it's a life I seem to have lost, a life stolen from me and now in ruins.

'It's very kind of you,' I reassure him.

My words seem to relax him a little.

'How are you feeling?' he asks.

I realise that I don't really know how to begin explaining my feelings and I'm not even sure that I want to burden him with the darkness inside my mind. Does he really want to know or is it just a display of politeness on his part? But then why else would he be here if not for support?

'Lost,' I proffer the solitary word, but it seems an appropriate and sufficient answer. At least it's an accurate one that shouldn't burden him too much.

'I suppose that's normal,' he replies. 'It's good that you're talking again. And the lady says you're responding well to treatment.'

I shake my head in response. 'Bill,' I say his name slowly. 'I forgot about Helen, forgot about her death.'

The words are painful to say, the reality of her death stirring emotions that I'm still struggling to control. I have to fight the will to breakdown again. This doesn't feel the right place for that, in front of him.

'I'm sorry,' Bill says.

'I can't even remember what happened,' I confess.

'I know, they told me,' Bill replies, sounding a little uncomfortable. 'I'm sorry. This must feel like going through it all over again for you.'

'I don't remember going through it the first time,' I explain. 'It just doesn't make any sense, none of this really does.'

'Don't you remember the accident at all?' Bill asks.

'My car accident?' I ask him.

Bill shakes his head. 'No, Helen's accident,' he corrects me. 'Or the funeral, what about that?'

A funeral? The thought hadn't even occurred to me. The final farewell to a life that has ended, my Helen's life and I can't even remember it. Desperately I try to think back and to recall something of the event, just a moment of the service or a conversation at the wake but my memory of that time is all blank. The harder I try to concentrate on remembering the darker and emptier my memory seems to be.

'You really can't remember anything can you?' Bill asks, interrupting my inner struggle but stirring my quest for knowledge.

'No, please tell me what happened to Helen,' I ask him, 'everything please.'

Bill leans back in his chair and takes a deep breath, puffing out the air from his lungs and hesitating for a moment before speaking. 'Okay Ewan, I'll try,' he says.

'Do you remember skydiving in Arizona?' he asks.

'Yes. Me and Helen went on holiday there once,' I reply, nodding as I remember fondly. 'She loves skydiving in America. I mean she did.'

'Well there was an accident on one of the dives,' Bill informs me. 'The two of you... collided in mid-air and Helen was, ummm....'

Bill smoothed his hands over his face for a second as if he is building up to something unpleasant but I have to know what happened.

'Helen was knocked unconscious in the collision,' Bill says sombrely, his words causing a feeling of nausea and horror to spread through my stomach. 'She wasn't able to, ummm.... open her parachute.'

Bill stops talking and begins rubbing his eyes with a blue handkerchief. His words form a horrifying image in my mind and I stare vacantly at the wall of the visitor's room, suddenly unable to face him, knowing he is Helen's brother.

I picture my unconscious wife, falling and unable to deploy her parachute. But I'm still alive. Helen and I had just started learning to do synchronised dives so we could travel down together in formation. It's an advanced skill and we were trying it ourselves on our own privately charted trip. If I had hit her somehow and knocked her unconscious then it was really me that killed her. The thought that I could be to blame is even more painful than the knowledge of her death.

I feel sick to my stomach and begin rubbing my eyes as tears start flowing from them. A hollow feeling of shame and emptiness is growing inside me fuelled by guilt. I feel almost lifeless and my leg starts shaking while Bill just remains silent and lost in his own thoughts, just the movement of his handkerchief out of the corner of my eyes reminding me he is even there. He should be angry and blaming me for taking his sister away and for killing her, not bringing me a magazine and some words of comfort.

The room feels solemnly empty to me now and my eyes see past everything into a vision of stark emptiness where Helen's smiling face is looking at me.

'I'm sorry,' Bill says, suddenly speaking but his voice is a little shaky. 'Shall I carry on or stop?'

My pain is fiercely intense but I need to experience and process the loss. I have to try and understand what happened to my darling Helen.

'No, I need to hear it,' I say quietly.

'She was killed instantly, there was no suffering,' Bill says bluntly and with stark clarity. 'It was ruled an accidental death.'

The revelation offers me no comfort and I suddenly think about my daughter and her hearing the news. 'Oh God, what about Jenny, is she alright?' I ask him.

'The funeral... was very tough on her,' Bill says. 'It was tough on you too, on all of us. Helen was my sister and so very... precious. But Jenny is alright, she's had some time to deal with it Ewan. She's been staying with me.'

'With you?' I ask. 'Why?'

Bill shuffles uncomfortably in his chair and looks away for a moment but when he continues his voice takes on a lower tone.

'After the funeral, you were very down Ewan,' he explains. 'You started drinking heavily and stopped going to work. There was a lot of pressure on you I suppose. I'm sorry but we should have realised sooner and tried to help. Perhaps if we had been there for you things would have been different. But it was all just grief you know? You were just grieving.'

I'm not sure I'm worthy or deserving of his apology. Drowning my sorrows doesn't sound like something I would do but then I had never experienced a loss like this, the loss of my Helen.

'It's alright Bill,' I assure him. 'I'm sure you were all suffering too and had enough to worry about without me.'

'You lost your job,' he continues. 'Or you quit, I'm not sure which. And then became very depressed. We didn't realise how bad you were until after your accident, not until Jenny came to stay with us and explained everything.'

'I crashed my car?' I ask, as I recall hitting a tractor, I remember that I think.

But Helen had been there and we were coming back from a picnic, she wasn't killed. It was all just a muddle in my mind, a jumble of moments that are twisted and out of sync.

'You were drunk Ewan,' he replies. 'You hit another car and were trapped.'

The shock of my drink driving actions is diluted by my overwhelming feeling of loss. It's as if anything else that happens to me is of little consequence now.

'You didn't hurt anyone else,' Bill adds, offering it as a consolation which is pitiful in its inadequacy. 'The other driver was only eighteen but he wasn't hurt. They had to cut you out of there though.'

'So I could have killed someone else as well as Helen,' I mutter in shame.

'You didn't though,' Bill replies. 'You were in a bad place Ewan.'

'What was wrong with me, with my head?' I ask.

'You were bleeding somewhere in your brain. You would have died without an operation. You probably don't know that Jenny was at the hospital all the time until you came out of a coma.'

'Jenny, my girl,' I say, tears stinging my eyes again, 'my poor little girl.'

'Take it easy Ewan,' he says.

Bill's words continue to lace my feelings with guilt and the pangs of it stick in my mind like emotional cement. Jenny's mother was dead and her father becomes an alcoholic who almost kills himself in a car crash. For the first time I have to face the shameful reality that I failed to care for my daughter and to support her, choosing to descend into my own self-pitying destruction instead. The normal decent fatherly thing to do would have been to remain strong for Jenny, the only parent she had left but I couldn't manage it. Helen was just too big a loss to bear and shamefully it broke me when I should have been there for Jenny. The extent of the failure is total and raw.

Bill stands up beside my chair and I feel his trembling hand on my shoulder. 'It's alright Buddy,' he says. 'It's not your fault.'

We stay like that for a while and he offers occasional words of comfort as I stare at the floor, sobbing. Eventually his trembling hand becomes still and my sobs slow down as I regain some of my fragile composure. But I lose none of my guilt. When Bill retakes his seat, I rub my sleeve over my eyes and take a few deep breaths.

'You were bought here when you came out of a coma,' he tells me. 'You were in some kind of... trance for a while.'

'I know,' I reply, nodding. 'Lily told me that, just not all the other stuff.

'I see,' he replies.

'Bill, where is Jenny?' I ask.

'She's still at mine,' he replies. 'But she is alright, don't worry.'

'I need to see her,' I say, but what I really mean is that I need to hold her and feel her presence, to show her that I'm here for her now and will never leave her again. We only have each other now, the two of us and our shared link with her mother, with my wife, with Helen. That is an unbreakable bond now.

'She hasn't been able to come since you came out of a coma,' Bill tells me.

'But why not?' I ask.

Bill sighs. 'She finds it... difficult,' he says.

'I can understand that,' I reply. 'But I'm alright now Bill, and I need to see her.'

'I'm sorry Ewan, I'll talk to her tonight,' he replies, 'but I'm afraid she still blames you for the accident and for what happened to her Mum.'

His words slice deep into the chambers of my heart like a blade. The emotional cuts hurt just as much as I remember the real blade doing when I was stabbed by Helen. Jenny rightly blames me for the skydiving accident and knows that I took her mother from her. She knows it's my fault and that must be her reason for pushing me off the apartment roof. That's how much she hates me, how much I deserve being hated. The realisation brings no more tears from me though, because sorrow won't help me now, nothing will help ease my guilt.

'I'll talk to her again Ewan, I promise' Bill says. 'And try to make her understand.'

Bill's words don't register with me as I feel like an empty, barren soul surrounded by stark loneliness. My heart feels hollow and for the first time in my life I can see little purpose in going on.

Sleep doesn't come easily for me tonight as the bed feels cold and empty in stark contrast to last night's heat. My throat feels dry as I struggle to sleep and I just can't seem to get comfortable. I also fear Virgil will be waiting for me in my dreams tonight. Lily told me that she suspects him to be a manifestation of guilt created by my traumatic experience. If she is right then that means that I created him and want him in my mind, which makes no sense at all. Virgil is a self-destructive pathway back into the dead loop and a doorway into my psychosis.

My heart longs deeply for Helen's touch and warmth, or at least the sound of her voice but she is all faded in my memory, muffled and distant. I switch my thoughts back to Jenny but her face is always cruel and cold in my mind, sometimes tearful. She is angry, disillusioned and disappointed with me because I took her mother from her and then failed her too. I can almost feel myself and Helen falling through the sky together and I beg death to take me instead of her.

Virgil wants to me to come back to him and I feel him closing in on my thoughts, pulling me back into the dead loop, luring me to embrace the shield of psychosis once more. His desire to force me back into psychosis is frightening but I'm sure he is winning the battle of wills. Hopefully I will die again tonight and then everything will be alright. Helen will still be alive and Jenny will love me again, with any luck.

23

Two Become One

The graveyard is cold this morning and soggy brown leaves clutter up the paved pathways as a gardener tries futilely to sweep them up. He labours with his broom, eyes downcast and oblivious to anything other than his task but for some reason I envy him. The well-trimmed grass that surrounds the generously spaced graves is a vibrant and healthy green. But the mood is made more sombre being underneath a pale sky of wispy cloud.

Helen's grave is surrounded with bouquets of fresh flowers and they look beautiful in the natural light. There is an arrangement of white and pink flowers shaped into the word 'Mum' obviously from Jenny and placed in the middle of them all. I know Helen would've loved that. The other flower bouquets could be from almost anybody but without reading the little cards it was impossible to tell. Every single one is beautiful and very much appreciated, whoever they're from.

To my left, the picturesque old church with its rough stone walls appears symbolically holy even to someone like me without a religious bone in my body. It makes for a beautiful scene in which to be laid to rest with the tall trees of the graveyard standing like protective sentinels over the deceased. The grave and the flowers evoke feelings of sadness in me but the graveyard offers a comfort that I have never appreciated before. I only wish the sky were blue and the sun were shining.

Helen's smooth headstone looks black and shiny, almost like obsidian and has words in gold lettering. Her name is engraved in huge letters but I avoid looking at the dates which will only highlight a life cut short.

'A loving wife and mother. Forever in our thoughts. An angel taken from us but always in our hearts and never forgotten.'

The words don't read like something that I would write because it feels a little clichéd although the sentiment is sort of special in its own way. Helen *was* always my angel. I kneel down at the grave in the soft damp grass and touch the flowers that spell out 'Mum'.

'I'm sorry Helen,' I whisper.

Kneeling at the grave is comforting and I close my eyes and think of my wife, picturing her smiling beautiful face and so many moments of happiness. I try to just remember the happy times and shut out the torturous darkness of recent months. I owe it to her to think about those happy times and send those memories down to her. It's a lonely but necessary vigil and I only begin to move when my legs start to cramp up.

After standing up I walk along the path a little way, looking at the neatly cropped bushes and trees while smelling the freshly cut grass. The morning is perfectly quiet and I think the methodical gardener may be the only other person in the graveyard. That is until the stillness is disturbed as Virgil suddenly appears on the pathway in front of me. There are tears streaming from his eyes as he approaches me.

'I'm sorry about your wife,' he says, resting a consoling hand on my shoulder. 'Truly I am.'

I slap his intrusive hand away and turn my back on him but he moves swiftly alongside me.

'I'm sorry for your loss Ewan,' he says. 'I lost my wife too, so I do know what you're going though.'

Now I do bring myself to look at him, his eyes terribly red and bleary, his face damp with tears and I realise that his suffering is genuine and real. That can't be faked.

'I'm sorry,' I reply, empathising with his pain.

Doing so somehow makes me feel a little stronger. Maybe I can help to support him in his grief now that I'm coming to terms with my own loss, coming to term with Helen's death.

'I'm sorry, what happened to her?' I ask him.

'She drowned,' Virgil replies softly, rubbing his sore eyes.

He looks deeply distraught now and an almost transparent shadow of a man, like his life is slowly being washed away. I can almost see the trees and the pathway through his body.

'You have to be strong,' I tell him, 'It takes time. I've been there but you can get through it just like I did. You need to be... patient. Maybe I can help you.'

'Do you remember all the good times we had Ewan?' he asks while sniffing. 'The first time you held a gun? Drinking good coffee? Running out of that bank?'

I do remember and it makes me begin to smile, in spite of where we are. Powerful good memories can do that.

'You tripped over an onion,' I remind him.

'And you couldn't even ask for the money,' he fires back, suddenly grinning. 'I think you asked them to check your balance didn't you?'

'They were good times,' I reply. 'All of them were good times.'

Virgil nods then puts an arm around my shoulder and walks me down the graveyard pathway, our shoes disturbing the wet leaves as we go.

'We could do it all again you know?' he says. 'After all, we're both completely alone now, outcasts from the world.'

'I don't think I can Virgil,' I tell him with a strange pang of disappointment. 'I have to look after my little girl now. I have to be there for her.'

'Don't be silly, she'll be fine Ewan,' he assures me. 'You can still keep an eye on her anyway. Things will be just like old times. You do miss it too right? It's not just me is it? You miss the dead loop too don't you?'

I ponder his question for a moment, comparing that situation to my current time of grief and sorrow. I remember that sometimes I found a purpose when I was dying every day. And unlike now, Helen was there too.

'Yes, I do miss it,' I confess.

'Everything was simple there,' Virgil says, 'bloody simple and bloody God honest perfect.'

He stops and turns to face me with eyes that are clear and focused now, devoid of any tears. 'Helen is still there you know,' he says, his voice taking on an insistent tone, 'in the dead loop. Helen and Adriana are both there, that's why we have to go back Ewan.'

'I really don't think I can,' I reply, glancing back at Helen's grave in the distance. 'I need... to move forward now... not go back.'

'What about me?' he snaps with a sudden flash of anger that takes me aback.

But before I can answer, he quickly raises his hands. 'I'm sorry about that Ewan,' he says, 'but I can't go back to the dead loop alone. It's that bitch Lily that drowned Adriana you see? My sweet Adriana, please Ewan you have got to help me.'

I shake my head. 'I don't know how to help you,' I tell him, 'I'm sorry Virgil.'

'Kill that bitch Lily for me,' he says insistently. 'That's that you can do. We make the rules remember?'

Virgil suddenly grabs one of my wrists and places a gun against my hand, closing my fingers around it. The gun feels cold and heavy in my hand but also oddly familiar. I'm not sure how it can help him reunite with his dead wife Adriana but he seems so desperate.

'That's it Old Man,' he says encouragingly.

'Lily?' I ask.

'Yeah, Lily,' he replies. 'Kill the fucking bitch.'

The woman smells like flowers this afternoon and I realise that I've never noticed her perfume smelling so strong before. Perhaps my senses are beginning to wake up or I'm just becoming attuned to the world again. My leg hasn't been shaking for two days and I only took two tablets last night instead of three. Lily's words are starting to make more sense now and are helping me to focus my mind and structure my thoughts so I can begin to stop them from controlling me.

'You're looking very well today Ewan,' she says smiling with an expression of satisfaction on her face.

'Thanks Lily,' I reply. 'I do feel different, much... stronger.'

'I'm pleased, because I've got some really good news for you,' she says.

'Have you? What's that?' I ask.

Lily smiles again but with an even broader look of satisfaction. 'Your brother in law called this morning,' she informs me. 'And told me your daughter is coming to see you today.'

Her words shatter my calm relaxed state as my stomach flutters with an odd butterfly feeling. It's a strange and odd sensation of broken serenity mixed with fear and I feel my eyes begin to water. I scrunch my eyes closed and cover them with my palms as tears of an uncertain nature begin to run down my face. Jenny's pale pretty face comes into my mind, my little girl.

I've stopped pacing agitatedly outside the visitors room now but I'm still not sure if I can bring myself to go in. I still feel nauseous and have to take deep breaths as I stand by the door, bracing myself against the wall with one hand. I've waited and waited for this moment, even bizarrely resorted to praying for it once or twice but now it's here I'm not sure I can actually believe it. Does Jenny still hate me? Is she coming here to deliver one final goodbye to me?

It was days ago that Bill told me that he would speak to her about visiting so what had he said to persuade her to come? What had he told her about my recovery? Was she just here to remind me how much she blames me for her Mum's accident?

I place my hand on the door handle and hesitate one last time but I have to find the courage to face her sometime even if I don't feel strong enough to take rejection. That would certainly crush me but I don't have an explanation that can justify or defend my failure to her. Slowly I open the door to find that the room is almost full with every table taken by visitors and patients but I can't see Jenny anywhere. Carefully I began to survey the room a little closer, paranoia spreading through me that she has perhaps changed her mind about seeing me. I tremble at the thought that she might not have come after all or simply just left while I was pacing the corridor outside. But then I spot her, just the side of her head but her long black hair and pale face are unmistakeable.

It's reassuring that Jenny isn't looking my way because it's easier to cope with seeing her in small stages but I know that I have to approach her. I'm terrified in anticipation of the moment that she will turn and I will see her face and whatever emotions her eyes betray. Any pretence she might still care will be exposed by her eyes. Will I see hatred and indifference or will a faint glimmer of love still remain for her father?

As I approach the table she turns her head as if somehow sensing my presence, making me freeze to the spot before I can reach her. Her pale face looks a little washed out but beautiful and innocent despite how tired she looks. And at first she manages to display no emotion at all, even in her eyes. Her whole face is unreadable and she wears a mask of hesitation and doubt. The blankness of her expression matches my own and for a moment neither of us do anything more than stare, our eyes locked together in unbreakable contact.

But then Jenny moves swiftly towards me, throwing her arms around me and burying her face into my shoulder. I hear her beginning to sob and feel her body trembling. At first I'm too scared to move and I can't even touch her. Her cuddle feels unfamiliar and I'm terrified of doing something to disturb her or that might cause me to lose her again. But then my arms are suddenly around her, clinging to her as my own eyes well up with tears and I cuddle my fragile daughter.

We remain together like that without eye contact, silently locked in an emotional embrace of mutual loss. There is no blame and for a moment I feel devoid of any guilt. This isn't a display of love or a time for hate either, I realise that it is nothing more than two people sharing a pure moment of grief and loss. It is best not to speak. There are no words that can be formulated to engage in this situation. I know in this moment that we are both here for Helen, not for our own benefit and deep down I'm sure that Jenny feels it too.

When I climb into bed I feel an immense sense of elation and relief, almost how I imagine narcotic bliss would be but I'm euphoric on forgiveness and love. The concept sounds almost evangelical but this is simply the love between a father and daughter who are unburdened and at peace with each other. Jenny has forgiven me for Helen's accident and buried the anger she carried with her, anger that I sought comfort at the bottom of a bottle.

I suspect it will be a long time before I can contemplate trying to forgive myself for not supporting Jenny after her mother's death. She may well have forgiven me for it but I still need to come to terms with the shame of my weaknesses that almost led to her losing both parents. In fact Jenny had as good as lost me during my alcoholism and for weeks while I was in a coma. Not to exclude my time in here on top of all that.

Jenny's forgiveness empowers me with a new determination to make a full recovery, something that I haven't felt before. My mental collapse and spiralling descent into self-destructive guilt has also been the catalyst that bought Jenny back to me. The path of recovery was treacherous and the mental price was high but the reward is priceless – I have my daughter back. I will never allow myself to lose her again. And after being given a rare second chance, I'm determined to ensure that I never need a third. I close my eyes and slowly drift to sleep.

The sun is shining in Pripyat this morning but although it's warm the silence is as oppressive as ever. My legs feel sluggish as if I've been wading through mud and I subconsciously check, expecting myself to be trapped in quicksand. Lifting one foot off the ground proves to me that I'm not stuck and there is no mud but the sensation still remains. When I look down though, it makes me wonder if the road this close to the ruined nuclear facility is pitted with radiation.

Virgil stands on the cracked tarmac facing me and obstructing the road ahead. The Chernobyl Sarcophagus lies beyond him in the distance while the ruins of Pripyat are behind me.

'We don't want to tarry here too long do we Ewan?' asks Virgil rhetorically.

His clothes are totally black and his hair seems almost yellow rather than blonde. Virgil has been with me for a long time now, like a parasite or a splinter of thought stuck so deep that no mental needle can prise it free. He is like an infection and a psychological thorn in my side. But finally I see him for what he is. I must destroy him, expel him from my mind and do whatever it takes to ensure than nothing can ever come between me and my family again. But he seems to read my thoughts, even though I haven't spoken a word.

'You can't get rid of me,' he says. 'I'm your salvation Ewan. And you need me.'

'I've never needed you,' I shout, pointing a finger at him. 'Not before and definitely not now.'

'You're nothing without me,' he replies, 'just a boring, empty shell of a man, not to mention a failure too.'

I feel my legs moving as previously suppressed rage boils up inside me and I close the short distance between us. As soon as I'm near enough I swing for him with my fist aimed at his face, but there is no contact and nothing solid to hit. There seems to be only cool still Ukrainian air where he once was.

Virgil suddenly reappears a little further down the road and now in closer proximity to the power plant.

'Is that how you thank me?' he sneers, a hint of disappointment on his face. 'I came back for you Ewan. I gave up my family to bring you back here into the dead loop. And this is how you thank me? Unbelievable.'

I charge towards him again only I'm much quicker this time, even more determined to smash him and to pummel his sneering face and lies out of existence. It's the only way to get Virgil out of my head – brute force. But once again my elusive nemesis disappears and then reappears further down the road. It's almost as if were some kind of entity and not a human being at all. It was Lily that first suggested that Virgil wasn't a real person and now I know she was telling the truth. Now I'm empowered and strengthened with that knowledge. Jenny's forgiveness proves that I don't need him anymore.

I snarl like an animal as frustration boils over at my apparent inability to catch my elusive tormentor.

'You know that you can have anyone you like,' says Virgil trying a different approach and a softer tone, but I'll never trust his misdirecting words again. 'I'm telling you Ewan, you can have Helen again. Or Tina if you prefer, hell you can even have both. What about my Adriana, she's cute right? What about Ali's girl would you prefer her instead?'

'You sick bastard. Don't you dare mention their names,' I growl as I advance towards him with cold murderous intent filling my heart.

These feelings should be unsettling and terrifying but there is no room in my emotions for doubt. I know that I would consciously murder him – even if he was a real man standing before me.

Virgil seems to slide backwards as I approach him, his legs not even moving and I don't appear to get any closer to him. The Sarcophagus is gradually getting nearer but I don't care about the radiation anymore, absorbing a lethal dose would be worthwhile if Virgil gets one too.

'What about that ass of Tina's though?' he taunts me, rubbing his hands together mockingly. 'Have you already forgotten how hot she looks in a tennis skirt? Or maybe you have even sampled her in the flesh.'

'You fucking disgust me,' I shout at his distasteful words. 'Leave me alone. You have to die, I want you dead.'

'I'm not going anywhere Ewan,' he taunts. 'I'm part of your thoughts and part of you. No one can hide from themselves, not from who they really are. And you are me Ewan. You can't be angry with yourself.'

I start to sprint towards him now, determined to catch him and silence him but he continues to slide backwards, preventing me from gaining any ground. Soon he will reach the power station and then he will have no option but to stop.

Virgil stops talking as we reach the Sarcophagus and he suddenly disappears into thin air. My nemesis is nowhere to be seen and I angrily shout out his name. But there is no response and the silence seems to taunt me as much as Virgil did with his words. For a moment the silence feels oppressive as I stand in the shadow of the Sarcophagus which seems to block out half of the sky. Up close I appreciate for the first time just how monstrous the building looks, the largest Pandora's Box in the world. I touch the concrete wall and it feels starkly industrial, cold but powdery smooth.

Walking around the Sarcophagus and tracing my hand along the concrete is strangely calming and my thoughts drift back to the people of Pripyat. Radiation had been their downfall and many of them left carrying a passenger inside them too. And just like me their passenger was a destructive force that was destroying them from within. But I won't be destroyed. Now that I know my enemy and understand him I can fight him. The poor people who fled from this place were already infected, already defeated in a battle they did not even know they were fighting. But I'm alive, I'm awake, I'm fighting and I see my enemy. I know him, I am him.

Pripyat is dead now and just a hollow symbol that needs erasing. Chernobyl is the painful scar of a tremendous wound, a failure and a dark stain on man's contribution to history, one that only time might eventually erase. But I don't have that much time; my battle must end here and now, once and for all. This cannot go on.

'Over here Old Man!' comes the shout.

I can see Virgil now off to my left, standing by an opening in the Sarcophagus. There appears to be some kind of doorway in the wall of the concrete structure leading inside and into the darkness. As I advance towards him I notice that he is holding something in his hands but this time he stays put and waits for me.

'Come and see what I've found Ewan,' he says waving the object at me.

She is long dead, her face blackened by dirt and exposure to the elements. One of her arms is all black and bent oddly. Her dirty hair is thick, brown and curly, just like my late mothers, but with flecks of what looks like ash in it. The little doll is broken and lifeless, with no clothing apart from a tattered pair of pink shorts.

'Give her to me,' I demand.

Virgil tosses the doll through the doorway and into the Sarcophagus with a wide grin on his face. 'Go and get her if you want her,' he says rather immaturely.

I barge past him, forfeiting the opportunity to get my hands on him as I plunge through the opening and into the darkness. Saving the doll is my immediate priority.

My eyes become accustomed to the dark almost immediately and I realise that I'm on a metal catwalk suspended inside the reactor building. Far below me are the reactor core and the ruined control room, shrouded in semi darkness and littered with piles of broken concrete and metal debris. It almost looks as if the building has been demolished from the inside and then had the walls of the Sarcophagus built around it. It seems a fairly accurate analogy I guess.

I glance over the railings and see the doll far below me in the gloom. Virgil's throw has sent her sailing cleanly into a deep pit containing the rubble of the ruined reactor core and the shattered control rods where I know the worst of the radiation lies.

She looks up at me from the darkness, lost, desperate and hopelessly alone and it reminds me of how Jenny must have felt. The thought of leaving her alone again for any moment longer than necessary abhors me.

Climbing over the catwalk railing, I begin to descend a rusty ladder into the darkness. The rungs seem like they have rusted and they leave some kind of dusty metal residue on my hands. Unfortunately the ladder has sheared off about halfway down and there is no easy way to reach the bottom. But the drop looks manageable.

Reluctantly I release my grip on the ladder, dropping down into the pit but landing more heavily on the concrete floor than I anticipate. I'm unable to suppress a yelp of pain as one leg collapses from under me. It feels as if my ankle is broken but at least I have one hand on the doll. I quickly pull her towards me, cradling her in my arms as I stroke her sad face. She smiles up at me and I wipe a tear from her cloudy little eyes. The reunion is shattered as a sudden stabbing in my ankle sears through my nerves, making me cry out again in a mixture of pain and frustration.

Suddenly I realise that Virgil is standing directly in front of me amongst the broken piles of rubble. His face is grey and epitomises a manifestation of evil in what little light reaches us down here in the gloomy heart of the Sarcophagus. I'm sure I can feel radiation silently passing through my skin and into my body with deadly and fatal intent.

'How touching,' Virgil sneers. 'What is it with you and that fucking doll?'

I ignore his question and clutch her protectively to my chest, unable to stand with my ankle still causing me fierce pain. In an attempt to keep Virgil away I hold out my hand with my palm raised. The doll needs me and I won't lose her again. I won't fail her again, not like before when I left her on that rooftop. I glance down at her comfortingly to make sure that she understands, and my eyes widen in surprise. Her face is changing, the features becoming more defined and less doll-like as she morphs into the face of someone else, someone familiar. As I watch, the doll's hair becomes much straighter and longer, cheekbones appear and big soulful eyes turn towards me. And then I suddenly realise that it's Jenny! The doll is my pretty little girl, ashen faced, staring up at me and pleading for me to save her.

'Keep back Virgil,' I warn him, defensively.

He laughs, making a cold cruel sound that echoes through the darkened halls and broken corridors of the reactor room.

'What is your morbid fascination with this shithole?' he asks. 'There is nothing here for you.'

But I'm not about to discuss my curiosity for Chernobyl and Pripyat with this animal. 'What the hell do you want?' I demand.

'I've told you over and over again,' he says. 'To bring you back to where you belong. And get you away from that bitch Lily.'

I begin to shuffle slowly towards him on my knees, desperate to reach him and somehow silence him or prove he isn't real. But he seems to sense the violent intent in my painful slow approach because he suddenly has a gun in his hand.

'Stay right there,' he warns me. 'I've seen that look in your eyes before Old Man. It was right before you shot me in the face I think.'

'Leave me alone,' I tell him in a defeated tone, 'can't you just go away?'

'I can't do that I'm afraid, Ewan,' he replies. 'We need each other remember?'

He sounds so sincere, so persistent in his nonsensical statements. But if there was ever any warmth of feeling or compassion in me for Virgil, it is long gone now. Cold hatred and disgust fill my mind as I stare at him and his gun.

'Go to hell,' I tell him. 'I don't need you.'

Virgil sighs impatiently and shakes his head. 'Maybe just killing you is the best thing to do after all,' he says. 'That will definitely reunite us in the dead loop for sure, just like old times.'

He raises his gun and aims it at my face from point blank range. I close my eyes as hatred is replaced by chilling fear. I'm not sure that I have the courage to face my final moments and embrace death.

'Don't worry,' I hear Virgil say. 'It'll be just like last time, you won't feel a thing at this range.'

I hear Virgil cock the gun, realise that he isn't bluffing and that he has never hesitated before when death is involved. For some reason Adriana's face appears in my mind, his wife. She seemed so normal. I picture her and him together. What would she think of him murdering me? Is she even real? I have met her, spoken to her and I can almost hear her voice in the gloom. 'So how do you two know each other?' she once asked me. I should have told her the truth. I don't know him at all.

Before Virgil fires, I feel my fingers close around something hard on the floor. 'Goodbye Ewan,' he says.

'Well it was nice to meet you Ewan,' I hear Adriana say.

I open my eyes and swing my hand upwards as hard as I can, smashing the broken control rod into Virgil's hand holding the gun. Virgil bellows in pain as I hear a bone crunching impact and the gun flies from his hand to clatter harmlessly somewhere in the rubble. Virgil backs away and massages his bleeding hand while still cursing at his intense pain. I remain on my knees, thankful to still be alive and clinging tightly onto Jenny.

'You bastard!' Virgil yells as fury helps him to control some of the pain in his hand. He cradles his hand and bares his teeth as I look up at him.

'I'll leave you to fucking die here,' he growls angrily, boiling in rage. 'How long do you think someone can survive here with this shitty radiation? A couple of hours maybe? When you're spitting out blood in pissing agony just remember that I offered you the quick way out. Before your times up you'll be crawling around and searching for that gun to finish yourself off.'

'I'll find my own way out,' I tell him.

'Only one of us can leave here Old Man,' he says, still simmering with spiteful venomous anger. 'You can't walk right? You'll never climb back up there.'

Defiantly I try and get to my feet to prove him wrong and manage to rise onto one knee but standing on the ankle is impossible. The movement of my legs is agony and merely confirms to me that the ankle is broken. Virgil is right.

'I'll close the door on my way out,' Virgil says coolly. 'I gave you every chance to join me Ewan. You just remember that, remember how selfish you were.'

He turns his back on me and begins to walk away towards the ladder that descends from the catwalk. I crawl painfully in the opposite direction, dragging my broken ankle behind me as I traverse the rubble littered floor. With Jenny still clutched in one hand I feel around the gloom, searching for the gun. A quick glance behind me reveals that Virgil is at the bottom of the sheared off ladder, jumping to try and reach it. It's plainly too high for him and he will never be getting out that way.

I continue with my desperate search, my ankle dragging behind me in agony as I scatter dust and broken bricks with my hand. My knuckles are bleeding from my frantic search but suddenly my hand comes across something cool and hard in the darkness, closing my fingers around it. I raise my arm gripping the gun tightly in my hand.

Kneeling up on the floor I grit my teeth and point the gun towards Virgil. Jenny is still safely cradled in my other arm, protected from the devastation and oppressive darkness around us.

'Virgil, wait!' I shout, causing him to turn around from another failed attempt to reach the ladder.

Seeing the gun, he shakes his head before returning and coming almost in touching distance of me.

'You can't shoot anybody,' he taunts. 'You couldn't even pull the trigger in the sports shop. You left me to get gunned down instead, remember? Like the coward you were born to be.'

'I want you to stay away from me forever,' I order him. 'Lily told me exactly what you are. I never want to see your smug face again, you sick bastard.'

'How many times do I have to say it? I'm not going anywhere Ewan,' he snaps. 'I'm part of you and you'll never get rid of me. Anything I did, you made me do. So it was you that must've thought about raping Tina. Just accept it and join me.'

'No!' I deny his words with clenched fists and every atom of my being. 'You're not me. You're a sick twisted freak. I'm nothing like you. I don't rape people. You'll never be a part of me.'

'I fucking am you!' he shouts furiously. 'And I'm not going anywhere.'

'A minute ago you threatened to leave me here,' I remind him. 'Changed your mind all of a sudden? Why don't you just go like you said? And never come back.'

Virgil stares at me for a second and grins. 'Because that's what you want,' he says. 'I'll never leave you. We belong together. We're one and the same. We have to be reunited. That can only happen when you come back with me into the dead loop. It's where we belong.'

'Psychosis,' I tell him. 'It's an illness. You're not even fucking real. I'm getting better and there's no place in my life for you.'

Virgil laughs, loud and mockingly at me. 'I'm not a bloody symptom,' he says. 'I *am* your life, your heart, your guile. You fucking need me.'

'I'll kill you,' I warn him.

'No you won't,' he replies, turning his back on me before beginning to walk towards an intact ladder that I hadn't previously noticed. 'I'll give your regards to Helen and Tina when I see them.'

But Virgil belongs here, not me. It's him that should remain in Chernobyl, forever entombed in the Sarcophagus. The ruined power station seems a fitting and symbolic place for someone like him. My hand is shaking holding the gun and the pain in my ankle is excruciating. Jenny slips out of my hand and falls onto the floor as I close both hands around the gun. I grit my teeth with a determined face and steady the weapon, aiming it at the climbing form of Virgil on the ladder.

For a split second I realise that I have never shot anybody before, excluding the basement suicide pact with Virgil. But I feel like I have walked through my own dark maelstrom to a perfect moment of peace. This is an action of necessity, a pure moment where I take back my life from the evil that would take it away from me. I have to do this for myself, for Tina most importantly and for Helen, but also I owe this to my Jenny. Without any further hesitation or any warning I squeeze the trigger twice and the deafening explosion of the two rounds assaults my eardrums. The gun smoke stings my eyes and I hear the empty shell casings clattering somewhere into the rubble nearby.

Virgil freezes in place for a moment on the ladder and stops climbing. I still have the gun pointing at him and my heart thumps furiously in my chest as he releases his grip on the ladder and falls backwards. A single tear runs out of one of my eyes as Virgil plunges into the radioactive darkness where he belongs. But suddenly I'm not even sure I meant to do it. I think deep down that I might still need him.

24
Homecoming

It's been nearly two weeks now since I last saw Virgil and committed him to an eternity inside the Chernobyl reactor building. I hardly acknowledge his existence now and can barely even remember his face. He is already becoming a fading memory, an unwelcome remnant of my mind that's nearly dispelled forever but I won't mourn his departure from my life.

They've reduced my psychosis medication to one tablet now and my physical strength has almost fully returned too. Bute more importantly for me, I've begun to understand my condition and what happened to me after the surgery and coma. I owe so much to Lily for breaking me out of catatonia and picking and delving into the fabric of my mind. She empowered me with the mental tools to face my psychosis. Without her I would never have been able to differentiate between reality and my delusional world. She restructured my thinking by encouraging me to talk about how I think about myself, the world and other people. Lily showed me how my actions affect my thoughts and armed me with the mental fortitude to overpower Virgil.

Jenny has been to see me almost every day this week and Bill came along with her yesterday too. I broached the subject of her moving back into my apartment but she still insists on waiting until I am home before talking about that. I'm pretty certain that I owe my life to my daughter and to Lily of course. It was Jenny's forgiveness that ultimately gave me the motivation and a purpose to resist Virgil. Although I don't like to think about him now it's impossible to remember how Jenny has helped me without being reminded of Virgil's lure. I feel certain that without her forgiveness he would surely have dragged me back deeper into the nightmare embrace of the dead loop where perhaps even Lily wouldn't have been able to reach me again.

Yesterday Jenny proofread a letter that I had composed to the surgeon, the man that stopped the bleeding in my head. He was just a faceless hero to me but I felt compelled to communicate my gratitude to him. Although it was little more than a politely worded thank you note and an insufficient gesture for his life saving expertise, it was very important to me. He deserved acknowledging. My dark times are past me now and Jenny is coming to the hospital again today. She's taking me home.

It feels almost like a farewell party in the visitor's room this morning. Bill has brought Jenny to the hospital and Lily and Brenda are here too, both of them smiling. Even Graham has come in today to shake my hand and congratulate me for leaving. It's an unfamiliar sensation wearing a coat for the first time in months but my faithful old leather jacket has a comfortingly familiar smell to it. Helen always liked this jacket on me but it feels a little looser than it used to. Jenny told me that I would just have to eat more to fill it back out. She is obviously still worried about my physical health which makes me self-conscious but Bill found her comment amusing, clapping me on the shoulder and suggesting that we find a good steak house straight away as the first order of business. But for me this moment is all about Lily. She looks every bit like some kind of guardian angel today, dressed as she is, all in white and seeming to have an aura of warmth around her.

'Remember you'll need to come back in on Monday for a chat, so we can see how you're doing,' she reminds me.

I realise that I welcome an opportunity to talk with her again, to share my thoughts and gain her encouragement.

'I wouldn't miss it for anything,' I assure her.

I hug her tightly and she doesn't seem to mind. 'Thank you for everything,' I whisper to her. 'You've saved my life.'

'I'm not quite sure I did that Ewan,' she replies modestly. 'But we were delighted to help.'

Jenny shakes Lily's hand and thanks her. 'You gave me back my Dad,' she says. 'And I promise I'll do something to raise money for your department. A marathon perhaps.'

Bill gives her a playful shove. 'You wouldn't make it five miles,' he teases.

'Good luck,' says Lily, shaking all of our hands one more time. 'And I'll see you on Monday Ewan.'

I insist that Jenny goes in the front of Bill's car and then sit myself in the back, needing to be alone on the drive home. It feels oddly comforting to be in a car again; even when I think that the last time was months ago when I was drunk and I had the accident. The memory of that day has never returned even though little pieces of other memories have, mostly just fragments and shards but enough for me to piece together a fractured timeline of my recent life.

The memories of Helen's skydiving accident have never returned but I do remember bits of our holiday such as the hotel we stayed in and chartering a plane. Unfortunately, memories of my weeks of alcoholism have started to leak back into my mind but they largely centre on arguments with Jenny or wallowing in the squalor of the apartment, with the occasional flash of noisy bars and cheap alcohol. That whole time is all a blurred jumble of mixed memories, none of them pleasant and all of them ones that I would rather forget.

But I'm grateful that I can recall a little of Helen's funeral at least, the time before all the drinking. I remember trying to make a speech at the service to talk about her life. About halfway through I'd found it too distressing and painful and so with my eulogy unfinished I limped back to my seat to respectful applause. I also remember arguing with someone at the wake but I can't remember who it was with or what it was about but I've decided never to ask Jenny to refresh my memory.

The majority of my other memories are all still a tangled blur except for selective chunks of the dead loop. I'm sure that I've forgotten parts of it but those that I do remember are so real, so vivid that it sometimes frightens me. It's quite unnerving that things that supposedly never happened can actually seem like memories. I wonder about the long term effects of being in such a condition of precarious mental unbalance.

Sometimes in hospital I would wake up from nightmares in a cold sweat feeling as though I'd just died. I wonder how accurate my experiences of death were, particularly the one about being stabbed in the back although I never can quite picture who stabbed me. I've deciding it was probably Virgil which at least helps me to process and deal with the memory.

I don't know how long the dead loop was being played out in my mind and whether it started when I was in a coma, in catatonia or if it was only during my psychosis. Lily explained it as a distorted collection of events related to my condition and life trauma, fuelled by my own negative feelings of guilt. But there are moments of it that still terrify me, incidents that I will never discuss with anyone and things that make me shudder to remember them. It's all worsened by the knowledge that it was my own supposedly normal mind that generated those events and created Virgil. My memory is so clouded that it's hard to separate my life before Helen's accident from experiences in the dead loop. But at least Lily says that it may improve over time. She has been right so many times already but I don't find her words on that reassuring. I still think my head is too muddled up right now.

I think about Tina sometimes and wonder why she was in my thoughts so often before. But for the moment I prefer to store my memories of her somewhere safe in the back of mind where they feel special but definitely never sordid.

I have accepted Bill's compassionate offer to take me to see Helen's grave before we go home. After only a short detour Bill pulls the car into the car park of a little church. Unlike me, both Jenny and Bill have been here many times already and so don't seem to mind when I tell them I want to walk to the grave alone. I need some time here alone.

Helen's grave has fresh flowers on it, a magnificent bouquet of different colours with six white lilies, perhaps placed here in anticipation of my visit. The smooth headstone looks black and shiny, almost like obsidian and with words in gold lettering. Helen's name is engraved in huge letters above the epitaph.

'A loving wife and mother. Forever in our thoughts. An angel taken from us but always in our hearts and never forgotten.'

It seems an inadequate few words to celebrate and remember the life of such a special person. I kneel at the grave and the sensation feels familiar as if I remember being here before. But I don't think I was as strong the last time I was here.

The graveyard smells of cut grass, a clean fresh smell mixed with flowers and the sun shines downs on us, on Helen and me. My fingers caress the short trimmed grass around the grave and I almost feel as if I'm stroking her red hair again.

As there is no one else around I begin to talk quietly, hoping Helen will hear the words and appreciate the sentiment.

'I'm sorry I've been away Helen,' I whisper. 'I'm sorry that I let you both down.'

I pause for a moment to allow my words to sink in and hope she can hear me explain myself.

'I've been pretty ill,' I tell her. 'But I'm better now so you don't need to worry about me. Or Jenny. We're going to be fine now. I swear to look after her properly, with everything I have... for both of us. I'm sorry... for everything.'

I place my hands flat on the green glasslike gravel that covers the surface of the grave plot, feeling its warmth absorbed from the sun as I send my inner thoughts down to her. It's the closest I can get to touching her now but the ground feels solid and warm under my hands, just like she used to.

'Are you alright Ewan?' says a man's voice behind me.

Slowly I stand up, my knees protesting slightly at the cramp caused by kneeling. Bill looks at me and offers a reassuring nod as I answer without even considering his question.

'Yes thank you,' I reply, rubbing my hands together to remove a few pieces of gravel that had stuck to them.

He places a consoling hand on my shoulder. 'Jenny was a little worried about you,' he tells me. 'She asked me to come and check on you. I don't think she wanted to disturb you herself. It's been quite a long time since you were here Ewan.'

Jenny's concern warms me inside. 'I'm fine Bill,' I try to reassure him as much as myself.

He puts his hands in his pockets and stands closer to the grave. 'She was no age was she?' he sighs. 'I still can't believe it sometimes. I'm so sorry Ewan.'

I never realised Bill was this sensitive or cared so much about his sister. He always seemed a little cold and disinterested in family other than his own children. Perhaps it just took something like this for him to demonstrate his feelings but I will always see him in a respectfully positive light in future.

'Bill, I never got round to properly thanking you,' I tell him, 'for looking after Jenny and letting her live with you. I mean, while I was in hospital. That means a lot to me.'

He turns around to face me and removes his hand from my shoulder. 'She's my niece,' he says matter-of-factly. 'I wouldn't have had it any other way. But she helped me as much as I helped her Ewan. With Helen gone it was kind of like having a little part of her still with us. She's a very special person your daughter.'

I've come to terms with my actions now but his words still remind me of my guilt and reinforce it. 'I know,' I reply quietly. 'But I didn't realise how special until now.'

Bill sighs and glances back towards the car park.

'Look Ewan, I wanted to say something in the car, but couldn't,' he says. 'You should know that we've arranged a little welcome home reception for you back at my place. Personally I wasn't sure it was the right thing to do, but Jenny insisted she wanted to make a big fuss about you coming home. It's just a few friends but I'd really like to check here that you're alright with it.'

A celebration seems grossly inappropriate somehow, but disappointing people is the last thing I can bring myself to do, especially if it means so much to Jenny.

'It's fine honestly, I'd like that Bill,' I assure him. 'But can you just give me a few minutes more here please?'

'Sure buddy, of course,' he replies. 'You take as long as you like. I'll meet you back in the car.'

I watch Bill amble slowly back down the path towards the car park before turning my attention back to Helen's grave. Deep down in my heart I sense that I have already mourned her loss before, although somehow I don't feel that I've ever done it properly. Being here today feels like losing her all over again, only this time the loss isn't quite so raw. In my mind I think I've already accepted her death but I know I haven't dealt with it in my heart.

I have to prove to Helen and myself that I can cope with life and move forward without her. I want to make Jenny proud and feel safe. The brutal reality of my failure to cope with grief and the solace I sought in alcohol fill me with shame, but I'm determined to become as worthy of Helen in death as I was in her life. Caring for Jenny is the only path to the redemption of my own self-worth.

'I miss you Helen and I'll always love you,' I whisper, before turning and slowly walking back towards the car.

The car journey is a silent affair. Bill is concentrating on driving and Jenny doesn't intrude upon my quiet contemplations. I stare out of the car window, watching people out walking in the afternoon sun or riding bicycles through the village. Bill doesn't live very far outside the city but we are already deep into the countryside. Being well away from London seems like a different world. How long has it been since I was anywhere other than our apartment or the hospital? I make a mental note to see more of our glorious green countryside when I'm better. Perhaps I can bring Jenny out here sometime or even take her on holiday somewhere if she will come.

Bill's house is much bigger than I remember although I've only been here a few times before. The huge detached house with its private gravel drive and double garage situated in a village probably costs less than my city apartment. As a retired builder Bill had done a lot of work on the house himself and Helen always said he had done well for himself in spite of his academic weaknesses. Apparently Bill was a tearaway teenager and his parents said he would never amount to anything.

The village and countryside setting make me feel a little envious of Bill and it is no surprise that both of his grown up sons still live at home. Bill had been self-employed running his own building company as long as I had known Helen and his son Dale just followed him into the family business. His other son Albert hadn't though, he commuted to the city every day. Jenny told me last week that he does something in graphic design. It's amazing how different two sons can be and it makes me wonder what our second child would have been like if we had tried for another after Jenny.

Once Bill switches off the ignition I wait a moment for him and Jenny to get out of the car first. I need every second possible to prepare myself to see people I know again, especially when I'm not even sure exactly who is going to be inside. When they collected me at the hospital, Bill invited me to spend the night in one of his spare rooms instead of my apartment and offered to take me back into London tomorrow. I'm not sure if I relish the company but I'm not ready to be alone in the apartment either. Staying here is the lesser of two evils and Jenny is here anyway. That was enough to swing the decision for me to accept his kind offer.

I need to stay close to Jenny. I haven't asked her yet, but I hope she will come back to the apartment to live with me, although I'll just have to try and understand if she doesn't want to straight away. But I know it will hurt and I don't know how to ask her.

As soon as I finally leave the car Jenny takes my hand and leads me towards the house. 'You'll never guess who is here,' she says, giving up any pretence of the surprise party. 'Come on Dad.'

The front door has a sign on it, just a simple foil banner that rustles slightly in the breeze and it reads 'Welcome Home'. I'm not home of course but the sentiment warms me inside and I interpret it to mean that they welcome me back to normal life and the real world.

Jenny reaches into her handbag and fumbles for her keys. I take a long deep breath as she opens the front door and steeps inside. Bill follows behind us as Jenny escorts me to the open plan lounge and dining room. If I remember correctly most of Bill's ground floor is one large area that he remodelled himself by knocking down walls and redesigning the whole floor plan. I wouldn't know where to start if it were me.

There are maybe ten people gathered expectantly in the lounge waiting for me, and most of them are holding a wine glass or a can of beer. In the corner of the room is a long table of unopened buffet food which is all still wrapped in cellophane. The welcome is initially muted as the room falls silent for a moment as numerous pairs of eyes watch me. But it is the strange selection of familiar faces that surprises me though.

'Here he is!' says Jenny, presenting me with proud smile.

I almost expect some kind of artificial cheer but everyone just claps slowly and methodically, a muted applause as if anything more might harm this fragile new arrival. I'm not too sure where to look or what to say and I smile politely but uncomfortably, unsure why I deserve any applause or appreciation.

But after allowing me time to absorb the moment, a woman bustles forward from the group and throws her arms around me.

'You look so well Ewan,' she gushes, kissing my cheek.

I'm a little overwhelmed at first but I focus my attention on her as I hear the clapping stop. It's Susan, Bill's wife who I've only met a few times before. They had separated as far as I could remember.

'Susan, it's good to see you,' I say politely.

She stops hugging me but still holds firmly onto my arms. 'You too Ewan,' she says. 'I'm so sorry about your illness, how are you feeling?'

'I'm much better thank you,' I reply. 'But I'm a little surprised to see you here.'

I guess it's not my most subtle response, more a clumsy attempt to divert the conversation away from me. I'm out of practice with social conventions.

Susan glances over her shoulder towards Bill who is busy talking to the other guests. 'We're giving things another go,' she explains with a faint smile. 'I moved back in last month and it's been... different.'

'That's good,' I reply, not intending to sound indifferent. 'Bill never said anything but I'm really pleased for you, both.'

'It's still early days,' she adds, 'and we're taking things slowly obviously. But come on Ewan, enough about us, everyone here is dying to see you.'

The word dying makes me wince but thankfully Susan doesn't seem to notice my discomfort. I've heard that word enough to last me a lifetime.

Susan seems a little more sedate than I remember. She was always very bubbly and sometimes a little overbearing, but tonight she seems calmer and more dignified. Her son Dale steps forward and shakes my hand, his strong working hands offering me a firm grip that's a reassuring reminder that I'm back in the real world.

'Alright Uncle,' he says, 'it's good to see you again.'

Dale's brother Albert and his wife are right behind him although I can't remember her name so I smile politely as they greet me. I think it might be Tracey, or maybe Tania – something like that but she has an uncomfortable smile on her face. It's fine, because I feel just as awkward.

'How's the job Albert?' I ask as his wife wraps her arm around his waist.

Albert shrugs. 'You know, still going,' he replies. 'Things are a bit slow as usual. I designed some jewellery adverts for Piccadilly station a few weeks ago.'

Dale peels away and I see him going to the fridge and removing a can of something.

'I'd like to hear more about it later Al,' I say, 'excuse me for a moment.'

My neighbour Ali is in the corner of the room, leaning casually against the patio doors but unlike some of the others, he doesn't approach me. He raises a glass in front of him and nods respectfully to me from across the room. I raise my hand and wave a salute at him as his latest girlfriend sips from a wine glass and simultaneously talks on her mobile phone. She seems oblivious to everything around her.

In the middle of the room is the oddest group of four people I could have expected to see and all four are looking at me with reassuring smiles on their faces. My Uncle Lionel and Aunt Mavis are here, but I doubt they've been out outside of Birmingham for years. I'm not even sure I've seen them since Helen and I got married and they must be at least in their eighties by now.

Engaged in conversation with them, bizarrely is David Stone, one of my many former bosses and one of the few who were truly sorry to let me go. He once told me that making me redundant was one of the toughest decisions he had ever had to make. His wife is standing next to him; at least I assume that's who she is. She must be one of the shortest women I've ever seen. I think she is a little older than him, although she looks very elegant, distinguished and formidable despite her short stature.

Jenny taps me on the shoulder and offers me an open bottle of Budweiser. 'One won't hurt you I'm sure,' she says, 'we are celebrating after all.'

I look at the beer as if it's my arch enemy and wonder at the logic of offering alcohol to someone who has so badly abused it. Jenny hesitates a moment in sudden realisation of her mistake and doesn't remove her hand from the bottle until I smile at her, offering some fatherly reassurance.

'It's been a very long time since I had a drink,' I tell her. 'It's fine honestly.'

Jenny relaxes and I take a small appreciative sip of the ice cold beer. I can't remember the last time I had a drink in a social gathering rather than alone and it's a refreshing experience. Being surrounded by a handful of relatives and friends isn't as relaxing as being at home, but it is perhaps more therapeutic. The turnout illustrates to me to that this handful of people at least cared enough to get together and welcome me out of hospital. But somehow I don't feel worthy or deserving of their sentiment. My feelings are a little deeper than guilt; I simply didn't expect these people to be here for me.

Their questions come at me gently and are not too personal in regards to the detail of my condition. Ali is the one exception as he directly probes me for detailed information into my illness. It doesn't bother me though because he was always upfront, to the point and a good friend. His latest girlfriend seems to study every word I utter in response to his questions, a lot like Lily used to do.

Throughout the whole evening, the resounding image in my mind is seeing Jenny smiling, relaxed and at ease chatting to everyone in the room. But she never strays too far away from me and doesn't stop glancing at me all evening when she doesn't think I can see her. She constantly checks up on me however many times I assure her that I'm perfectly fine. Eventually I concede defeat and stop telling her not to do it.

Before the evening is finished, I decide to have a second beer. Standing alone in the corner of Bill's conservatory, I gaze distantly into the semi darkness of the garden and slowly exhale. With no one watching me for once, I raise my bottle in a silent toast and respectful farewell to the dead loop.

25
A New Beginning

It's now been almost four weeks since I left the hospital. Jenny and I have returned to the apartment and settled back in although it took some monumental cleaning, which Jenny insisted on doing herself and forcing me to relax. She treats me like I'm still fragile and unwell which I hope will wear off fast.

I've spent a lot of time reading during these last few weeks, skimming through old National Geographic's and tearing through a good few novels while sitting out on the apartment balcony. Eric had kindly saved me a copy of all the National Geographic's since my accident, convinced he said that I would recover and be back to collect them in a few months. His gesture was a considerable surprise to me and the small bundle of magazines he gave me was a significant symbol of kindness, particularly as he insisted on me not paying for them.

Without Helen the apartment seems too quiet during the day especially when Jenny is out but I keep myself active by ensuring that I go for a walk or take the tube into the city. Ali visits whenever he has an occasional day off from the hospital but it's important for me to be out of the apartment once a day in the real world and to embrace reality.

Seeing Lily once a week is a real break from the daily monotony of reading in the apartment although she tells me that I won't actually need to visit her much longer. I've stopped taking medication now but feel an impending sense of disappointment that my time with Lily will soon be over. She is the final link to my old life and concluding our time together will leave me to face the reality of my new life without her as a lifeline. It's a daunting prospect.

I haven't really heard anything much from Bill since coming home but Jenny tells me that Susan had unfortunately moved back out. Looks like things between them hadn't worked out after all.

David Stone telephoned this morning and invited me to go and meet him to discuss a job opportunity. I'm not sure I'm ready for that yet, but I promised I would at least go and have a chat with him about it. Part of me wonders whether it is some kind of sympathetic gesture on his part but I try to persuade myself that it's because he remembers my good work ethic. The thought of working all day and meeting so many people is a frightening one but Lily says that getting into some kind of meaningful routine is important. I owe it to Jenny to try. Maybe I should talk to Lily about it at our next meeting and see if she can help me think more positively about taking that step.

Ali came round last night, bringing a few cans of beer with him even though I prefer soft drinks these days. He has yet another new girlfriend, a pretty Italian girl that he met on the Internet apparently. I've only seen a picture so far and it probably won't last knowing him. I didn't realise what a good friend he was until now. He is still the only person who pushes me to find out more about what happened to me and I even told him about the dead loop. It's refreshing to talk with someone other than Lily who doesn't tiptoe around my illness. I guess Helen is the only subject that he doesn't ever bring up.

Jenny came with me to the cemetery last Friday as it was Helen's birthday. We took some fresh flowers and a card that Jenny had laminated to keep it dry. She cried on and off all morning before we went out but she cheered up when I persuaded her to sing Happy Birthday at the grave. Neither of us can sing so we were both embarrassed but Helen would have enjoyed our performance I'm sure. After our poor singing we both had our own private moments of quiet reflection at the grave. Neither of us talked about our thoughts but I'm sure the sentiments were similar, in assuring Helen that we would each look after the other now.

Jenny hasn't begun training for any marathon yet and I assume she has probably forgotten what she said to Lily about raising money for the hospital. Perhaps I should do something myself but I will have to think of something much easier than running the London marathon!

The sound of the front door bell disturbs my thoughts and I put down my magazine and switch off the television. I'm sure Ali is definitely working today so I wonder who it could be. I open the door and experience a heartening feeling of joy, albeit surprise to see Tina standing there.

She is dressed in smart blue jeans and a tight fitting, short red jacket. I notice her black hair is quite a bit shorter than usual but the style definitely works on her. As usual her face is immaculately made up and she looks as attractive and full of life as ever.

After my initial surprise, seeing her on my doorstep evokes mixed feelings in me. The memory of kissing her once comes into my mind along but it is jaded by her horrific end in France at the hands of Virgil. I also can't dismiss the flashes of memory I have of turning up drunk at her house. My vague memories of that time are embarrassing and I feel uncomfortable wondering what her recollection of it may be. I try to display any bad thoughts though, as her presence tugs at the warmer feelings in my heart.

'Hello Ewan,' she says warmly.

I step forward and give her a brief hug but the sensation feels a little unnatural. She smiles a little awkwardly when I release her, making me feel a little self-conscious.

'It's good to see you,' I tell her. 'What are you doing here? Would you like to come in?'

Tina could bring some much needed life into my eerily quiet apartment. It needs a woman's presence if only for an hour.

'I'm sorry Ewan I can't,' she says, 'I've got someone waiting downstairs.'

'Oh, okay,' I say, my voice trailing off with undisguised disappointment.

'So how are you feeling?' she asks quickly.

It's a question I'm already fed up with being asked but I can forgive her for it as I haven't seen her for so long.

'I'm okay now,' I tell her, needing to assure her that I'm once again the old Ewan she used to like. 'I guess it's just a little quiet for me around here I suppose.'

'Yes, you look well,' she says, although I'm not too sure how sincere she sounds. 'Ewan, I'm truly sorry about what happened.'

My thoughts switch back to the loss of Helen for a moment. 'That's okay, thank you Tina,' I reply.

'I should've been a lot tougher on you,' she says. 'Maybe then you would have got some help before your accident.'

I realise now that she's talking about my alcoholism and not Helen's death. I remember Tina trying very hard to get through to me but I still can't separate waking up in her bathroom, probably in the dead loop from the reality of going to her house drunk. There are too many fragmented memories of being drunk and I don't think I will ever know which of them are real.

'I think you were pretty tough on me Tina,' I assure her. 'It was just that I wasn't listening. I think you did everything you could.'

Being reminded of my spiralling descent into alcoholism is disconcerting and an uncomfortable feeling, certainly not a subject that I want to talk to her about. I wonder how badly her opinion of me has changed since our flirtatious days together at D.G.E.C.

'I'm still not sure I did enough,' Tina replies, placing a hand on my arm and gently squeezing. 'But I'm glad you're okay Ewan. After the accident, I mean... I felt so guilty...'

'Don't be stupid,' I tell her, enjoying the comforting warmth of her hand on my arm. 'It's hardly your fault what happened to me.'

'How is Jenny?' she asks, 'now you're home?'

The question makes me picture Helen and realise how much Tina is just like her in so many ways. They're both strong and attractive women with fierce, confident personalities, more than a match for any man in the world. I would never have found happiness with a dizzy or quiet woman who didn't have her own mind and a strong personality. For a moment I have the urge to cuddle Tina and to feel her warmth and strength. I miss the comforting feeling of a woman in my arms but feel a tinge of shame at thinking like that with the loss of Helen still so fresh in my mind. The mere thought of holding Tina feels like a betrayal but I realise how the silence of the apartment is not what's hurting me, it's my loneliness.

'Ewan?' asks Tina. 'I asked how your daughter is.'

'I'm sorry, I was miles away. She's fine thank you,' I tell her. 'She has a new boyfriend and has applied for quite a few jobs. It keeps her mind off things so she's doing well.'

Tina smiles with what looks like a sort of a relieved expression.

'Are you sure you don't want to come in, maybe for a quick coffee?' I ask her, 'Just for old time's sake?'

'I really can't Ewan,' she says. 'I'm actually on my way to the airport.'

'Airport?' I repeat the word a little bluntly.

'I've been offered a job in Dubai,' she informs me with an air of finality. 'It's only a year's contract but it's bloody lucrative. And if goes well then who knows?'

Her words reinforce my intensifying feelings of disappointment. She is only a former work colleague but I feel so close to her and the thought of her being so far away is painful. But we have never been more than colleagues, despite that kiss in France. But was that kiss even real? I can't seem to remember if it just happened in the dead loop or if it happened in reality. But I know that right now I'm losing her and I don't want to.

'Good for you Tina,' I reply. 'I wish I had a job out there.'

Tina rubs my arm gently. 'I'm sure you'll get back on your feet in no time,' she reassures me. 'But I really do have to get going. I was only passing anyway and just wanted to make sure you were alright before I left.'

'Oh, I'm perfectly fine,' I tell her, trying to disguise my hollow feelings from manifesting themselves in the tone of my voice.

Tina kisses my cheek, the scent of her perfume and the warmth of her lips are intoxicating. 'Take care of yourself Tiger,' she says, giving me a little wink.

'I will,' I murmur quietly as she turns and walks down the corridor and away from my hollow and empty life.

I feel tears beginning to form in my eyes. 'Good luck Tina,' I whisper as soon as she is out of sight.

Five minutes after Tina has left, the doorbell rings again. It can't be her again can it? I do hope so, but why would she come back so quickly? I hastily open the door to find a young man standing outside with an I.D. badge hanging round his neck. He is casually dressed and looks only a few years older than Jenny. In one hand he has a bundle of thin pamphlets and a bible is clutched in the other. I feel a massive twinge of disappointment that it isn't Tina at the door, but he only smiles as he begins his religious sales pitch.

'Good afternoon,' he says cheerfully. 'Could you spare me a few minutes to talk about God?'

'I'm not really religious,' I warn him politely.

'That's okay,' he replies, apparently undeterred by my statement. 'Have you ever thought about God?'

I shrug indifferently, looking at him while trying to be polite but somehow I'm unwilling to shut the door. Perhaps I just don't want to go back to my quiet reflection in the apartment. I'm definitely not a man of faith but being on my own so much in the day makes me relish a little friendly conversation, even this kind.

'I've thought about a lot of things lately,' I tell him, 'but not God specifically.'

I lean back casually against the door frame with my arms folded and he seems encouraged by my relaxed body language.

'Would you like to be closer to Jesus?' he asks, offering me one of his pamphlets.

The front cover is glossy and the feel of it in my fingers reminds me of the National Geographic I was just reading. I glance briefly at the bright yellow sun on the front cover as he continues talking, sufficiently encouraged by my polite indifference.

'So, do you believe in God?' he asks.

The thought occurs to me to invite him into the apartment and indulge in a religious discussion with him. It might be interesting to debate his beliefs and understand what his faith really has to offer. But I realise that if I lose interest then I might not be able to get rid of him quite so easily once he is inside. Anyway, he would have his work cut out to convince me about the existence of God. Recent events make me open minded to new ideas and thoughts, but I think I'm unlikely to embrace religion too easily. As he talks to me I quickly reach the conclusion that any conversation on this subject would be best conducted at the door where I can easily end it any time I like.

'What's your name son?' I ask him.

The young man transfers his pamphlets into the same hand as his bible and then holds up his I.D. badge in front of him. He looks very different in the photograph, a little younger than he is now and his hair was blonde then, not dark like it is now. He smiles at me as he displays the badge.

'My name is Virgil,' he says.

For a moment I just stare at his badge, my eyes burning into it and a vacant look appears on my face. Virgil. The badge holds my attention for a few more moments until I look back at his smiling and relaxed young face.

After a long pause with neither of us speaking, I open my front door a littler wider and stand to one side.

'Would you like to come in?' I ask.

Printed in Great Britain
by Amazon